MARKED

JEWELS OF THE NORTH - BOOK ONE

SIERRA LANE

For everyone who took the time to listen to me whine about this book and how I was never going to finish it.
You were right.

CONTENT WARNINGS

This story contains content that may be difficult for some readers to consume. That content includes:

- Alcohol consumption
- Pseudo-incest (two adopted brothers participating in sex with a third and fourth partner)
- Penetrative cis male/cis female sexual intercourse, vaginal, oral, and anal.
- Threesomes and foursomes
- Double penetration
- Discussion of kink and sexual submission
- Dubious consent due to alcohol use
- Rough sex
- Bondage

- Mild dominance/submission
- Dirty talk implying exhibitionism and voyeurism, and calling a woman a slut
- Consenting non-consent (character gives consent to be immobilized/bound but gets off on feeling helpless and her partners telling her she is)
- Unprotected penetrative sex
- Sexual spanking
- Character walking in on another character during phone sex
- Tentacle bondage
- Tentacles touching people during sex
- Implied romantic feelings between two cis men
- Magical mind control violating a character's free will, both references and on-page description
- Entering someone's thoughts without their explicit consent
- Nightmares
- PTSD
- Character death
- Murder
- Blood mention
- Depression
- Suicidal ideation
- Memories of psychological torture
- Negative self-talk

- Memories of childhood body shaming, verbal abuse, etc.
- Religious (Protestant Christian) language

Some of these warnings may seem unnecessary for some, but please keep in mind that it isn't possible to know what is or is not hurtful for someone to read. This warning is included out of respect for those who are sex-averse and do not enjoy reading sexual content, as well as those who may be triggered by certain sexual acts.

Even if something isn't a trigger for you, please respect that it may be for someone else. If you need to heed these warnings, please take care of yourself first; your mental health is the first priority.

1

Taking a deep breath and exhaling slowly, I lean over the pool table and line up my shot. The cue ball slices neatly past the 9-ball, dropping the 1 into the side pocket.

Straightening back up, my focus expands again to take in the bar around me. Aerosmith plays from the jukebox, the smells of beer, bar food, and leftover cigarette smoke from before it was illegal to smoke inside mingle in the air.

The rest of the bar is too dimly lit for me to see much outside the lights shining down on the two pool tables, but the college town dance of mating, socializing, and coping rituals is probably carrying on as usual. It's so much like the places Jake and I used to visit that I have to viciously suppress the memories trying to rise up. That's not what tonight is about.

Wendy, the younger waitress, detours past the pool tables to pick up my empty shot glasses, replacing them with a margarita without being asked.

"Busy tonight." I lick salt off the rim of the glass before taking a sip, savoring the sweetness that washes away the burn of the earlier shots. I'm just hitting the perfect glow, enough to make everything just a little easier, not enough to really impair me.

Wendy leans a hip against the pool table, balancing her tray of empty glasses on the other. "Yeah, even for Wednesday, this is a lot. Good for tips, but my feet are killing me."

I grimace in sympathy, "Honey, you couldn't pay me enough to wear those heels for half an hour, much less your entire shift."

"But they look so pretty." Wendy groans as the closest table of college boys waves her over with their empty pitcher. "Duty calls. Maybe this time nobody will pinch my ass."

Setting my drink down on the side of the table, I return to my abandoned game. If I can roll the 5 down the bumper and into the corner pocket, I'll have sunk all the solids and none of the stripes, winning the game I'm playing against myself.

Before I can take the shot, a stack of quarters clinks onto the bumper.

I turn and look up—and then up some more. The guy standing there is tall, easily a foot taller than my perfectly respectable five foot six, with warm brown skin and eyes that look like they smile a lot behind wire-rimmed glasses. Hot, slightly nerdy, and so very much my type that I shove a hand in my pocket to touch the little charm bag there. I'm not interested in falling for a Fae glamour. Not tonight, of all nights.

Nothing about him changes when I touch the charm bag, except that the once-over he's giving me is more blatant. It's been awhile since I've felt that prickle of response to anyone, guy or girl. Longer than I'd care to admit.

But as attractive as he is, I'm only here because the alternative is wallowing in my apartment; I'm not interested in picking up. I gesture to the other pool table, empty under the pendant lights. "That table's free."

He shrugs wide shoulders. "I don't like playing with myself."

I smirk at him disbelievingly.

Dimples flash with a sheepish smile as he ducks his head. "By myself," he corrects. "I don't like playing by myself."

"Well, I do." I turn back to bend over the table again, doing my best to ignore the little tug of want in my stomach. "So when I'm done here, you can have this table and I'll move over to that one."

"Just one game?" he asks. "Please?"

Despite the distraction he presents, I manage to drop the 5, leaving only the stripes. Shrugging, I move around the table to get a better angle on the 10. "One game. But I have to warn you—fuck!" I curse as I scratch, the cue ball dropping into the corner pocket.

"You have to warn me?" He leans against the table right next to where the cue ball falls into its slot with a thunk.

I circle the table to get to it, deliberately invading his personal space. "I am very, very, extremely…mediocre at this game."

Retrieving the cue ball, I turn away from him to plonk it on the table and survey my options.

"Well, hell, I'm definitely not betting with you." He pulls up a stool from somewhere, folding himself onto it. "I'm Ben."

Even sitting, I have to look up a ridiculous amount to meet his eyes. "Claire."

He eyes the table. "You could bank it and drop the 12 in the corner pocket there."

I roll my eyes. "What part of mediocre don't you understand? Do I look like I can make bank shots reliably?"

"It's not that hard, really." The dimples make another appearance, only this time the grin is less sheepish and more—I stop myself before thinking the word hot. Or sexy. Challenging, that's it. His grin is challenging. "I can help you out if you want. Give you a few pointers."

Hands on my hips, I turn to face him. "Are you seri-ously going to pull that whole 'oh, let me show you, baby' routine? The one that's just an excuse for the guy to wrap himself around the girl.

If anything, the grin deepens, going past challenging and straight into wicked. "Only if you want me to." He stands, walking slowly toward me and bracing his hands against the pool table on either side of me, leaning down until his lips brush against my ear. "Do you want me to?"

My stomach somersaults. Trying to think clearly is almost impossible with his breath whispering over my ear, the solid heat of him behind me, almost close enough to touch. Then again, parts of me haven't been thinking clearly since the first moment I met his eyes.

Just to be on the safe side, I touch the charm bag again, but he's still there, larger than life and twice as sexy. I may not have come looking for this, but if I want to forget, there are definitely worse ways to do it. I lean back until I can meet his eyes squarely. "You know, I think I really do."

He waits until I turn to face the table, then moves up until he's pressed against my back, hands sliding down my bare arms until they cover mine on the cue stick. The thin cotton of my tank top is no match for the warmth of his body; I have to fight not to shiver against him.

"So how much do you know about bank shots?" he asks.

Breathe, I order myself. "I know I suck at them. I know you bounce the ball off the bumper and try to get it to hit the ball you want." I shrug. "Half the time I can't get it anywhere near the ball I want, much less make the shot."

"The cue ball is going to come off the bumper at the same angle it hits, so you have to get good at figuring angles." Ben taps the cue gently on the bumper across the table. "If we aim it right…there…"

I let him guide my hands on the stick, making the shot and watching as the cue ball banks neatly off the bumper, slicing past the 12 just enough to send it rolling toward the corner pocket. The cue ball keeps going, coming to a stop in the perfect position behind the 15 so I can drop it in the other corner.

"See? Easy."

"Well, sure, when you're good at it." My good-natured grumble is derailed a little; something else has caught my attention. "Um, that guy over there is watching us, kind of intensely, actually."

I don't want to point, but honestly there's only one guy I could be talking about. Lounging back against the seat of a nearby booth, his fingers wrapped loosely around a beer bottle, he's just as hot as Ben, in a completely different way. Less hot and nerdy, more like a bad boy who's good in bed. And he's watching us like we're his own private show, his eyes hot and focused, their light color contrasting with his dark hair. "Do you know him?"

"Yeah, that's Jack." Ben leans down until his mouth is at my ear again. "He likes to watch. Does that bother you?"

Holy shit. My mind locks up for a moment, trying to process what I just heard and everything it implies. Once I work through the fact that yes, he really said that, and yes, it seems like he meant it, I can finally think about the question itself. Does it bother me? Strangely, it doesn't take me long to decide. "No. It doesn't bother me."

Ben spins me around, boosting me up to sit on the pool table. "Good answer."

Stepping up between my knees, he pauses for a minute, giving me time to protest, pull back, say something. But now that I've decided, I don't want to wait. Fisting my hands in his dark gray button-down, I pull him down to me.

The kiss isn't gentle or tentative. He catches my lower lip in his teeth, scraping lightly over it before licking into my mouth. I shudder, sliding my fingers up into his hair until he shivers in return, his big hands coming up to cradle my head and hold me in place. Not that I'm trying to get away; I push closer, pressing myself up against the hard muscle of his chest as he explores my mouth with single-minded intensity.

We break apart, both breathing hard. Ben strokes his thumb over my cheekbone, his rich brown eyes never leaving mine. "Come with me?"

I inhale and brace myself for attitude. "I think first we should establish some ground rules."

His forehead furrows. Well, with a face like that, he probably doesn't get turned down very often. And he looks confused, not mad, so that's something. "Ground rules? Like what?"

"Like your friend over there. You said he likes to watch. Is that all he does? Or is he going to want to join in at some point? Because I'd rather not have that sprung on me in the middle."

"Um." He drops his eyes, and I'm close enough to feel the heat on the back of his neck. "Sometimes, yeah."

"I'm not saying I don't want this," I tell him; I can feel the tension in his body, the way he's starting to withdraw from me. "But I don't really know you, and you don't really know me. This will be a lot more satisfying for both —for all of us if we take a couple of minutes and talk about what is and isn't on the table."

His muscles relax under my hands and the grin makes another appearance. I'm beginning to think it should be classified as a lethal weapon, or an intoxicant at the very least. I don't think I'm that drunk, but it's possible this is the tequila talking.

"You're saying you want to tell me what you like and don't like? I don't have to figure it out by trial and error? I don't have to try to read your mind?" Ben swings me down from the pool table and grabs my hand, leading me over to the booth where Jack sits. "Never let it be said I stopped a pretty woman who wanted to talk dirty to me."

He waits for me to slide into the booth first before sitting next to me. "Jack, this is Claire. Claire, Jack."

Seen up close, there's a weird resemblance between Jack

and Ben. It's hard to figure out why; superficially the only resemblance between them is that they both have black hair. Skin color, eye color, facial features are all different. But something in their body language, the way they hold themselves and move their hands, speaks of a closeness, familiarity.

"You two looked pretty cozy over there on the pool table." Jack gives me the same blatant appraisal I was subjecting him to. "I figured you'd be headed out about now."

"Claire wanted to set some ground rules first." Ben picks up the other beer on the table, sipping it and watching Jack expectantly.

"Ground rules?" Jack says with a smirk. "If you could be having perfectly good sex, why would you stop to talk about it instead?"

"Why have perfectly good sex when you can have amazing, mind-blowing sex?" I counter, dropping my voice almost to a purr. "You saying you don't like a woman talking to you about all the dirty, sexy things she wants you to do to her?"

Jack swallows visibly. When he speaks again, his voice is noticeably lower and rougher. "What exactly are we talking about here?"

I drop my eyes to the table; this never gets any easier to talk about. But future me will thank me for being honest. "I have a big submissive streak, sexually; I like my partners to control what's happening. I want to be told exactly what to do. I don't want to have to guess what will make my partner feel good."

Both of them shift slightly in their seats at my words, inhaling sharply. Jack reaches across the table, lifting my chin until I meet his eyes, even hotter and more intense than before. "Benny told you I like to watch? And sometimes I like to play, too? You're okay with that?"

I nod, my mouth suddenly dry at the mental image of him "playing" with me.

"How submissive are we talking?" Ben asks. He slides one big hand over my thigh under the table, holding me gently in place. Even that hint of restraint has my heart beating faster. "You just want to be told what to do? Or do you want more, maybe to be tied up?"

Jack smiles slowly, his eyes never leaving mine. "Her pupils just dilated. I think she likes that, too."

I swallow hard, nodding. "Tied up, tied down, held down. Not sure why, but it really works for me."

Ben's hand tightens on my leg. Jack's thumb strokes down my jaw and under my ear, finding the spot that makes me shiver. "Kinky girl." My face heats, but his eyes are steady and approving on mine. "If you want us to be in control, what happens when we ask you for something you absolutely, positively, will not do?"

"I say 'red.' Red means stop."

They nod in unison, just one of those little quirks that tugs at my attention. "Any definite limits we should know about before we start?" Ben asks.

"I'm not into serious pain. A little spanking, a little rough, sure, but nothing hardcore." I glance between them. "What about you two? Anything you want to throw out there?"

"Well, as it happens, sweetheart," Jack drawls, "this is your lucky day. You found yourself two guys who like to be in control. In fact, I think Ben's about ready to take control right now."

Ben slides out of the booth, tugging me after him. "You got the drinks?"

"It's covered. You two go have some fun." Catching my free hand, Jack lifts it to his mouth, slowly kissing the palm, his eyes never leaving mine. "I'll be there shortly."

2

Ben pauses outside the motel room door, still holding my hand. "Last chance to back out."

I grin up at him, anticipation coiling in my belly. "Not a chance."

He takes me at my word, unlocking the door and pulling me inside. As soon as the door closes behind us, he has me pressed up against the wall, his mouth fierce and hot on mine. It's so easy to get lost in the kiss, lips and teeth and tongue meeting and exploring, all while I'm pinned to the wall by the hard, muscled length of him.

Ben slides his hands under my ass, lifting me almost effortlessly as he tears his mouth away from mine. "Wrap your legs around me," he growls.

We both groan as he settles between my legs, his erection pressing hard and hot against me. Closing his mouth over the side of my neck, he scrapes his teeth across my skin. I arch into him, unable to do anything but respond.

Drawing back briefly, he pulls my tank up over my head, sucking in a breath at the sight of my lacy purple bra, tracing the line where lace meets skin with his fingertips. "You know," he murmurs, "every time you leaned over to take a shot, I got a little peek at this thing. I really appreciate the role it played in driving me insane tonight, but it's got to go."

He kisses me again, and the next thing I know my bra is hitting the floor. Ben bites my earlobe lightly, then licks and kisses his way down my neck, over my collarbone, into the space between my breasts.

Pausing to scrape one fingernail gently across my nipple, he smiles against my skin as I jerk in reaction. "You're a little sensitive there, baby. You like it when I play with these pretty tits?"

Before I can respond, his mouth closes over one nipple and his fingers stroke the other. I writhe helplessly, trapped between Ben and the wall, unable to do anything but moan.

He licks and sucks, squeezes and strokes, moving between my breasts until my hips arch desperately against him, the seam of my jeans rubbing against my clit. When he finally stops teasing, pinching one nipple and closing his teeth on the other, I come screaming.

Stroking my arms gently, he eases me down until my breath no longer comes in huge sobbing gasps, resting his forehead against mine. "Goddamn, woman. Did you seriously come just from me playing with your tits?"

I flush, dropping my eyes, but he tips my chin up until I meet his gaze. "Hey, look at me. That was the hottest thing I've seen in a long time." His grin is definitely evil this time. "Of course, now that I know you can come like that, I'm going to have to do it again later, so Jack can watch."

I swallow, unbelievably aroused by the thought of it. Ben lets me slide slowly down the wall until my feet hit the floor, then leads me over to the small table in the kitchenette area.

"But for now, bend over and put your hands on the table," he says, a snap of command in his voice.

I shiver at his tone, bending over and planting my hands on the wood. Ben's hand strokes approvingly down my back. "Good girl. Stay there. I'll be right back."

True to his word, he's back in next to no time, holding two striped ties. He knots one gently around my left wrist, tying it to a table leg, then repeats the process with my right, leaving me just enough slack to keep my hands planted on the tabletop.

Tugging experimentally at the bindings tells me what I already knew from watching him; he obviously knows his knots. The loop around my wrist is loose enough not to cut off my circulation, but tight enough that I'm not going anywhere. I feel my whole being relax into that knowledge, slumping against the tabletop—only to tense again when a pocketknife lands on the surface next to me.

"Relax, baby." Ben says. He's grinning again, but I'm not really able to appreciate it as it deserves, distracted by watching him unbutton his shirt. "The knife is just for emergencies, if we have to get you out for some reason. You're not into pain or blood, and neither are we."

He shucks off his shirt and undershirt, revealing an impressively muscular chest and arms, but moves back behind me before I really have time to appreciate the view. "Now then," he says, his palms stroking down my back. "I think you're a little overdressed for this party."

I jump a little when his hands move under me to unbutton my jeans. He takes his time peeling them down my legs, pausing to slide my shoes off before removing the jeans completely.

There's a moment of suspense, but before I can get antsy I feel his thumbs slide under the waistband of my purple panties. His hands stroke over the curves of my ass and all the way down my legs, taking the panties with them and leaving me completely naked, shivering in anticipation as he kneels on the floor behind me.

"Oh, yeah," Ben exhales slowly. "That's what I've been thinking about ever since I walked into the bar and saw you bent over that pool table."

I squeak in surprise when he grabs my thighs, lifting me up until my knees are on the tabletop.

"Now I'm going to lick this pretty pussy until you

come for me again," he says, nipping at my ass. "Lean down on your elbows—yeah, just like that."

He keeps his hands wrapped around my thighs, using his thumbs to spread me open to his gaze. I shudder as his tongue licks a torturously slow, wet path from my clit all the way up to my ass and then back down.

Ben settles in like he has all the time in the world, lazily circling my clit with the tip of his tongue before delving inside my pussy, deeper each time. I slowly become aware of my own voice, moaning, breath sobbing out of me as he brings me higher and higher, alternating strokes of his tongue and his fingers.

Just when I think I can't take any more, Ben crooks two long fingers inside of me just as he closes his mouth over my clit and finally, finally sucks. I come with his name on my lips, clenching around him.

"Damn, that was hot," Jack says from the direction of the door.

I should probably be worried about the fact that I didn't notice him come in, but my brain dismisses that as unimportant, awash in the endorphin rush of two back-to-back orgasms.

Jack's gaze moves behind me and I feel Ben stand up, although he leaves his fingers where they are. "I miss anything fun, Benny?"

"She came just from me playing with her tits." The post-orgasm fog must finally be clearing from my brain, because I swear I can hear the smug grin on his face, even if I can't see it.

One side of Jack's mouth quirks up as he moves to the table, curling his hand around the nape of my neck. "Is that so?" he murmurs. "We can have some fun with that later on, can't we? Maybe I'll suck on one and Ben will suck on the other and we'll see how long it takes you to get off like that."

Ben chuckles behind me. "I think she likes that idea. You're even wetter than before, baby."

Jack's fingers stroke the side of my neck and I suck in a breath, his touch raising goosebumps on my skin. He looks over his shoulder at Ben. "How many fingers?"

"Three now." Ben pushes another inside of me, thrusting lazily in and out.

I push back as far as the ties allow, trying to increase the pace, then jump when Ben's hand smacks my ass, hard.

"You're not calling the shots here, Claire," he growls, grabbing my hip with his free hand to hold me in place as he moves his fingers deliberately in and out of my pussy. "I am."

"You like that, don't you," Jack purrs in my ear. "You like Ben fucking you with his fingers while you're tied down."

I nod, even though it wasn't a question, dropping my forehead to the table.

"What do you want, sweetheart?" Jack asks. "You want Ben to fuck you?"

I nod again, overwhelmed with sensation.

Jack moves in so close that his mouth touches my ear. "Here's the deal. Ben'll fuck you—but you have to ask for it." He licks my ear, nipping gently at the lobe. "And you have to use the bad words. Talk dirty to us. Tell us what you want."

Swallowing hard, I try to find my voice, when every drag of Ben's fingertips inside me steals my breath. "Please, fuck me, Ben." Shit, was that my voice, all breathy and soft?

"You can do better than that, sweetheart," Jack chuckles in my ear. "C'mon, I know you know the dirty words. Tell Ben exactly what you want and you'll get it."

I hesitate, the words clogging in my throat. What if they think I'm a freak?

The small part of my brain still functioning points out that I'm tied to a table in a motel room, about to fuck one man while another one watches or maybe joins in. That ship has probably sailed.

Turning my head to meet Jack's eyes, I open my mouth. "I want you to fuck me, Ben. I want you to bend me over this table and pound your big, hard cock into my pussy until I scream. Please, fuck me, Ben. Please."

With every word, Jack's eyes darken and his grip on the back of my neck tightens. The last word is barely out of my mouth before he drags me toward him, devouring my mouth like a starving man at a feast. I'm so absorbed in the kiss that I almost don't notice Ben's fingers leaving me entirely until they're gone.

I moan into Jack's mouth in protest. Laughing softly, he breaks the kiss. "Don't worry, sweetheart, Ben's going to fuck you. Aren't you, Benny?" He glances up at Ben.

"Well, she did beg so nicely," Ben lifts me gently down until my feet are on the floor, then pushes inside me in one rough, surprising thrust. "That what you want, baby? Want me to fuck you hard and fast?"

"Oh, God, yes, Ben, please." I drop my head to the table again. Even after two orgasms, my pussy is still so tight that he has to work his way in with short, hard thrusts. I have a fleeting moment to be grateful that he used a condom, but practical considerations are soon overwhelmed with waves of sensation.

Once he gets the full, thick length of his cock inside me, he keeps the same speed but fucks me harder. His big hands grip my waist, positioning me at the perfect angle for his thrusts, holding me so I don't slam into the edge of the table.

"Look at me, Claire," Jack orders.

I open my eyes reluctantly, not sure exactly when I closed them. Jack sits in one of the cheap hotel chairs in my line of sight, jeans unzipped, fisting his cock almost lazily. I can't help but groan, the visual pushing me even higher.

"Do you know how hot this is?" he asks. "You, bent over that table with your pretty ass in the air, moaning and begging while Ben fucks you? This is better than porn. I'm gonna wake up horny for months, maybe years, and have to jack myself off, remembering how you sound, how you're so wet I can smell you from here. I can't wait to taste you later, hear how you sound when I've got my tongue buried deep in your pretty pussy. Does she taste good, Benny?"

"Oh, yeah," Ben groans, still fucking me relentlessly. "She feels even better. Hot and wet and tight, like you wouldn't believe. Keep talking. She likes it, don't you, Claire? Like Jack talking dirty to you?"

I nod.

Smack! Ben spanks me again, harder this time, never pausing his thrusts. "What was that? I couldn't hear you."

"Yes!" I grit out.

"Yes, what?" Jack smirks at me, like the smug bastard he is.

"Yes, I like you talking dirty to me," I gasp, incredibly aroused and so close to coming I can almost taste it. Ben lifts me just a little higher, his cock sliding over the perfect spot inside me once, twice. The third time I come, shocked breathless by the intensity. He fucks me mercilessly through the orgasm and the aftershocks, holding the same steady rhythm.

"Eyes open." Jack's hand strokes gently through my hair. I open my eyes to see him standing directly in front of me, his cock hard and thick in his other hand. "Gonna fuck your mouth now, sweetheart. Open up."

I open my mouth obediently and he slides in, shallow and gentle at first. Then deeper, until I'm timing my breaths by his thrusts, his cock sliding all the way to the back of my throat. Swallowing hard, I try to push back my gag reflex, loving the way he looks down at me, like he can't stop watching his cock disappear between my lips.

Soon they're moving in rhythm, Ben's thrusts pushing me further onto Jack's cock, Jack's rocking me back toward Ben. Jack cradles my head in his hands as he fucks my mouth, Ben holds my hips as he fucks my pussy. I'm surrounded by them, completely under their control, and knowing that is almost enough to make me come all by itself.

"Fuck," Jack groans. "This is even better than watching. Wish I could fuck your mouth forever. I'm gonna come and you're gonna swallow it all for me, aren't you?"

I hum my agreement, making him shudder at the vibrations on his cock. He looks up and over my head, probably sharing a look with Ben, and they both pick up the pace.

When Ben's finger ghosts over my ass, teasing and prodding, I suck in a breath around Jack, tensing up. Ben smacks my ass again, hard. "You're trying to call the shots again, baby. You're not making the decisions here. We are. If you want to stop, we'll stop. Otherwise, relax and let me in."

I do what I'm told, relaxing and bearing down slightly as Ben's finger slips past the ring of muscle. It's slick with something, but I still hiss slightly at the burn. His finger picks up the same rhythm as their cocks inside me, lighting up nerve endings I'd all but forgotten about.

"Want you to come for us again, like this." Ben's voice is deep and rough; I almost think I could come just listening to him. "Jack's cock in your mouth, mine in your pussy, my fingers in your ass. And you love every second of it, don't you?"

He adds a second finger, chuckling smugly at the sounds I make, the way I can't decide whether to pull away or push closer. When he starts to thrust harder, Jack matches him thrust for thrust, like they share one brain. "Oh, yeah. You love it. Maybe next time I'll let Jack fuck your pussy while I fuck this tight little ass. You're going to scream yourself hoarse from coming and you'll—love—every—second."

Jack's hands fist in my hair and his hips buck, filling my mouth as he groans above me. I swallow, doing my best not to choke as he pulls back, finally letting me draw a breath. Then Ben twists his fingers, thrusts deep, and growls, "Come for us," and I am, flying helplessly over the edge one last time.

When I can see again, Jack is gently untying my hands, calloused fingers rubbing gently over the faint pink marks on my wrists. I lie limply on the table, thinking vaguely about moving, and he strokes a hand down my back, smiling smugly. "I think we wore her out, Benny."

Ben's answering laugh is my only warning before he

lifts me and carries me to one of the beds, lying me gently down and stretching out next to me, one arm cradling me close. "Seems only fair. I'm about ready for a nap myself." He drops a kiss on the top of my head. "That was incredibly hot, in case you didn't realize."

Jack curls himself into my other side, his hand resting on my belly. "Nap does sound pretty good," he mumbles, his voice muffled as he tucks his face into my neck. "Game called on account of nap."

I'm worn out enough that all I manage is a noise of agreement before sleep claims me.

3

My eyes fly open as two mouths close over my nipples at the same time. Before I'm even fully awake, I'm writhing under the contrasting sensations. Ben scrapes his teeth over my nipple, lightly at first, then harder, while Jack sucks and licks with long strokes of his tongue.

My hips buck, seeking more sensation as they drive me higher and higher. Then they each pin one of my wrists to the bed, leaning their weight on my thighs, making it so much worse and so much better all at the same time. I'm begging, high and breathless, "Ben," and "Jack," and "Please," and "God," and "Fuck," and when they both bite down lightly, I come.

When I can breathe again, the first thing I see is Jack's face, wearing that ridiculously sexy smirk. "My turn to eat that pretty pussy. You gonna scream for me like you did for Ben?"

I'm recovered enough to give him the smirk right back. "Maybe. Are you as good at it as he is?"

"Benny, go get those ties. We're gonna need 'em." Jack threads his fingers through my hair and leans down to kiss me, gentle and sweet.

Something soft wraps around my wrist as he breaks the kiss, expertly knotting my wrist into the tie, then fastening it around my thigh. He makes quick work of my other wrist, then sits back to admire his handiwork before meeting my eyes again.

"Let me tell you a little secret, sweetheart." He leans in, never breaking eye contact. "I taught Benny everything he knows—"

"Hey!" Ben settles back against the headboard next to me, looking both amused and affronted. "I know some girls who would beg to differ."

Jack's smirk is back, full force. "Yeah, whatever, dude. But I didn't teach him everything I know. And because you decided to be a little smart-ass, you're gonna come for me twice before I fuck you. Now..." Jack looks me over, a leisurely appraisal. "Where to start?"

He skims his fingertips down my legs, barely touching. The corner of his mouth tilts upward even further as I shiver at his touch.

Sliding down to the foot of the bed, he places a soft kiss on the inside of my ankle, licking and nipping his way up the inside of my leg. He pauses at the back of my knee, lavishing attention on the sensitive skin there until I'm writhing against him before continuing his slow path upward.

By the time he makes it to my pussy I'm shuddering, my hips hitching up off the bed. But he skips right over it, working his way down my other leg, holding my ankles down as he feasts on my skin.

"Fuck, please, Jack," I groan brokenly. I have just enough awareness left to feel his lips curve against the back of my knee, just before his teeth scrape over it.

I would have jumped off the bed without his hands on my ankles to anchor me. It's so much, but not nearly enough to come. I need more, and he knows it.

"Please, Jack, what?" He grins up at me. "What do you want, sweetheart? Want me to lick your clit and your pussy? Want me to fuck you with my tongue and fingers? Want me to make you come?"

"God, yes, please." I'm beyond being embarrassed at the words and sounds coming out of my mouth, beyond thinking about about anything but needing to come.

Jack moves up, settling between my legs. His broad, muscular shoulders spread my legs wide, his breath on my pussy making my hips roll shamelessly toward his mouth. Looking up my body, he meets my eyes, all confidence and heat and anticipation. "You ready to scream for me?"

Without waiting for an answer, he spreads me wide and licks, slow, exploratory swipes up and down before circling my clit. Feels so good, so wet and hot. "Jack—God —please—don't stop—"

He licks his way back down and inside me, curling his tongue to find the perfect spot.

I do scream, then, his name the only sound that escapes as I come, the sensations so sharp and clear they almost hurt.

"Good girl," he murmurs, lifting his face to smile at me, his mouth wet. "Benny, you can help me with this next one. Your turn for the dirty talk, since my mouth is gonna be occupied."

I shudder as Jack's mouth latches onto my clit. I'm still almost painfully sensitive; I can feel my legs start to shake from his unrelenting attentions. My next orgasm isn't going to take long at all at this rate, I think—and then Ben starts purring filthy words into my ear.

"Jack was right; this is better than porn. Fuck, Claire, I could get off just listening to the sounds you make. Everybody in this motel can hear you, how turned on you are, how much you want us. I guarantee every guy here is jerking off right now, wishing he was the reason you keep screaming."

I moan, the combination of Jack's mouth on my clit and Ben's voice in my ear almost too much to take. Jack crooks two fingers inside my pussy and starts thrusting, never letting up on my clit. My hips jerk, tension rising as he strokes my g-spot perfectly with every thrust.

Ben's voice darkens even more as he moves closer, the

hard line of his dick pressing into my hip, one big hand splayed over my stomach to hold me down. "God, so greedy. Just came once and you're already about to come again. Gonna come for us whenever we want, aren't you baby? Come all over Jack's face while he fucks you with his fingers. And we're not gonna stop there."

The mental image he's building with his words is almost overwhelming, torturing me with the need for an orgasm that's just out of reach.

"I'm gonna hold you down while Jack fucks you," Ben promises, nipping at my earlobe. "Pin you down so you can't move. You'll just have to take it, take however he fucks you. And you'll know you can stop it, any time you want. All you have to do is say the word and we'll stop."

I whimper, little noises punched out of me with every stroke of Jack's fingers inside me, every slide of his tongue over and around my clit.

"But you won't want us to stop, will you? You want us to hold you down and fuck you until you come again and again and again. Until you've forgotten what it feels like not to have us fucking you."

I buck helplessly against Ben's restraining hands, against the ties on my wrists and thighs. The scream that rips out of my throat is so high-pitched it's almost inaudible.

The only things that are real to me are the hard restraint of Ben's body, anchoring me, the feeling of Jack's mouth on my clit and his fingers curled into my pussy. I don't realize they've untied me until they start gently rubbing at my wrists and thighs, soothing the faint marks where I pulled and twisted against the bonds.

It makes something warm rise in my chest, being cared for like I haven't been in a long time. I shove the feeling away, opening my eyes to focus on the reality. This isn't a relationship. This is a really hot one-night stand that isn't over yet.

I slowly stroke a hand up Ben's arm, then Jack's, enjoying the chance to finally touch, to let my hands linger on the swell and dip of their muscles, to feel them flex restlessly under my hands.

Threading my fingers through Jack's hair, I tug him down for a kiss, lazily twining my tongue with his. I can taste my own salty flavor on his mouth. When I break the kiss and lick my lips, I can't stop a smile as his eyes darken in response.

Turning my head, I pull Ben in for a kiss this time, letting him taste the traces of musk left on my tongue. He growls against my lips, exploring every last corner of my mouth, like I'm the best thing he's ever tasted and he doesn't want to miss any of it.

An eternity later he lifts his head, glancing toward the end of the bed. Jack is standing there, rolling a condom slowly down onto his cock and watching us with intent.

"How do you want her, Jack?"

He closes his hands over my ankles, tugging me down

until my hips are almost at the edge of the bed. "There we go. Hold her arms down for me, Benny."

Ben moves until he's kneeling by my head, pinning my wrists to the mattress in a gentle but implacable grip. The fact that he can hold both of my wrists in one big hand makes me shiver, almost as much as the sensation of him holding me down. "Like this?" he asks.

"Just like that," Jack purrs. Sliding into me in one smooth stroke, he never breaks eye contact as I pull and tug on my arms, testing Ben's grip. "You should've felt how wet she got when you were talking to her. I thought she was gonna come right there when you told her you were gonna hold her down, the way her pussy clamped down on my fingers."

He presses my knees back toward my chest, holding me open for his thrusts. "Shit, sweetheart, I didn't think anything would feel better than fucking your mouth, but I'm enjoying this almost as much as you are. Benny definitely is."

I roll my head to the side to see that Ben has taken matters into his own hands, his free fist squeezing his cock. When I lick my lips, both of them groan.

Jack turns my face back to him, speeding up his thrusts. "You want to suck him off, I'll let you, but not yet. Right now, I'm gonna fuck you and you can't stop me. Can you?"

I shudder. I can feel the rush of wetness, the involuntary reaction to the question, as well as he can. My whole face goes hot when he chuckles, my eyes sliding closed.

"Look at me, Claire," he commands. My eyes open almost of their own volition. "I asked you a question."

"No." My voice is ragged, almost unrecognizable. "I can't stop you."

He rewards me with a slow, lingering lick over one nipple. "And you love that, don't you? You love Benny holding you down while I fuck you. You're dripping wet because you're helpless. I could fuck you slow and gentle, so it takes you an hour to come, or I can pound you into the mattress. You don't know what I'm gonna do, but it's up to me, and that gets you so hot you could almost come right now, couldn't you?"

I groan, but I know better than to deny him the answer. "Yes."

"Yes, what?" Jack's mouth hovers over my other nipple. He smiles as I shiver, his breath whispering over my skin.

"Fuck." I groan. "Yes, I love it. I love you—shit—fucking me while Ben holds me down. I love knowing you can do whatever you want to me. I'm—oh God—I'm about to come just thinking about it."

I feel more than hear the stroke of Ben's hand speeding up next to me. Jack hums his approval, licking over my nipple with slow, rasping strokes, matching the thrusts of his cock in my pussy.

He scrapes his teeth over the other nipple, chuckling as

I arch up underneath him. "Good girl. I think you deserve a reward for that. What do you think, Ben?"

Ben groans. "I think she deserves a fucking medal. But I'm not gonna be able to take much more of this."

Jack pulls out of me, smirking at the protesting noise I make, and climbs up onto the bed, bracing his back against the headboard. "Go ahead and let her up. C'mere, sweetheart."

Ben releases my arms and sits back, waiting.

I crawl hesitantly toward Jack, incredibly aware of their eyes on me. He pulls me into his lap for a heated kiss that doesn't end until we're both gasping and grinding against each other.

His hands urge me to turn around until my back is against his chest, my legs straddling his, guiding me down onto his cock. We both groan as I sink the last few inches, his cock hot and hard inside my pussy.

"That's it," he murmurs in my ear. I shiver as his breath ghosts across the sensitive skin of my neck. "Fuck, you feel amazing. Wish I could stay like this forever. But poor Benny's been left out. Gonna let you suck him now, okay?"

I nod, squirming as his hands close over my breasts.

"Get over here, Benny," he orders, teasing at my nipples.

Ben doesn't wait to be told twice, kneeling in front of me. He's so tall that he can slide his cock right into my mouth, shallowly at first, then deeper and harder until I'm taking almost his full length with each thrust.

He laces his fingers in my hair, tugging gently to set the pace. I never realized hair-pulling was something that turned me on before this, but right now it's one more sensation, one more thing driving me higher.

I try my best to stay focused on Ben, at least enough to make sure it's good for him. But Jack is hitting the perfect spot with every thrust, his fingers playing my nipples like he's touched me a million times. Like he's inside my mind, can feel what I want before I can ask for it.

The sounds I'm making, even with Ben's cock in my mouth, are kind of unbelievable, but I can't focus on that. I can't focus on anything except my next orgasm, hovering just out of reach.

Jack slides one hand down to stroke my clit as he bites down on my neck. All it takes is a few touches before I come. In front of me, Ben groans, fingers tightening in my hair, holding me in place for his final thrust. I swallow instinctively as he comes, hot and salty-bitter all over my tongue.

Before I can process that, before my brain is even functioning again, Jack's hands slide down to my hips, holding me down, and he buries himself deep inside me as he comes, too.

For a moment I'm trapped, pinned between two hard, male bodies. Even as wrung out as I am from the last several hours, that's almost enough to get me worked up again.

But then Ben pulls out, his thumb wiping at the corner

of my mouth before he guides me down to the bed, wrapping himself around me. Jack follows us, flopping down on my other side.

We lie there in a tangle of sweaty limbs and gasping, shuddering breaths, my heart pounding to match the rhythm I can feel under my hand, where it rests on Ben's chest.

I think vaguely about getting up, finding my clothes. It's probably about time for the walk of "fuck yeah, I got laid." But Ben's arm is around my waist, Jack's legs tangled with mine. Gods, it's so good, just to touch and be touched, skin on skin. To not feel lonely, to not be alone, just for a little while.

I feel myself drifting off, and instead of getting up, I let it happen.

Just for a little while.

4

ᚷᚱᚺ

orning light filtering around the edge of the curtains wakes me, pulling me gently toward awareness. I do my best to go back to sleep; I'm warm and comfortable and I don't want to lose that. But the half-seen unfamiliar shapes around me, and the sound of not one, but two other people breathing, finally finish the job, bringing me awake enough that there's no chance of drifting off again.

We aren't quite as entangled as we were when I fell asleep. Sometime during the night, Jack shifted to sleep on his stomach, although he still has one leg hooked over mine. Ben is sprawled on his back now, with me lying almost on top of him.

I let myself savor the warmth of skin and the feeling of

breathing bodies for a few minutes longer. But eventually I have to start extricating myself.

I bite my lip to keep from giggling when I remember the last time I needed to use these ninja skills—my sister Amanda refused to nap when she was three unless I'd lie down with her. Ben and Jack are a bit bigger than Amanda was, but I manage to successfully navigate my way to the foot of the bed with no more reaction than a quiet grunt from Jack.

They both look so good, two well-muscled bodies that somehow manage to cover almost the entire surface of a very large bed. I have to stop for a moment to appreciate the view before I start the scavenger hunt for my clothes.

My jeans, underwear, and shoes are all scattered round the room, apparently left wherever Ben tossed them after taking them off me. My bra is on the floor, too, but my tank top somehow managed to land on top of the light fixture by the door.

Once I have everything, I start to get dressed, but then I pause and glance back at the bed. Neither of them has so much as twitched while I've been moving around the room, even letting out the occasional soft snore. I should just put my clothes on and start the walk back to the bar, but my skin feels caked with dried sweat and, probably, other evidence of our night-time activities.

I slip quietly into the bathroom, closing the door softly behind me. Turning on the water, I pull my hair up with the elastic from the pocket of my jeans while I wait for it to warm. It takes awhile, but when I finally step into the surprisingly roomy shower I have to bite back a moan as the hot spray hits my back. It feels so good I want to stay here forever, but I force myself to scrub off quickly, hoping the shower hasn't woken them.

When I've cleaned every part of my body, I kill the water reluctantly, drying off briskly with one of the scratchy motel towels. Pulling my clothes on and wiping the steam from the mirror, I let my hair down and make a face at the mess. Two marathon sessions left me with sex hair, and not the sexy Hollywood kind. Putting it back in a messy ponytail is the best I can do.

Clean and looking halfway respectable, I turn off the light and pull the door open cautiously, only to freeze in the doorway.

"Trying to sneak out on us?" Ben lounges on the bed, his voice amused. He stretches slowly, still completely naked, and grins as I blush, doing my best not to stare at his erection. "If you want to go, no problem, but I'd really like to buy you breakfast first."

I grin back, trying to keep my eyes on his face, as much to be polite as because I'm not sure my poor pussy is up to another round just now. Although it's tempting. "I wasn't sure what the morning-after etiquette was. We didn't really discuss it."

Rolling out of bed, he crosses the room to me, ducking his head for a long, steamy kiss that leaves me breathless and wishing I hadn't gotten dressed. "Well, I lost my copy of Emily Post, but I'm pretty sure breakfast is allowed."

"Or you could take your clothes off and come back to bed," Jack says, scrubbing a hand over his face as he sits up on the side of the bed. "Or in the shower with us. We haven't done shower sex yet."

I cock my head to the side, staring at him incredulously. "Are you seriously trying to talk me into the shower with you before your eyes are even open?"

He pries them open long enough to shoot me an irritated look. "I'm not a morning person. So sue me. I'm usually a lot happier after morning sex, but somebody has too many clothes on for that."

I'm about to suggest that he should come over and take them back off me, but my stomach picks that point to make a loud, embarrassing rumble, clearly audible to all three of us. And then Jack's stomach does too, as if in answer, and we all start laughing helplessly.

"Fine, we'll do breakfast," Jack grumbles. Standing up, he shoves past us into the bathroom, completely unselfconsious of his nakedness and his very obvious erection. "But if I have to jerk off in the shower, so do you, Benny. No blow jobs while I'm in there, or we'll never get out of here before we starve to death."

"Well, damn," Ben murmurs, kissing me one more time, his mouth lingering over mine before he finally raises his head. "There goes my plan for the morning. You're blushing again."

For probably the billionth time in my life, I curse my fair skin and how easily it shows every bit of color. "Curse of the redhead." I tug on the ends of my brown hair. "I can change the color, but I've still got the skin."

He grins, tapping the tip of my nose with one finger. "And the freckles. It's cute."

I roll my eyes as he turns away, pulling clean clothes out of a duffel bag on the floor. "Great. That's exactly what every woman wants to hear from the guy she just fucked. That she's cute."

"You are cute." Ben turns with his hands full of clothes just as the water shuts off in the bathroom. "You're also hot. Sexy. And if Jack wouldn't kick my ass for getting between him and bacon, I'd throw you down on that bed and prove it."

"Don't tempt me," Jack growls, toweling himself off as he walks out of the bathroom. "Get your ass in the shower, Ben, or so help me gods, I'll leave you here."

ᛋᚱᚼ

I TAKE them to my favorite diner, a tiny place almost exactly halfway between the motel and the bar. It's early enough that the hungover college students haven't dragged themselves out of bed yet, so we actually manage to score one of the booths.

The waitress, Susan, appears almost as soon as we're settled in, Jack ushering me into the booth ahead of him.

She slaps menus down in front of Ben and Jack, filling my coffee cup almost in the same motion, then both of theirs when they nod. "Hey, sweetie. Dave's got your bacon on the grill. I'll be right back with the cream."

"Come here often?" Jack asks. As she bustles away, he starts scanning the single-page menu without waiting for an answer.

"This is the only place in town that cooks bacon the way I like it," I say, leaning back against the booth. "I like my bacon crispy, but not burnt. You'd be surprised how hard it is to find a restaurant that can manage that."

They both smirk a little at that, exchanging a look. "So, besides the bacon, what's good here?" Ben asks.

"Honestly, I've never tried anything that wasn't good. If you like greasy diner breakfasts, this is basically heaven."

He grins at me. "We may have to roll Jack out of here, then."

Jack rolls his eyes across the table, his expression fond. "Yeah, yeah. Like you didn't almost cry over the waffles in that last place."

"Whatever."

Susan comes back with the small jug of heavy cream, setting it down next to my coffee cup. "You boys ready to order?"

Ben hands her his menu. "Three eggs, medium, hash-browns and toast, please."

"You got it, hon," she says, turning to Jack. "And you?"

"Same for me, but biscuits and gravy instead of toast,

and a side of bacon," Jack says, passing his menu over as well."

Susan collects them with practiced ease. "Sure thing, hon. It'll be out pretty quick, but let me know if you need anything." She bustles off toward the kitchen, clearing plates off an empty table on her way.

Silence settles over the booth, heavy even under the hubbub of the diner. I draw circles with my fingertip in the condensation from my water glass. "So, uh, you guys do this a lot?"

"Breakfast in greasy diners? Yeah." Jack stretches his arm across the back of the booth, curling his hand around my shoulder. "Or did you mean breakfast in greasy diners with hot women we picked up and fucked?"

I blush again; I swear I can feel Ben grinning at me from across the table. I peek. Yup. Dimples and all. It's unfair.

"Really more of the second, I guess." My voice trails off. "I'm really nosy sometimes, and it's none of my business. But last night doesn't seem like the first time you two have done that."

"We had, ah, kind of a weird childhood," Ben says, his voice cautious.

I snort. "Join the club. We meet at the bar." This time I'm the one grinning at him, although he returns it with interest.

"Our moms traveled a lot, for work—" Jack starts.

"Wait. 'Our' moms? So you all traveled together?" I interrupt.

Jack grins. "Our moms are married. They adopted us out of foster care."

"You're brothers?" I feel like my head is on a swivel, looking between them. This is a curveball I wasn't expecting.

Ben holds a hand out, wiggling it back and forth. "Technically, I guess yeah? I'm a changeling, so no blood relation, though. Which is why I'm better-looking than this loser."

I bite my tongue to hold back a lot of really inappropriately nosy questions. I've never met a changeling before, but now doesn't seem like the time. Probably I should be more weirded out by the fact that they're technically brothers, but whatever.

"Benny!" Jack says, pressing a hand to his chest with a mock gasp. "How could you deny our deep brotherly bond? It's so much deeper than blood!"

"Yeah, yeah," Ben sighs. "Anyway, Mom and Mama didn't have anyone they trusted to take care of us long-term, so we basically grew up on the road, living out of motel rooms and short-term apartments, so not a lot of privacy. We, ah, figured out pretty early that we both like to watch, and it kind of grew into this."

Jack sips his coffee, shrugging. "It's not what most people consider normal, but everybody's got their kinks. We're not hurting anyone. I like to think of it as live porn. And, bonus, sometimes I get to be part of the action."

Ben shrugs, too. "We make sure the people we fuck know what they're getting into, that they're okay with it and having a good time. Everybody wins."

Before I can say more, Susan is back with our food, loading the table with plates. I can't help smirking a little when Ben and Jack look between their breakfasts and mine.

"You're gonna eat all that?" Jack asks, eyeing my three eggs, double order of bacon, hashbrowns, and short stack of pancakes like he's trying to decide what he can steal.

"Hell yeah I am." I drizzle syrup over the pancakes, spreading it evenly between each layer. Cutting off a bite, I follow it with egg and hashbrowns, then bacon, the balance of salty and sweet perfect on my tongue. "You guys wore me out. I need fuel if I'm gonna hit the gym later."

Jack takes a bite of his own bacon and groans happily. "You were right. This is heaven, and I'm never leaving."

"So what do you do at the gym?" Ben asks between bites of his own breakfast, eyeing their bacon covetously. "Yoga? Pilates?"

I smile sweetly, cutting off another bite of pancake. "Powerlifting."

They both stop and stare at me. It's very satisfying. "Powerlifting?" Jack asks. "Like with the bars and the big weights?"

Swallowing the food in my mouth, I let myself bask in

their surprise. "I placed third in my weight class at the last competition I did. I don't have as much time to train as I'd like with work, but if I can get my bench press up, I should be able to start winning some."

"Damn," Ben says, eyeing me appraisingly. "You don't look like She-Hulk."

"I'm not really interested in getting my body fat down low enough that I look super ripped. I perform better with a decent reserve," I say with a shrug, forking up the last bite of my pancakes. "Plus, I'd like to keep my boobs."

"Amen to that." Jack finishes the last of his biscuits and gravy, sitting back with a contented sigh. "You should definitely keep your boobs. I'm kind of a big fan."

I echo his sigh, scraping the last bits of food into a pile with my fork. "I definitely got that impression. Not that this hasn't been fun, guys, but unless you're planning on sweeping me off to your vacation home to be your kept woman, I have things I need to do before Monday rolls around and it's back to reality."

"Sure we can't interest you in round three?" Ben makes hopeful eyes at me.

Regretfully, I shake my head. "Probably not a good idea. It's been amazing, really, but even super hot sex isn't going to buy my groceries or clean my bathroom."

"Need a ride?" Jack asks.

"Nah, my apartment's not far from here. That's why I was at that bar in the first place; if I decide to get drunk, I don't have to worry about driving." I slide out of the booth and smile down at both of them. "Seriously, nice to meet you two. Best night I've had in awhile."

Ben smiles back, treating me to that grin one more time. "Us, too."

I turn and walk out the door.

5

Opening the door to my tiny lab in the library basement the next morning is like the reverse of the Wizard of Oz, stepping back to black and white when, for a little bit, everything was in color. But fucking random dudes doesn't pay the bills, so unless I want to start a new career as a call girl, I guess it's time to get back to work.

Adjusting the volume on my Bluetooth speaker, I hit play and tuck my phone into my pocket. I pull on gloves, singing along softly to Five Finger Death Punch, and open the first box sitting on the stainless steel table, spreading the flaps wide.

The 16th-century manuscript inside has been really well preserved, but the pages are still yellowed with time. I lift it carefully, holding my breath as I transfer it to the waiting cradle, easing it open to the first page.

Stepping back, I press the button, watching as the glass platen lowers, the cradle adjusting. When the scan appears on the computer screen, I double-check the quality and that it's uploaded to my cloud backup, then turn the page and start the process again.

"Two down, a hundred seventy-nine to go," I mutter to myself. Rolling my neck from side to side, I try to release some of the tension that always creeps into my shoulders while I work.

As always, there's the temptation to look at the scan, to try and read it or get lost in the beauty of the illuminated text. But I'm here to work, so I turn back toward the table, my hips swaying slightly to the beat.

"Excuse me, ma'am, we're looking for Dr. Ryan?"

I jump, reaching for the volume control on my phone before turning to see who has invaded my climate-controlled archive. For a minute I think I'm hallucinating. But no, it's Ben and Jack, dressed in cheap black suits, gaping at me.

"Claire?" Ben obviously wasn't expecting me either. "You're Dr Ryan?"

I shrug, a little self-consciously. "That's what it says on my student loans."

"You're a librarian?" Jack nudges Ben with his elbow. "Well, there's one for your bucket list, Benny."

Ben smacks him on the shoulder. "Shut up, jackass."

"You shut up."

"Boys," I fight back a smile. "As nice as it is to see you again, what brings you to my humble lab?"

They turn back to me and reach into their jackets, pulling out badge folios with FBI emblems and ID cards. "Agents Wayne and Parker, FBI," Jack says.

My brain pushes through the surprise and kicks into gear, my eyes narrowing. "Bullshit."

Both of them flinch. Ben tries for an appealing grin, but it looks a little ragged around the edges.

"Excuse me?"

"I'm pretty sure the FBI doesn't send brothers, even adopted brothers, out as partners. If only for the same reason the military doesn't let family members serve together. You're not FBI. You're hunters."

They stare at me, and the penny drops.

"Ben and Jack. Shit, how could I be so stupid?" I strip off my gloves tossing them in the bin to be washed. "And they say men think with their dicks. Brothers named Ben and Jack. Only I could go out for a drink and end up fucking the goddamn Andersons."

Visibly bemused, they tuck their badges away. Jack purses his lips, staring at me. "You're not a hunter."

"No shit, Sherlock," I snap. Pacing away for a minute, I try to get myself under control.

"So how do you know about hunters?" he persists. "Hell, how do you know about us?"

I snort out a humorless laugh. "You're kidding, right?

Everybody who knows anything about the supernatural knows about you two. You stopped the fucking Fae invasion—you know, after you started it."

"Yeah, but how do you know?" Ben's eyes have gone hard and suspicious. "Most people have no idea there was almost a Fae invasion. You're not a hunter. Are you human?"

"As human as you are." I say, then roll my eyes in the face of their disbelief. "Fine, test me. Might as well get it out of the way."

A swig of holy water, a shallow cut to my forearm with a silver blade, then an iron one later, I slap band-aids over the cuts. "Satisfied?"

Jack looks stubborn. "You still haven't explained how you know about the Fae."

"That—is a long story, and I don't want to tell it here." I glance at my phone. "I'm gonna need a drink to get through it. How about I buy you lunch and you can hear my sob story, if you really want to know."

Ben sweeps a hand toward the door. "Lead the way."

ᛋᚱᚺ

THEY FOLLOW me to the restaurant in their car, Jack holding the door for me as we walk inside. We don't talk when the waitress settles us into a corner booth or while we wait for our drinks. The silence feels heavier with every moment, but I have no desire to start talking. Just thinking about it is like a lead weight in my stomach.

The restaurant is still sparsely populated, the lunch crowd thin on the ground on a Thursday. The waitress returns with two beers and a margarita, takes our food orders, and vanishes again.

I take a long drink, feeling the clear burn of the tequila down my throat, then a deep breath.

"I was married." I feel, rather than see, them flinch, but push ahead, trying to get it out. "We met in college, and—it was good, you know? Not like rom-com, throwing shit and crying and making out in the rain, not fairy-tale perfect, but good. Not a lot of drama and bullshit. We just—clicked."

I take another drink, trying to organize my thoughts. "I grew up in a really religious family, and I pretty much got away from that in college, but Jake was never a believer. And then last year, when the minor Fae came through—"

They both wince, all the confirmation I need of the rumors I've heard about their involvement. Ben covers my hand with his, Jack moves closer until his leg is pressed against mine, their touch a quiet comfort.

"Gods, I thought he was having an affair, can you believe that?" I shake my head. "He was distant, he kept making excuses for not being around. I had no idea about the Fae, not then. But even if I had—he had such a strong will."

"Those are the easiest ones for the Fae to glamour," Ben says grimly. "Especially if they don't believe in supernatural things."

I sigh. "Yeah. By the time I figured out what was going on—it was too late. I warded the house, started carrying iron and salt with me. I tried—I found a witch who would try to break the glamour, but he disappeared. I don't know if he's alive or dead, on Earth or Underhill."

"I'm sorry," Jack says. "That sucks."

"Yeah." I drain the last of my drink. "So after that, I set myself to learning everything I could about the supernatural, about the Fae specifically, although I picked up stuff about shifters and human magic, too. With my degrees and my connections in academia, I was able to dig deeper than most people can. And for some reason, when you start looking into Fae shit over the last few years, two people always seem to come up."

They have the grace to look a little embarrassed, at least. "Shit does seem to keep happening to us," Jack allows. "What are you a doctor of, exactly?"

"Anthropology and Medieval History, so basically how to ask 'do you want fries with that?'" I say. "Thankfully my masters is in library science, which makes me a little more employable. Tens of thousands of dollars in student loans, jobs that pay just enough to clear them around the time I get to retire. What else could I want?"

Ben gives me an answering grimace, rubbing his thumb comfortingly over my wrist, while Jack leans his shoulder into mine. I'm not going to look up; if either of them is looking the least bit sympathetic, I'm going to cry. I don't want to cry.

"So anyway, that's how I know who you are. Care to tell me what you were doing in my lab with your bullshit fake FBI badges?"

I can practically feel them exchanging glances over my head.

"How much do you know about what happened, after the Fae came through?" Jack finally asks.

"Bits and pieces," I answer honestly. "I heard you were trying to seal off access to Underhill?"

Ben nods. "It was a little more complicated than that. But yeah, there was a spell—a series of spells—that would divide our dimension from Underhill forever. No more Fae snatching babies and leaving changelings in their place, no more Wild Hunt riding through, no more kelpies drowning people in streams."

"Sounds great." I run my fingertip through the salt left on the edge of my glass and lick it off. "So what's the catch?"

"Two things," Jack says gruffly. "First, we discovered along the way that the final spell requires the caster to sacrifice their life. And I'm kind of used to having this asshole around; I'd rather not lose him. Even if it gets rid of the Fae."

Ben sighs like they've had this discussion a lot. "And the other thing is, when we didn't do the final spell, it didn't just allow more Fae to come through. It also rebounded, and this idiot took it instead of me."

"It would've killed you," Jack says simply. Like that's enough of an answer. Maybe, for them, it is.

"So now he's cursed."

At Ben's nod, Jack shrugs out of his cheap suit jacket and rolls up his sleeve, tilting his arm toward me.

The mark on his forearm looks like a tattoo at first glance, which is probably why it didn't stand out to me the other night. Deceptively simple from a distance, I can see that it's made up of intricate sigils on a closer look. "Are those moon phases?" I ask, leaning in to inspect it.

"Yeah," Jack sighs. "I don't shift, don't have any of a wolf shifter's normal weaknesses. But on the full moon, I go berserk. If Ben hadn't acted fast the first time, I don't know how many people I would've killed."

"And I'm processing a collection of spellbooks and histories from the library of a notable Fae scholar." I sit back up, squashing the desire to run my fingers over the mark, just for the chance to touch him. "You're hoping there might be something in there to help you break the curse, so you want copies."

They exchange glances again—a slight eyebrow lift from Ben, a tiny shrug from Jack. "Not bad," Jack says.

"Not bad?" Ben scoffs. "She's exactly right and you know it."

"Fine," Jack says, taking another drink of his beer. "So, can we have copies?"

I shrug. "Yeah, sure. I can give you access to my cloud backup of the scans so you can download them for yourself. How's your Old English and medieval French?"

Both of them do their best to keep a straight face, but I can see the slight slump of their shoulders. Probably that's why I make my offer. I've always been a sucker.

"I can translate them for you. Not right now; I have another three weeks on my contract with the library before I'd have time to really work on it. I can email them to you when they're done, so you don't have to hang around."

"I can try to help, but my French is pretty rusty," Ben says.

Our conversation cuts off as the food arrives. We devote ourselves to eating for a few minutes, waiting until the waitress is out of earshot before picking it back up again.

"So you said your contract with the library will be up," Ben notes, pouring dressing on his salad. "You don't work there full-time?"

I swallow a bite of my own salad before answering. "Nope. I'm kind of a specialist; most places don't need someone like me full-time. I'd love to get on with a museum, but there's a lot of competition."

"How does that work out for money?" Jack asks, chewing his burger. "Do you travel around a lot?"

"If I need to," I answer. "I do a lot of freelance translating, some tech writing, consulting for private collectors, that kind of thing. Most months it adds up to enough.

And when I get a contract like this, it lets me build up a cushion. Most of what I do can be done pretty much anywhere there's a decent Internet connection."

I can see them having a whole conversation in facial expressions and body language. The anthropologist in me itches to study them, to catalog what Ben's eye roll and Jack's smirk mean, but I force myself to drop my eyes to my food. Getting any more mixed up with them isn't a good idea. Not if I want any shot at a normal life.

No matter how good the sex was.

6

I close the flaps on the last manuscript box, fastening it carefully before slipping it back into its sealed case. The past few weeks have flown by even faster than usual, and now it's time to say goodbye. As usual when I finish a project successfully, I feel accomplished, but also a little bit of a loss; I got to have these books for a little while, but they were never really mine.

Removing my gloves, I glance around the climate-controlled lab one last time. And then it's time to gather all the little personal items that somehow always migrate into my work space—hair elastics and business cards and my favorite pens that I'm not going to leave behind, plus an embarrassing number of reusable coffee cups. Stuffing them into my messenger bag, I turn off the lights and leave, locking the door behind me.

For the last time.

Thankfully, before I can descend into full-blown wallowing, my phone vibrates in my pocket. When I fish it out, there's a text notification from Ben on the screen. *Got the last scan. Finished?*

Smiling, I text back. *Yup! Now the real work can begin! ...tomorrow*

The phone vibrates in my hand. *Slacker*

Hey, a girl's gotta eat, I text back, rolling my eyes. *And we both know how much I like to eat.*

And be eaten, is the near-instant response.

A blush spreads hot over my face as I stare at the screen. Ben had given me phone numbers and email addresses to contact them before they left town to do whatever they were doing in between trying to remove Jack's curse. Since then, Ben and I have fallen into an easy routine of texts and emails back and forth, usually him asking questions about the pages I scanned that day. Sometimes I ask what they're up to and he tells me about their latest hunt.

But this is the first time he's ever referenced the night we met. Not that I've forgotten. Sometimes I think every erotic detail is burned into my memory, but my brain has compartmentalized. The Ben who texts me with questions about medieval French and substitutes for spell ingredients is a separate person from the Ben who fucked me so hard I screamed.

At least in my mind.

But now, one tiny text message, three little words, and those dividing walls come crashing down. All I can think about is Ben's mouth on me, or Jack's head between my legs while Ben's deep, rich voice purrs filthy words in my ear.

I have no idea how long I stand there, staring blankly at my phone, but when I drag myself out of my reverie, the screen has gone black. Shaking my head, I stuff the phone back in my pocket and head to the library director's office for my final report.

I'll think about it later

ᛋᚱᚻ

ONCE I GET HOME, I sink into my couch with a sigh. Normally after finishing a contract, I take some time to rest my brain, to switch gears from one project to another; it's prime binge-watching time. But tonight I'm restless, unable to settle and relax like I usually do. I even think about heading down to the bar for a couple of drinks and some solo games of pool. But that reminds me of Ben and Jack, which makes me even more restless.

My phone rings, startling me. It's probably a telemarketer, but as twitchy as I'm feeling, even that is a welcome distraction. I answer it without checking the screen. "Hello?"

"Hi, Claire." Ben's voice is warm and somehow familiar in my ear, even though we haven't spoken in weeks.

"Ben?" Surprise makes my voice squeak. Great. Way to make a good impression. "Uh, hi."

I can hear the grin in his voice, see his dimples flashing in my mind's eye. "Were you expecting someone else?"

"No," I say. "No, I, uh, don't really get a lot of calls. I was just surprised it was an actual person and not a robot telemarketer."

"I—" it's apparently Ben's turn to sound uncertain, which is a surprise. "I wanted to apologize about that last text. If it offended you, or made you uncomfortable. I just…"

Silence.

"Ben? You still there?"

"Yeah. You know—forget it. I just wanted to say sorry if it bothered you. We're going to be working together on these translations. I don't want you to be uncomfortable."

I curl into the corner of the couch. "What were you going to say before?"

He inhales, hesitating again for so long that I almost think he isn't going to say anything.

"I was going to say that I know you were upset when you found out who we are, but—gods, Claire. Being with you—it was good," he finally says. "Great. Amazing. Mind-blowing. If you hadn't figured out we were hunters, we probably would've tried to talk you into another round, or more, for as long as we were in town."

His voice drops to that low purr that does such unbelievable things to my insides, rumbling dark and rich with just that hint of raspiness. "I want to fuck you again. I think about it when I'm jerking off in the shower in the morning, or at night when I can't sleep. I think about how your pussy felt around my cock and about how much I loved fucking your mouth. I think about all the things we didn't get to try, and I imagine how hard you'd scream for us if we did them."

"I—" My mouth is dry and my voice has gone breathy. "I don't know what to say."

"You don't have to say anything. I just—I wanted to be honest with you. If you're not interested, you're not interested. I'm not going to try and pressure you into anything, and neither is Jack. This can be all business, if that's what you want."

I swallow. "What about Jack. What does he want?"

Ben laughs softly. "Baby, I can count the number of women Jack's taken to breakfast on the fingers of one hand. I'd have fingers left over, too. I guarantee you he wants to fuck you again, too."

Jack's voice sounds, indistinct in the background.

"What, Jack, are you saying you don't want to?" Ben asks, his voice quieter, like his mouth is further from the receiver. I strain my ears, but all I hear is silence. "That's what I thought. Claire, I'm gonna put you on speaker, okay?"

"So what," I ask, "you want to be fuck-buddies? Friends with benefits? What are we talking about, exactly?"

Instead of answering me, he turns it around. "What do

you want, Claire? You're good at telling us what you want in bed. How about now? What do you want from us?"

My heart is pounding like I've been running for my life. "I—I don't know."

"That's okay," he says, his voice gentle. "Start small. Do you want to be with us again?"

"Yes." The answer slips out before I can second-guess it, before I can take it back. The truth, hanging there in the open where anyone can take it, use it to beat and batter me.

Ben exhales, like he's been holding his breath. "Okay. Do you want to spend time with us? Get to know us, not just the rumors you've heard? Or do you want it to be just sex, and then just business."

It takes me two tries to get my answer out, and not just because of the pang of guilt I can't quite shake. But Jake is gone. He's never coming back. I have to accept that, or I'll go crazy with wondering. "I don't want it to be just sex. I —I like you, both of you. I want to get to know you."

"We do, too," Ben says. "Both of us."

In the background I can hear Jack again, and this time I can understand that he's saying "hopefully naked."

I laugh helplessly, and Ben laughs with me, his deep voice reassuring in my ear. But when the laughter ends and silence falls again, insecurity comes creeping back in with it.

"Why me?" I ask, leaning my head back against the couch and closing my eyes. "I think I can safely assume I'm not the first girl you two have picked up. And maybe all I know is rumors, but they tend to agree that the only long-term relationship you do is with each other."

I rub the heel of my hand against my forehead, trying to dissipate the ache that's settled there. "I'm a mess, Ben. I've only been in one relationship in my life, and now I'm a 34-year-old widow. I'm so fucked up in the head that I get lost in there sometimes. You guys should be running for the hills instead of trying to get to know me."

Ben's answering laugh is completely humorless. "Baby, you want to talk fucked up in the head? I'm a changeling; the only reason I have this life is because someone's real kid got stolen and I was left in his place. Jack's not any better, either."

"Hey!" Jack says in the background. I don't know what it says about me that I can picture the looks they're exchanging.

"We're not exactly prizes, Claire. Most of the people I've fallen for ended up dead. I should be telling you to run as far away from us as possible, not talking you into giving us a shot."

My heart aches in my chest at the pain in his voice. It echoes in the raw, hurting place inside me where Jake had been ripped out of my life. Maybe we're more alike than I thought.

When I can speak without crying, my voice is small, but it's steady. "I don't want to run."

"Me either," Ben says.

7

ᚷᚱᚼ

One of the best things about being between jobs is plenty of time to cook. The weather is turning cool, changing colors on the trees and bringing out my urge to bake all of the things. After a couple of days of buckling down, I need a break from translating grimoires. Snickerdoodles sound like just the thing.

Of course my phone would start ringing when my hands are covered in cinnamon and sugar, vibrating itself toward the edge of the counter.

"Shit," I curse. Hastily rinsing my hands clean in the sink and wiping them dry, I manage to grab the phone and swipe to answer just before it goes to voicemail. "Hello?"

"Hey, baby," Ben says. "Everything okay? You sound a little out of breath."

"Yeah, I'm fine," I say, tucking the phone between my ear and my shoulder. "It's nice and cool here, which triggered my annual urge to bake. I'm making snickerdoodles, but I had to clean off my hands before I answered the phone."

He laughs. "Well, now that I know you're making cookies—"

Jack says something unintelligible in the background, only the excitement in his tone coming through.

"Yes, cookies. Gods, Jack, you're like a five-year-old. Anyway, we finally took out that kelpie and we're only about 3, maybe 4 hours away. We don't have a line on anything else that needs checking out right now. I was going to see if you were cool with us hanging out for a bit and working on the translations with you?"

"Sure thing." I return to rolling the cookie dough into balls, then coating them with cinnamon sugar. "Today's a good day for that, actually. I've been on a cooking binge lately, trying to clean out the fridge before the food goes bad, and I made a pie yesterday. It'd be nice to have some extra mouths around here so I don't eat all of it myself."

Ben laughs again. "I probably shouldn't tell Jack about the pie or he'll speed the whole way there."

Jack's voice comes through the phone, along with the sounds of a scuffle. "I don't know! Ow, fine, jerk, keep your eyes on the road! Jack wants to know what kind of pie."

I can't help grinning. "Apple. And I have ice cream to go with it."

Ben groans. "That did it. If we don't show up, you'll know we're dead in a ditch because this asshole was speeding. And if we do show up, you're probably not getting rid of us until the pie is gone."

"I'm okay with that." I adjusting the balls of cookie dough on the baking sheet until they're evenly spaced. "I've been running the scans through the OCR program so we can try auto-translating them. I'll show you what I've got once you get here."

"Sounds good." Ben drops his voice to the low, intimate tone that always drives me crazy. "Maybe we can find time for a game of pool or something while we're there."

I take a breath, trying and failing to quiet the butterflies in my stomach. "Maybe we can."

He chuckles. "Now Jack's really speeding. See you soon."

ᛋᚱ

THE KNOCK on my door startles me, tearing my focus away from the computer screen and the half-translated page on it.

I know it's Ben and Jack; one of the reasons I love living in this area is that we hardly ever get people going door-to-door. Getting to my feet, I resist the urge to dash into my room and change clothes. They've already seen me naked, I remind myself as I head toward the door. Jeans and a t-shirt covered in flour aren't going to scare them away. Probably.

When I open it, I'm gratified to see that they both look a little nervous, too. At least I'm not the only one. "Come in." I step back to let them in, trying to remember what normal people do with their hands. Do I kiss them? Hug them? What?

"Damn," Jack says with a whistle as he comes through the door, Ben on his heels. "I thought you said you had an apartment. This is huge."

I smile, closing the door behind them. "Technically it is an apartment. It's just a big one. With two floors."

"It's nice," Ben says, hesitating halfway down when he leans in for a kiss.

Fuck it. I go up on my tiptoes to close the distance between us. Of course, what starts as a simple press of lips quickly becomes heated. Ben gets his hands on my waist and pulls me in against him and licks into my mouth like it's been years, not weeks, since the last time we kissed.

When we break apart, breathing hard, Jack is watching us with a look on his face that I can't quite decipher. I move to him before I can think too hard about it, pulling his head down. He goes willingly, kissing me gently, almost tentatively, but no less hungry than Ben was.

He's smiling when he lifts his head, his eyes clear again. "Somebody said something about pie?"

"Dinner first." I slip my hand into his, reaching for

Ben with my other hand, and leading them through the living area toward my dining table. "I've got meat and potatoes. You'll have to suffer through that before you have your pie."

"Oh, no." Ben's monotone voice belies the amusement dancing in his eyes. "You monster. Please don't make us eat that home-cooked meal. Have mercy."

I smack him on the shoulder, shoving him gently into a chair. "Shut up and let me feed you."

"Yes, ma'am," they say simultaneously.

"But seriously, Claire, do you need help with anything?" Ben asks.

I pull the serving dishes out of the oven where I'd put them to keep warm. "Not right now. I'll let you help with dishes after, though. Do you guys want beer?"

"That sounds great," Jack says. "In the fridge?"

"Yeah, help yourself." I set the platter of roast beef, potatoes, and carrots on the table, returning to the kitchen for the broccoli and cauliflower.

Jack takes two beers from the fridge and pops the lids off with the opener on the door. Carrying them back to the table, he hands one to Ben before taking a long pull from his own.

"Help yourself." I set the last dish on the table and slide into a chair between them.

Jack makes a face at the other vegetables, but helps himself to the roast and potatoes. Ben takes some of everything, trying the broccoli first while I'm dishing up my own food, watching him surreptitiously. I can't help smirking when he lets out the kind of noise I've only heard from him in bed.

"What did you do to this broccoli?" He forks up a bite of cauliflower and pops it into his mouth. The moan is louder this time. "And the cauliflower. Jack, you have to try this. I swear it doesn't taste like vegetables."

Jack makes another face, but stabs a tiny broccoli floret with his fork. Although he starts out chewing hesitantly, delight slowly dawns over his face. "Seriously, what did you do? That's incredible."

"I roasted it in bacon grease." I take my own bite, enjoying the contrast between the savory bacon flavor and the sweet caramelization of the vegetables. "You can use oil instead, but the bacon grease gives it a really good flavor. When I do asparagus, I wrap the bacon around it. It's ridiculously good."

"Hate to say it, Benny," Jack looks over at Ben with a smirk, "but I think maybe those kelpies got us. We met a woman who likes kinky sex with both of us, buys us beer, likes bacon, and makes broccoli taste good. We've obviously died and gone to heaven."

I blush.

Ben looks thoughtful. "You might have a point. Except we met Claire before we went after the kelpies."

"True." Jack chews his vegetables, lost in thought for a minute, then shrugs. "Either way, there's pie, right?"

By unspoken agreement, we keep dinner conversation

light. Ben and Jack tell me stories. Like the time a witch cast an animal attraction spell on them so they were attacked by amorous squirrels—"You wouldn't believe the looks you get when five squirrels are all humping your leg at once."

My stories have a lot less supernatural mayhem, but they seem equally amused by the freshman who thought he bought weed but was actually smoking oregano.

I thought I would be too nervous and on edge to eat, but before I know it, the food has disappeared and Jack is making obscene noises over his apple pie. Ben and I share an amused glance before we turn our attention to our own desserts.

Both of them help clean up, Jack loading the dishwasher while Ben wipes the table. But once all the cleaning is done, a palpable awkwardness settles over us, all distractions gone.

Finally, I'm unable to deal with the silence any longer. "So. I guess it's time for me to say we should set some ground rules—again?"

Jack shoots me an amused glance. "You and your ground rules."

I roll my eyes. "There are three of us. That's literally six times as many chances for misunderstanding and drama. If this is going to work, we're going to have to talk about things. And the beginning seems like a good place to start."

"So what do you want to start with?" Ben laces his fingers through mine.

I hesitate. "I guess by asking, I mean, is this a relationship? Are we exclusive?"

"Yes," they say simultaneously almost before I'm done talking, no pause or hesitation. There's a moment of silence while they share one of those speaking looks, but then Jack gestures for his brother to continue.

"I'm not gonna tell you we haven't done the casual hook-up thing before," Ben says, lifting my chin gently until I meet his gaze. "But that's not what we're after here. We want you. Just you."

Jack slides his hand around the back of my neck. "We're probably gonna fuck things up somehow, but it's not gonna be by cheating on you. Nobody else, unless we all agree"

"Okay," I say, breathing a little easier. "Then I guess my next question is, how does this work? Do we only have sex when it's the three of us? Is one of you going to get jealous if you're gone somewhere and I have sex with the other one?"

They look a little baffled at the question. "Uh," Jack says. "That hasn't ever really come up before. I don't think I'd care if you fuck Benny when I'm not here. Now if I am here and I'm not invited, I might get a little testy."

"Yeah, same for me," Ben says. He grins wickedly. "But if that happens, when I get back, you have to tell me exactly what he did to you. In detail. With the dirty words."

I blush again.

"That'll be a fun time. I may have to send you somewhere on purpose," Jack smirks. He squeezes the back of my neck gently. "Any more questions? Cause it's been weeks since I got to fuck you, and all this talk is giving me ideas."

He gives me a moment to reply, then pulls me closer for a kiss. There's nothing tentative this time about the way he nips and licks, devouring my mouth. I moan, nerve endings sparking to life, as he hauls me off my chair and onto his lap.

The hard ridge of his cock inside his jeans fits perfectly between my legs, pressure just where I want it. He tears his mouth away and rests his forehead on mine, breathing hard. "Here? Or do you wanna take this to a bed?"

Jack grins when he steps into my bedroom and sees the king-size bed. "Now that's what I'm talkin' about!"

"I like to sprawl." I lead Ben through the door, following Jack's lead. "And this way there's plenty of room for everyone."

Ben closes the door behind us and leans down to kiss me. It's long and deep and dirty, our tongues and lips sliding against each other, leaving me whimpering when he pulls back. My brains are so scrambled by the kiss that it takes me a few minutes to realize Jack is tugging him away from me to sit on the foot of the bed, eyeing me with that dirty smirk.

"I think we need to see how good you are at following directions," he purrs. Sitting down next to Ben, he pulls his boots off, his eyes never leaving mine. "You like to do what you're told, right, Claire?"

Mouth dry, I nod, unable to speak.

"Good girl," he says. "Take off your jeans. Slowly."

I fumble with the button on my jeans for a second, until I can get my hands to work. Lowering the zipper slowly, I shimmy the tight denim down my legs, stepping out carefully. I'm still wearing my blue button-down shirt, long enough to cover my underwear, but as I straighten back up, I feel more naked than if they'd stripped me to the skin.

Ben starts to remove his boots as well, maintaining eye contact with me the whole time. "Unbutton your blouse, but leave it on."

I obey with shaking fingers. They haven't touched me except for a couple of kisses, but I'm already on edge, just from their eyes on me, from this slow tease of their orders. And they know exactly how turned on I am; I can see it on their faces.

"Leave the shirt, but take off your bra," Jack says, pulling his own shirt up and over his head.

Shivering from the dark rasp of his voice, the way it builds my arousal higher, I reach behind me. Getting the bra unhooked goes smoothly, but I have to concentrate to pull it out of my sleeve, acutely aware that I'm nearly naked.

Both of them suck in a breath as the bra drops to the floor. I feel a sudden surge of confidence, a feeling of power. Their cocks are pressing hard against their jeans, a clear visual of how turned on they are by me.

The last bits of my uncertainty and insecurity fall away, lost in this heady rush. I shake my hair back, smiling as their eyes go to my breasts.

"Doing so good for us, baby," Ben murmurs, tugging his shirt off and tossing it to the floor. "Take off your panties, too."

I slide them down my legs, bending at the hips and arching my back to make sure they get a good show, then slowly straighten back up.

Jack's nostrils flare as he inhales. "Damn, sweetheart, I can smell your pussy from here. Are you that wet just from stripping for us?"

Swallowing, I nod, watching Jack's hands fist in my comforter while Ben shifts next to him.

"Come over here," Jack growls.

Letting my trembling legs carry me to the bed, I obey. He fists his hands in my hair, pulling me down for a rough kiss. When it ends, he uses his grip on my hair to tug my head back, scraping his teeth over my neck and smiling when I shudder under his touch.

"I wanna watch you give Benny a lap dance," he breathes in my ear. "You gonna do that for me? Get him all worked up, make him beg?"

The thought, the mental picture, makes me groan. How does he know exactly how to push my buttons?

Jack chuckles mercilessly in my ear. "What's that, sweetheart? I can't hear you."

"Yes." I arch under his hands as he nips at my earlobe, my voice soft and breathy.

"Good." He guides me back up off his lap, turning me to face Ben. "You ever done this before?"

I shake my head, blushing.

"First thing we're gonna need is music," Jack says. He pulls his phone out of his pocket, tapping at the screen for a moment.

Ben huffs out a laugh as the opening riff of "Pour Some Sugar On Me" fills the room. "Really, Jack?"

"Hey, it's a classic for a reason." Jack gets up and moves behind me, his hand trailing up my arm and over my shoulders. "Now remember, Benny, no touching. Hands on the bed."

Rolling his eyes, Ben complies, moving his hands from where they rest on his thighs and pressing them flat on the bed.

Jack pulls my hair back over my shoulder, leaning down to speak directly into my ear. His breath ghosts over the sensitive skin of my neck, raising goosebumps everywhere, making me shiver.

"First, I want you to go over and ride his leg. Let him get a good look at those pretty tits."

Sucking in a breath, I nod stepping toward the bed and straddling his thigh. My hips circle against him, in time to the music, and I smooth my hands down the front of my body, over the shirt.

He digs his fingers into the comforter like he's fighting not to grab me, his eyes following the movement of my hands. Encouraged, I slide them back up even slower, spreading my shirt wider until my breasts are completely uncovered, nipples so hard they ache a little.

"Oh, baby, you're gonna pay for this when I get my hands on you," he promises, eyes gone dark as he watches me move.

"That's it, sweetheart," Jack says from behind me. "Now turn around. Grind that pretty little ass up against him."

I turn around as ordered, but I shoot Jack a glare. "My ass is not little."

"And thank the gods for that," Ben says. He gasps a little when I lean back, reaching up to wrap one hand against the back of his neck for balance, but keeps talking. "I love your ass. I can just grab on and fuck you as hard as I want. And you'll take it, won't you, baby? Take everything we give you and beg for more?"

"I don't think I'm supposed to be the one begging here," I say. The grinding is nice, his cock hard under me, but I decide to up the ante. Sliding my hands down to my breasts, I cup them in my hands, stroking my thumbs across my nipples. "I guess I can if you want me to, though."

"Fuck," Ben mutters. His hands flex against the bed in my peripheral vision. "Jack, you're gonna pay for this, too."

Jack smirks. "I don't think he's gonna last much longer, Claire. Why don't you show him where he can touch?"

Reaching down, I lace my fingers through Ben's larger ones, dragging his hands slowly up my thighs, over my rib cage, until they're cupping my breasts. Together we lift them like an offering for Jack's hungry gaze.

He leans forward, swiping his tongue slowly over first one nipple, then the other, smiling wolfishly at the noises he drags out of me.

I retaliate by sliding one of Ben's hands down between my legs. We groan together as his fingers slide wetly across my clit.

"Shit, baby." His voice is a deep, hungry rasp in my ear. He frees his fingers to move further down, nudging inside my pussy. "You're so fucking wet for us, dripping all over my jeans. Wanna fuck you right here, just like this, make Jack watch."

I whimper as he crooks his fingers expertly inside me, his thumb still on my clit. When I look up, Jack is completely naked, stroking his cock as he watches us with a predatory gaze.

Ben chuckles wickedly in my ear. "Oh, you like that, don't you? C'mon, baby. Come for us now. Let Jack see how much you love it. Let me feel how much you love it. Want you to come all over my hand, wanna be able to smell your pussy on these jeans even after I wash 'em."

He works me over like that, one hand inside my pussy, one hand on my breast, murmuring filthy endearments and promises into my ear. When he pinches my nipple and orders me to come again, I do.

I'm vaguely aware of being shifted, my body pliable and melting. Before I've entirely recovered, I feel myself sinking down onto Ben's cock. I groan as he pushes into my pussy, feeling myself stretch and ease around him until he's fully inside, as deep as he can go.

And then he starts to move, one hand on my breast and one on my clit. His strong arms pin me like that, with my back to his chest, holding me immobile so all I can do is take it as he fucks up into me.

Jack moves toward us, one hand wrapped around his cock, but Ben snaps, "No," stopping him in his tracks.

"I said you were gonna pay. You get to watch me fuck our girl. You get to hear her, smell her, watch her pretty tits bounce, but you don't get to touch. Not this time."

"Fuck, Benny," Jack snarls. His fists clench at his side, but he doesn't come closer.

I can feel Ben grin against my neck. "Hands to yourself, or maybe next time I'll cuff you to the bed and make you watch while I fuck her." Jack's cock jerks in his hand as I whimper. Ben chuckles again. "Or maybe I will anyway, since it looks like both of you really like that idea."

He turns his mouth back toward my ear, his voice dropping back to that dark, velvety rasp. I can tell from the direction of Jack's eyes that he maintains eye contact with his brother the whole time.

"You want that, baby? Wanna see him all stretched out on your bed so you can play with him however you want and he can't move? I bet he'll go crazy while I fuck you and he can't even get a hand free to get himself off. You could make him beg you to touch him."

Shuddering, I come apart under Ben's talented hands and dirty voice, the desperate intensity of Jack's regard. Ben's thrusts speed up, fucking me straight through my orgasm and into another. Finally his hips stutter and he bites down on my shoulder, thrusting up inside me one final time as he comes.

I notice when he eases us back to lie on the bed. I just don't care. When Jack joins us, I barely muster up the energy to ask "All right?"

He captures my mouth in a blistering kiss, muttering something about being better than porn. I'm pretty sure he'd let me know if he hadn't come, so I relax, enjoying the comfort of having them there with me.

Some indeterminate, lazy amount of time later, I giggle, massaging my fingers through Jack's hair and watching him arch like a cat under my ministrations.

"What's so funny?" Ben asks, propping himself on one elbow to watch.

"All these stories about the big, bad Andersons. Fighting the Fae, saving the world. And nobody has any idea how cuddly you two get after sex." I giggle again. "If I had a secret camera in here, I'd have blackmail material for days. I'd never have to work again."

"If you had a secret camera in here, you'd have the best porno ever," Jack says, his eyes still closed. "I'd pay good money for that."

"Dude, nobody wants to see your scrawny white boy ass when they're watching porn," Ben says, his eyes crinkling at the corner.

Jack smirks. "My ass isn't scrawny, it's magnificent. And so is my hair."

I roll my eyes. "Oh my gods. I take it all back. Nobody said anything about a secret camera. Who wants more pie?"

9

I wake up sometime in the small hours of the morning, when the barest hint of light seeps in around the edge of my curtains, just enough to realize that I'm not alone. Ben is curled around my back, his arm heavy over my waist. I'm sprawled half across Jack, his heartbeat strong and steady under my ear. My muscles are more relaxed than they've been in a long time. Maybe from last night's sex, maybe from sleep.

Maybe it's them.

I let myself drift back into sleep, warm and content in their arms.

ᛋᚱᚼ

WHEN I WAKE AGAIN, later that morning, it's almost

bright in the room despite my heavy curtains, sunlight filtering around the edges. Both of the guys are still asleep. I consider my approach for a moment before rolling onto my side and sliding slowly down to take Jack's cock in my mouth. He hardens almost immediately under my tongue, but doesn't wake up until after he's started thrusting gently.

"Jesus, fuck, Claire," he babbles brokenly, his voice still thick with sleep. "Shit, sweetheart, feels so good. Don't stop—oh gods—don't stop—"

Ben's big hand threads into my hair, urging me down further onto Jack's dick, holding me gently in place when I would've pulled back. Breathing through my nose, I focus on pulling in air, swallowing around him.

"That's it, baby." Ben's voice is dark and rich, his approval making arousal coil in my belly. "Swallow for him, let him feel it. Feels so good when you do that. Take care of Jack and I'll take care of you."

He starts licking his way down my spine, peppering my skin with tiny kisses and nips. Curling himself around, he lifts my leg, sliding his head down to lick at my clit.

I moan around Jack's cock, which just makes him thrust harder into my mouth.

"So good, sweetheart, don't stop," Jack growls. "Gods, wish I could fuck your mouth forever. So hot—feels so good—"

The combination of Jack's words with Ben's fingers pushing into my pussy, his tongue on my clit, has me coming almost before I realize it. Jack keeps thrusting into my mouth while Ben slips out from between my legs.

I hear a crinkling sound and then Ben is back, straddling one of my legs and lifting the other to rest on his shoulder as he curls two long fingers inside my pussy again. He chuckles when I moan around Jack's cock. "Don't worry, baby, I've got you."

With me lying on my side like this, it's an even tighter fit than usual. Ben has to work his way inside my pussy with short snaps of his hips until his cock is as deep as it can go. Then he starts fucking me in earnest, matching Jack's thrusts into my mouth.

Ben fucks me relentlessly through one orgasm and straight into another before he comes, thrusting even deeper inside me. Seconds later, Jack finally loses it, coming in my mouth with a loud groan.

We lie there for a few moments, catching our breath. Eventually Jack drags me up for a kiss, apparently unbothered by the taste of his semen in my mouth. "That was amazing." His voice is still a little slurred from sleep or orgasm or both, his hands stroking up and down my back. "You're officially the only person who ever gets to wake me up."

I settle in against his side while Ben gets up, still panting, to deal with the condom. "You know that's not gonna happen every morning, right?"

"Aww." Ben pouts as he crosses the room to back into

the bed behind me. "Please? We'll make it worth your while."

Pursing my lips, I pretend to mull it over. "I'll consider it."

We lie in surprisingly comfortable silence for some time, hands moving idly over skin, until our breathing has slowed back down to normal. I can't figure out how to ask what I want to know, so I finally just blurt out, "So—"

Jack props himself up on one elbow, his other hand tracing patterns on my stomach. "What's up, sweetheart?"

"I should start by saying I'm super nosy, I guess." Of course now I'm fumbling to try and find the right words. Way to kill the afterglow. "If I ask about something you're not willing to share, just let me know. I'm a big girl, I can stand being told to butt out."

"Okay, now I'm a little worried about what you're gonna ask," Ben says, running his fingers through my hair.

Jack rolls his eyes. "What do you want to know?"

"We talked about it a little before, that first morning but—how did you guys figure out that you liked..." I gesture to the bed, the way the three of us are entangled, "...this?"

They share one of those looks full of communication that I can't quite parse. Ben arches an eyebrow, Jack shrugs minutely. Then their attention is back on me, and I let out a breath I didn't realize I was holding.

"What we told you was true," Ben says. "You know

who we are and what we do. Have you heard anything else about the way we grew up?"

"Just what you told me, and what's common knowledge. You know how the community likes a gossip. You were in foster care until your moms saved you, took you in and started teaching you?"

Ben nods. "Yeah. We really grew up in each other's pockets. I must've been, what, sixteen the first time Jack brought someone back to our hotel room?"

"Sounds about right." Jack smirks a little. "I wasn't sure he was actually interested in sex, until I saw him peeking at her. Made sure to give him a real good show. She really liked it, too."

I watch, fascinated, as Ben drops his eyes. If his skin was as pale as mine, I'm pretty sure he'd be blushing. "I liked it. I thought it was just because I'd never seen a real girl naked before but—it was better. Even after I'd had sex, it was better when I brought someone back, when Jack was watching." He grins wickedly, dimples flashing. "You should've seen his face the first time I asked him if he wanted a taste. Thought he was gonna have a heart attack."

"You coulda given me some warning," Jack grumbles. "One second I'm watching this girl begging him to let her come, next thing I know he's calling me over."

Ben smirks. "You didn't waste any time, though. Practically teleported across the room."

"Yeah, yeah," Jack says. "Anyway, after that, it just

kinda got to be a habit. Like I said, it's like live porn, and sometimes I get to play, too."

Ben strokes his hand up and down my arm. "I don't really know why it works. Maybe because we had drilled into us that we were safer together for so long that we can't really relax unless we are. And I'm always a little scared I'm going to be too rough, so knowing Jack can stop me if I start to go too far—" He shrugs. "It helps. It's better."

"Yeah. It just makes sense for us. We're a team for everything else; it figures we're a team for this, too." He smirks. "Never had any complaints, anyway."

"It sounds so logical when you explain it like that." I'm only teasing a little as I snuggle in closer between them. "And I definitely don't have any complaints."

"Good." Jack leans in and kisses me.

"But—" My voice trails off as I try to think of how to phrase the next question without giving too much away. "Never mind."

"What is it, baby?" Ben presses a kiss to my hair. "You want to know something, we'll tell you."

"Well, obviously you guys have done the threesome thing before. Have you ever—"

"Have we ever tried dating someone?" Jack finishes for me. "No. Most of the girls we picked up weren't interested in anything serious. And the ones that might've been, well, we weren't there long enough for anything to have a chance."

I feel Ben nodding behind me. "You know the kind of

life we've been living, basically as long as we can remember. We've both tried to get out, different times, different ways. It never worked. Both tried to pretend we were normal, to be normal. How well do you think that went?"

"Hell, maybe that's the real reason we do this. For most of our fucking lives, Ben was the only permanent thing I knew," Jack says. "It's a little less lonely when someone who knows you, who loves you, is there. Makes it feel a little less empty."

I pull him closer, my chest aching from the remembered loneliness I see on his face, echoed in Ben's eyes. I don't have any kind of healing power in my touch, but I try my best. "I'm sorry. I shouldn't have asked."

"No, you should," Ben says. He wraps his arms around me, snuggling closer as well. "If we're gonna do this, you need to be able to ask. It's not going to work if we can't be honest. Jack and I—we're both a little broken. We've just learned to work around the sharp edges."

Curling my other arm around Ben, I hold him to me, fingers threaded through his hair. "I just—I'm just trying to understand. You guys have been with lots of girls—lots of women," I correct myself. "I'm not anything special. Why me?"

"I beg to differ, and I'm pretty sure Jack does, too. You understand exactly how fucked up we are, and you're still willing to give us a shot."

"We couldn't make relationships work on our own." Jack starts to trace patterns across my stomach again.

"We're too used to being together. It was like half of me was missing; we just fit. So if we're ever going to have a shot at a relationship, at something that lasts, it's gonna have to be together. With someone that fits us. You fit."

Ben nods his agreement. "This isn't just a matter of opportunity. It's not just, oh, there's this woman here, right place, right time, any woman would work. We've had chances before, but it's never been right. This?" He lifts one shoulder. "It feels right."

I lace the fingers of my free hand through Jack's, the other one stroking comfortingly down Ben's back. "Yeah. It does."

10

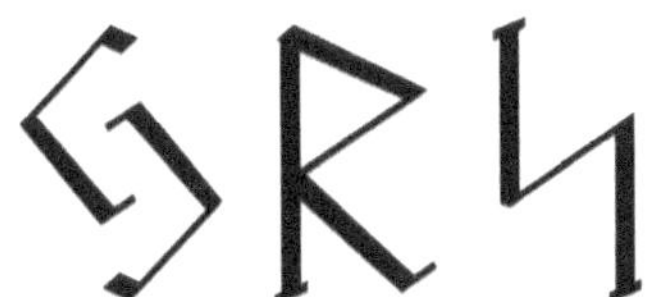

"Huh." I straighten my back and wincing a little at the ache. Gods only know how long I was hunched over the computer, staring at scans, this time.

Ben glances up from his laptop, eyebrows raised.

I gesture toward my screen. "This one is by a priest who made an extensive study of curses, traveling around to gather stories of people who'd been cursed and then cured. Might have something useful.

He brightens. "Is it in Latin?"

"Yeah," I say, glancing down at the paper. "It looks like this is the original work, too, not a copy. So less chance of shit getting lost in translation or transcription."

"How can you tell?" he asks curiously.

"Same way you tell that someone was killed by a

redcap versus a rusalka." I smile a little. "This is what I do. Come here, and I'll show you."

I point to the way the lines waver slightly across the page as he comes to lean over my shoulder. "Medieval monks would have been more precise than this. Our priest was good, but he wasn't that good. And here?" I point out a place where the pen has bobbled, making a slightly misshapen T.

"Okay," he says. "So there might be something in there about the curse, if something like it happened before?"

"Could be." I'm only half paying attention, pulling up the rough translation my computer program had generated. Splitting the screen between that and the original, I start making notes, crossing out words and replacing them with others. "He was pretty thorough, so this could take awhile, but there's a chance."

Ben returns to his own spot and the manuscript he's translating, flipping to another page in the Greek-to-English dictionary he'd dug up from somewhere.

I'm so absorbed in the translation process that I barely notice when Jack comes back into the apartment from wherever he was and starts working in the kitchen. Some part of my brain registers the sound of cabinets opening and closing, the smell of cooking meat and onions. But I still jolt in surprise when Jack sets three plates on the table, blinking a little as I come back to reality.

"Wow." My mouth watering, I take in the patty melts covered in beautifully caramelized onions and perfectly

melted cheese, accompanied with piles of what look like
—"Did you make sweet potato fries? Like slice them and
everything?"

He shrugs like it's no big deal, but I can see the pleasure in his eyes and the slight flush across his cheekbones.
"It's not that hard. Not like I don't have lots of practice
with a knife."

"Not just a pretty face, I see." I pull one of the plates
closer to me, enjoying the way his blush deepens. Cutting
off a bite of the patty melt, I maybe moan just a little when
the flavors hit my tongue. "Gods, Jack, this is so good.
Forget hunting; you should just live here and be my
personal chef. I can keep you in the style you're accus-
tomed to."

"Yeah, cheap beer and cheaper motel rooms are hard to
come by," Ben smirks. But I notice he doesn't waste any
time closing his laptop and grabbing his own plate. After
he takes a bite, he admits, "this is really good, man."

Jack sits down with us and claims the last plate, unable
to entirely suppress a pleased smile. "I'm not exactly fluent
in French or Latin, so I figured I should do my part a
different way. They also serve who grocery shop and cook."

I devote myself to my food for several blissful
moments, enjoying the flavors that burst across my tongue.
It just so happens that I glance up in time to catch the last
of one of those silent conversations—Ben's raised eyebrow,
Jack's answering nod, the matching wicked grins that make
it clear they are, in fact if not in blood, brothers.

"Do I want to know?" Even though I asked, most of my attention is on finding the perfect patty-melt-to-sweet-potato-fry flavor ration.

"Later," Jack promises. I should probably be more worried that he's turning that smile on me. But that look in his eyes usually means I end up enjoying myself pretty thoroughly. "Any luck with the translations?"

I chew and swallow the last bite of food, setting down my fork. "Maybe. The one I'm working on is promising, but so far the only story I thought would be helpful is pretty clearly a werewolf and not an actual literal curse."

Both of them slump back in their chairs. "Well, it was a long shot." Jack is doing his best to hide his disappointment, but it's still pretty obvious.

"I've still got a lot of it to get through," I clarify. "I'm going to get back to it after lunch. But if we don't find anything in these books, I know some people in the community who might be able to help us out, since they owe me a favor. Sorry it's not more."

"Hey." Ben takes my hand in his. "It's more than we've managed to find. Even if we're just talking the speed of translation, you'd still be helping. The fact that you have contacts to reach out to is a bonus on top of that.

Jack nods agreement, pressing his knee against mine. "I'd love it if we could find the magic solution, instantly do it, and call it a day, but things as powerful as this curse don't usually work that way. You're getting us closer than we were, and definitely closer than we would've gotten on our own."

It's my turn to blush. "I just wish it was more. Wish I could do more," I say quietly.

Jack leans over to kiss me softly, making my heart ache from the sweetness of it. "We'll find a way," he says quietly. "There's an answer out there. If anybody can find it, you and Research Boy over there can."

Ben rolls his eyes. "He says, like he's never done a day of research in his life."

"I've done it." Jack waves a hand, picking up his last fry with the other and popping it into his mouth. "Doesn't mean I like it. You actually do."

"Sometimes." Ben stacks up our empty plates and carries them to the sink. "But right now, I think we could all use a break from research."

I reach for my computer. "Sure, just give me a minute. I'm almost done with this page."

Jack takes my hand, pulling me out of the chair and leading me toward the bedroom. "It can wait, sweetheart. We've got a little surprise for you."

"And suddenly I'm worried." I'm only half-joking, my nerves suddenly thrumming with anticipation.

Ben follows us into the room, pulling me close for a long, hot, hungry kiss. "Remember our first time?" He nibbles on my neck the way he knows drives me crazy, breathing the words into my ear. "Remember what I said I wanted to do?"

Jack moves in behind me. I catch my breath, half at the memory of Ben's words and half at the feeling of being trapped between two hard, muscular bodies. I nod, wordlessly.

"C'mon, baby," Ben's lips vibrate against my throat when he chuckles. "You can do better than that. What did I say I wanted?"

I swallow hard, my mouth suddenly dry, as Jack presses in closer against my back. "You said—you said you wanted to fuck my ass while Jack fucks my pussy."

Ben rewards me with another kiss. "Good girl. You did remember. I still want to. I know Jack still wants to."

"You're fucking right I do," Jack growls in my ear.

"So the question is," Ben says softly, "do you want to? This is completely up to you. What we're already doing is amazing; I could keep it up the rest of my life and die a happy man. We don't have to do anything else if you don't want to."

I take a deep breath, letting it out slowly. There's still the part of me that tells me I shouldn't want this, but that part of me is usually full of shit I haven't unlearned yet. Standing here, surrounded by them, protected by them, I find the strength to be brave. "Yes. I want to."

"You sure, sweetheart?" Jack's voice is gentle as he kisses my shoulder. "If you're not sure, we can wait. No rush. No pressure."

Twisting around to face him, I go up on tiptoe for a kiss. "I'm sure. I want this. Want both of you."

"We're still not gonna rush into this." Ben fits himself flush against my back, somehow even closer than before. "We have time to get you ready. I want—we both want this to be good for you. So I had Jack pick up some toys while he was out today."

Jack chuckles, taking my face in his hands. "Don't ever play poker, sweetheart. I can see exactly what you're thinking." He kisses me long and hard, until I feel myself melting into them again. "Don't worry. We'll make it good for you. If anything hurts, you say 'red,' right?"

"Right," I agree absently, most of my attention focused on the way they're working together to remove my clothes. Ben peels of my shirt and tosses my bra aside, his hands coming up to cup my breasts and play lightly—too lightly —with my nipples. In the meantime, Jack unbuttons my jeans and slides them down my legs, steadying me while I step out of them before tossing them aside.

"But first, we're gonna have some fun. Lie down on the bed, on your back," Jack orders. "Hands above your head."

I blink at him for a moment before complying, settling back against the pillows and lifting my arms above my head. When Jack pulls out a set of leather cuffs from somewhere, I crane my neck to see the rather large bag sitting next to the bed, my eyes widening. How the fuck did I not notice him carrying that in here?

"I might have gotten a little carried away," he admits. Buckling one cuff around my right wrist, he smiles wolfishly as I shiver, not sure if it's from the brush of the soft lining against my skin or the way it sits snugly around my wrist. "Benny just asked me to find some plugs so we could ease you into things. But then I saw these, and I remembered how much you liked us tying you down. So I picked up a few extra things."

"Can't complain." Ben says. Sitting down on the other side of the bed, he watches, stroking a hand absently up and down my leg, as Jack threads the chain through the slats on my headboard, then buckles the other cuff. "Why the long chain?"

Jack winks at him. "So she can turn over. If we want her to."

Ben smiles slowly back. "Good call."

"But in the meantime—" Jack leans down to kiss me, his tongue lazily twining with mine, pinning me to the mattress with the weight of his body. He sits up just long enough to pull his shirt over his head, tossing it aside before leaning down to nip gently at my neck. "Not that I'm complaining about your mouth on my dick, sweetheart, but I'd really like to fuck you this time."

"Okay," I gasp. My breath catches in my throat when he licks a circle around one nipple before sucking it into his mouth. When Ben joins in, leaning down to scrape his teeth over the other nipple, I buck up underneath them, pulling fruitlessly against the cuffs.

Jack kisses his way down my belly, leaving my breasts to Ben, who uses his hand to make sure neither of them feel neglected. I'm already on the verge of coming just from the feeling of restraint when Jack licks at my clit. All it takes is him curling two fingers inside my pussy to send me over the edge.

Ben releases my nipple with one last suck that has me arching up as much as the cuffs will permit. Sliding further up, he captures my mouth in a long, sumptuous kiss. The mattress shifts as Jack moves away for a moment and something crinkles—condom, my brain supplies.

I moan into Ben's mouth when I feel Jack's cock press slowly inside my pussy, inch by torturous inch, too much and too slow all at the same time.

"That's it, baby," Ben murmurs. Kissing my neck, he goes back to playing with my breasts. "Jack's gonna fuck you, get you good and turned on, and then we're gonna put a plug in that pretty ass of yours, start getting you ready. And then we'll take turns fucking you."

Jack lifts my legs until they're propped on his shoulders, pushing still deeper inside of her. "Oh, she likes that idea." Reaching down, he rolls one of my nipples between his fingers. "I can feel you getting wetter just thinking about it, sweetheart. It won't be quite the same, but it'll give you an idea of what to expect, having us both inside you."

Ben turns his attention to my other nipple, scraping his teeth lightly over it before sucking it inside his mouth. His other hand slides down my belly, finding my clit and stroking it in time to Jack's thrusts. Before long I'm coming, shuddering under their hands.

They stroke and pet me as I come down from it, but I still whimper a little when Jack pulls out and their strong hands urge me over onto my stomach, arms still stretched above my head.

"Up on your knees for us, baby," Ben urges. His hand slides down my back and over the curve of my ass, lighting up already-sensitive nerve endings.

I do as he asks, leaving my head and shoulders on the bed as I get my knees under me. Nerves start to rise, coiling electric in my belly, heightened by the sound of the lube clicking open behind me.

"No, baby, it's okay." Ben begins his soothing strokes over my skin again. "Don't worry, don't tense up. You can do this, you're gonna love it. Gonna make you feel so full, so good."

There's a blunt, cool pressure against my ass and, despite my best intentions, I start to tense up. But Ben doesn't press it inside, just teases it against me. "Jack, why don't you see if you can distract her, huh?"

"My pleasure," Jack says.

I smile when I realize I can hear the smirk that must be on his face. It disappears quickly when his fingers slide up my thigh, unerringly finding their way to the spot at the base of my clit that makes my legs shake.

He focuses mercilessly on that spot, driving me higher and higher. My moans climb along with my arousal until I'm not even making a sound as I come, just gasping as I shake under his hand. I'm still vaguely aware of the plug, that Ben is pressing it gently but firmly into my ass until it's fully seated inside me, but it doesn't hurt. It's just one more sensation.

"Good girl." Ben's thumb rubs circles on my hip, grounding me with his touch. "So good for us. Can't wait until that's me inside you, til I can fuck that tight little ass."

Jack pushes inside my pussy again before I can respond, so I can't do anything but moan when his thrusts move the plug deeper into my ass. "Fuck, sweetheart, you're so wet. You like that, don't you?"

It takes two tries for me to reply; each time I start to, he thrusts a little deeper, stealing my breath. "Yes," I finally gasp. "Gods, Jack, please—"

"I like it when you beg," he rasps. His big hands grip my hips to hold me in place while he fucks me. "I'm gonna fuck you til I come, then Benny's gonna fuck you til he comes. That what you want?"

I nod into the bed, so turned on I can't speak.

Ben threads his fingers through my hair, tugging gently until I lift my head. "That's nice, baby," he says gently, "but it doesn't really matter what you want, does it? You're chained to the bed. We can do whatever we want with you, can't we?"

I moan, and his grip in my hair tightens. "I asked you a question," he growls.

"Yes," I breathe. My face is so hot I'm pretty sure it's going to catch fire.

"Yes, what?" he prompts.

I don't want to say it, but somehow that makes it even better, the fact that he's forcing me to say it driving my arousal to places it's never been before. "You can do whatever you want," I moan. Jack's hands tighten on my hips as he picks up speed. I'm so close…

"That's right." Ben's voice is dark and low, purring into my ear. "And you like that, don't you, you little slut? Want us to use you however we want?"

That's all I can take; Ben's voice, his words, his hands fisted in my hair, Jack's cock inside me, the plug in my ass, all of it comes together and pushes me over the edge.

Jack fucks me unrelentingly through it, taking me up again before I've even come down. "Such a slut for us," he growls, "letting us fuck you however we want. You want to come again?"

"Fuck, yes, please, Jack." I'm babbling brokenly, trying desperately to arrange words into a coherent sentence.

"Ask me before you come," he orders. "If you come without permission, Benny's not gonna fuck your pussy tonight. Understand?"

I nod frantically, but that's not enough of an answer. Jack smacks my ass, hard. "Answer me."

"Yes," I gasp. "I understand. Please, Jack—"

"Good." He fucks me harder, his hips snapping. Before long I'm shaking under him with the effort of holding back my orgasm.

"Can I come?" I moan, barely holding onto control.

He doesn't even pause. "Not yet. Ask me politely next time."

I barely make it three more thrusts. "Please can—please can I come?" My voice breaks when Ben tugs on my hair again, lighting up nerves all over my body.

"Jack, please, please let me come," I beg, gasping for air, unable to stop the words falling out of my mouth. "Please, please, please, oh fuck, please—"

"Come for me," he orders.

And I do, screaming into the bed as he fucks me through it. I barely even notice when he thrusts deep inside me one last time, shuddering with the force of his own orgasm. When Jack withdraws, I collapse limply onto the bed, too wrung out to even lift my head.

Ben presses a kiss to my hair and turns me gently to lie on my back again. I moan as he sinks all the way into my pussy with one quick thrust, his cock sliding over my over-sensitive nerves.

"Not gonna last long after that." He grits the words out, gripping my thighs and pushing them back toward my chest, bending me almost double. "Fuck, baby, that was so hot I almost came before I got inside you."

Despite his words, he takes the time to find my g-spot and nail it with each thrust, fucking me until I'm shaking and sobbing underneath him, pulling against the cuffs. But I can't get away. I'm helpless, chained to the bed, pinned under his body.

It's that, as much as the physical sensations, that makes

me come one more time. He comes only a couple of thrusts later, letting go of my legs and all but collapsing on top of me, the weight of his body pressing me into the mattress.

I fall asleep before Jack finishes taking the cuffs off.

11

It's the middle of the night when I come awake gradually, a vague sense of wrongness refusing to let me sink back into sleep. Ben still snores softly next to me, one arm holding me close to his side, but the other side of the bed is empty.

I glance at the window, but it's still night, no light coming in around the edge of the curtains. The bathroom door is open and dark, but the door to the living room is closed, dim light shining underneath it.

Slipping slowly out of Ben's grasp, I watch carefully as I ease off the side of the bed, his breath slow and even the entire time. Grabbing someone's shirt from the floor—it must be Ben's, since it actually fits over my boobs with enough room to button—I pull it on, not wanting to parade naked through the living room, since the blinds are probably still open.

Making sure the light from the living room doesn't fall on Ben's face, I crack the door open just enough to slip through, closing it softly behind me.

Jack is sitting on the couch when I turn, arms braced on his knees, infinite weariness in every line of his body. For a second I think about retreating, pretending I never woke up, never saw him like this.

When he turns his head and meets my eyes, the pain on his face has me forgetting my self-consciousness. Moving across the room, I curl up beside him, pressing close for warmth, for comfort.

"Hey." I keep my voice soft, leaning my head on his shoulder.

He hesitates for a moment, then leans back and slides his arm around my shoulder. "Hey."

"Can't sleep?" I ask after a few more silent moments, cringing a little at the awkwardness of the question.

"Nightmare." His tone is half-dismissive, half-weary, and all heartbreaking. "Comes with the territory when you're a hunter. PTSD, flashbacks, and a whole lot of triggers no therapist knows how to help you deal with."

I nod, not really sure how to respond to that.

We sit like that for awhile before he sighs and leans back against the couch, pulling me with him. "It's the curse." His voice is barely audible. "It—"

He shudders, closing his eyes. "I—when I dream,

everyone is dead. Ben, you, Mal—everyone. I've killed everyone. And it—it feels so good. I want to go back and do it over again, slower, so I can enjoy it."

I turn more toward him, wrapping my arms around him and holding on as tight as I can. He buries his face in my hair, clinging desperately.

"I don't know if I can stop it," he says after a moment. "I don't know how to stop it. Hunting helps for awhile. Sex, too, but nothing works for long. I hope like hell we can find an answer. I don't know—do you know about the time I spent Underhill?"

"Somehow that never came up." I have no idea where this came from, but I'm not about to stop him when he's opening up to me.

He nods. "It was before—before all of this. Around the time Benny and I started hunting on our own. We were chasing down a lead on the Fae who left him here and— well, it doesn't matter how. He got hurt. Badly. He was dying."

Even after only knowing them for a few weeks, I can't imagine him taking that well.

"So I—I made a deal."

"Jack!"

He sighs. "I know. It was dumb. But—even before our moms, he was there, you know? I always looked out for him. So I made the deal. And she kept her side. She healed him, like nothing ever happened. But the price—the price was that I would go Underhill with her, to be her Knight."

Part of me, the part that isn't horrified by the prospect of Jack being trapped Underhill, wants to ask questions. But now isn't the time for most of them. Still, I have to hold up my side of the conversation, so I ask the least loaded one I can think of. "How long were you there?"

"Time is different there, but I think a hundred years? Maybe more. I lost track, after awhile. I didn't want to remember, because it hurt too much. And—I didn't want to think about anyone I knew, anyone I loved, seeing what I'd become."

"How did you get out?"

His face does something complicated that I can't quite interpret. "Ben. The stupid bastard managed to break me out, with Mal's help—"

"Mal?" That's the second time he's mentioned that name, but this time there's enough space to ask.

"Malak." Jack's voice sounds different when he says the name, I think. But he moves on before I can parse it. "He's a dragon shifter. Ben never would have found me without him. They both almost died, getting me out. But—this curse, it feels like being back there. I can't do it again, Claire. I can't be that thing again."

"We'll find a way," I promise. I just hope it's not a lie. "There's an answer out there. Somewhere. We won't let you fall."

He sucks in a shuddering breath as I stroke my hands up and down his back, thread my fingers through his hair. We both pretend he isn't crying.

As I know all too well, you can't cry forever, no matter how much it feels like you will sometimes. Finally his breath evens out and he relaxes in my arms. "C'mon," I say, urging him up. "This couch is kind of awesome, but the bed's even more comfortable."

"Yeah, okay," he says, scrubbing his face as he stands and pulls me to my feet with his other hand.

Once I'm steady on my feet, he tries to let go, but I hold on, tugging him toward the bedroom.

Ben rouses, just a little, as we settle back into the bed. "Everything okay?" He pulls me back toward him, his eyes still closed.

"It's fine, Benny." Jack says. Pulling the covers up over us, he drapes his arm across my waist. "Sleep."

"'Kay," Ben mumbles. His snoring resumes almost immediately.

I only have to shift about an inch to kiss Jack's cheek. "You too. We're here, we're fine. Sleep now."

He nods, closing his eyes with a sigh. "Yes, ma'am."

ᛋᚱᚺ

THE NEXT TIME I wake up, it's with Jack's mouth on mine and Ben's fingers moving gently inside my pussy.

"There she is." Ben murmurs. He leans down for his own kiss as Jack pulls back. "You awake now, baby?"

Grinning wickedly, he curls his fingers up to stroke over my g-spot as I start to answer.

"I think so." I manage to get the words out despite his best efforts, gasping as Jack licks over my nipple. "You should—ah!—probably make sure, though."

Jack lifts his head. They're both grinning at me and I feel it like a punch in my chest, like a hand wrapped around my heart.

Something must have shown on my face, because their expressions shift instantly to concern. "Claire? You okay?" Jack asks softly, sliding a comforting hand up my arm.

I shake it off and do my best to smile at them—plenty of time for panic later. "I'm fine," I say as reassuringly as I can, reaching for their hands. "This is a hell of a way to wake up."

"Give it a minute," Ben says.

His grin is firmly back in place as he adds a third finger, only Jack's hand on my stomach keeping me on the bed. My hips push up toward him, a sound that can only be described as a whimper coming out of my mouth when he slides his thumb over my clit.

Not to be outdone, Jack returns his attention to my breasts, licking and suckling and nibbling until I completely lose it, shuddering under their hands as I come.

I'm vaguely aware that they're moving me, pulling me a little further from the headboard. Then Ben pushes inside me, bottoming out in one long thrust. "It's gonna be hard and fast, baby," he warns, matching actions to words as he sets a pace just on the right side of brutal.

The speed and force is so overwhelming that I lose track of Jack until he's leaning over me, his fingers shiny with lube, slicking the valley between my breasts. "Wanna fuck these pretty tits," he says, spreading the lube meticulously over my skin. "You gonna let me do that, sweetheart?"

He grins ferally when I nod, pouring more lube into his hand and slicking it over his cock before straddling my chest, careful not to drop all of his weight onto me. Taking my hands, he brings them to my breasts, pressing them together until his cock is engulfed between them.

"Hold 'em for me," he orders, beginning to thrust.

I have no idea if he picks up the same rhythm as Ben or if Ben just slows to his pace. Honestly, it's like asking if the chicken or the egg came first; they just always fall in sync.

Tucking my chin down to watch the head of Jack's cock appear and disappear between my breasts, I can't resist sticking my tongue out and licking it, smiling at his groan. Encouraged, I manage to get my mouth open, catching the head on his next thrust.

"Jesus fuck," Jack swears, his voice strangled. He makes his thrusts shallower so the head stays in my mouth; his hands come up to cover mine, pressing my breasts closer together. "You're gonna kill me, sweetheart. Gotta see this, Benny. Letting me fuck her tits and her mouth at the same time. Fucking amazing."

Ben looks over Jack's shoulder and groans, his fingers

digging into my hips as he does his best to fuck me into the mattress. "Shit. I wanna do that, too."

"Next time," Jack promises for me. He swallows hard, his eyes fluttering closed as I hum my agreement.

My concentration starts slipping after that. Ben's hard, pounding thrusts build me higher and higher, especially when he gets a finger on my clit, rubbing it until I come.

I do my best to keep my mouth relaxed for Jack, but I'm not sure how well I manage. The slide of his cock over my skin, the way his weight on my chest, is almost too much stimulation in my hypersensitive state.

Ben fucks me harder and faster, his finger still on my clit until he buries himself deeper inside me and comes.

"Suck on me," Jack orders.

I do as I'm told, sucking the head of his cock deeper into my mouth.

He groans above me, letting go of my breasts and pushing further into my mouth as he comes, filling my mouth until I swallow it down.

We lie in sweaty, content silence for awhile, hands roaming idly over whatever skin they can reach, until Jack's stomach growls. He grins sheepishly as Ben and I laugh.

"Breakfast?" I ask, pushing myself to a sitting position.

"Shower first," Jack says, rolling off the bed and steering me into the bathroom, with Ben following close behind.

ᛋᚱᚺ

"THAT'S WEIRD."

I look up from my computer to see Ben frowning at his own screen while Jack loads the breakfast dishes into the dishwasher. "What's up?"

"Maybe nothing," he says.

It's not even a little convincing. He finally admits defeat after I stare at him for a couple of minutes. "Murder, pretty bloody. Witnesses saw 'a fiery shape' flying toward the house before the murder and then away afterward."

"Sounds like our kind of thing," Jack says. "Where was it?"

Ben's eyes scan over the screen again. "Oklahoma. Not a town, just out in the country. Probably—" he taps at the keyboard for a second "—about 6 hours drive or so."

"Okay," Jack says. He pauses when Ben gives him a look. They have another one of those silent conversations, this one a bit longer than normal.

"You guys know I'm sitting right here, right?" I ask dryly.

They have the good grace to look a little embarrassed. "If we go—we wanted to ask—" Ben stutters to a halt, fiddling with his pen as he takes a breath and tries again. "We're a little worried about you being here alone while we're gone. We'd feel better if you were at our place."

I purse my lips, torn between annoyance and amusement. "I am a reasonably adult woman. I've been on my own for awhile, you know."

"We know," Jack says. "But you've been helping us research the curse. Asking questions. Sooner or later that's gonna get back to the kind of people—things that would much rather I did something to get myself put down. We've made a lot of enemies. A lot of powerful Fae would be just as happy for me to self-destruct, and they'd love to take out somebody we care about."

I sigh. "I'm not stupid." Focusing my concentration, I push just enough energy into my wards to make them visible, glowing on the walls and the windows. They're the only bit of magic I can do successfully, and I might be unreasonably proud of them. "I did the whole place when I moved in, and I keep them up. Plus you aren't the only people I've helped with research. Nothing is getting in here that I don't invite in.

They inspect the wards for a moment before nodding in approval. "But you're not gonna be in here the whole time we're gone," Jack says. "You'll have to go out sometimes."

"We're not saying you're stupid, or that you can't take care of yourself under normal life circumstances," Ben continues. Sincerity rings in every word; he really means it. "But these aren't normal circumstances. The kind of things that might be gunning for you, we'd have a hard time with them. And we've been training for this most of our lives."

I waver, torn between the knowledge that they're right and my attachment to this space, this home that I've slowly and painfully made for myself.

"Please." Jack's voice is soft, something raw and hurting in his eyes. "If you get hurt…"

I swallow hard, blinking back sympathetic tears. Goddamnit, I'm such a sucker. "Okay," I whisper.

Ben pulls me into a hug, his hands rubbing soothing circles into my back. "Thank you," he whispers in my ear before pulling back. "And hey, while we're gone, you can play in the library."

"You have a library?" I ask. In my experience, that means a bookshelf or two. Not enough to keep me entertained while they're out and about.

"Biggest collection of magic texts and supernatural lore we know of." Jack's smug grin is annoying, but it feels good to see him smiling again.

I roll my eyes. "So, like, 50 books?"

The smile Ben gives me is one I normally only see in bed. "Multiply that by a thousand or so. And it all needs to be cataloged. It's not even on cards."

It's Jack's turn to roll his eyes. "You two can talk nerdy to each other some other time. Claire, how soon can you be ready to go?"

I think about it for a minute. "Am I going to be coming back eventually, or do I need to get all the important stuff today?"

"We can come back," Ben promises.

"In that case, give me an hour and I'll be good to go."

12

"Home, sweet home." Jack opens the door to the small cabin with a flourish.

"Somehow this isn't what I was expecting," I say. I follow him inside anyway; anything that's not the car after our four-hour drive is nice. There's no Tardis-style bigger-on-the-inside moment. It's a cabin. Somewhere on the nicer end of cabins; it's clearly insulated and appears to have electricity and indoor plumbing. There's one bookcase on the wall, which both of them should know better than to call a library. I'm decidedly underwhelmed.

Ben grins at me like he knows what I'm thinking. Honestly, he probably does; I've never been very good at having a poker face. "Come on." he says. Crossing the room, he presses his hand against the bookshelf.

A spell glows to life at his touch, swirling in the air

around his hand before settling back into the wood. I have just enough time to recognize what I think are warding and locking symbols before the bookcase swings toward us, revealing a space behind it.

I let Ben take my hand and lead me through the doorway onto—a balcony? I stop dead in my tracks, hands clutching the balcony railing as I look down into the room below. There's so much to see that I barely notice Jack following us, the door closing behind us.

It looks like a museum, more than anything else, although there's definitely a war-like slant. Displays of various weapons, from swords and daggers that might be actual ancient artifacts to modern machine guns and bazookas, line the walls. Everything is clearly organized, but there's so much I don't get more than brief impressions, although I see something that looks suspiciously like a Star-Wars-style blaster.

They give me a moment to take it all in. When I look up, they're wearing identical boyish grins. "Come on." Ben hitches one of my bags higher on his shoulder, gesturing me down the stairs ahead of him. "You can't even see the library from here."

I follow them down the stairs and deeper into whatever this space is. The library is even bigger than the room I could see from above, shelf after shelf of books stretching out into the distance. Moving to the nearest one, I can't resist running my finger over the spines, letting out a pleased sigh.

"I think I'm jealous." Jack nudges Ben, still grinning. "She usually only makes that noise in bed."

"You have no room to talk." Ben retorts, winking at me. "We all know how you talk to your car."

Jack shrugs. "She's a special lady."

I pull out a book at random, my eyes widening at the spell diagrams on the pages where it falls open. "You guys get me the best presents. Nobody's ever gotten me a whole library before."

"Well, anybody can do flowers and candy," Jack says.

Ben sets down the bags he was holding and moves to stand behind me, sliding his arms around my waist. "Think you can keep yourself occupied while we're gone?"

"I guess." I roll my eyes and draw the word out like my most annoying teenage self. Honestly, now he's just fishing for compliments. "How long do you think it'll take?"

They shrug in unison. "No way to know, really," Jack says. "Could be days, could be weeks. Usually somewhere in between."

"Well then." I make my voice brisk, turning in Ben's arms to kiss him, then pulling Jack in for one as well. "You should probably show me around so you can get going. The bad guys aren't gonna hunt themselves."

"Oh, I see how it is." Jack laughs, slinging an arm around my shoulders as Ben picks up the bags again. "You and the library just want to be alone."

"Maaaybe."

Ben shakes his head fondly at us, unable to hide his

smile, and leads the way deeper into their place. They show me the kitchen, the bedrooms, including one I can use if I'm not comfortable in their rooms, the bathrooms and the garage and a couple of storerooms that make my fingers itch to organize them. But we all know my attention is back in the library.

We end up back in the room full of weapons, standing in an awkward little triangle. It makes sense, when I take a second to stop and think about it. They've never had anyone to say goodbye to, anyone to leave behind. Just like I'm not use to saying goodbye.

I pull first Jack, then Ben, into a kiss, lingering just a little. "Drive safe. Come back soon."

"Yes, ma'am." Ben gives me a little squeeze before he lets go.

"Definitely got a good reason to now." Jack smirks at me, and then they're gone.

At least I'm never really alone when I have books.

ᛋᚱᚻ

I PICK up the phone absently when it starts to vibrate and swipe to answer, my eyes never leaving my computer screen.

"Hello?"

"Hey, baby," Ben says.

My eyes slide closed at the sheer relief of hearing his

voice, having real evidence that he's alive and fine. "Hey," I answer, trying to keep my tone light. "How's it going?"

"It's weird," he admits. "The family and neighbors all claim they saw a 'fiery shape' fly into the house right before the murder. Pretty sure we've ruled out a ghost or a poltergeist. There's no local urban legends about anything like this. So we have no idea what this thing is, or how to stop it."

"That sucks." I set aside the book I'd been cataloging when he called. "Want me to dig through here and see if I find anything that matches?"

He lets out a breath. "That would be great. We're kind of spinning our wheels here until something else happens. And the locals aren't very cooperative."

"Where did you say you were, exactly?" I ask.

"Middle of nowhere Oklahoma," he says. "Pretty country, but redneck central."

"Oklahoma." I tap my pen against my teeth, grimacing when I notice I'm doing it. "I grew up in Arkansas, close to the border. What part of Oklahoma?"

He pauses for a minute. "Uh—north…east?"

I minimize my database and open Google Maps, thanking whatever gods are listening that their weird Batcave lair has good wifi. "What's the nearest town?"

"Brushy," he answers. "I swear I'm not making this up."

"Oh, I know you aren't. I've driven through Brushy before; it's basically a wide spot in the road. The reason I ask is, not a lot of people realize that Oklahoma has a huge number of Native American tribes."

"Oh yeah?" he says, interest clear in his voice. It's so nice not to have to lead a dude around by the hand until he gets what I'm thinking.

I nod before I forget he can't see me. "If I remember correctly—yeah, that area is mostly Cherokee, thanks to the fucking Trail of Tears, although a lot of people are descended from multiple tribes. Do you think there's anything in here on Cherokee myths?"

"I wouldn't be surprised," he says. "We haven't gotten through half of it, but from what I can tell, there's a little bit of everything. If you have time to look, that might be a good place to start. We sure haven't found anything to go on."

I bite back a question about where all this came from; now isn't the time. A cursory search through what little I've gotten cataloged doesn't turn up anything. I pick up the hand-written 'catalog' I found yesterday, paging slowly through while I tuck the phone between my ear and my shoulder. "So the local police aren't cooperating with the 'FBI?' I'm shocked."

I can practically hear Ben's eyes rolling through the phone. "Yeah, local law enforcement, what there is of it, actually isn't too bad. They want this solved. But the family isn't interested in talking to us at all. You'd think they'd want to find out what killed their kid."

I grab the nearest piece of scrap paper, noting down a

couple of titles that might be useful. "This is the part of the country that has a long, proud heritage of being unco-operative to authority. Moonshiners, outlaws—actually, you're only a few hours away from, I kid you not, Robber's Cave. Jesse James used to hide out there. And even without that history, most of the time anyone around there deals with the government, it's not a good experience."

"I guess." The line is silent for a few moments, except for our breathing. "I miss you."

A goofy smile spreads across my face. Thank fuck there's no one else here to see it. "I miss you, too. Let's get this figured out so you guys can come back home, okay?"

"Okay," he agrees.

ᛋᚱᚼ

I RUB my eyes and flip another page, struggling to focus on the cramped handwriting. I'm halfway down the page when the meaning of what I just read finally sinks in.

Grabbing my phone, I start at the top of the page again, reading more closely, then punch the air in triumph before hitting Ben's number in my contacts.

He answers practically on the first ring. "Hey, baby. You find something?"

"I think so. It's a little complicated, though."

"Okay, hold on," he says. "I'm gonna put you on speaker so Jack can hear, too."

I wait impatiently until I hear Jack's tinny voice through the phone. "Okay, sweetheart, go."

"So in Cherokee mythology, there are these giant antlered snakes called uktena that live in rivers," I begin.

"Snakes with antlers? Sounds kinda badass," Jack says.

I can't help grinning, even though missing them is an ache in my chest. "The legend goes that the first one was a man who tried to kill the sun and was transformed into that shape. Anyway, they're supposed to have spots all down their body. They're unkillable unless you shoot them in the seventh spot back from the head, because the heart's under there."

"Are you saying a giant river snake is killing these people?" Ben asks. "Cause nobody's seen that. And it doesn't explain the fiery thing they have seen."

Forgetting for a moment that they can't see me, I shake my head. We really need to see if Skype will work for these conversations. "No, actually the opposite. Apparently when someone kills an uktena, they can get the diamond that's embedded in their forehead. Which they have to keep wrapped in a deerskin in a cave."

"O-kay," Jack says slowly. "I'm guessing weird forehead diamonds aren't the end of it."

"You are correct." I look back down at the page. Even after two reads, I can still hardly believe I'm reading it right. "Every week they have to, and I quote, 'feed it with the blood of small game.' Plus the blood of a bigger animal every six months."

One of them lets out a low whistle. "Shit," Ben says.

"And, get this, 'should he forget to feed it at the proper time, it shall emerge from its cave in a shape of fire, flying through the air to slake its thirst with the lifeblood of the conjurer or some one of his people."

"Huh," Ben says. "So, what, someone in this family killed an uktena and forgot to feed the diamond? And now it's killing them?"

I lean back in my chair. "It's the only thing I could find that fits what's going on. And they might not have known what to do. I'm a member of the Cherokee Nation, tribally enrolled and everything, but my parents didn't teach us anything about what it means. I've picked up a little here and there, but I had to do it on my own."

"Okay," Jack says. "How do we kill a fucking diamond?"

"I don't know if you can," I admit. "The book says that whoever uses it can 'put it to sleep.' And if the conjuror dies, it's supposed to be buried with him. If it isn't, it'll try to find his grave for seven years before it 'sleeps forever.'"

Ben makes a disgruntled noise. "Why would anybody want this thing in the first place? Or is it like a cursed object, something they can't get rid of?"

I flip back through the book, scanning for something else I saw earlier. "Apparently if it's used correctly it's a luck talisman. And whoever owns it can also see the future."

"Still not sure it's worth all the blood," Jack grumbles.

"So we're pretty sure that's what it is. How do we stop it, if we can't kill it. Can we feed it?"

"Probably not, unless there's some Native American somewhere in your family," I say. "Says 'no white man must ever see it.' Ben, I know you're not white, but I'm pretty sure the implication is that it's only for Cherokees or maybe one of the related tribes."

"Well, shit," Ben says. "So, what? We just walk away?"

I sigh. "Maybe you could talk to the family. Tell the truth about who you are and tell them what we think is going on. Maybe they know someone who knows a traditional medicine man or woman. Somebody who could take charge of this thing. Unless one of you can figure out how to kill a diamond, that's probably going to be your best bet."

The line is silent for a moment, so quiet I almost think the call was dropped.

"You know," Jack says finally, "that's a good idea."

I roll my eyes. "Of course it is. Have you met me? I have great ideas."

"You do," Ben agrees. I can hear the smile in his voice. "We'll go see what we can do about this. Call you tomorrow, okay, baby?"

"You'd better," I say, mock-threatening. "If you don't check in on a regular basis I'm gonna drive down there myself."

"We'll be good," Jack promises, his voice amused. "Miss you."

I have to pause long enough to keep a word starting with L from slipping out. "Miss you, too," I say instead. "Go save the day."

I'd much rather have found a solution for Jack's curse, but it's still nice to feel useful, even a little bit. I'm not just a liability, someone who has to be kept safe because I can't fully protect myself. I can help.

13

___

"What the fuck is this twangy redneck shit?" Jack yells.

I jump, turning down the volume on the country song—when did that start playing? Despite the stabbing pain in my head, I launch myself out of the chair where I'd been sitting. Jack oofs a little as I thump into his chest, but he drops his duffel and hugs me back.

When I finally pull away, he's grinning, and so is Ben when he gets the same treatment a few seconds later.

"Missed you." My voice is thick where my cheek presses against Ben's shirt, his heart beating steadily under my ear. I tell myself that it's stupid to have missed them so much, when they were only gone a couple of weeks. "Both of you."

Ben kisses the top of my head. "We missed you too, baby."

I don't pull back from Ben until I'm sure I'm not going to cry.

"But seriously, sweetheart." Jack's face is completely serious, and not in the way that he pretends when he's trolling me. "You can't just play this kind of shit around here. We have standards."

I narrow my eyes at him. "First of all, you're the one who wanted me to be here instead of in my apartment. Where I go, my music goes. Secondly, you really want to go there?"

Ben sits down in a chair, one hand rubbing over his mouth and completely failing to hide his grin.

Jack blinks at me incredulously. "Uh, yeah?"

"So the man who owns everything ever produced by the Eagles and Creedence Clearwater Revival is calling my music 'twangy redneck shit?'"

"Hey," he protests. "That's different. Those are classics."

I smile at him as patronizingly as I can manage, patting his cheek and trying to ignore the queasiness in my stomach and the throbbing ache in my head. "Whatever you say, dear."

Gathering up my computer, I head down the hall to the room where I've been sleeping, singing under my breath as I go. "It's okay to not like things. It's okay, but don't be a dick about it."

Behind me, Ben bursts into laughter.

ᛋᚱᚼ

I GLANCE up at the knock on my door, then back down at my Kindle. "Come in."

The door opens, then silence. When I finally look up, Jack is hovering in the doorway in a clean t-shirt, jeans, and bare feet, hair still damp from the shower and an uncertain look on his face.

I let the silence stretch for a few minutes.

"I—" he trails off, rubbing a hand over the back of his neck. "I—I was a dick."

Turning off my Kindle, I set it aside. "Yeah, you were," I agree evenly.

He meets my eyes for a moment before dropping them again. "I'm sorry," he says finally. "I'm sorry the first thing I said to you after being gone for almost two weeks was me being a dick."

I sigh, patting the bed next to me. He crosses the room gingerly and sits down, still acting like he's walking on eggshells.

"I'm sorry I went all passive-aggressive on you and stormed off to my room like a teenager having a bitch-fit. I've got a nasty migraine—seems like I had one every day while you guys were gone." I smile wryly. "I get bitchy when I'm hurting. Sorry."

He smirks, seeming to regain a little of his confidence. "Headache, huh? You know what the best thing is for that?"

"What?" I ask cautiously, waiting for the punchline.

"Orgasm." Leaning into my space, he kisses me possessively, licking his way into my mouth, exploring it like he's never tasted me before, only pulling back when we're both breathing heavily. "Preferably multiple."

"Oh really?" I say as skeptically as I can manage, raising my eyebrows.

He nods solemnly, his eyes crinkling with a smile he won't let out. "Scientifically proven."

Despite feeling like someone is tightening a clamp around my skull, I still find myself smiling at him. "Well, who am I to argue with science?"

He grins back, lifting me until I'm straddling him and pulling me in for another kiss. I moan into his mouth when I realize he's already hard, his cock pressing against me even through the layers of fabric between us. Breaking the kiss, he peels my t-shirt off, unhooking my bra with one deft motion.

"Constricting clothes can make it worse," he murmurs. His hands on my hips hold me firmly against him as he kisses his way down my chest. "You really should be naked."

"I'll—ah!—keep that in mind." I gasp as he licks a slow, tightening circle around my breast.

He teases at my nipple, barely-there licks until I'm almost twisting out of his grasp, trying to get his tongue where I need it. Finally he takes pity on me, closing his mouth over my nipple, sucking for a minute before closing his teeth on it.

I feel him smile against my skin as I curse, shaking with sensation. His mouth on my breasts, his hands on my hips, the long, hard line of his cock pressing against my clit —I can't escape his touch. It's so much, almost enough, but not quite there. When he finally releases my nipple, leaning back a bit to admire his handiwork, I'm shaking.

"Yeah, we should probably get you out of those pants," he murmurs, rolling us over so we're lying on the bed and he can tug the waistband of my yoga pants down. "Not saying I didn't enjoy watching you walk away in 'em. But naked is better."

Between the two of us, we manage to make short work of my pants and underwear. I even have time to pull his shirt up and over his head before he leans back down for another long, hungry kiss, the weight of his body so good as it presses me into the mattress.

"Where was I?" he purrs, tracing the shell of my ear with his tongue and chuckling softly when I shiver underneath him.

"Here?" he asks, scraping his teeth lightly over the side of my neck. I tilt my head back to give him better access, but he just shakes his head, sliding down my body and cupping the breast he hadn't played with before. "Oh, that's right. Don't want it to feel neglected."

He alternates between my breasts for what feels like forever, his clever fingers tormenting whichever one his mouth isn't on. He completely ignores my moans and the frantic movements of my hips under him, never quite giving me enough stimulation to come.

"Please, Jack." When I finally beg, I'm a little shocked at how wrecked my voice is.

Smiling wickedly, he shifts up enough for a quick, hard kiss. "I like it when you beg," he rasps, sliding back down my body until he settles between my legs, his shoulders pressing them apart.

I'm expecting more of the teasing, but he licks at my clit immediately, making my legs shake and try to close on his head. He stays focused there, using lips and teeth and tongue until I come so hard I can't even scream, my breath catching in my throat.

When I finally have to shove him away, too sensitive to handle the sensation, he grins up at me. Crawling up my body, he leans in for a long, filthy kiss, letting me taste myself on his tongue. "That's one." he says. "How's your head?"

"What head?" I ask, earning another grin.

"That's what I like to hear. You gonna come in, Benny?" He doesn't turn around as he asks the question. "Or just lurk in the doorway the whole time?"

I look over at the door to see that yes, Ben is standing there, one hand pressed against the bulge in his jeans as he watches us.

He catches my eye, grins, and crosses the room, dropping into the chair by the bed and unzipping his jeans carefully. "Don't mind me," he says cheerfully, pulling out his cock, already hard and wet at the tip. "I'll just sit here and watch."

Jack grins back at him, pulling a condom packet from his jeans before dropping them to the floor. Sliding the condom on, he rolls us over so I'm on top. "Wanna see you ride me, sweetheart. Let's give Benny a show, huh?"

I return his smile as I sit up, positioning his cock between my legs. When I start to slip slowly, teasingly down on him, I can tell that I'm wet enough to take him in all the way. But I work my way down slowly anyway, enjoying the way both of them watch me.

Jack bites his lip, but keeps his hands on the bed, fisting them in the blanket as he lets me set the pace.

Once he's fully inside, I circle my hips a little, sinking down just that fraction of an inch further.

He groans. "So that's how we're gonna do this?" He thrusts up into me. "Gonna make me do all the work?"

"Maybe," I say, lifting up just a little and then back down, enjoying the slick slide of his cock inside my pussy.

"Fine, then," he says. Smiing evilly, he slides his hands up my thighs, over my stomach, up my torso to cup my breasts.

I can't help but suck in a breath when he closes his hands just enough that his fingers brush my areolae—and stops. I whimper, just a little, and he chuckles.

"Need something, sweetheart?"

Rolling my hips, I grind my clit against him, trying to

arch my breasts into his grip, move his fingers closer to my nipples, with no success.

"You want something, you're gonna have to ask nicely," he purrs, his fingers stroking tiny circles on the increasingly sensitive skin of my breasts, every inch lighting up with the slightest touch.

I look over at Ben, but he shakes his head with a wicked grin of his own. "Don't look at me, baby," he says. "This is between you and Jack. I'm just here for the show."

"You and me, sweetheart." Jack's voice pulls my attention back to him. "What do you want?"

I huff out a frustrated breath. "I want you to play with my tits."

"Like this?" he squeezes my breasts gently. Too gently

"No!" I snap, moving faster, trying to get enough pressure on my clit to come.

"Ask me nicely," he orders. "Ask nicely and I'll let you come."

Shuddering, I give in. "Please play with my nipples, Jack. Please."

"I do like it when you beg," he says. Closing his fingers on my nipples, he smiles when I suck in a breath and move faster. "Like this?"

"Harder, please—oh, fuck, yes—Jack, just like that." I let my eyes fall closed, fucking myself faster still on his cock. My hands come up to grip his wrists, keeping his hands exactly where they are.

I can feel the orgasm building, hovering just out of

reach, hear myself chanting "please, please, please." When Jack squeezes my nipples perfectly, thrusts up just right to grind against my clit, I come, clenching around him.

I shudder over him, trying to recover, but he keeps moving, fucking up into me. It only takes a few more strokes before he groans, thrusting up into me hard, deep enough to trigger another orgasm when he presses against my already sensitive clit.

My muscles feel like liquid as I collapse on top of Jack, our chests heaving together. The bed dips when Ben joins us, making me shiver a little when his hand strokes down my back.

"Is that how we're doing apologies now?" he asks after a few minutes.

"I could get behind that," Jack snorts His heart thunders beneath my ear. "How's the headache, sweetheart?"

I lift my head experimentally, slowly at first but then faster, smiling when there's no more stabbing pain. "Seems to be gone. I guess you really do know your science.

He kisses me. "I'm happy to repeat the cure anytime you need it.

14

"So here's where we're at." I look from Ben to Jack, trying my best not to feel like a failure. "It's been almost two months. We haven't found anything in the books I was scanning. There might be something in the library, but unless I know how to whip up a database spell, it could take years to find. With just me, or even with your help, a cataloging project like this is a lot, and we'd have to basically read every book, one at a time."

Jack's face is carefully blank in the way it only is when he's hiding his feelings. "Okay."

"So what's our next step?" Ben is nearly vibrating out of his skin with the need to move, to do something. "There's a witch in Arizona; she's got a bad reputation, but maybe—"

"Actually," I interrupt, "I was going to call in a favor from some friends."

Both of them sit up a little straighter.

"What kind of favor?" Jack asks.

"What kind of friends?" Ben demands at the same time.

I can't help smiling, even though I'm nervous. This time with them, even with the specter of the curse hanging over our heads, has been almost honeymoon-like. I'm not sure how the different pieces of my life will fit together when they meet. But really there's only one way to find out.

"It's easier to just show you," I say, pulling out my phone and scrolling through my contacts until I find the number I'm looking for.

A click echoes in my ear, followed by a mellifluous baritone with a British accent. "Doctor Ryan, how lovely to hear from you again."

"Hi, Jeeves." I do my best to ignore the curious looks on the guys' faces. Easier to just let them meet Jeeves than to explain that I'm using my phone to talk to a disembodied household spirit. Besides, Jeeves is one of a kind; even if they think they know what to expect, they'll be wrong. "Can you tell Ethan I want to call in my favor? There's a really complex curse that I can't get a handle on and I'd like him to take a look, when he has time."

"Certainly," Jeeves replies. "One moment."

I can't help laughing when I hear the music; Jeeves is

more than capable of speaking to me and Ethan at the same time. The fact that he's faking hold music is honestly kind of petty and completely in character. His snark and pettiness are two of my favorite things about him.

"Dr. Barren will be delighted to see you at your earliest convenience," Jeeves says after a few moments. "Will you be coming alone?"

"I'm fairly sure you know the answer to that question," I reply. "But no, I'll have two people with me. Can they find me here? Or do I need to get to somewhere that's not warded?"

Jeeves' tone takes on an even more condescending edge. "We will contrive. Is now convenient for you?"

"Sure, now's good," I raise an eyebrow at the guys, doing my best to convey "don't freak out" without actually saying it. "See you soon, Jeeves."

"I will be delighted to speak to you in person, as it were, and to make the acquaintance of your companions," he replies. The line goes dead just as four people walk through the wall.

Gabe smiles at me, his grin stretching cheeks that are almost as dark as Ben's, one hand protectively on Wynn's shoulder, just under the wildly curling mane of her dark hair. They're both a few steps behind Max and Jamie, whose eyes are sweeping the area for threats, just for a second before they relax.

Jack and Ben are on their feet instantly, hands on their guns, before I can reassure them. I'm not sure how I ended up collecting strays with PTSD, but apparently this is my life. Maybe I should've explained better "It's okay. It's okay, guys. These are the people I was calling."

"Where I come from, people knock." Jack grumbles, but he slides his gun back into the holster at the small of his back. After a couple of seconds, Ben makes his disappear as well.

"Sorry," Jamie says, winking at me. "Next time we can come through the front door, if you want."

I shake my head at him at the same moment that Wynn smacks him in the arm. "I'd apologize for my partner," she says darkly. "But if I got started, I'd never be done apologizing for all of them. Hi, Claire."

"Hi, Wynn." I return her smile, just as contagious as I remember. "Jack, Ben, this is Wynn, Gabe, Max, and the guy with the questionable sense of humor is Jamie. Everyone, Jack and Ben Anderson."

"Damn, Claire." Gabe lets out a low whistle, grinning as he crosses the room to pull me into a hug. "You make the coolest friends."

I roll my eyes, but return the hug. "I'm friends with you, aren't I?"

It's his turn to wink at me while Max rolls his eyes in the background. "Exactly."

"Okay, not to be a dick." Jack's fingers twitch at his sides until Gabe lets go of me and steps back to Wynn, wrapping an arm around her waist. "But who exactly are these people and what makes you think they can help?"

"They're part of the Seven." I say.

Watching understanding dawn over his face is kind of fun. I haven't gotten to surprise either of them like this in awhile. Sure, Jack and Ben are legendary in supernatural circles, in a way I can't compete with—that I don't want to compete with, to be honest. But I was doing just fine before I met them. It's not everyone who can call up the seven most powerful magic-users in the world, the supernatural equivalent of the Swiss banking system.

Ben lets out a low whistle. "The Seven owe you a favor? How the hell does that happen?"

"Everybody needs librarians." Wynn says it before I can, with a saucy grin on her face. "Also I should clarify that I'm not technically one of the Seven. Seven-adjacent, maybe."

"You are." Max politely ignores my surprise that he's actually speaking up; the first time I met them it was three days before I heard him talk. "Or are you going to claim that Tori and Livvy aren't, either? Maybe we should start saying The Eight instead."

Wynn's mouth sets in an obstinate line. From the tone of Max's voice, this is an argument they've had before. But before she can really get into it, Jamie cuts her off, turning to me. "Are you ready to go?"

"Where—oh, damn." Ben interrupts himself as he realizes the answer to his question, his whole face lighting up.

"What?" Jack asks, looking from one person to the next.

Ben rolls his eyes. "The Seven have their own pocket dimension. Nobody can get to them if they don't want them to. It's how they're able to remain neutral."

"Well, that and the dirt Ethan has on pretty much everyone," Jamie allows. "He's interested to hear about this curse of yours, Claire."

"Technically it's Jack's," I tell him. "Old Fae magic."

Wynn links her arm with mine, grinning. "Even better. He's gonna love this. He hasn't had anything really complex to play with since my whole thing."

Since Wynn's "whole thing" had involved her taking down a Fae Queen in Underhill and burning out her magic for the better part of a year, that doesn't make me feel better. But Ethan is one of the best theoretical mages alive. Maybe the best. If anyone can figure out what's going on with Jack, it's him.

Jack looks hesitant. "Do we need to pack a bag or anything?"

"This shouldn't take long," Wynn promises. I do my best not to bristle when she smiles at him; I know she's perfectly happy with her guys. "And if it does, Jeeves can get you whatever you need. He's very handy to have around."

"Well, okay then." Jack takes my free hand, squeezing gently. Probably no one but Ben or I can tell how tense he is under the casual mask. "Let's go see the wizard."

As USUAL, the main living area of the Seven's place (it's easier for me to think of it as a house, because I do not have the kind of brain that enjoys thinking about a pocket dimension floating in the magical equivalent of outer space) is stunning.

It looks like something out of a magazine spread. The living area is full of comfortable couches artfully draped with soft pillows and softer blankets, looking out through a wall of windows on a gorgeous beach scene. The kitchen is further back from where we came in—the Seven like walking through walls in other people's houses but prefer to use doors in theirs—but equally perfect and luxurious, all bright white cabinets, granite countertops, and stainless steel appliances large enough to feed a small army.

And that's just the window dressing.

"Welcome back, Dr. Ryan," Jeeves says. "Would you care to introduce your companions?"

"Good to be back, Jeeves," I say. Possibly I smile a little at how wide Ben and Jack's eyes are, and how they're trying not to obviously scan the area for the source of Jeeves' voice. "This is Jack and Ben Anderson. Jack, Ben, meet Jeeves. Don't let Ethan fool you; Jeeves is the one who runs everything around here."

They look only marginally less confused, which I guess is fair. I didn't really explain anything.

"To answer the question Dr. Ryan didn't, I function primarily as a household spirit," Jeeves says. It might be my imagination, but I think he sounds amused as well. "Since

Dr. Barron thought the best use of a knowledge spirit would be to make me into a glorified intercom-cum-butler. If you need anything during your stay, you have only to ask."

"Jeeves is great," Wynn says. I'd forgotten how perky she gets sometimes; it's always a weird contrast to her t-shirt and jeans look when she turns on the pep. "I don't know how I lived without him, honestly."

"You're too kind, Miss Wynn." Jeeves sounds marginally more mollified. But only a little. "In the meantime, I believe Dr. Barron—"

"Is here!" Ethan speed-walks out of the hallway and into the common area. "What did you bring me, Claire?"

His wife Tori rolls her eyes as she follows in his wake. "Hi, Claire. Welcome back. How are you?"

Now it's Ethan's turn to roll his eyes. "Yes, yes, manners or whatever. Blah blah blah. You said something about a curse?"

"On Jack." I lift the hand that he's still holding by way of indicating which one he is. "A spell rebounded on him and now he's experiencing effects every full moon."

Ethan's eyes go unfocused and he mutters something under his breath, looking intently at Jack when he's finished. "Huh. Okay, you have my attention. But we'd better do this in my lab. Let's go."

Turning on his heel, he heads back down the hallway, not looking behind him. Jack hesitates, but when I start to follow, he comes with me, Ben following on our heels.

"Tell me about this spell that rebounded." Ethan comes to a stop at one of the many almost-identical doors, pressing his hand to the lock-plate and waiting as the spell recognizes him and opens the door. "Ritual? Witch magic? Fae magic? Do you have a copy?"

"We found it in a book of medieval spells," Ben says. "If somebody can take me back to our library, I can get it and show you."

Ethan manages not to snort audibly at the idea of something so pedestrian as Ben running his own errands. "Or you can just tell Jeeves where it is and he can get it."

"Oh. Right." Despite the way Jack is looking around like he's expecting the thumbscrews to come out any moment, Ben looks like a kid in a candy store. "Uh, Jeeves, it's on the second shelf from the left, leather bound—"

He cuts off as a book appears in his hands.

"This one?" Jeeves sounds like he's not trying particularly hard to hide his smugness.

"Yeah." Ben opens the cover, flipping through the pages to find the one he's looking for. "That's amazing."

Jeeves sniffs. "I exist only to serve. Thank you for making a simple household spirit very happy."

"Gods, who let you read Douglas Adams?" Ethan shakes his head. "Show me this spell before he really gets on a roll."

As he and Ben put their heads together over the spellbook, I squeeze Jack's hand. "You okay?"

"Yeah." He keeps his voice low, too. "You trust these people?"

"I really do. Ethan might not be able to find the answer, but he'll try. He loves puzzles and figuring spells out. The only problem we'll have is if he gets so interested he forgets to sleep, or eat. Tori might get mad at us."

I can practically see Jack picturing Tori, every part of her appearance carefully crafted to convey the impression that she could buy and sell you without blinking an eye. "That would be bad."

"Yup. Hopefully it doesn't come to that."

"You! Mister Artful Stubble!" Ethan snaps his fingers at Jack. "Get your ass in the spell circle. I need to run some tests."

With a last squeeze, Jack lets go of my hand and does as he's told, even though I can see the muscles jumping as he clenches his teeth.

For all our sakes, I hope Ethan can find an answer soon.

ᛋᚱᚴ

"YOU OKAY, SWEETHEART?" Jack asks from his place inside the spell circle. He'd been on high alert for the first half hour or so, watching every move Ethan made. But eventually boredom set in. He's already disassembled and reassembled his gun at least four times. And now he's watching me more closely than I'd like.

"You're the one being magically poked and prodded." I do my best to hide my wince as Ethan does something that makes the circle flare brightly for just a second, intensifying the throbbing in my head into a needle of fire lancing through my skull.

From the look on Jack's face as I blink away the afterimages, I need to work on my poker face.

"Headache again." It's not really a question.

"I'll be okay," I tell him.

"Hey." He doesn't bother to call me on the lie, turning to Ethan instead. "Don't you have some kind of magic migraine pill around here somewhere?"

Ethan blinks at him for a second, then turns to look at me. "We might," he says slowly. "Are your headaches persistent, Claire?"

"She's been having them for weeks." Jack answers before I can say anything. "She won't go to the doctor."

"Well, most doctors are hacks," Ethan says. "Might as well still be using leeches. Lucky for you, we happen to have one of the best bio-mages in the world. Jeeves, can you let Livvy know we'll need her help?"

Jeeves' smooth baritone says, "Certainly. Will you be joining Dr. Adams in her lab, or should I have her come to you, Dr. Ryan?"

"I can—" I start.

"Unless he's gonna let me out of this thing so I can go with you, have her come here," Jack says. His eyes drop to the floor when he catches the look I'm giving him. "Please, Jeeves?"

After a barely perceptible pause, Jeeves says, "Dr. Adams is on her way."

Sure enough, it's only a couple of minutes later when Livvy steps through the lab door, crossing to me with a smile. "Hi, Claire. I didn't know you were visiting. Jeeves said something about recurring headaches?"

"It's just been a couple of weeks—"

"Every day for a couple of weeks," Jack interjects. "I haven't been able to talk her into going to the doctor."

Livvy smiles sympathetically, nudging me into a chair. "Well, now the doctor has come to you. Sit tight and we'll see what we can figure out."

Within a few minutes I'm sitting inside my own spell circle, with Jack's eyes intent on me, ignoring Ethan in favor of trying to, I don't know, help Livvy figure out what's wrong with me with the power of his mind or some shit.

It's possible that repeated painful headaches make me the tiniest bit bitchy.

I take deep breaths and do my best to be a model patient. It's not like I like being in pain. I really would like Livvy to find some kind of cause, some kind of solution. I just don't believe she'll be able to.

Sure enough, eventually she steps back and meets my eyes. "Well, there's no physiological cause that I can find."

Even though some part of me was sure that's what

she'd say, I still find myself slumping, disappointed. Each of the Seven has always seemed larger than life to me ever since we first met a couple of years ago; I really wanted Livvy to pull out a miracle cure.

"That doesn't mean we're out of options," she says. Breaking the circle, she squeezes my shoulder gently. "There could still be a magical cause; if I can get some blood, I'll run as many tests as I can think of."

"Sure." I push up my sleeve.

Jack looks like he wants to protest, but subsides when I shake my head at him. He hasn't though through the implications yet, but my blood is a lot safer here than it would be in a doctor's office, mundane or otherwise. Nobody who has the magical oomph to use my blood to hurt me would risk pissing off the Seven.

Livvy produces a blood draw kit from thin air and gets to work; I'm not especially squeamish about needles, but watching the blood go down the little tube into the vial makes me feel light-headed. Anyway, it's a lot more interesting to watch Jack and Ethan, to try and figure out what Ethan is doing to look at the curse. Jack is so bored he's started flipping his knife end-over end without looking, his fingers moving with the speed of muscle memory.

"Done." Livvy makes the small mound of blood vials vanish before I can get a good look at how many there are. "Jeeves, can we get a snack for Claire to get her blood sugar back up?"

"Certainly," Jeeves says. In the same moment, a small

table appears at my elbow with a plate of cookies and a glass of juice. Livvy gives me a smile before she disappears out the door again, presumably to start those tests in her own lab.

The throbbing in my head makes the idea of food seem terrible, added to the vague nausea from having so much blood drawn, but I know eating will help. So I force myself to sip the juice until I'm feeling more human, then start nibbling on the cookies, chasing them with drinks from the glass of milk that replaced my empty juice glass.

"Time for a break," Ethan announces just as I'm finishing the last cookie. "Jeeves, did somebody order lunch?"

"I believe Ms. Ador has ordered sushi."

He fist-pumps and breaks the circle around Jack in the same motion. "Hot damn! Come on, average height, dark, and grumpy. And you, too, Claire. Let's go stuff our faces. We can get back to this after lunch."

I know better than to rush Ethan, but I can't help but ask. "Anything?"

"Maybe." He shoots me a sharp look. "Nothing I'm willing to swear to yet. It's an interesting puzzle you brought me, Claire. Almost interesting enough that I'd say you don't have to call in your favor for it."

"But only almost?" I do my best to match his joking tone when I reply.

His smile is more sympathetic than I expect. "We'll see. We'll see."

ᛋᚱᚻ

"Like this?" I ask, doing my best to copy the eyeshadow blending trick Wynn had made look so easy. Spoiler alert: not easy. This is why I don't usually fuck with makeup. I'm not convinced that Wynn isn't using her witchy powers to make her makeup look so good, but trying to mimic her is helping distract me from wondering what Ethan is doing in his lab.

Kind of.

"Almost," she says. "Try blending with your finger instead of the brush. Sometimes that helps."

I turn my eyes back to the mirror floating helpfully about three inches in front of my face. My fingertip has just made contact with my eyelid when Ethan bursts into the common room.

Ben and Jack look up from the table where they were geeking out over weapons with Wynn's guys. Wynn and I turn to face him at the same time, makeup tips forgotten.

"Okay." Ethan says. He starts to pace in a way that probably doesn't mean good news. "So I have good news and I have bad news. The good news is, because I'm a genius, I figured out what's up with your curse thingy."

'And?" Ben asks after a few seconds, interrupting Ethan's overly dramatic pause.

Ethan sighs. "Kids these days. No patience. Just to confirm, Skippy, you said you served as a Fae Knight for awhile, yeah?"

"Yeah."

"Right. So, most Knights are already some flavor of supernatural critter. A regular garden-variety human isn't gonna last long. Unless they get some juice. So the Queen you served did a spell that plugged you directly into Underhill."

He pauses expectantly again, only to sigh when met with our blank or confused expressions. "Okay, fine. Basic dimensional theory 101. Our Earth is connected to Underhill, magically. That's where the ambient power comes from, slipping through those bonds. But in Underhill—it's like the difference between a house outlet and one of those big power stations. The Queen connected you to that power, so you'd be stronger, heal faster. Basically superhuman."

"So why—?" Ben snaps his mouth shut when Ethan holds up a hand.

"Wasn't finished. You said it goes in and out with moon phases. Which is because the connection between our world and Underhill waxes and wanes with the moon. So when you're feeling the craziest, Underhill is the closest. When that spell rebounded on you, it must have blasted those power channels wide open."

We all wait, but this time he actually seems to be done, looking around expectantly.

"So how do we fix it?" I ask.

The look on Ethan's face confirms the sinking feeling

in my gut. "That's the bad news. He was a Knight for how long? In Underhill time."

"Don't know exactly. I stopped counting, after awhile."

"A hundred years, give or take," Ben says quietly. "I asked Mal."

Ethan nods. "Yeah, so if you break the spell, all of those years he lived catch up with him, all at once. Best-case scenario, you're taking care of a guy who's a hundred and thirty something. Worst case? He drops dead."

Silence falls.

"Well." Jack pushes to his feet and shoves his pistol back into its holster. "I need a drink."

"Solid plan, buddy." Ethan crosses to the wet bar. "What's your poison?"

Conversation slowly resumes around the room, but I can't look away from the slump of Jack's shoulders as he throws back the shot Ethan pours him.

Which means I'm the one who sees him pull out his phone, stiffening when he reads what's on the screen. Not the only one, though, because Ben crosses to his side before I can even stand up.

"We, uh, we need to go," Jack says. He sets the shot glass back down on the bar with the kind of elaborate care that makes me think he wants to break it instead. "This has been great, but we need to get home."

"No problem," Ethan says. "Everything okay?"

The motion Jack makes is somewhere between a nod and a shrug. "Nothing we can't handle."

Ethan clearly wants to press for more details, like the busybody he is, but he subsides, probably thanks to a significant look from someone else in the room. "Feel free to come back anytime, or give us a call if you run into something that needs some more firepower. Mi pocket dimension es su pocket dimension, etc. The doors should take you back to your place."

"Thanks." Jack heads for the door, Ben at his heels as usual.

I have to scramble a little to catch up with them, but they slow their pace when they notice. Jack waits until I'm there before reaching for the door, hesitating for an infinitesimal second before making contact with the door-knob and opening it.

Seeing their bunker through the opening gives me a weird sort of homesick feeling. I haven't been there for long, but it already feels more like home than anywhere I've lived since Jake died.

"Ready?" Jack asks, reaching for my hand and threading our fingers together.

"Let's do it."

We step through together.

15

"What's up?" Ben asks as soon as we're safely in our own space, with no prying ears to listen in.

Jack hands him the phone by way of answer, a text message visible on the screen. I lean over to read it along with Ben, snuggling in closer when he wraps an arm around my shoulders and pulls me in.

The text message is from an unknown number. All the words make sense individually, but I have no idea what they mean in this context.

payback time. One week. Bring your brother. 37.386447, -121.743163. -Khari

"When do we leave?" Ben asks. Still holding onto me with one arm, he hands the phone back.

"Wait, who's Khari?"

Jack sighs. "First of all, you're not going, Benny. Secondly, Khari was another Knight at Iorwen's court. He helped Ben and Mal break me out, said I would owe him. Apparently it's time to pay him back. Alone."

Ben's mouth flattens into a mutinous line. "If you don't take me, I'm just gonna follow you. You need someone to watch your back. Besides, he said to bring me. What happens if you don't?"

"Worst case scenario?" Jack shrugs. "He takes me out so we don't have to worry about this curse fuckery anymore."

"Not an option," I snap. "Ben's right. He needs to go."

"What, now you're both ganging up on me?"

I stretch up on my toes and kiss his scowling mouth. "Only when we're right and you're being stubborn."

His phone rings before he can argue any longer. "Hello? Oh, yeah, one sec."

I watch as he hangs up the phone and sprints up the stairs to the bunker door. Yanking it open, he pulls the brown-skinned man standing there into a hug.

"Mal, man, good to see you," he says when they finally separate—which takes a little longer than I expected. But then, if this is Malak, he's one of the most important people in Jack's life. I'm pretty sure Jack and Ben haven't told me about even half of the things they've taken out together since rescuing Jack from Iorwen's court

"Claire, this is Malak," Jack says. Leading Mal down

the stairs, he slips an arm around my waist when he gets close enough, squeezing gently. "Mal, this is Claire, our —girlfriend?"

"I dunno," I say. "That sounds awfully high-school. And I don't know if we've ever technically seen on a date. I can't think of a better word for it, though?"

Mal's rich brown eyes dart back and forth between us, the corners of his mouth quirked up. "I've always been partial to 'paramour.' But whatever you call it, it's nice to meet you, Claire."

"Likewise." I shake his offered hand, somehow surprised by the warmth even though it makes sense for a dragon shifter to run hot. "Thanks for keeping my boys alive."

"I do my best." he says. His tone is mournful, but his eyes dance with amusement. "It's a tough job, though."

I can't help grinning back. "I bet."

"Hey," Ben protests. "At least I'm usually trying not to die. Unlike some people."

"That's true, dear." I make my voice as patronizing as I can, patting his cheek gently. "I just wish you were a little better at it."

Ben snorts but doesn't bother denying it, turning his attention to Mal as he drapes an arm around my shoulders. "Hey, man, what's up?"

"It's been some time, and I had a feeling you needed my help."

"Yeah, we do," Jack says. "Khari wants to meet. But

what if it's a trap? Maybe somebody's pretending to be Khari, to lure us out so they can get at the bunker, or get access to Claire. I'd feel better if there was someone here to help in case of an attack."

Mal nods. "I'm happy to help. I wish I could go with you, though. Just in case."

Jack squeezes Mal's shoulder, his hand lingering. "Me too, buddy. Next time I have to go meet a half-crazy Fae Knight, I'll definitely take you."

"Very well," Mal sighs. "I'll go put my things in y—a bedroom, then, if that's all right?"

"Go for it, man." Jack's hand finally falls away. "Dinner in about an hour."

Ben nods. "Come on, man, I'll show you where they're at."

Jack is still watching when the two of them disappear down the hall.

�ᚱ�

AFTER DINNER, I settle back into the my seat in the library, determined to get some work done.

I look up from my computer some time later to see Ben standing there, a fond smile on his face. "Sorry, what did you say?"

"I was wondering if you wanted to hang out and watch something, since we're leaving in the morning. Jack's showing Mal the garage and the rest of the bunker, so it'll just be the two of us."

"What's up with them?" This is the first moment of privacy since Mal got here, so I'm finally free to get out the question that's been on my mind since Mal showed up.

He offers me a hand out of my chair. "Man, I don't even know. I thought there was something there after we rescued Jack, but I can't tell if they're actually fucking or just exchanging longing glances like they're starring in a gay version of Twilight."

"Huh."

"Does it bother you?" He looks back over his shoulder as he leads me to his room. "I know we said we weren't going to be hooking up with randos, but—"

I have to think about it for a moment before I'm sure of my answer, following him through the door and inside. "I don't think so? I mean, he obviously feels something for Mal, and you've both known him longer than you've known me. Anyway, it'd be pretty hypocritical of me to be bothered by it, considering I'm with both of you. Does it bother you?"

"Nah." He finally lets go of my hand, leaving me to make myself comfortable on the bed while he grabs the necessary remotes. "Mal's good people. You know we don't have much in the way of family, but he's definitely part of it. Besides, he's good for Jack."

"I've noticed that." I arrange the pillows to my liking before lying back. "What are we watching?"

"You can pick," he says, turning on the TV and the laptop hooked up to it. "I really don't care."

I smile hopefully. "Avengers?"

When he steps back, it's already showing on the screen. He presses play with a shit-eating grin before joining me on the bed. "How did I know what you were gonna say?"

"Because you know me," I say simply, snuggling into his side.

He presses a kiss into my hair. "Yeah. I do."

Sometime around Thor's big entrance I realize that, as much as I love the movie, I'm having trouble focusing. Ben's big hand rubs circles on my back, occasionally pulling the back of my t-shirt up enough for his fingers to skim lightly over my skin. I can't help but squirm against him every time.

"You okay?" he asks the third or fourth time it happens. His tone is innocent, but the glint in his eye says he knows exactly what's going on.

"I'm fine," I say sweetly. Two can play at this game. "Just feeling a little warm."

I sit up enough to strip off my shirt and toss it to the floor. When I cuddle back up against Ben, I make sure to press my breasts firmly against him, letting him get a good look at the cleavage framed by my red lace bra. "That's better. You don't mind, do you?"

"Not at all," he says, his voice taking on a telltale rasp.

He goes back to rubbing those maddening circles on

my back, but his rhythm falters every time I take a deep breath.

Finally, just as I'm about ready to crawl on top of him and kiss him until he agrees to touch me everywhere else, he lets out a long breath.

"Fuck this," he growls. Rolling us over, he presses me into the mattress, kissing me long and deep, wet and filthy. The soft cotton of his t-shirt slides against my exposed skin, just another sensation driving me higher.

I moan into his mouth when he rolls his hips, pressing the long, hard line of his cock down between my legs until he's grinding directly against my clit.

When he lifts his head, we're both breathing like we've just finished a marathon. He pulls back just long enough to strip his t-shirt off and send it flying across the room. Lowering his head, he runs his tongue along the edge where the lace on my bra meets skin. He grins up at me when I moan and arch up under him.

The next time he licks my skin, his tongue slides under the lace, teasing and testing until I say "Fuck, Ben, please."

He sits up enough to shuck off his jeans and start unbuttoning mine, since apparently I'm incapable of anything but lying on the bed and breathing right now. And even breathing is tricky. I never get tired of looking at him like this, naked and aroused and mine.

"Jack's not the only one who likes it when you beg," he says. Pulling the zipper down on my jeans, he peels them and panties off. "Wish we had time to play, but Jack and

Mal could be back from the garage anytime. So this is gonna have to be quick."

Pushing two fingers inside me, he pumps them lazily in and out, humming his approval of the noises I make. With his other hand, he reaches for the bedside table and retrieves a condom. "You're already so wet for me, baby."

I try to answer, really I do, but then he slides a third finger into me and I moan instead, pushing my hips up to take him deeper.

"That's it," he croons. Ripping the condom packet open with his teeth, he rolls it on one-handed, his other hand still fucking me. "You like that don't you? But it's not enough. You want more."

I nod, almost frantic, because he's right. I need more.

His grin becomes predatory. "What do you want, baby? Can you tell me?"

Licking my lips, I swallow hard, trying to find my voice. "I want you to fuck me."

"Oh, you can do better than that." His fingers stop moving inside me. "We've been through this before. Be specific, baby. What do you want me to do?

I close my eyes, feeling the flush bleed from my cheeks down my neck, a wash of heat. "Want you to hold me down, fuck me into the mattress. Want your cock in my pussy. Feels so good, makes me so wet when you fuck me. Please, Ben."

He pulls his fingers out, replacing them with his cock at my entrance. "This what you want?"

"Yes, please, Ben, fuck me."

"Like this?" He slides slowly inside, fucking me with short, shallow thrusts.

"More," I beg. "More, please."

Taking my wrists in one big hand, he pins them to the mattress, thrusting harder. "That what you want?"

I twist under him, pulling at his hold. The rush of sensation that goes through me when I can't pull free is like lightning in my veins. "Please, Ben, I need more."

He leans into me harder, pressing me down into the mattress with is weight. "More what, baby?" he breathes in my ear. "Tell me what you want."

"God, Ben, please fuck me harder," I groan, closing my eyes. "Want every inch of your cock inside me. Want you to fuck me hard and fast."

I can feel his smile against my ear. "You're a greedy little slut, aren't you, baby? Don't care if Jack and Mal hear all the noise you're making. You just want me to fuck you."

He nips at my earlobe as I shudder under him. "Oh, you like that." He never stops fucking me just like I'd asked, hard, fast snaps of his hips. "Like thinking about Jack and Mal hearing the way you beg for my cock? Maybe we should just call them in here and let them watch. Let them see how much you love it."

I'm not sure if it's Ben's words, or his forceful, demanding thrusts, or his grip on my wrists, or a combination of all three. It doesn't really matter what causes it, the result is the same. I come, shaking under him. He fucks me through it before groaning my name and thrusting deep into me one more time, collapsing on top of me.

After a few moments, he lifts his head, still breathing hard, but it takes a second before he meets my eyes. "Hey," he says. "Was that—did I go too far there?"

With an effort, I bludgeon my few remaining brain cells into something like working order. "No," I say slowly, shuddering a little as I replay that last bit in my head. "I don't think so."

"Good."

"I'm a little surprised, honestly. I never thought I was an exhibitionist, but thinking about Jack and Mal walking in on us…" I shiver again. "I wouldn't want to do something like that for real without all of us talking about it first. I know you and Jack are a package deal, and I wouldn't want to choose between you even if you asked me to. And Jack and Mal have their whatever-it-is. But bringing someone else in with us—"

He leans down to steal a kiss. "Definitely fair."

Pulling out, he climbs off the bed to deal with the condom while I stretch, enjoying the pleasant soreness in my muscles.

"Want to finish the movie?" he asks. Settling down next to me, he pulls the covers up over both of us.

"Sure." My voice cracks on a yawn in the middle of the word. "Not sure how long I'll be able to stay awake, since someone wore me out, but let's give it a shot."

He pulls me closer, his hand stroking up and down my arm. "Stay here as long as you want."

"Careful," I joke. My eyes are already sliding closed. "Keep saying stuff like that and you'll never get rid of me."

The last thing I remember before sliding into sleep is him pressing a kiss to my hair and whispering, "I'm counting on it."

16

Standing on the balcony, I kiss Jack fiercely, cradling his face in my hands. "You listen to me, Jack Anderson." I pull back to look him in the eyes, making my voice as serious as possible. "I don't care what it takes, you're coming back to me. Understand?"

"Yes, ma'am," he says. But his cocky smirk doesn't quite reach his eyes.

I kiss him one more time before pulling away and turning to Ben. Standing on tiptoe, I pull him down for a kiss of his own. "That goes for you too, Ben. I don't care who or what you have to kill, maim, or threaten. I expect to see both of you walking through that door before the end of the week."

"Got it." He reels me back in for one more kiss. "See you soon."

Jack hesitates for a moment before giving Mal a quick hug. "Take care of our girl, huh, Mal?"

"I will ensure she is safe," Mal says. His hands linger, just for a second, as Jack pulls away. "Be careful, both of you."

"Aren't we always?" Jack hitches his bag up onto his shoulder. "Don't worry. Back before you know it."

And then they were gone, the door slamming shut behind them in a way I try very hard not to think of as ominous or final.

The problem with knowing that magic is real is that everything seems like a portent, and usually not a good one.

"Well." It sounds more like a sigh than a word, but I'm pretty sure Mal understands what I'm feeling. "I guess it's time to get back to work."

"Will it bother you if I am also in the library?" he asks.

I laugh. "I had eight siblings. The only thing that will bother me is if you expect me to make your food or clean up after you. Being in the same room isn't even on the radar. Although I do appreciate you asking."

"Of course." He follows me down the stairs. "What are you working on down here?"

Explaining my cataloging project, and the different collections of data used to categorize things in libraries, doesn't help me forget, exactly, that Jack and Ben are heading into a dangerous situation. But it's a nice distraction.

From the number of questions Mal asks, I think he needs the distraction, too.

ᛋᚱᛈ

"Can I ask you a question?"

Mal's voice brings me back to awareness of my surroundings. Judging from the soreness in my butt, I've been sitting at this computer at least an hour. I take a minute to save the bibliographic record I just created before answering. "Sure, go for it."

"I apologize if this seems rude or offensive," he says. "I—do not always fully grasp the nuances of human communication. You are engaged in a sexual and romantic relationship with both Ben and Jack, correct?"

I can't help but smile at his careful phrasing. "Yes, I am."

He tilts his head a little to one side, a gesture that makes it suddenly obvious that he isn't entirely human, whatever his current form looks like. "That—is not the norm for this human culture, is it?"

I snort, rolling my eyes. "It's not a choice the majority of people make, true, but it's not like there really is such a thing as normal. You've been kicking around with Jack and Ben for long enough, I'd think you would have noticed that."

"Not a choice the majority would make. So why did you?"

Suddenly I'm having one of those weird moments of cognitive dissonance; I'm explaining my sex life and relationship choices to a freaking dragon. Somehow this is my actual life. "Honestly? At first I was trying to forget—well. Things from my past. Sex is good for that, at least for a little while."

"You said 'at first.'" His gaze sharpens. "So things have changed since then?"

I shrug, trying to find words for what I feel, what I know to be true. "It works. And I'm not just talking about the sex. Ben and Jack—it's like they're two parts of a whole. Except that makes it sound like they're not complete on their own, which is wrong. If I'd met either of them alone, I still would've fallen, hard. But together—they're more, you know?"

Mal nods. "Their souls are linked. They are individuals; they can stand on their own. But they're stronger together, always."

"Huh." That—makes a lot of sense. "I didn't know that. Do they know that?"

It's his turn to shrug. "I'm not certain. Do you think it important that they know?"

"If they don't already, then yeah, I think it's the kind of information they should have."

"When they return, I will communicate it to them," he promises. "But you said at first, it was just sex. Is that all the relationship is to you?"

I pause a moment, examining his face. "Malak, are you

asking me what my intentions are?"

He doesn't blush, at least not visibly, but he ducks his head a little. "Jack and Ben have both been hurt a great deal in the past. They seem very fond of you; I'd rather not see them hurt again if I can help it."

"It's not just sex," I say. Holding his gaze, I will sincerity into every word. "I care about them, a lot."

His smile is small, but the happiness and relief in it are almost blinding. I nearly don't notice the wistful look in his eyes. "Good."

I'm about to return to my computer when something occurs to me. "Can I ask you a question now?"

"Certainly," he says. His voice is polite, but his eyes are wary.

"Can I see your dragon form?" My face heats as soon as the words leave my mouth. "Sorry, that's probably rude. Never mind, I'll—"

He interrupts me with a hand on my arm. "Claire. I am not offended, and you can certainly see my dragon form. But perhaps we should relocate to the garage; I would hate to damage anything in here."

"Yeah, of course," I say. Following him, I eyeing the large open space in the middle of all the weapons displays. It's easily big enough for a Jeep or a small truck. How big is his dragon form?

Biting my lip to hold back the questions fighting to get out, I follow him through the hallways until we come to the garage. Mal lets go of my arm, walking out into the center of the cavernous space.

His footsteps should probably echo in the large, empty room, walking on the concrete floor, but he's absolutely silent. When he turns to face me, there's something about his eyes that activates every latent, primal instinct in the back of my mind.

I'm in the presence of a predator.

"Are you certain?" he asks. "If it will bother you, or disturb you—

Rubbing my hands over my arms where goosebumps are rising on the skin, I nod. "I'm sure."

"Very well."

Even though I'm watching closely, I'm not really sure what happens. I'm not sure why I expected some big ritual; like all shifters, dragons' magic is inherent, built into who they are. One moment, Mal stands in the center of the room, perfectly still. The next, space seems to—to fold, almost—and instead of the human body, there's a motherfucking dragon sitting calmly and watching me with wide, somehow familiar eyes.

"Mal?"

I can change back if you wish, Mal says, somehow. His draconic mouth doesn't move, but I can hear his voice anyway. Or maybe I just think I can. *You seem...uncomfortable.*

"No, no," I say. Hesitantly, I take a step closer. "Can I —is it okay if I come closer?"

Of course. I never was the type to eat virgins.

That startles a snort out of me. "I'm definitely no virgin."

You are unmarried. That is all it used to mean. Sexual virginity is a useless human concept.

"Fucking right." I come to a stop less than an arm's length from Mal. His scales don't look hard, like I thought they might, but almost—soft. My hand lifts without conscious thought, but I force it down. "Can I touch you?"

I am entirely at your disposal. Mal lays his huge dragon head down on the floor, and holy hell, his eye is still almost on a level with the top of my head. He's huge.

Gathering my courage, I reach out and let my fingertips brush against his neck. The surface of the scales is almost soft, with a sort of tanned-leather texture, but I can feel the inflexible armor underneath. And the warmth radiating off him, even more so than in his human body.

When my hand trails down toward his shoulder, Mal makes a rumbling noise that, aside from the volume, is remarkably like a cat's purr. "Is that okay?"

It feels very nice, Mal says, his huge eye sliding closed. *You may feel free to do that as often and as much as you like.*

I have no idea how much time we spend down there, Mal patiently answering my questions and eventually letting me climb up onto his back like a kid on a jungle gym, perching between the bases of his wings.

"This is amazing," I say. Rubbing gently at the skin in front of my crossed legs, I savor the texture under my fingers, the little vibrations as he purrs contentedly.

This is my favorite form. Mal sounds like he's about three strokes away from falling asleep. *Some of my cousins prefer the water form, they say the tentacles are more useful than talons. But there's nothing like flying. I'll take you, sometime.*

"I'd like that." With one last rub, I straighten up reluctantly. "But for now, I should probably get back to work."

Mal waits politely until I've made my way back to the floor to change into his human form. But now that I've seen him as a dragon, I can't stop noticing it. The way his eyes, warm and liquid brown, have the same expression as the huge golden slit-pupiled dragon eyes. Even though he's back in a body that's normal human size, albeit on the large end of that scale, it's like I can feel the wing of his dragon body, wrapped around me and sheltering me close.

It's the safest I've felt in years.

ᛋᚱᚺ

AFTER DINNER and giving up on the cataloging—I can only do so much before my eyes start crossing—I flop down on Ben's bed and check the time. It's late enough that the guys have probably stopped for the night, since Jack said they were going to take the drive in easy stages.

Before I can second-guess myself any longer, I pick up my phone and hit Jack's number.

He answers almost as soon as it starts ringing. "Hey, sweetheart. What's up?"

"Missing you." The honest answer slips out before I can stop it. "Are you still on the road?"

He chuckles, something soft rustling in the background. "Nah, we got a room for the night. No point killing ourselves to get there when the meet isn't til day after tomorrow. Everything okay there?"

I roll over onto my back, closing my eyes and pretending he's lying next to me, not hundreds of miles away. "Yeah, nothing weird or scary. I'm about a quarter done with the library database. Mal watches a lot of movies."

"Yeah." The smile is even clearer in his voice now. "He said he was trying to understand humans better, but at this point I think it's just a habit."

Silence falls for a few moments. It could have been awkward, but it isn't. The steady sound of Jack's breathing on the other end of the call is comforting. Like I'm not alone.

"I should probably let you go," I finally say.

"You don't have to. I'll stay on the phone as long as you want."

I can't help smiling. "That could get difficult when you have to go shower."

"I already showered," he says. His voice drops to that low, intimate purr that always makes me shiver. "This room looks a lot like the one we had that first night we met you. Even got the same little table. I had to jerk off in the shower, remembering you bent over that table, begging Benny to fuck you."

Over my sharp inhale, I hear the rumble of Ben's voice in the background, but I can't make out the words.

"Fine," Jack says with a laugh. The phone beeps, and when his voice comes back, it sounds further away. "Benny says if we're gonna have phone sex, he wants you on speaker so he can hear, too. "That okay with you?"

I swallow, hard. "Yeah, that's—that's fine."

"Where are you, baby?" Ben asks. Even with the slight tinniness from the speaker, I can hear the familiar rasp in his voice.

"In your room. Lying on the bed."

He chuckles, low and dark. "I bet it still smells like sex from when I fucked you last night, doesn't it?"

"A little bit."

"You should've seen her, Jack," he says. It should not be that hot to hear him talking about me like that, like I'm not even here. Like it's a private conversation with Jack that I just happened to overhear. "Begging for my cock, for me to fuck her. And she got so wet when I mentioned you and Mal might walk in on us. I thought she was gonna come right then and there."

"That so?" Jack's breathing is faster now, clearly audible. "You like thinking about getting caught, sweetheart?"

I actually whimper, which would be embarrassing if I wasn't so turned on. "Y—yeah."

"Take off your shirt," Jack orders.

I pull my t-shirt over my head, tucking the phone back between my ear and shoulder as soon as I'm done.

"What bra are you wearing?" he asks.

"I'm not. I was getting ready for bed, and I was tired of wearing it, so I took it off."

They both groan at that. "When we get back, I want you to show us how you get yourself off," Ben says. "Lay you down in my bed and watch you touch yourself until you come."

"Only if I get to watch you, too," I shoot back.

Jack chuckles. "Whatever you want, sweetheart. Play with your tits for us. Nice and gentle at first, okay?"

"Okay." I cup my breasts in my hands, letting my thumbs skate lightly over my nipples.

"Tell us how it feels," Ben says.

Closing my eyes, I bite my lower lip. "Feels good, but I want more. Want it harder."

"Go ahead," he says.

I squeeze my nipples harder as soon as I have permission, flicking my nails across the tips.

"That's it, baby," Ben says. Apparently he can hear me moan just fine. "Are your nipples nice and hard?"

"Yes." I gasp, rolling them between my fingers and thumbs before squeezing down again. "So hard it almost hurts. Wish you were here to touch them."

"So do we," Jack rasps. "Unbutton your jeans for us, take them off."

Somehow I manage to obey, unbuttoning my jeans and

wriggling out of them without dropping the phone. "They're off," I report, breathless.

"Good girl," he says. "Slide your fingers down into your panties. Is your pussy wet for us?"

I do as he says, making a little noise when my fingers brush the sensitive spot at the base of my clit, my legs shaking. "Yes."

"Yes, what?"

The smile in Ben's voice makes me swallow hard. "Yes, my pussy's wet," I mumble. My face flushes just from saying the words, which is ridiculous.

"Good," Ben purrs. "Want you to slide your fingers back up and play with your clit. Can you do that for us, baby?"

I obey, feeling the fine tremble in my thighs as my fingers find that spot again. "Y-yes," I gasp, my other hand moving back to my breast.

"What are you doing with your other hand, sweetheart?" Jack asks.

"Playing with my nipples," I admit, squeezing one before moving my hand to the other.

"Dirty girl," he says. "Gonna come for us like this? Touching yourself for us?"

I gasp in a breath, my finger moving faster against my clit. "Yes," I moan, my voice growing higher.

"Want you to be loud for us," Ben commands. He's breathing almost as fast as I am. "Let us hear you, baby."

Throwing my head back against the pillow, I stop

trying to be quiet. "Yes, yes, yes," I chant. My hips arch up off the bed as I work myself up further. Like this, I can pretend they're here, can remember every hot, dirty thing they've done with me. I can pretend Ben's hands are pinning me to the bed, Jack's mouth on my pussy. Can replay the sensation of being so trapped between them that there's nowhere to go, nothing to do except feel.

I think maybe I scream their names as I come.

The door opens a second later. "Claire? Do you require assistance? I thought I heard—"

Mal stops mid-sentence, staring at me with hungry eyes, his nostrils flaring as he scents the air, his lips parted

I have just long enough to think about the picture I must make, sprawled across Ben's bed, nearly naked, one hand on my breast and one down my panties. Just long enough to think *maybe* and *yes, please*—

"I—I'm sorry—I thought—"

I never find out what he thought, because he backs out abruptly, closing the door quickly behind him.

"Was that Mal?" Ben asks.

I'd momentarily forgotten about the phone. "Did you do that on purpose?"

The words were supposed to come out accusatory, but apparently I can't snarl or snap so soon after an orgasm.

"Hey, Jack started this," he says. "I didn't plan it out with Mal or anything, if that's what you're asking. We miss you already. And phone sex is a lot better than just jerking off in the shower while thinking about you."

"Are you okay?" Jack asks. It sounds like there's something in his voice, but it could just be the speaker.

I sigh. "Yeah, I was just surprised. But next time, I'm locking the door."

"So you're saying that didn't do anything for you?" Ben asks. I can faintly hear the slick sound of his hand on his cock, then it gets louder when Jack joins in. "Not even for a second?"

My face flames hotter. "Did it do something for you?"

Jack groans, a short, bitten-off noise.

"It sure did," Ben confirms. "And Jack won't admit it, but he nearly came when he heard Mal talking."

A thud sounds down the line.

"Don't hit me! You know I'm right," Ben says. He sounds far too smug. "Too bad Mal left."

"Nah," Jack says after a pause. "I want to see, the first time he fucks her."

I roll over, burying my face in the pillow even though there's no one to see. "You're trying to kill me."

"Just wait," Ben promises. His breath is coming faster now, despite his conversational tone. "Can't wait to watch Mal fuck you, let him see how gorgeous you are when you come for us."

I hear Jack's telltale groan as he comes, the sound choked off in his throat.

"Shit," Ben says, breathless. "I'm close. Wish—wish you were here, baby. Wanna see you—fuck you—"

The room is quiet then, except for the sound of their breathing in my ear. "I miss you, too," I finally say.

"Get some sleep, sweetheart," Jack says. His voice is soft and warm and I want to wrap myself up in it like a blanket. "We'll call you soon."

Ben murmurs his goodbyes, too, and then I really am alone.

17

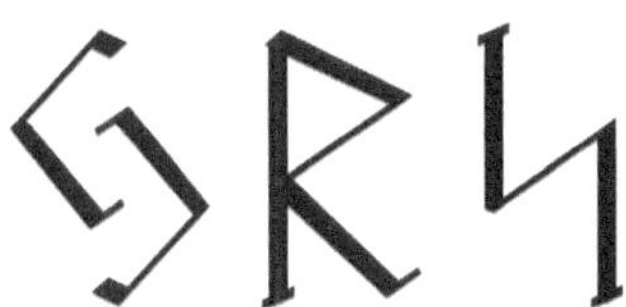

Pushing back my hair, I stand up to take the stack of books I was working on back to the shelf. I only make it about halfway before the migraine crashes down on me, demanding my full attention now that I'm no longer tightly focused on my work.

I can't help the whimper that escapes me. Sliding the books back onto the shelf with clumsy hands, I lean my forehead against the cool wood, trying to take deep breaths.

It doesn't help. The pain is like a band clamped around my head, screwing infinitesimally tighter with each torturous throb of my heart.

"Claire? Are you okay?" Mal's voice is hesitant. He's apologized for busting in on me the night before, several times, but I can still nearly feel the awkwardness between us, hanging heavy in the air.

"Headache," I manage, still trying to breathe through the pain. "I get them sometimes."

It's interesting—it would be a lot more interesting if my head would stop that fucking throbbing—that I can actually hear the slight frown in Mal's voice without looking. "Jack mentioned that you've been having them frequently. Is this something you were prone to in the past?"

I shake my head without thinking, immediately regretting it when the pain somehow becomes stabbier. "Not this often, not this severe. Maybe I'm allergic to something here, but I haven't had any other signs of an allergic reaction."

"It could be many things, I suppose," Mal says. His voice comes closer. "I am not trained in healing, but I do have some magics. Would you allow me to at least try and determine why these are happening so frequently?"

This time I catch myself before I can nod, thank fuck. "Yeah, please. If you can tell me for sure that I don't have an inoperable tumor or something—that would be good."

Mal's warm hand gently guides my head up, turning my face toward him. He rests two fingers lightly between my eyebrows, his eyes sliding closed with a slight frown still wrinkling his forehead.

We stay like that for some time. I fins myself closing my eyes, too. Without the light stabbing into my eyeballs, it's easier to focus on Mal's magic moving through my head. It's a weird feeling, like the wash of cool water when you take a drink, only inside my brain.

Finally he drops his hand, opening his eyes. "You do not have an inoperable tumor," he says. His his forehead is still furrowed, though. "There is no injury or disease that I can locate causing your headaches."

"I'm sensing a but here," I say.

He grins at me, like we both heard the joke about butts Jack would make if he was in the room. "I'm not entirely certain what's causing your headaches, but, once Ben and Jack return, I can consult with some other people who might have an answer."

"Not even going to guess?" I tease gently. It's nice to feel that comfort we had started to find coming back, instead of the awkward distance that's been the norm for today.

He shakes his head. "No, I don't wish to hazard your health on a 'guess.'"

"You did something, though," I say. "It's more bearable now."

Ducking his head, he drops his eyes to the floor. "I— you were in a great deal of pain. And as I said, I have some magics."

I touch his cheek, waiting until he meets my eyes again. "Thanks, Mal. Really."

He shrugs, looking like a bashful schoolboy instead of

a powerful dragon shifter who's probably been around for hundreds of years. "I just wish I could do more."

"We're all just doing the best we can." I hesitate for a second before going up on my toes to kiss his cheek. "This is a lot better than curling up under a blanket, whimpering and wishing for sleep or death. So, thanks."

His hands come up to wrap around my upper arms, steadying me as I settle back down to the floor. "You're very welcome."

ᛋᚱᚼ

GETTING to the end of my page, I realize, once again, that I haven't read a single word.

"I just wish I knew what was happening." I say it out loud this time, instead of thinking it for probably the fiftieth time in the past few hours.

"I can arrange that." Mal says it casually, as if that's a regular thing people say. Well, maybe it is regular for dragons.

He smiles a little at the surprise on my face. "Scrying is a magic I have practiced quite a bit, over the years. And Jack and I do have a...unique bond. Give me a moment."

I jump a little when an oval mirror appears on the table between us, flat and shiny, with a simple gold border around the edges. Mal sets his hands on either side of it, closing his eyes.

After a few seconds, clouds fill the surface of the mirror, obscuring the reflection of the ceiling.

When they clear, parting as if blown away by a stiff breeze, the view is of Jack and Ben, as if we were in the back seat of the car as they drive along a narrow, two-lane road.

"Pull over here," Ben says. Looking up from his phone, he points off to the side.

Jack grumbles about the paint job and the dust, but complies. He manages to find a relatively flat place to pull off the road, parking his baby under the slight shade of some scrubby trees. They both have to cover their eyes against the glare of the setting sun as they step out of the car, the viewpoint in the mirror following behind Jack like he's a character in a video game.

Ben consults his phone again. "We'll have to hike the rest of the way. About half a mile up that hill."

Circling around to the back of the car, Jack rummages around in the trunk. He fishes out a couple of canteens and refills them from a jug of water, tossing one to Ben. "All right then." He lets the trunk lid slam shut. "Let's move out."

Ben eyes him uncertainly. "You're not taking anything else?"

Jack shrugs, heading up the hill. "I've got an iron blade, salt and holy water. We don't have anything else that could do more to Khari than piss him off, and I'm not even sure those will work on someone as old as he is. If he decides he wants to kill us, I'll go down fighting, but no point in weighing ourselves down. It's hot."

Ben falls into step beside him, eyebrow still quirked. "What do you think he wants?"

"Hell if I know," Jack mutters.

"I don't like it."

"Me either," Jack says.

Mal and I echo the words at the same time.

Jack continues. "But this is the best hand we've got."

Ben sighs. "I guess we'd better go play it out, huh?"

Mal and I watch in silence as they hike up through the trees, pausing when they come out into a clearer area. It almost looks like they're appreciating the view of the hills spread out before them. But I can see the tension in Ben's shoulders, the way Jack's fingers twitch, and the lone figure waiting for them on the ridge ahead.

When they finally move forward, Ben falls back slightly, covering their right side and leaving Jack to watch the left as they approach the man.

"Hello, Ben," Khari says. "It's been a long time."

"We came," Jack says. "What do you want?"

Khari makes a soft tsking noise as they come to a stop, just out of arm's reach. "I'm disappointed in you, Jack. You were a Knight, albeit for only a small fraction of the time I have been one. What do you think I want? What did you long for, during each endless moment of Underhill time? What would you have given anything to have, that your Queen would never allow?"

"Jack?"

Ignoring Ben's question, Jack nods slightly. "Not a Knight anymore," he points out, pulling a short sword out of a sheath hidden under his jacket. "I don't think this is gonna cut it."

Khari actually smiles then. "Oh, Jack. One doesn't simply stop being a Knight. The Sword is there, waiting for you. All you have to do is call it."

Jack huffs out a breath, glancing over his shoulder at Ben. In the same moment, Ben moves up closer, until his left shoulder was just touching Jack's right, giving him a little nod.

When Jack looks back at Khari, our viewpoint changes as well, like we're behind his eyes. But more than that, I can feel what Jack is feeling. Not all of it, but enough. The loneliness and pain he went through during his time Underhill, the despair and depression that grew and grew until death seemed like a welcome release.

"Yes," Khari says. "You know what I want. I freed you. Now it's your turn. Call it."

Jack closes his eyes—I can feel his slight embarrass-ment at doing so—and opens his hand. I can't quite iden-tify what I'm feeling from him. Somehow, without moving, he *reaches*, and then his hand isn't empty anymore.

The sword in his hand seems simultaneously more real and more unreal than anything else around them. It should look ridiculous, like something from a video game come to life, but instead it just looks right. Like Jack is the only person who could hold it, like this is the only place it could exist.

Of course, I'm a little distracted by what I'm feeling from Jack, the anger rising up inside him like an unstoppable tide. The way he's clearly fighting himself not to lash out, even though he's standing perfectly still. Something growls at the back of his head, something that wants to rage and kill until there's nothing left. Jack fights it back, clinging to his sanity and his control with ragged, bleeding fingernails until he finally opens his eyes again.

"Is that—is that what he's feeling all the time?" I ask Mal. My voice is hushed, like I'm afraid they can hear us.

"I do not know." His forehead furrows.

In the mirror, Ben is watching him too, the worried wrinkle between his eyebrows deeper than I've seen it in awhile. But he stays where he is, a solid foundation for Jack, and jerks his chin slightly toward Khari.

Khari sighs, staring at the sword in Jack's hand, then looks up with a wry twist to his mouth. "I was going to say you have no idea how long I've waited for this. But I imagine you do."

Jack clears his throat once, then again. "Maybe a little bit."

Taking a deep breath, Khari looks out across the hillsides, then back at Jack. "I'm ready."

Jack takes a deep breath of his own. When he steps

forward, I can feel the way he already misses Ben's warmth at his back.

Khari surprises him by reaching out, laying a hand gently on his shoulder."Thank you."

Jack nods, raising the sword.

I look away from the mirror. The peaceful expression on Khari's face is the last thing I see, a sharp contrast to the wet, grisly sounds I hear before Mal lets go of the mirror and the connection is lost.

18

Even though nothing shows in the mirror, Mal's eyes aren't focused on me or the room around us, almost like he's still seeing whatever is happening.

I'm not sure if I should disturb him or not; I don't have a lot of experience being around dragon shifters, or people with the ability to scry. "Mal?"

He lets out a breath, nostrils flaring, still not really looking at me. "Jack is—struggling."

"Okay." Still not really sure what to do with that. "Can I ask what that means? Do I need to leave you alone?"

After a moment of hesitation, he shakes his head and takes my hand. When he speaks again, it's not out loud, but in my head, like he did when he was in dragon form. *If*

199

you truly wish to be with him, this is something you should know.

I open my mouth to ask what he's talking about, but before I can speak, I'm—we're—somewhere else. I can feel Mal, a strong, warm presence with me, holding me safe and secure. Which is the only reason I don't panic when I suddenly find myself in Jack's head.

ᛋᚱᚼ

"Jack? Jack, give me the sword, okay? Just open your hand, let me have it. I'm here, man. Just let it go."

Slowly, the noise in Jack's ears becomes a voice (Ben), the sounds the voice makes slowly taking on meaning ("Drop it, Jack, let it go"). The exulting, hungry rage echoing inside him looks through his eyes, sees the man standing in front of him. Sees a target.

Him kill him kill him kill them all of them kill him kill him need to kill kill him now gut him stab him slice his throat rip him open cut him kill him kill—

A shock of rejection, a "No!" rips out of his throat. His fingers loosen on the sword, let it fall to the ground. He scrambles back out of arm's reach, shuddering at the mental picture of Ben, torn and broken and bloody on the ground, that paints itself behind his eyelids. Nausea rises in his stomach at how much, so much of him, that wants it to be real.

Ben gathers up the sword, wrapping it in his overshirt like he's afraid the sight of it will turn Jack berserk. He watches, cautiously, and Jack wants to say something, to reassure him. But right now every bit of his willpower is needed to fight back the curse, the burning need to kill and rend and destroy.

Deep inside, down in the darkness that he hates about himself, the small part of him that gloried in being a Knight, in the pain and blood and violence, has awoken. If anyone other than Ben had been standing there, he might not have been able to stop. Might never have stopped until he bathed the world in blood.

But ever since that night, standing in the street, watching their foster home burn down, protecting Ben has been his true North, the one fixed point that his world revolves around. Fae and vampires and werewolves haven't been able to sway him from this one simple truth. And he will be damned—at least he still has enough of a soul left to find that funny—if a curse, even one laid by a Face queen, can manage it.

When he has enough self-control left to pay attention to what's around him, Ben is still standing there, whole and alive. Jack takes a swallow from his canteen, the water cool and soothing on his throat, raw as if he'd been screaming his denials to the open sky.

The sun has almost dropped completely behind the low hills to the west, scrubby trees casting long shadows across the ridge.

"Let's get back to the car while we can still see where we're going." The words scrape roughly out of him, but it's something of a relief to know that he can still speak.

Ben just nods, worried frown still wrinkling his forehead.

He falls into step behind Jack, as usual, a warm, solid presence at his back.

Down the hill, into the car, starting down the highway toward home. Jack closes his eyes in the passenger seat and does his best to pretend he doesn't still feel the curse screaming in his blood, his bones, behind his eyes.

—kill kill kill him kill him stab slash cut him hurt him kill him bathe in his blood kill them all of them burn the world down—

ᛋᚱᛡ

I JERK awake as the light turns on, startling me out of fitful sleep and dreams of Jack, smiling with a sword in his hand as he kills us all.

"Sorry, sweetheart," Jack says.

He turns the light back off, and that's almost worse, leaving him a dark silhouette in the doorway.

"She's in here, Benny," he calls down the hallway.

It's a little better when he comes inside, close enough that I can see him in the light from the open door. He drops heavily onto the side of the bed, like he doesn't have the energy to stand any longer. "Mal said you went to bed early, but we got a little worried when you weren't in your room."

"Sorry." I rub my eyes. "Hard to sleep by myself. Works a little better in your bed."

I can just barely make out his quirked eyebrow. "Not Ben's?"

"Your mattress is nicer."

"Fair enough." He pulls off his boots and shirt, barely finishing before he collapses back onto the pillow.

Now that I'm more awake, I can hear the way his voice slurs—with exhaustion, since I can't smell any alcohol, even with him on the pillow next to me. "I wasn't expecting you guys back until tomorrow."

He sighs, pulling me close against his side. "Took turns sleeping, drove straight through. Wanted to be home."

"You okay?" I'm not sure how much I should say of what I saw, what I felt. What Mal felt. Does Jack even know how much Mal can see through their bond? He must, right?

Ben comes in, closing the door behind him and interrupting my train of thought.

Jack shrugs. "Who the fuck knows? As okay as I ever am, I guess."

I wrap my arm around his waist, pressing my cheek to his chest. "Okay. Sleep now?"

Fabric rustles as Ben pulls his boots and clothes off, too. He slips under the covers behind me, warm and solid and safe. I'm surrounded by them, lifting the last bit of crushing fear off my chest. Inhaling, I take what feels like my first full breath since they walked out the door.

"Sleep," Jack agrees. His voice is thick with fatigue, his eyes already closed.

"Sleep," Ben says.

His kiss on my hair is the last thing I remember before sleep pulls me under again.

ᛋᚱᚻ

Jack kisses me awake, slow and sweet. His hands frame my face, his mouth moving over mine almost reverently as we lie facing each other.

"Good morning," he murmurs. His breath whispers over my lips, his thumb strokes over my cheekbone.

"Good morning."

He smiles and kisses me again, rolling me to my back and bracing himself above me. Despite the hardness of his erection, hot and insistent against me, he kisses me tenderly. Like nothing could be more important than this, his mouth on mine, lips and tongues sliding gently together.

"Need you." He kisses a slow, teasing path down my neck and across my shoulder. "Can I?"

I let my hips roll up under him, the rough denim of his jeans rasping against the soft cotton of my panties. "Yes. Whatever you need. Whatever you want."

He comes back to my mouth for another long, sumptuous kiss, tasting me until I'm wriggling impatiently beneath him, desperate for more.

Finally lifting his head, he smiles lazily and slides

down, trailing soft kisses down my chest, over the swell of my breasts.

He circles them with kisses and nibbles and licks, never enough pressure or stimulation, his weight pinning me firmly to the bed. When he finally closes his mouth gently over my nipple, my eyes slide closed, my breath sobbing out in relief.

He torments me gently for what seems like hours, hands and mouth skimming over my body as he moves slowly, inexorably down. I come, gasping out his name, almost as soon as he closes his mouth over my clit.

Ben stirs next to me, probably because of the noise we're making.

Jack lifts his head enough to smile at me. "How about a hand here, Benny?"

Ben's hands skim over me in turn, coaxing and teasing. His touch leaves me shaking while Jack pushes one finger, then two, into my pussy, matching the slow, almost languid rhythm of his tongue on my clit.

They build me up again together. Ben falls into sync with his brother without any words passing between them, until I'm shaking under them, begging "please, please, please" into Ben's mouth, my hips arching helplessly off the bed as I come. But even as I fall apart, their hands and mouths on my skin keep me grounded, hold me together.

I can't focus enough to hear what Jack says, or maybe he doesn't say anything. Maybe Ben just knows. Either way, gentle hands pull me back against Ben's chest, arrange a pillow under my hips. A condom packet rips open, then Jack is sliding into me, moving in slow, teasing thrusts. He leans in to kiss me, one hand braced on Ben's shoulder, the other one on mine. Touching us both. Connected to us both.

"Need you," he breathes. Sweat glistens on his skin as he starts to move faster.

I slide my hands up his arms, trying to reassure him with my touch.

He hisses as my thumb slides over the Mark, the moons dark against his skin. Never breaking eye contact, I lean forward and press my lips to it. I don't stop even when I feel it throbbing under my mouth, unnaturally hot and angry, burning with the force of the magic that's trapping him.

When he tries to pull away, I hold him there. He could break my grip if he wanted to, but he stays. "Whatever you need, Jack. Just come back to us. You're ours. It can't have you."

Jack's eyes flick up to meet Ben's over my head. He nods, pressing a kiss to my neck.

"Ours," Ben murmurs in my ear.

"Ours," Jack growls. He thrusts impossibly deep inside me as he comes.

"Yours." I have to close my eyes against the tears prickling at them. "You're mine. And I'm yours."

19

My phone vibrates across the library table with the force of its silent ringing. Grabbing it, I swipe absently at the screen, not looking up from my computer. "Hello?"

"Am I speaking to Claire Ryan?"

"Yes, this is she."

There's the tiniest hesitation before the voice on the other end speaks again. "Ms. Ryan, this is Janelle Dyer, the nurse from Dr. Dickson's office. I'm calling to tell you that we have your test results back and everything looks normal."

"Okay. I see."

"Dr. Dickson has called in a referral for you to a neurologist specializing in these kind of cases," she says. "I have that number for you."

I bite back a retort. It's not this perfectly nice nurse's fault that my head is fucked. More fucked. "Sure. Go ahead and give me that number."

I don't bother writing it down.

"Have a great day," the nurse chirps.

"Thanks. You too."

I end the call and set the phone down on the table instead of slamming it like I want to. It doesn't do any good. Ben is still watching me like a hawk. "What's up?"

I sigh, rubbing my forehead and leaning back in my chair, trying to loosen up my lower back muscles. "The doctor has no idea what's causing my headaches. There's no physical or neurological reason they can find for them. Just like Mal said. Just like Livvy said."

"What number did they give you?"

"Some brain specialist they want me to go see."

He raises his eyebrows. "I notice you didn't write it down."

"What for?" I snap. "So I can rack up hundreds of thousands of dollars in medical bills for him to tell us there's nothing causing them? Mal and Livvy already told me it's not an injury or a disease, and the doctor just confirmed it. This is just a thing that sometimes happens to people. Nothing we can do about it."

"You're not…" Ben bits his lip. "Have you been having like, weird dreams?"

I haven't, not that I remember. "Like what?"

"Like very realistic, detailed? Almost like you're seeing something that's actually happening?"

"No, I haven't," I say slowly. "Any particular reason? That's a really specific question."

He looks down at the table. "Sometimes I have visions. Dreaming the future. I think it's something the Fae did to me—you know, before they dropped me off like a bag of trash. Anyway, I didn't realize that's what was happening until they started to come true. I just asked because I used to have headaches, too."

"Do you still have them? The visions?"

"Not for a long time," he says quietly. "It freaked Jack out, when it happened. Made me too much like the things we hunted."

"You don't have to tell me." I'm out of my chair to hug him before I even realize I've moved.

He pulls me into his lap, a hand smoothing over my hair as my head falls on his shoulder. "It was rough. But we're better now. Someday. Someday I want to tell you. Just—not today."

ᛋᚱᚼ

I turn off the shower and dry off, wrapping a towel around myself before brushing my teeth. Say what you will about survivalist-style bunkers, but at least the water pressure's good.

I'm halfway back to my room when I realize I need to go. Part of my mind, the part that questions and snarks and has second thoughts, says *Go where? You're wrapped in a towel. What are you doing?*

But it's like that part is trapped, locked in a glass box where it can only watch. I'm almost through the library and to the stairs leading up and out when Jack sees me.

At first his eyes are appreciative, moving over the towel that's the only thing I'm wearing. It only takes a few seconds for that gaze to sharpen, for him to catch my arm as I move past him.

"What's the rush, sweetheart?" His voice is low and calm.

"I have to go," I hear myself say. It's true. I *have* to go. I need—I don't know what I need. But I have to go get it. "I have to go."

"Okay," he says easily. But he doesn't let go. "You're not gonna get far without shoes. Why don't we go to your room and get you dressed? You can tell me where we're going."

I allow myself to be led back to my room. "I don't know where it is. But I have to find it. I have to, Jack."

He nods like this makes perfect sense, guiding me to sit on the bed. "If I let go, are you gonna sit there while I find you some clothes?"

"I'll—I'll try." I honestly don't know, and that should terrify me. But all I can feel is that urgency, like a drumbeat in my blood, in my ears, in my fingertips. "But we have to hurry."

"Okay." He releases my arm slowly, poised to block any movement toward the door. We eye each other warily for a minute, but I manage to stay on the bed. Even though my foot starts shaking with the need to *go*.

Jack turns and starts rummaging in my dresser while still somehow keeping an eye on me and staying between me and the door. After a few seconds, he tosses a bra and some underwear onto the bed. "Put those on while I find you some clothes, okay?"

I nod, grabbing them. Ignoring that inner voice— *usually he's trying to get your clothes off, not on. Something is wrong*—I do as he suggests

By the time I have the bra and underwear on, he's back with a t-shirt and jeans.

"Give me your hand, sweetheart," he says as I'm pulling up the zipper on my jeans.

I do so automatically, then stare blankly as he fastens a leather cuff around my wrist, the other end already attached to the headboard.

"But—I need to go."

He takes advantage of my momentary confusion to shift me up further onto the bed and secure my other wrist. "Sorry, sweetheart. But you're not yourself. I don't know what's going on, how something got through our warding to get to you. But you're staying here, where it's safe, until we figure this out."

I jerk against the cuffs, testing them. But he didn't fasten my wrists together like he usually does, to make it easier for me to get out if anything happens. My hands are cuffed to opposite sides of the headboard, my arms spread so I don't have enough leverage to yank them free.

"I have to go!" I yell. Even though I know it won't work, I can't keep from jerking again, dull pain in my wrists. It's rising in me, the need, the panic. "I have to find it!"

"Gods." He rubs a hand over his face, looking more tired than maybe I've ever seen him. "Maybe we are cursed."

ᚴᚱᚼ

BEN AND JACK are in the hall outside. Their low voices float in through the open door, just quiet enough that I can't hear what they're saying.

I try to stop myself from pulling against the cuffs, but I start again as soon as I'm not focusing on being still. Why don't they understand. I *have* to go!

A phone rings in the hallway, breaking through their quiet conversation.

"Hello?" Jack's voice is louder now, enough that I can hear the words, barely. "Mal, man, we need some help. I know you said there wasn't anything wrong with Claire, but she's lost it. She tried to leave in a fucking towel!"

Ben say something, still too quiet for me to understand.

"About an hour ago," Jack says. "You are? Thank fuck."

There's a soft noise I can't quite place, then Mal's deep voice. "Would you like me to see if I can help?"

"Please." I've never heard Ben's voice sound like that before. It would scare me, if there was room in my mind for fear, or anything other than the need to leave.

Mal appears in the doorway, his forehead furrowed. "Claire?"

"I have to go," I say. Well. I mean to say it. It comes out more like a sob as I jerk against the cuffs again.

He nods, closing his eyes for a moment, then opens them again. Moving his hand in a circle, he says something under his breath.

It feels like my ears popping, like the air going perfectly still. Suddenly I can think again, I can make my hands be still instead of pulling at the restraints.

My whole body goes limp with the relief of it, the inexplicable pull finally disappearing.

"What—?"

"Give me a moment and we'll have you out of those." Mal reaches for my left wrist, unbuckling the cuff. "And then I will endeavor to explain."

"Mal—" Jack starts.

Mal never pauses, freeing my hand and rubbing gently at the marks from where I'd strained against the cuffs. "It's fine, Jack. Shielding isn't one of my inherent magics, but I can maintain it indefinitely. You're not going anywhere, are you, Claire?"

I nod, my free hand coming down to rest in my lap as Mal leans across my body to unbuckle the other cuff. "Yeah, I—I'm good. What the fuck?"

"I'd like to know that too," Ben says. I've never heard that edge in his voice before. It's apparently a day of firsts.

"I don't know everything," Mal says. "But I suspect that talking about what I do know is a conversation best had over drinks."

ᛋᚱᚻ

ONCE WE'RE ALL SETTLED around the kitchen table, bottle of whiskey in the center and four glasses half-filled with the amber liquid, Jack points at Mal. "Okay. Spill."

"I believe that the roots of this go back to before you met Claire." Mal turns his glass around in his hands. The light turns his eyes the same warm amber as the whiskey, the same color as his dragon form, when he looks up at me. "Claire, what happened to your husband?"

I open my mouth to answer, then stop. Because I was going to say the same thing that I told Ben and Jack during that first lunch. That he'd disappeared, that I had no idea if he was alive or dead.

Except none of that is true.

And I forgot.

"How—?"

"Someone—someone with extraordinary skill at magic and tremendous power—planted false memories in your head," Mal says. "Along with a magical compulsion, which I am currently shielding you from. So tell us. What do you remember about what happened to your husband?"

"Jake really was glamoured." I speak slowly, trying to separate what I thought I remembered from the new-old memories sitting alongside them in my head. "But—he didn't just disappear. I went after him."

It hurts, remembering. Telling them.

But the memories are clear, like it all happened yesterday, sharp and new. Jake telling me he was leaving, that he was going Underhill to be with his Queen. Me begging him to reconsider, following him out of the house and into the doorway that opened in thin air.

The way the Queen frowned when she saw me, then the smile, beautiful and terrible, like a knife slicing across my skin.

"She said—" I have to stop and swallow. "She said as long as I was there, I could serve her purposes. And then…"

I have to stop again, to breathe through the memory of my mind being ripped apart and reformed. The worst part had been how easy it was for her. She sat there the entire time, lounging on her throne while I screamed and begged and vomited. At the end, when it was over, she didn't have so much as a hair out of place.

"She said that, since I wouldn't remember, she'd tell

me. Called me her hound, said I would follow the scent and bring her the Treasures. She laughed, and said how funny it was, that one of the humans he loved so much would be the thing that undid his great work."

I open my eyes. I'm not sure when I closed them. "The next thing I remember is waking up in my house, believing that Jake just disappeared. Why—why do I remember it now?"

Mal looks a little embarrassed. "I believe that may be at least partially my fault. The Queen no doubt meant to have you lie in wait until a time of her choosing, at which point she would activate your compulsion. But without her around to reinforce it, the block walling off your real memories became weakened."

"Okay, but how is that your fault?" Jack asks.

"Dragons radiate a powerful magical aura when shifted into their human form," Mal says. "That no doubt weakened the barrier even further. I apologize, Claire. I had no idea my proximity to you would have such an effect."

I manage a smile. "No apology needed. I'd rather know. Although I guess we don't really know what we know. She didn't exactly explain what Treasures she was sending me after."

Mal smiles back at me, but it looks forced. "For a Fae Queen, there are only four she could be speaking of. But I thought they were legend; even the oldest dragon shifter histories never contained any evidence that they existed.

"That what existed?" Ben's voice is impatient. His

hands are gentle, though, when he wraps an arm around my shoulders and pulls me close. "Dude, I know you're like a hundred years old, but can you knock it off with the cryptic bullshit, just this once?"

"The Jewels of the North," Mal says. "Humanity's last defense against the Fae."

20

Jack knocks back his whiskey and pours more before speaking. "Okay. Maybe start at the beginning? Or close to it, anyway."

Mal nods. "In the earlier days of your recorded history, there was a human hero named Arthur. Legends of him have persisted to this day, although they are largely incorrect, as legends tend to be."

"Wasn't he actually a British king who fought the Romans?" I ask. The warmth of Ben's body, his arms around me, is helping calm the small tremors running through me, but I'm still jittery.

"That's what most historians believe," Mal agrees. "But the truth is that he and his men primarily fought against the Fae. Where once the queens and their servants had the run of this world, hunting humans and shifters with impunity, the iron swords of Arthur's knights allowed humans to hold their own, to triumph. The Fae were eventually driven back Underhill, the connections between our worlds weakened."

Ben shakes his head. "How? Even with iron weapons—the Fae should have overrun them."

"Merlin," Mal says. "The story goes that he brought the Four Treasures of the Tuatha de Danaan from the North. Some said they were gifts from the gods, some said they were powerful magical artifacts that Merlin crafted. But either way, he used them to set up a magical protection around the Isles, one strong enough to hold even a Queen at bay. And, when Arthur fell battling a Fae Queen, Merlin worked his greatest magic. He hid the Treasures, the four great Jewels, in secret locations around the world, anchors for a spell that would protect our world from the Fae. That would allow us to live in peace."

"But you said that's just a legend," Jack says.

Ben snorts. "Well, someone believes it's true. Enough to fuck with Claire's head to try and find them."

"I'm probably not going to like the answer to this question," I say. "But what could a Fae Queen do, if the Jewels were real? If she had them?"

Mal's face sets in hard lines. "This world would no longer be protected. Despite the fact that we are closer to Underhill now than before, the Queens are still limited. They can only act through intermediaries; to set foot outside of Underhill would be to die, blocked from the magic that sustains them. There's been some debate about what keeps them away. But the Queen who took you clearly believes she knows."

"What was her name?" Jack asks quietly. "Did she tell you? They usually like to brag."

The tremors start up again at the question, deep in my gut where it feels like I'll never be warm again. "Yeah, she—she said her name was Talaith"

He frowns. "If Talaith is involved in this, Iorwen isn't going to be far. They fight over shit like dogs over a bone."

"Although Iorwen would doubtless sear your eyes from your head for that comparison, you're not incorrect," Mal says. "However, since Talaith's compulsion has revealed itself early, we have an opportunity."

"What kind of opportunity?" Ben asks.

Mal looks at me for a moment, his eyes sharp and intense. "If Claire is willing, we could locate the Jewels before Talaith. Whatever their origins, whether or not they do, in fact, protect our world from the Fae, they are powerful objects. Possibly powerful enough to remove Jack's curse without causing his instant demise. Certainly powerful enough to end this compulsion before it damages her mind."

"It's too dangerous," Jack says instantly. "Claire should stay here, where it's safe."

"Excuse you, I'm sitting right fucking here," I say. I can't muster as much snap to my voice as I'd like, but it's enough to make Jack wince, so that'll have to do. "And last

I checked, I was an adult who got to make my own decisions."

Ben squeezes me gently. "You haven't eaten yet today, though. No decisions on an empty stomach."

My stomach, traitorous as always, chooses that moment to growl. "Fine. Can we have bacon?"

"That's my girl," Jack says.

He shoots me an apologetic grin as he gets up and makes his way to the stove, but I'm reserving my forgiveness for after breakfast.

There'd better be a lot of bacon.

ᛋᚱᚼ

I WAIT until we're done with breakfast, half out of courtesy, half because I'm too busy stuffing my face. There is, in fact, a lot of bacon. Maybe Jack thinks that will change my mind. I hope not. I'd like to think he knows me better than that by now.

Pushing back from the table, I load my dishes into the dishwasher and come back to my chair before clearing my throat.

Three sets of eyes turn my way instantly.

"I'm doing it."

Jack opens his mouth to say something, probably to try to talk me out of it, so I just keep going. "It's my choice. I've thought about it, and I'm doing it. Besides, if Talaith figures out I've found a way to beat the compulsion, she'll probably come after me. At least this way I'll have a chance."

Ben sets a hand on Jack's arm, shooting him a meaningful look. "We know it's your choice. But I hope you'll let us help."

"I don't even know where to start," I admit. "I'll take all the help I can get."

"We should probably see if we can determine the location of the stones through scrying," Mal says. "I can teach you."

I feel bad about worrying Jack and Ben. I can see it in the pinched looks on their faces and the stiffness in their body language. But it's such a relief to be actually doing something, to have a path to follow, steps to take. I'm not going to stay locked up in here for the rest of my life like some fairy-tale princess. I can't.

"You know you don't have to do this for me, right?" Jack reaches out to take my hand, his eyes searching mine.

"I know." I squeeze his fingers, willing him to understand. "I'm doing it for me."

He still doesn't look convinced, but he doesn't stop me when Mal leads me off to the library for scrying lessons.

ᛋᚱᚼ

"Claire."

I don't look up from the mirror where I've been trying —and failing—to scry for the last couple of hours until

Ben yanks it out from between my hands. I growl at him, but he only shakes his head and pulls it back further out of my reach.

"Nope," he says. "You don't get this back until you've had at least 8 hours of sleep."

I briefly consider trying to make a grab for it. But Ben has a good foot of height and a ridiculous reach on me. The only thing I'd accomplish would be to embarrass myself.

"Fine." I shove back from the table, trying, and failing, not to feel like a three-year-old throwing a tantrum. "I'm not gonna be able to sleep, though."

Something rattles behind me as Ben hides the mirror, but I don't look back as I head down the hall toward the bedrooms. He catches up quickly, though, his long legs eating up the distance until we're walking side by side, his hand settling warmly onto the small of my back and steering me into Jack's room.

"I think we can help with that," he murmurs. "Sleep is important. You need your rest."

I pull in a breath to snark back at him, but something catches my eye and the air leaves me in a rush before I can speak.

Because there's Jack, stark naked, stretched out on the bed with his hands cuffed above him. He gives me his usual cocky smirk, but with an edge of uncertainty to it that I'm not used to seeing. His body doesn't seem to have any qualms about the situation, however; his cock is already so hard it looks like it hurts, standing straight up from his body.

"How long?" I ask. My voice is softer than I expected, hushed, almost, as I kneel on the edge of the bed. "How long have you been waiting?"

"Not long." Ben closes the door and comes up behind me, hands landing on my shoulders and stroking slowly down my arms. "Just enough time for him to start thinking about what you might want to do to him while he's like this."

Jack closes his eyes, shuddering. "Benny, I swear to God—"

I lean over and kiss him, cutting off his words. Hesitantly at first, but for once he doesn't try to take over the kiss, letting me set the pace. The chance to play like I don't usually get to makes me bolder, more willing to try things. Catching his lower lip between my teeth, I nibble at it gently until he groans. When I finally lick inside with little teasing flicks of my tongue, it's warm and familiar, the taste of Jack mixed with whiskey.

Ben's hands urge me up gently, just long enough to pull my t-shirt over my head. I go back to kissing Jack as soon as I can, letting Ben peel me out of the rest of my clothes. When I'm finally completely naked, I crawl up, straddling Jack's stomach. Licking my way down his neck, I sink my teeth into the muscle where his neck meets his shoulder, smiling against his skin as he arches and shudders under me.

The bed shifts under us as Ben sits down, stroking a hand down my back. "That's it," he murmurs. "You can do whatever you want."

I let go, sliding down slightly until I can lick a circle around his nipple. I have no idea how long I tease him like that, but it's long enough that he rasps out "Please," his hips thrusting up, his cock just barely grazing my ass and making him moan at the friction.

I sit up, pressing my ass back more firmly against his cock, smiling wickedly. "Please what?" I prompt.

"Fuck," he growls. He can't move much with my weight pinning him to the bed, just enough to thrust up against me again. "Please fuck me."

"Well, since you ask so nicely," I tease. It's a weird echo, this role reversal, and maybe another night I wouldn't be into it, but right now it feels good, right. And clearly Jack's into it. I wriggle back, dragging the wet softness of my pussy across his dick, feeling his hardness spread me apart as I start to sink down onto him.

"You sure?" Ben asks. His hand squeezes the back of my neck, pulling me to a stop. "We can keep using condoms. We're used to it."

I can't help smiling. "Just as sure as I was the last time we talked about it. And the time before that. The tests all came back clean, my IUD is good for another two years. I want this."

He searches my eyes for a long moment, but whatever he sees there must reassure him. "Okay."

I rise up over Jack, lowering myself down his cock in one long, slick glide. My eyes close as I savor the sensation, the feeling of no barriers between us.

He shudders underneath me once, then again as I shift my weight, taking him as deep inside as I possibly can.

"Fuck, sweetheart." His eyes flutter shut, his head arching back on the pillow, arms straining against the cuffs. "Jesus fuck, that feels so good."

I lift up slowly, then slide back down even slower this time, my nerves lighting up with every movement of his cock inside me. I keep the slow, torturous pace as long as I can stand it, not sure if I'm doing it to torment Jack or myself.

But then Ben is behind me, the muscled plane of his chest pressed warm against my back, the hard, thick line of his cock nudging my ass. He reaches around, cupping my breasts in his big hands, thumbs brushing too lightly over my nipples.

I whimper and start moving faster, taking Jack fully inside my pussy on each downstroke. Ben rewards me by scraping his nails lightly over my nipples, then rolling them between fingers and thumbs, giving me the sensation I need.

"That's it, baby," he breathes in my ear. "You're driving him crazy. Look at him."

I force my eyes open, vaguely wondering when I'd shut them. But that's not important now. What's important is

Jack's eyes on me, the muscles in his arms and chest flexing as he strains against the cuffs.

"You want your hands free, Jack?" I'm a little shocked at the low rasp of my voice

"Yes," he grits out. A muscle jumps in his jaw as Ben squeezes my nipples, making me moan and arch back against him.

I have to swallow a couple of times before I speak again. "What would you do if you had your hands free?" I roll my hips a little faster. "I'm already fucking you; what else do you want?"

He narrows his eyes, then smiles wickedly, licking his lips. "Want to get my hands and my mouth on those pretty tits of yours." He thrusts up into me, just a little, smiling when I moan. "Know you love it; you get so wet when we do it. Practically dripping just from us licking and sucking and biting. Maybe one day Benny and I should have a contest, see who can get you off fastest just by playing with your tits."

Behind me, Ben groans, dropping his head to nibble on my neck. His clever fingers are still busy on my breasts, making me pick up the pace, chase the orgasm hovering just out of reach.

"There you go, sweetheart," Jack says. He keeps fucking up into me, his timing perfect, making sure my clit rubs up against him with every stroke. "Ride me. Wanna see you come for me, wanna hear you. You like this position, don't you? Talk to me, tell me. Use the dirty words, since you won't let me touch you."

"Oh, fuck." I moan, letting my head fall back against Ben. "Feels so good, Jack. I feel every inch of your cock like this. Makes me so wet, your huge, thick cock inside my pussy."

Both men groan at the same time, Ben's cock twitching against my ass and his hands tightening on my breasts. Jack matches my speed, his face twisting almost like he's in pain. "Shit, Benny, you gonna make her come? I'm not gonna last long here."

"Always rushing," Ben says. But when Jack thrusts up into me, hard, pressing against my clit just perfectly, Ben squeezes my nipples and bites down lightly on my neck. And just like that, I'm gone, writhing between them as the combined sensations push me over the edge.

Ben eases me down until I'm draped across Jack's chest. Just as I realize that Jack hasn't come yet, I feel Ben's fingers teasing across my ass.

"Relax," Ben murmurs. His other hand strokes gently up and down my back as he presses one finger slowly inside. "Gonna get you used to being filled up like this."

Jack captures my mouth in a kiss, distracting me as he starts slowly thrusting up into me again. "Gonna feel so good, sweetheart, both of us fucking you at the same time."

Ben eases a second finger in, stretching and twisting. It

feels strange, but he's right. It does feel good. I'm surprised to realize I'm more than halfway to coming again.

I whimper a little as Ben's fingers slide out before I can stop myself, He chuckles darkly behind me, his other hand still warm and firm on the small of my back. "Don't worry, baby."

The plug presses gently but firmly against my ass, the tip just sliding in. "I'm gonna fuck you with this plug until you come. It's almost as big as I am, and you're gonna take it for us, aren't you?"

I nod against Jack's chest, my eyes closed as I try to breathe through the stretch.

"Good girl." Ben presses the plug in and pulls it out in tiny increments. He goes infinitesimally deeper with each thrust, matching Jack's pace inside my pussy.

Jack bucks up under me as the plug goes deeper. "Shit, Benny, I can feel that."

Ben leans over so he can murmur in my ear, all while never stopping his inexorable rhythm. "Jack likes to think he's straight as an arrow," he says. "But when we're both fucking you, there's not gonna be much between us. I'll be able to feel his cock rubbing against mine inside you, and so will he."

Jack closes his eyes, and Ben drops his voice even lower. "And he fucking loves it."

Shuddering, Jack thrusts up inside me, his rhythm becoming a stutter as he comes. I find myself coming as well from the combination of Jack's deep, erratic thrusts and Ben finally seating the plug firmly inside my ass.

My heart is still hammering in my chest when I hear the slick sounds of Ben jerking off behind me, followed quickly by his groan as he comes, hot and wet, over the small of my back.

"Really?" Jack's voice is still a little breathless, but when I manage to lift my head he's making an impressively bitchy face. "Was that really necessary, Benny?"

"Like you wouldn't have done the same," Ben says.

Jack snorts, but doesn't attempt to argue. "You're cleaning it up, buddy."

Ben lifts me off Jack, setting me down gently and reaching for the cuffs. "Whatever you say, man."

I could lie here forever like this, listening to them bicker gently. Maybe I will. I don't feel tired at all, despite the vigorous exercise.

I'm asleep before Ben finishes uncuffing Jack.

21

"Maybe you should take a break," Ben says from across the library table the next morning after Mal has left to do some kind of mysterious dragon shifter shit.

Whatever image was starting to form in the scrying mirror disappears with the distraction. I shoot him a look. "I've only been working on this for an hour, Ben."

"Yeah, okay." He drops his eyes to his computer screen, but the set of his jaw says he's not convinced.

I don't have time for this. Sighing, I return to the mirror, trying to focus my concentration like Mal showed me.

"Do you want something to drink?" he asks ten minutes later.

I have to count to twenty before I can trust myself not to snap. "No thanks, I'm good."

"You sure?"

"I'm sure." It takes a valiant effort of will not to clench my teeth, and I only mostly succeed.

ᛋᚱᚺ

"I'm hungry. Are you hungry? What do you want for lunch?" Ben asks five minutes later—yes, I'm keeping track, because he's being weird. Even Jack is side-eyeing him from his seat at the next table over, disassembled pistol pieces abandoned in front of him.

I close my eyes and rub my forehead. Seriously, what the hell?

"Do you have a headache? Want me to get your meds? Maybe you should lie down for a little while—"

"The only headache I have right now is you," I snap. "Godsdamnit, Ben, just because you're fucking me doesn't mean you have to wrap me in bubble wrap and baby me. I'm a grown woman who's been taking care of herself for quite a few years now. I'm not gonna break!"

Ben flinches. I feel a little guilty, but this shit seriously has to stop. He's been ridiculously solicitous ever since Mal dropped his little bombshell and it's driving me up the fucking wall.

I shove my chair back from the table, leaving the mirror lying there. Ben opens his mouth, probably to ask where I'm going, takes a good look at my face, and closes it again.

"I'm going to go work out," I say. Without looking behind me, because I can't look at him right now without saying something I'll regret. Something else I'll regret. "Don't wait up.

SR4

THE ROOM they set aside for my squat rack and other equipment is too quiet, my footsteps echoing off the wall, but music blaring through my Bluetooth speaker fixes that. I move through my warmup quickly, pacing circles around the room between sets as I slowly add more and more weight to the bar.

Taking a deep breath, I swing myself under the bar, settling it across my shoulders. Another breath in, keeping my core firm, and I stand all the way up, lifting it off the rack.

A few steps back, one more breath. Holding air in my lungs as I drop down, knees out, chest up, breathing out with the force of pushing up, up, up against the weight holding me down.

I step forward and let the bar drop onto the rack. My body feels limp, wrung out, my quadriceps loose and shaky. I reach for my water bottle and take several drinks, turning to set it back down—and I freeze.

"How much was that?" Ben leans against the wall, looking as hesitant as a man his size is capable of looking.

I briefly consider not answering, just to drive home how irritated I am with him, but I'm pretty fucking proud of myself. "Three seventy-five!"

His eyes widen. "Holy shit!"

I can feel my smile becoming incredibly smug, but I'm honestly okay with that. I think I'm allowed to be a little smug. But as the silence stretches between us, my smile starts to fade.

"Anyway," he says. "I'm sorry I was—"

"Hovering? Smothering? Driving me up the wall?" I somehow, barely, resist the temptation to soften the words. I don't want to have to deal with this shit on the regular. If we're going to make this work, he can't keep acting like this.

He rubs a hand over the back of his neck, giving me his best sheepish grin. "Yeah. That."

I sigh. "I'ms sorry I blew up at you. But seriously, that's not okay. I can't work like that. I can't live like that."

"I know." He takes a seat on my bench, currently shoved against the wall. His long legs sprawl wide, arms dangling between. "And I really am sorry."

After a moment's hesitation, I sit down next to him. "I guess I just don't understand why the change all of a sudden. I mean, I know you've already been looking out for me, and when it's normal, I like it. What took it up to crazy serial-killer stalker level?"

He looks down at his hands. "I'm, uh, not really sure. Maybe it's the Fae thing?"

"Okay, but what does that have to do with anything?"

"The queen who took Jack—that wasn't her only price for healing me." He closes his eyes, a pained expression on her face.

I slide closer, lifting his arm around my shoulders and cuddling close into his side. "I'm guessing I'm not going to like where this story is going."

His face grows grimmer, which I didn't think was possible."She glamoured me, used me to take out a woman —I have no idea why. But it—I killed her. In front of her children. While they screamed and cried."

I do my best not to react outwardly; now isn't the time for my feelings about this. "It wasn't your choice, Ben. You would never—"

"I keep people safe." His mouth takes on the stubborn set I've come to know only too well. "That's what we do. We keep people safe. But I killed her."

"So all the people glamoured by the Fae, they're responsible for their actions?"

"What?" He shakes his head. "No, of course not. That's ridiculous."

I poke him in the chest. "Then why the fuck would you be?"

He sighs, deflating back against the wall. "You're right.

I know you're right. It just—I remember doing it. I remember—fuck. I remember how much she enjoyed it. It —it felt like it was me, you know?"

I lean in closer, doing my best to project comfort, not to remember what it felt like to be a passenger in my own head. "I know."

"It's not just that," he admits after another moment of silence. "Hunting doesn't exactly lend itself to relationships. I've had to watch too many people I care about die, because they got in the way, or because someone wanted to prove a point, wanted to see me bleed."

"Ben—"

His arm tightens around me. "What we have, the three of us, it's more than I ever thought I could have in my life. I don't want to lose you, too."

I swallow down the ache in my chest until I can speak. "We both know there aren't any guarantees. I could get hit by a truck, or choke on my dinner."

"Or get food poisoning, or a thousand other things. I know," he agrees. "But now that we know about the Jewels, you're in even more danger. Like Jack said, Talaith and Iorwen are always competing over shit. We can protect you against a lot, but not two fucking courts of Fae."

"What do you want, Ben?" I ask. My voice is as soft as I can make it. "Do you want me to promise never to leave here alone? Want me to stay locked up in here for the rest of my life?"

He sighs. "Part of me does. But—" he holds up a hand "—I'm not asking for that. Just—be careful?"

I nod. "I'll try. For what it's worth, I don't want to be tortured by Fae, or see them overrun Earth."

"Good. I don't want you to be tortured by Fae either." He kisses me lightly, pulling back to look into my eyes. "I love you. You don't have to say it back. I'm not trying to rush you. I just wanted to say it."

I choke out a laugh. "I love you too. God, I think I've been falling in love with you two ever since you caught me trying to sneak out that first morning."

He pulls me in for a longer, deeper kiss. "I've been falling in love with you ever since you sat us down and told us exactly how you wanted us to fuck you."

His phone vibrates between us, a startling interruption that has both of us jumping. He sighs as he fishes it out of his pocket, then bursts out laughing, turning the screen so I can see.

There are two text messages on the screen, both from Jack. The first one says, *if you're still alive, dinner in 10.* The second one says *if not, Claire, let's eat first then I'll help you with the body after.*

I laugh too, getting to my feet and crossing to the weight rack. "Come on then, help me put these weights up. If we're late, he's gonna pout about how it would've been so much better when it was fresh."

Ben joins me, taking the plates I hand him and carrying them over to the rack. Together we get the bar stripped down and plates back in place in no time, heading toward the kitchen hand in hand.

ᛋᚱᚺ

"How many times did you have to hit him over the head before he calmed the fuck down?" Jack slides the dinner plates onto the table with a flourish.

I grin up at him. "Only a couple. Good thing he's got such a hard head, huh?"

"Hey."

"Aww." I lean over and kiss him. "It's okay. I still love you. But if you pull that shit again, we're going to have words."

"Understood." He smiles at me. "Love you, too."

Jack clears his throat. "What am I, chopped liver?"

I eye him, trying to gauge his mood. "I figured you for the type to run for the hills if a girl even looks like saying the L word."

He shifts uneasily in his seat, like even the idea makes him uncomfortable. "Maybe."

"Let's see, then." I reach over and lay my hand on his arm, waiting until he meets my eyes. "I love you, Jack."

And yeah, there's the expected panic in his eyes. But he doesn't pull away, and as the moment passes, the panic fades into something else. Something that warms me from the inside. Something that feels like home.

He's smiling when he says it back.

22

"Ugh." I shove the scrying mirror away from me. Just a little, not enough to send it flying. I'm not interested in finding out what Mal would do if I broke one of his possessions. Maybe the whole "dragons hoard" thing is bullshit—I keep forgetting to ask—but maybe it isn't. "This isn't working."

"Scrying is a skill that develops over time, even when the innate ability is already there," Mal says. His voice is mild, but the way he straightens the mirror a bare fraction of an inch makes me think that maybe I was smart to be gentle. "You've only been trying for a week. Did you learn to walk in a week?"

"Yeah, but I've got a direct line to the Jewels." I only barely resist the urge to cross my arms like a child.

Although compared to Mal, I guess I am. We all are. "Mal, how old are you?"

He blinks a little at the sudden change of subject. "Somewhere between five and six hundred years old. I no longer keep track, particularly given the number of times I have moved between Underhill and the human world. Why do you ask?"

"Just wondering." I sigh, running my hand over the ornamental frame around the mirror. "But seriously, if a Fae queen is going to fuck with my life and my memories, it'd be nice if I could actually, I don't know, find the damn magic rocks."

"I could lift my shielding—"

Mal cuts off at the sudden, loud protests from both Jack and Ben. They subside when he raises a hand, which surprises me. I keep forgetting that the three of them have a history before I came on the scene. "—but I do not think that would be wise. Even if you were restrained, Claire, Talaith would not have bothered to safeguard the spell to prevent you from harming yourself accidentally."

"That doesn't sound like a good time." I sigh again. "I guess you can't lift the shield just a little?"

"I am reluctant to risk that."

Jack makes an impatient growling noise. "Yeah, fucking seconded. We can find these things without that."

I roll my eyes. "Can we? Because I'm not getting that impression. Neither Ben or I have turned up anything research-wise. Not to mention this isn't getting us any closer to figuring out how to deal with your curse."

"Perhaps there is something else that we could try to find the Jewels," Mal says. "A different form of scrying."

"As long as it doesn't involve me rushing out of here in a towel, I'm willing to give it a shot." I shoot Jack and Ben a quelling glare when they open their mouths. "Although I'll probably be shit at this too, just like regular scrying."

Mal shakes his head. "I have the ability to induce a light trance state in a willing subject. What Talaith did—your brain was fundamentally altered, to allow you to sense the Jewels. Being in this state might allow you to find the connection, to follow it."

"Worth a shot. Are we doing this now?"

"You should be physically comfortable," Mal says. "Perhaps a bedroom?"

When I meet his eyes, I'm deeply certain that he's also remembering that frozen moment when he burst in on me while I was half-naked and just barely post-orgasm. My face heats but I can't look away from him, the way his eyes go dark with the memory. As humiliating as it is, though, the space in my brain that likes it when Ben calls me a slut, talks about how greedy I am, also finds it excruciatingly hot.

And now is definitely not the time for this.

"Sure. I think there's a path between my bed and the door."

I push to my feet and all three men mirror me.

"Will it mess this up if we're there too?" Jack asks. His voice is low and rough enough that I can't help wondering if he picked up on the energy between me and Mal. Or maybe he's just remembering that we had discussed Mal joining us.

"As long as you're quiet, it should be fine." Mal gestures me ahead of him down the hallway. "Do you think you can manage that?"

Ben and I exchange a look that lets me know I'm not the only one who noted the suggestive tone in Mal's voice, or the flush on Jack's cheeks.

"I'll try," Jack mumbles.

Mal wraps a hand around the back of his neck and squeezes. "You can do it."

Their interplay is enough to distract me from what we're about to do until I'm stretched out on my bed, Mal sitting next to my hip. Jack and Ben hesitate in the doorway for a moment, one of those silent conversations passing between them. Some conclusion must have been reached, since they close the door behind them and lean against the wall, one on either side of the doorway.

"Are you comfortable?" Mal's voice is low and resonant, drawing my attention back to him.

I wriggle against the mattress a little, the question drawing my attention to minor points of tension in my body. "I think so. As much as I can be with all three of you staring at me."

As soon as the words are out of my mouth I regret it,

especially since Jack is visibly struggling with the need to make a dirty joke. He manages to control himself, however.

When I look back at Mal he nods. "Yes, I can see where that would make things difficult. You may close your eyes, if it helps."

The dimly lit room that I still don't quite feel at home in disappears, replaced by the backs of my eyelids. I do feel more comfortable this way, even though I know that they're all still looking at me. At least with my eyes closed, I don't have to see it.

"I'm going to touch your forehead, like I did that time in the library." Mal's voice is quiet, but I don't have to strain to hear it. Almost before he finishes speaking, his fingertips make contact with my skin, two points of warmth between my eyebrows. "Try to relax your body for me, starting with your toes and moving upward.

This, at least, is familiar, from yoga classes and guided meditation videos. I do my best to follow his directions. The focus on relaxation distracts a little me from the cool-water sensation of his magic moving behind my eyes.

I'm not sure how long it takes before he speaks again, drawing my attention from the floaty sensation. "Very good, Claire. Now I want you to think about that moment, when you knew you had to go. Go back to that memory."

It's not like remembering. Suddenly I'm there again,

standing in front of the mirror, gripped by the sudden realization that I have to go--

A warm hand wraps around my wrist where my pulse is hammering. "You're safe." Mal's voice is firm, his touch grounding. "It's just a memory, Claire. It can't hurt you. We're here. Do you feel it? The impulse, the thing telling you to go?"

"Yeah." I do my best to slow my breathing down. I can't feel anything but the need pulling me out the door. Mal's hand is the only thing holding me in place. "I feel it."

"Where do you feel it? Which part of your body?"

Stopping to think is hard. I start at my feet again, force of habit and repetition. I don't feel it there, although they are shifting restlessly against the covers. Not in my legs, either. I move my scan upward, probing each body part in turn but coming up empty.

Until I hit the place behind my eyes, directly below Mal's fingertips. "What the fuck is that?"

"Tell me what you see."

I open and close my mouth a few times, trying to put it into words. "I--don't see it, exactly. But there's something. It feels almost like--like the time I got a fishhook stuck in my finger. It's not me, but it's attached to me. Pulling on me."

"That sounds like our spell," Mal agrees. "Can you tell which way it wants you to go?"

Even after trying everything I can think of, I shake my head. "Just out."

He makes a little whuffing noise. "Most likely this being a pocket dimension is throwing things off. Are you up for a little trip?"

"All of us," Jack says, the first sound he's made since entering the room. "We're coming, too."

"Of course."

"If you're sure it's safe." I blink my eyes open. Even the dim light of my lamp is a lot, after so long with them closed.

Mal shrugs, offering me a hand to sit up. "As safe as anything else. As we will be in the human world, I don't believe you to be in any further danger from Talaith. But our best bet for finding the jewel is most likely to be a triangulation of sorts."

"Take Claire to different locations and see which direction the spell is pulling her?" Ben nods slowly. "That could work. I'll get a map and a compass."

As he slips out the door, Jack moves toward the bed, sitting on my other side and taking the hand Mal isn't holding. "How are you holding up?"

I shrug. "Okay, I think. It's better, having a way to try and move forward. Not just sitting here, spinning our wheels. You know?"

"Yeah, I know." He lifts my hand to his lips, pressing a kiss to the back of it. "But don't kill yourself, okay? We'll find another way if we need one."

Ben returns before I can come up with an answer that won't start a fight. He crosses the room to take Mal's other hand--

--and between one blink and the next, we're no longer in my room.

The three of us are still sitting on a bed, with Ben standing next to Mal. But the room is different, light and airy, with a window open to admit the sound of--is that the ocean?

"Where are we?" Jack asks before I can.

"I maintain a number of safe houses at different locations on Earth," Mal says. His voice is casual, like that's something normal people do. Or maybe it is for dragons. How the hell would I know? "This one is in South America, near the Caribbean."

As much as I want to go to the window and look out, I want to get to the bottom of this more. Pulling my hands free, I stretch out on the bed. This mattress is much more comfortable than mine, cradling my body in such softness that I feel like I could go to sleep right here and now. "You so owe me a beach vacation after all this is over."

"Deal," Mal says. "Are you comfortable?"

We go through the whole process again. It's easier this time, now that I know what and where I'm looking for. Easy to find the hooked tug, the need to go. Easy to point in the direction it's trying to pull me.

By the time Mal pulls me out of the trance, I'm shaking a little from restraining myself. Even with his hand on me, grounding me, I can feel the strength of the impulse. It's terrifying, not knowing how much I can trust my own mind. The way the compulsion disappears when the trance is lifted is a relief I can feel down to my bones.

"How do you feel?" Mal asks as I look over at where Ben is drawing a line on his map. "Do you need to take a break?"

I shake my head. "No, I want--let's finish this."

As soon as Ben gathers his things, we join hands again. Even though I'm watching for it this time, I still can't clock the moment of transition. It's like something out of a movie, the change in our surroundings while we remain the same.

This room is different from the last. Just as luxurious, but pale wood floors and creamy white walls, with floor-to-ceiling windows looking out on a snowy mountain scene.

"Where's this love nest?" Jack leaves us on the bed and crosses the room to get a better look outside.

"The Swiss Alps," Mal says. With a snap of his fingers, a fire bursts to life in the fireplace, warmth radiating outward and taking the edge off the slight chill in the air. "Ready, Claire?"

Lying back, I go through the whole process again. And again, from a safe house in Sri Lanka, and one in Tanzania.

"Well?" I ask after the last one.

Ben looks up from the map. "The lines all meet in the same place, but it doesn't make any sense."

"Why not?" Jack asks, joining me in looking over Ben's shoulder.

We can all see the answer before he says anything else. The lines meet, unmistakably, in the same place. The Atlantic Ocean, off the coast of Portugal.

"We can't exactly rent a submarine and go looking on the ocean floor for this jewel," Jack says. "What the fuck do we do now?"

"I wonder--" Mal cuts himself off, turning to me. "Claire, do you have the energy to attempt one more trance?"

As much as the idea scares me, as much as it seemed the pull was getting stronger with every attempt we made, I nod. Right now this is our only lead; I can't chicken out. "Yeah, but after that, dinner, okay?"

"Agreed." Mal sits next to me as I return to the bed. "Jack, Ben, this time I would like you to help me anchor Claire."

"How do we do that?" Ben sets down his pencil and circles the bed, climbing up to sit next to me. Jack joins him, sitting opposite Mal.

"Touch her," Mal says. "Skin contact. Remind her body of where it is, so she doesn't get lost."

Jack looks at him doubtfully, even as his hand settles on my ankle, warm and comforting. "Lost? What are we doing?"

"Claire, this time you're going to attempt to follow the spell--" Mal raises his free hand to cut off whatever Ben and Jack were about to say. "Not physically, with your mind."

"Is that safe?" I feel stupid even asking the question, but this is so far outside anything I've done that I would feel stupider if I didn't. "You said so I don't get lost?"

He purses his lips, clearly searching for words. "If I'm correct, there shouldn't be a risk. But it might be similar enough to astral projection for there to be problems. Best not to risk it, particularly since you haven't done this sort of thing before."

"What if I do get lost?" I feel dumb asking the question, like a little kid, but it slips out anyway.

"Then I will come after you."

Something in the tone of his voice, the light flashing in his eyes, says that anyone who tries to prevent him from finding me will regret it. It's comforting, especially when I contemplate possibly--what, leaving my body? Gods, how is this my life?

I shake myself out of my reverie and lie back on the bed. Ben's hand curls comfortingly around my wrist, Jack's rests on my ankle. Mal takes my other hand, talking me through entering the trance state for hopefully the last time.

It gets easier every time. I don't know if that's a good sign or not, but after so much practice, I can actually see the spell, a little bit. it's like a beam of light, shining faintly and still pulling me in the same direction as before. I take a deep mental breath and follow.

The sensation is something like flying in a dream, but not as fast. More like floating, in a way. I follow the thread of light through the wall, wincing a little even though I have friends who can literally walk through walls and I've done it myself. Still, it never gets any less weird.

Once I'm out of the building, I pick up speed. It's less like I'm following the pull and more like it's pulling me which is--not great. I focus on slowing down, the panic subsiding when I'm able to. Even though I have no idea where I am, being in control of my movements is good. Everything looks gray and misty, like a heavy fog where I have to strain my eyes to see anything. Although technically, I guess "I" am lying on a bed back in Tanzania. When I pay attention, I can feel the three hands holding onto me, can see the silver cord stretching back the way I've come.

For a second I want to give up on the whole thing, to head back to my body and say that we'll find another way. It's an incredibly vulnerable feeling, floating in a vague nothingness. But then I remember what it felt like to be inside Jack's head, to fight the curse that wants him to destroy everything he loves. That wants to break him.

If he can live with that, every day, I can do this.

Once I stop holding myself in place, I pick up speed again. I have a vague impression of sand, endless dunes rippling out under a hot sun, but then it's gone, replaced by choppy, blue water, then land again. As I slow, the land below me becomes clearer; green, rolling hills giving way to white buildings with red tile roofs. First small clusters, then a larger city.

Even though I saw the map, the lines Ben had drawn, I'm still somewhat surprised when I move past the city without slowing further. Then I'm over what must be the Atlantic, my astral self or what the fuck ever I am right now dipping lower and lower toward the waves.

It's stupid to hold my breath as I move below the surface, but I do. Or I think I do. When I think too hard about it, I feel the panic rising again, so I stop and focus on my surroundings to distract myself.

The strangest thing is how not-strange it seems. It's strangely like watching an ocean life documentary. The blue of the water, darkening the deeper I go, even though I can still see perfectly well, is familiar. Fish and other sea creatures move around me, undisturbed by my passage--a shark of some kind cruises by close enough to touch, if I had hands, scattering a school of smaller fish when they notice it coming.

Soon I'm deep enough that I can see the sea floor, a line of underwater mountains that seem to be my destination. There's nothing special about them that I can see, even when I get closer. My path leads me straight for what looks like some kind of volcanic caldera, the sides eroded enough that it's clearly been dormant for a long time. Probably. I'm not a geologist, or a vulcanologist.

Before I can quibble any longer with the comforting

lies my brain wants to tell me, I pass over the rim of the caldera and find myself--somewhere else.

Or, no, not exactly. I'm still over the caldera. There and there are the eroded spots I'd noticed before, in exactly the same place. But instead of a mostly empty bowl of stone, I'm now floating over a bustling city made out of columns and buildings in a style I recognize belatedly from the semester I studied abroad in Athens.

Whatever is pulling on me is stronger now, moving me even faster. I don't have time to take in details, only the fact that somehow this impossible city is full of life, people bustling here and there. I think that maybe a few heads turn to watch my progress, but that's impossible.

Right?

I'm moving toward the far wall of the caldera at a nearly dizzying speed. As I get closer, it becomes clear that only one building could be my destination. It looks like it was dug into the side of the caldera, with nine columns supporting a massive arch on the front.

I slow down as I pass under the arch and into the building. There are enough arched openings off this room that I'm sure the building goes back who knows how far. But I can't really focus on that right now. All of my attention is on the statue that towers under the vaulted ceiling. A man of indeterminate age, holding a staff in one hand, a carved stone hood hiding one of his eyes.

His other hand outstretched, holding a stone that

swirls liquid blue and green and white and gray, the colors moving like waves crashing on a beach.

"Welcome," a woman says. "We've been expecting you."

When I tear my eyes--or whatever I'm seeing with--away from the stone, I see her. The statue, huge as it is, should dwarf her, but something, maybe the way she carries herself, maybe the aura of power crackling around her, makes her just as impossible to look away from.

"Um. Hi."

She smiles. "We have much to do and time grows short. Have your dragon mate bring you here."

I start to protest that Mal isn't my anything, but the look she gives me stops the words before they can begin. "I--you want me to come? You should be protecting the stone from me, so I don't take it to Talaith."

That smile grows wider, more knowing. "Many things are happening, Claire, and Talaith is the least of the players on the board. Bring your erastés, my dear, but come swiftly. It is not safe for you to linger unprotected in this way."

"I'm not sure I know how," I admit, unable to give her anything but the truth.

"Yes, you do." Her voice is firm but gentle, like she can tell how close I am to a freak-out. "I can feel your anchors from here; surely you can as well. Return to them, then to us. I will assist you."

"Wait," I blurt out. "What--where is this?"

She tells me, her smile widening even further at my reaction.

The flick of her fingers is the last thing I see before I open my eyes in Tanzania, gasping like I just ran a marathon.

"Are you well?" Mal asks. His hand pulls me up to sitting, his eyes warm and concerned.

"Yeah, I think so." I do a quick check of my body to make sure I'm not lying to him, but everything seems to be working normally. "And I found one of the jewels."

Ben and Jack sit up straighter. "Oh yeah?" Ben's hand squeezes mine. "Where is it?"

I take a breath, feeling the weight of three sets of eyes on me. "We have to go to Atlantis."

23

As soon as Mal zaps us back home, Jack heads for the kitchen. I follow him, desperate for something to quiet my growling stomach. Somehow I manage to scrounge up enough leftovers out of the fridge to take the edge off, while he starts frying bacon in one pan and cracking eggs into another.

"Breakfast for dinner?"

"You got it." He moves around the kitchen with quick, competent motions, flipping bacon and eggs, mixing something in a bowl that turns out to be pancake batter.

I perch on a barstool, working my way through my snack; it's not often that I just get to watch him like this. It's a full ten minutes, according to the clock on my phone, before he notices that I'm still there.

"What's up?"

"Nothing," I say. "Just--this is nice."

He ducks his head, his cheeks flushing darker as he turns back to the stove. "Yeah. It is."

By some kind of mutual unspoken agreement, we don't discuss anything heavy until the food is cooked, the four of us gathered around the table.

"So Atlantis is real?" Ben puts a generous number of bacon slices on my plate before serving himself. "Like, in our world?"

I shrug. "Your guess is as good as mine. I've never astrally projected or whatever that was before. And maybe it's a pocket dimension or something But it's a big-ass, Greek-looking city under the ocean. And that's what--well, what she told me it was."

"Can you tell us what happened?" Mal asks. I don't think he even notices that he's putting food on Jack's plate before his own, but Ben and I share another raised-eyebrow look.

"Sure, If you think it'll help."

Mal shrugs, one of the most human gestures I've ever seen him make. "This is uncharted territory for all of us. I thought the Jewels were a legend; that's how I had always heard of them. A--what is the word--an allegory, to explain why the Fae failed to conquer this world. And I most certainly did not know of Atlantis, or any other under-water city. The more details we share, the more chances to make sense of this."

I chew the food in my mouth, savoring the mix of

flavors, salty and sweet in perfect balance on my tongue. It's a lot like that first breakfast with Jack and Ben, back before life got so much stranger. "Okay. So, it was weird. Kind of like flying, but also not..."

I take them through what I remember, which is a surprising amount. The memory seems sharper, clearer than normal, like it was burned on my brain. I tell them how there was nothing to see until "I" was over the caldera, then suddenly the city appeared. I'm even able to describe the weird mingling of old-fashioned and modern clothes I saw on the people going about their business.

When I get to describing the temple, Mal stops me. "You're sure there were nine pillars?"

"I could see it from a long way away." If I close my eyes, I can still see it. "There were definitely nine."

"That is--odd."

Ben frowns. "What's odd about it?"

Mal purses his lips. "The Greeks, and after them, the Romans, tended to build in particular formulas. Even if this building is dug into the side of the crater, as Claire said, there would either be five, or six, or eight columns supporting the pediment. Nine is--I don't like to say 'unheard of,' but I've certainly never seen or heard of it. It may not be relevant, though. Did you go inside the temple, Claire?"

"Yeah. There was a statue, an old man holding a staff. I guess he was maybe Merlin?" I close my eyes again, trying to draw up the mental image. Even in memory, though, the stone holds my attention, the hypnotic swirls of color inside it. "I was too focused on the stone, but it didn't look like any statue of Zeus I'd ever seen."

"Zeus would most likely be depicted holding a lightning bolt," Mal agrees. "Then what?"

I bite my lip. This part sounds ridiculous, even to me. "There was a woman. She could see me. She said--she said they'd been expecting me. And that I should have--should have you bring me there."

Something in Mal's eyes says he knows I'm hiding something, but thankfully he lets it go. I'm not interested in telling him that some strange woman in a vision called him my mate. Mostly because then I might have to tell him how okay I am with the idea.

"She wanted you to come?" Ben asks. "Does she know Talaith wants you to get the stone?"

"Yeah, that seemed weird to me, too." I cut off another bite of pancake, swirling it through the syrup puddled on my plate. "She said that things were happening, and that I should come and bring my--my erastés. Whatever those are."

Mal coughs. "It's a Greek term for lovers. So she thinks we should all come, then?"

"Commanded is the word I'd use." I follow the pancake with more bacon and eggs, then a bite of perfectly buttered toast. "She said she would help."

"Can you even take us there?" Jack turns to Mal. "I thought you could only go to places you'd been before.

Mal shakes his head. "Technically that is the case. I could possibly take the vision of the city from Claire's head, with her consent, but I'm not certain I'm willing to trust your safety, any of you, to a possibility."

"Something tells me we're going to have to take some risks," I say. "Not that I like the idea of ending up like a bug on a magical windshield, but if either Jack or I is ever going to have a normal life, we've got to try something."

"She's right," Jack says. "We can't just sit here--I can't just sit here, waiting for this to drive me crazy. This is a chance to do something. We need to try."

Mal sighs. "Very well. But not tonight. We will rest, and make the attempt tomorrow. And I will go first, alone."

I haven't known him for long, but even I can tell that there's going to be no arguing him out of this. This time it's both Jack and Ben exchanging glances with me before we nod.

"Deal," Ben says for all of us. "Tomorrow."

ᛋᚱᚻ

"So." Ben closes the bedroom door behind us. "Tomorrow we go to Atlantis."

"If I'm not hallucinating from whatever Talaith did to my brain." I wince as soon as the words are out, but it's a worry that's been lingering in the back of my mind. I might as well forge ahead, since it's out in the open now.

"Seriously, are we going to base an entire plan on something that may or may not be real?"

Jack shrugs, peeling out of his overshirt. "Mal's going to check it out first. He seems pretty confident he can deal with it if it's a trap."

"Yeah, but what if there's just...nothing?"

Ben starts undressing too. Between the two of them there's a lot of skin and muscle on display. It's distracting. "Then we make a new plan. But we won't know until we check it out."

"I guess." I sigh. "It just sucks, you know."

"I know." Jack pulls me into his arms. "Knowing that someone's been fucking around inside your head...it's kind of the worst. It stays with you."

I stand there, frozen in place, unable to return his hug, a terrible suspicion eating into my brain like a worm boring inside an apple. What if Talaith's mind-fuckery is the only reason they were interested in me?

I'd asked why me, and Ben hadn't been able to give me an answer. What if this was it? It makes a horrible, sickening sense. More sense than thinking they want to be with me, what, because of my sparkling personality? I'm not ugly, but I'm not even close to being on the same level as them in terms of looks.

"Claire? Claire, what is it?"

The worry in their voices snaps me out of my self-pitying downward spiral. I shove the question to the back of my mind--thanks, super conservative childhood, for teaching me how to repress my feelings--and smile. "Sorry. Got lost in thought there for a minute."

"Are you sure you're okay?" Ben reaches out, tucking my hair behind my ear. "The last few days have been a lot. It's okay if you're not."

"We know what it's like to not be," Jack adds.

I do my best to make my smile as convincing as possible. "Yeah, it's been weird, but my brain just went down one of those rabbit holes. I swear, I'm good."

They exchange a look I can't interpret. For a second, I think I need to come up with more reassurance, but then they nod and continue taking off their clothes. Which, for the record, I am always in favor of.

We go about getting ready for bed in silence, nobody speaking until we're tucked in together.

"You're amazing, you know that?" Jack asks.

I shrug. "Not really."

He pulls back a little until he can look me in the eyes. "I mean it. Your whole life has changed, and you're not curled up in the corner crying, you're working your ass off trying to help."

"You really are," Ben agrees, snuggling closer on my other side.

All I can think to do is shrug again. "Well, what else am I going to do? Sit around whining about how it's not fair? I'm not twelve anymore. I can help. I want to help."

He leans down to kiss my forehead, taking a breath before saying, "And that's why we love you."

"Well, one of the reasons."

It takes a second before I realize what he just said, but I can feel my whole face light up. "I love you too, Jack."

I can practically feel Ben rolling his eyes. "What am I, chopped liver?"

"Shut up." There's no heat in Jack's voice, even as he reaches over to flick Ben on the ear. "We're having a moment."

Turning, I kiss Ben's cheek. "I love you, too, Ben. Both of you."

The warmth in my chest lasts until I drift off, safe between them.

ᛋᚱᚻ

THE NEXT MORNING, we're a sweaty, satisfied tangle across the bed, breathing just starting to even out, when Ben says, "Next time we should ask Mal if he wants to watch."

I can feel my body try to jerk back without my conscious direction. But between Jack's legs draped over mine and Ben's arms holding me close, I'm pretty much immobilized, which at least saves me from an embarrassing fall to the floor. My face still heats at the thought, the blush moving down my neck and across my chest.

"Works for me," Jack rumbles. He doesn't even open his eyes, the asshole.

Ben smiles. "Well, baby? What do you think?"

I open my mouth, close it for a moment, then open it again once I actually figure out what I'm going to say and I'm pretty sure I can match their casual attitude. "First off, what makes you think he'd even want to?"

Jack snorts. "Mal's fascinated by humans. I'm surprised he hasn't asked to watch us before now."

"And I've seen the way he watches you," Ben adds. His smirk widens when my face heats up again. "He wants to."

"Do dragons even--even have sex? With humans?"

"He's spending a good chunk of time in a very human body," Ben points out. "And he's hundreds of years old. I think he might surprise you."

Another snort from Jack. "Sure as hell surprised me a couple of times."

I giggle, raising my eyebrows at Ben, who shrugs in return.

"But the question wasn't 'does he want to?' The question was, what do you think about this?"

"It's okay if it's not something you want to do," Jack says. His face has gone serious all of a sudden. "But if you're just thinking you're not supposed to want it, or if you're worried what we'll think of you for wanting it, that's different.

I close my eyes as they hold me closer. "I'd--I'd like to try. But there's a big part of me telling me I shouldn't want to."

Ben leans in, kissing me gently. "You don't have to do

anything you don't want to. But I think you might really enjoy this. I know we would."

Draping himself over my back, Jack kisses the side of my neck. "Look at it this way. How did you feel when Mal busted in on you while we were having phone sex?"

"Embarrassed." My voice is barely audible. Fuck, why is this so hard?

"And what else?" Jack's voice is low and coaxing in my ear. "Were you just embarrassed?"

When I finally get the "no" out, my voice is even quieter.

They wait for me to continue, letting the silence draw out until it feels stretched, vibrating with the tension of the unanswered question hanging there.

I have to close my eyes to admit it.

"I liked it. If I hadn't just come, that would've made me."

Ben's hand rubs soothing circles on my arm. "I'm glad you trust us enough to tell us that."

"It's hard." I force myself to open my eyes again. To look at them. "The way I was raised, sex was a wonderful thing--for making babies. Hell, I don't think I ever heard either of my parents ever use the word. The closest my mom ever got to telling me about sex was that when I was married, it'd be okay for my husband to see me naked."

"Wow," Jack says, kissing my shoulder. "Hell, you're lucky you didn't end up a pregnant teenager.

Ben smacks him in the head.

"Hey!"

"You can't just say shit like that."

Laughter bubbles up, undeniable. "No, he's right. I was a huge ball of hormones and had no idea what to do with them. All it would've taken was one-guy sweet-talking me. I would've been knocked up so fast."

Jack looks a little shamefaced. "You might not have gotten pregnant."

"No, with my genetics I probably would've. I have nine brothers and sisters, you know."

The "holy shit" comes from both of them at the same time. It makes me smile, even though thinking about my family doesn't usually lead to smiles.

"My parents believed that kids were blessings from God, so why wouldn't you want all the blessings you could get?"

"Quality over quantity," Jack mutters.

"Nine?" Ben's face is still shocked-looking. "How do you keep up with each other?"

That's enough to quiet my laughter. "We don't. Well, I don't. When I decided I wasn't sure if I believed in God, my parents said I wasn't part of the family anymore, and not to contact anyone who was. They didn't want me to lead my siblings 'away from the truth.'" My mouth twists, but I manage to keep my flippant tone. "Came in handy with the whole Fae mess, though. No family around to ask inconvenient questions when Jake went missing."

Ben pulls me in a little tighter. I can tell that he and

Jack are exchanging a look over my head, but I can't care about that right now. "So how did you learn about sex, then? School?"

"Oh, hell no." I snort a little, grateful for the change of subject. "We were homeschooled. Can't have those precious young minds exposed to dangerous ideas like evolution and sex ed. I started college at seventeen, and if my scholarship hadn't required me to live in the dorms, I'd probably have taken a lot longer to stop drinking the kool-aid. No, I learned about sex from books."

"Kinda surprised your parents let that happen," Jack says.

I shrug. "They had no idea. I read so many books my mom would've had trouble keeping up even if I was the only kid. Multiply me by ten and she didn't have a chance. I did slip up sometimes, and she'd keep an eye on me for awhile after. But I got really good at hiding them. It was my only real rebellion while I lived at home. And even after, reading was still how I learned about--things."

Ben raises his eyebrows. "You're telling me that you sat us down in a bar and had a very calm, clear negotiation about your specific kinks--which you learned about from books?"

"Not just from books," I protest. "The Internet is a valuable resource. And it's not like you two were the first guys I slept with."

"Hey, I'm impressed," he says. "You know I love that

you trust us enough to admit what you want. It's almost as much of a turn-on as the actual sex."

"Speak for yourself," Jack says. "Nothing's as much of a turn-on as the sex."

Ben rolls his eyes. "I said almost."

Jack starts pressing kisses to my shoulder. He groans a little bit when I arch back against him, like he hadn't just come a few minutes ago. "Shit, sweetheart, I can't wait to see Mal's face when he gets a load of you. What do you think? Should we cuff you? Let him see how much you like it?"

"Or maybe we should just hold you down," Ben muses. "You always go nuts for that."

I shiver between them, jerking in surprise as Ben pulls back enough to slide a hand up my thigh and press two fingers inside my pussy. At the same time, Jack cups my breasts in his hands, thumbs skating lightly over my nipples.

"Always so wet for us, baby." Ben starts a steady rhythm with his fingers as his thumb slides up to find my clit. "Gonna blow Mal's mind, the way you look when we're fucking you, the sounds you make."

"You'll beg us for it, won't you?" Jack's voice is a low purr in my ear. "Let him hear how much you want it, the way you beg us to fuck you, beg to have our cocks inside."

All I can do is moan, overwhelmed by the mental picture their words are painting.

Jack pinches my nipples, just barely hard enough to sting. "Answer me, sweetheart."

"Yes," I pant. I can't catch my breath as they drive me higher. "Yes, whatever you want, do whatever you want."

"Good girl." Ben leans in to kiss me, pushing a third finger inside me.

I'm right on the edge, shaking with the sensations, the intensity, the idea of what we're discussing. When they each lean in, their teeth scraping lightly over the side of my neck at the exact same moment, I come, shuddering between them.

They stroke and pet me as I come back down, their hands gentle on my oversensitive skin. When Jack whispers "love you" in my ear, I feel Ben's mouth curve against my shoulder.

We fall asleep like that, still connected.

24

"We should all go together."

Jack's jaw is set in a stubborn line that I've come to know all too well in the months we've known each other, his body tense as he paces back and forth across the library floor. Mal's face is outwardly serene, but I can see the frustration growing in his eyes.

"It simply makes sense for me to go alone first. I am impervious to many dangers that would damage or kill a human."

"I don't care," Jack snaps. "I don't want you going without backup. Not until we're sure it's not a trap."

Mal reaches out, stopping Jack's restless movements with a hand on his shoulder. "And how do you propose we determine that, without someone going to see?"

Jack makes a frustrated noise, but he doesn't break free from Mal's touch, light as it is. "I--fuck."

Ben clears his throat. "Are you sure about this, Mal?"

"You--both of you--keep saying I'm family." Mal answers Ben, but his eyes don't leave Jack's, one corner of his mouth tipping up in a crooked smile. "Would you let anything stop you if you thought there was a chance to save Jack, or to protect Claire?"

"No." Ben doesn't hesitate.

Mal turns more toward Jack. "We already know what you would do to save Ben, or to save me."

Jack closes his eyes briefly, but he doesn't argue.

"If I'm part of your family, then I get to choose. Let me choose this. "

Taking a deep breath, Jack reaches out, groping blindly until he finds my hand, squeezing hard enough to steal my breath.

"Okay," he says.

The word is barely audible, more breath than voice.

Mal doesn't hesitate, doesn't give him any more chances to quibble. One second he's there, the next he's gone, the air in the room rushing in to fill the space where he was.

Just as Jack's grip on my hand is starting to become a problem, aching in my bones, Mal returns, reappearing with no fanfare.

"Well?" Jack asks.

Mal smiles, his eyes wide and wondering. "I have seen

the city of Atlantis. We can return whenever you are ready."

Jack looks at me, then Ben, then back to Mal. "We already packed our bags, you know."

"I know." Mal grins. "So, ready?"

He takes Jack's other hand and reaches for Ben's. Ben's fingers lace with mine, and Mal turns that grin on me.

And just like that, we aren't in the library any more.

ᛋᚱᚼ

"Holy shit."

Ben's voice is low and reverent as he looks around the inside of the temple, taking it all in.

"Yeah," Jack agrees. "It's not that I didn't believe you, sweetheart--"

"I know." I squeeze his hand where it's still holding mine. "Honestly, I didn't quite believe me."

But here we are. Standing in the temple that I almost thought I had dreamed, with the statue and the carvings, everything I remember and more. And the stone. I have trouble taking my eyes off the stone. Whatever shielding Mal had done stopped the relentless pull, but I think anyone would have been drawn to it.

Before I can ponder that too long, the woman from my vision enters the room, wearing a drapey robe kind of thing. "Good. You've arrived."

Jack and Ben both move to place themselves between

us. "Hi, I'm Ben, this is my brother Jack." Ben's smile is pleasant, but it doesn't reach his eyes. "It's nice to meet you."

The woman smiles back, faint lines appearing around her eyes and mouth, breaking the illusion of agelessness. Her skin is a few shades lighter than Ben's or Mal's, a warm golden brown that nearly glows against the pale fabric of her gown. "I am Rhea, the high priestess here. And you are the erastes of the Chosen."

"What does that mean?" I recognize the word from the last time I was here, but I still don't know what she's saying. Although if I'm getting the context right, it might prompt and awkward conversation with Mal.

"Erastes? The Greeks used it to mean lovers, but over the years here it has come to mean something more. Your mates, the chosen of your heart."

Part of me wants to quibble with her wording, but a much bigger part of my brain has latched onto something else. "Chosen--what did you mean when you said 'the Chosen?' Who is the Chosen?"

Rhea looks at me, smiling slightly, like she's never seen anything so funny. "You are, of course."

"Chosen for what?" Jack demands, a second before Ben and Mal ask the same thing.

Through it all, Rhea keeps smiling. If I wasn't so desperate for answers, the knowing smile would seriously be getting on my nerves. "The tale is a long one, and can be told more comfortably elsewhere. Will you come with me? No harm will come to any of you in the temple of the Father."

Jack is still bristling with suspicion, but Mal's hand on his shoulder keeps him from blurting out anything too aggressive. "We accept your hospitality," Mal says.

"Excellent!" Rhea turns, her robe sweeping behind her. "Come, then."

We exchange glances, but this is what we came here for. Mal takes the first step, and we follow her deeper into the temple.

ᛋᚱᚻ

"YOU KNOW the story of the jewels?" Rhea asks once we're seated in a group of chairs with strange, curving legs, on a balcony overlooking the city.

"We know the legend," Mal answers. "I believe the version my people tell is the least corrupted, but--"

She nods at his shrug. "Many things have been lost that once were known. So I will tell you the story as we know it here in Atlantis."

I can practically feel Ben quivering with the need to ask questions, but when I slip my hand into his, he manages to keep quiet.

"Long ago, when the Fae sought to take this world by force, there was a king in the Northern Isles." Her voice falls into a storyteller's cadence as she begins, taking on the rhythms of something memorized so long ago it's practically muscle memory. "But weapons of bronze could not hold them back. This king, Arthur, he had a wizard to fight at his side, a wise man with great power."

"Merlin," Ben breathes. "Shit, sorry."

Rhea nods in his direction. "Merlin knew that Arthur was doomed. No human army, no matter how mighty or well-armed, could hold back the full might of the Fae Queens. But he loved Arthur, and Arthur loved humanity. So, for Arthur's sake, Merlin sought out the four great treasures of the Tuatha Dé Danann, gifts from the gods of the north. Those treasures took their power from four magic stones. How Merlin found them in their hiding places is a story for another time. But find them he did, and he used them as the foundation for a great enchantment, one which protects our world to this day."

"That stone, in the statue--" I bite my lip. "Sorry."

"Dŵr," Rhea says. "The Stone of Water. Taken from the Cauldron of the Dagda and placed here, in Atlantis, for us to guard. Until the Chosen would come."

Jack scowls. "You keep saying that. Chosen for what? And why do you think Claire is this Chosen?"

"Merlin knew the Queens would search for the Jewels," Rhea says. "But before he passed from this world, he looked to the future and left us a prophecy. One day, a woman would come. A human, who could pass the Trials he set. Who could use the Jewels to make our world safe from the Fae forever."

"And you think that's me?" I choke back hysterical

laughter. "Something must have gotten mixed up in the last thousand years or so. I'm just some pawn a Queen sent after the Jewels because I'm expendable."

Rhea's eyes are uncomfortably shrewd on mine. "So you do not wish to face the Trials?"

"I'm the last person you should be handing one of the Jewels to." I have to make her see, to make her understand. This--ancient magic and legends and prophecies--this isn't me. I'm a librarian, for fuck's sake. "I literally had my brain chewed up and spit out again by a Fae Queen so I could bring them to her. You should be hiding it from me."

"I know," Rhea says. "It was prophesied."

I drop my head into my hands. "Of course it was."

"Merlin knew that his spell would not last forever." Rhea continues to speak as if I'm taking this super well. She's probably a mom. She has that mom air of unflappable calm to her. "Even without the Fae Queens seeking to weaken it, the passage of time and changes in the natural magical field would erode it. HE only ever intended the spell to be a stopgap measure until the Chosen came."

"And what, exactly, is this Chosen supposed to do?" Ben persists, asking the question before I can.

I lift my head again just in time to see Rhea smile as she says, "The Chosen will finish what Arthur started and close our world to the Fae once and for all."

"Cool." My voice sounds flat and unnatural in my ears, echoing like it's coming from far away. "I need a drink."

ᚦᚱᚼ

"So," Mal says. We're alone, in a spacious room we'd been shown to by a pair of girls dressed in less elaborate versions of the robes Rhea wore. One of them had brought a large pitcher of wine and four metal cups before saying we would be called for dinner, bowing, and closing the door behind her.

Jack pours us all generous glasses of the wine, passing them around. "I can honestly say that this isn't what I expected."

"I don't think any of us did." Ben takes my free hand in his, squeezing gently. "Claire? How are you holding up?"

"Well, let's see." I feel brittle, like I might break into pieces at any moment. "A Fae Queen fucked with my head so I'd find her some magical rocks and she could take over Earth and enslave the humans. We found the first one, it's in the lost city of Atlantis, which actually fucking exists. And these idiots are just going to hand it over to me because they say Merlin left a prophecy that I can do what King fucking Arthur didn't, what none of you could do, alone or together. It must be Tuesday."

Mal gives me a sympathetic look. "We can leave, if you

wish. There are no magical protections keeping us here. You have only to say the word."

Jack nods and Ben does too, like he hasn't been visibly itching to get out and walk the streets of Atlantis. For that matter, I am, too. This city is everything I ever dreamed, back when I was a nerdy teenager hiding books about magic from my parents and dreaming of a bigger world.

But I left wanting to be the Chosen One behind a long time ago, along with believing in God and hoping for contact with my family.

"No," I say slowly. "I'm pretty sure this is all bullshit. But...if I can pass these Trials, whatever they are, and get the Jewels--I don't know. If they're powerful enough to keep the Fae Queens in Underhill where they belong, maybe they're powerful enough to break this compulsion. Or maybe we can find a way to break Jack's curse without killing him."

"You don't--"

I raise a hand and Jack, for once, falls silent. "Don't even start with me, Jack Anderson. You know damn well you'd be doing the exact same thing if it was you they were calling the Chosen One."

He grimaces, but doesn't argue the point. "Yeah. And I fucked it up. You'll probably do better."

"It'd be hard for her to do worse," Ben teases.

Mal opens his mouth like he's going to protest, but seems to think better of it. "I do feel we should investigate these Trials before Claire undertakes them, however."

"Definitely." Ben practically vibrates with excitement. "And do some research, see if we can find anything about them. I can't believe there's no record of this prophecy anywhere."

"It might have been hidden along with the Jewels," Mal points out. "Even my people only knew of a rumor of the Jewels' existence."

Jack drains the last of his wine. "Well, maybe the people here have a library we can go through."

"I guess we can ask at dinner," I say.

The room they gave us must be on the outside of the temple, since it has tall arched windows looking down on the bustling city. It's spacious and everything about it looks luxurious. But as the silence falls, it's impossible for me to ignore the fact that, aside from our chairs, the only furniture in the room is one enormous bed.

When I manage to tear my eyes away, catch the end of a silent conversation, Jack's raised eyebrows and twitch of the head, Jack's answering nod.

Ben turns to me. Despite the many hot, kinky, sometimes embarrassing things we've done together, the possessive, hungry look in his eyes is enough to make me blush.

Before I can so much as squeak, he pulls me out of my chair and onto his lap. His big hands wrap around my legs, tugging me forward until I'm straddling him, his mouth devouring mine.

I can feel the thick, hard length of his cock pressing up against me. He rolls his hips up into me and I moan into his mouth. When he fists a hand in my hair, letting his mouth trail down my neck, I moan again. His wordless growl of approval vibrates against my skin, resonating with the delicate scrape of his teeth.

"Um," Mal says. "Perhaps I should go."

I open my eyes enough to see that he's gotten to his feet, looking fixedly out the window. When Ben's free hand slides up to cup my breast, his thumb skimming over my nipple, I gasp. Mal's eyes dart up, as if drawn to me against his will, his lips parting as his eyes rake over my body.

"You could go." Jack's casual tone belies the tension in his eyes as he saunters toward Mal, circling behind him to speak directly in his ear. "Or you could stay and watch."

25

M al shudders. I have a moment of sympathy, watching him. Watching them. Having Jack purring seductive suggestions into your ear is pretty overwhelming, as I know firsthand.

He forces his eyes away from me. "I--I'm going to go."

But he stands there, his hands clenched into fists. Not moving. Watching Ben, watching me, like a starving man offered an all-you-can-eat buffet.

"That's a shame." Jack's voice is still that low, dark rasp that always sends shivers down my spine. But I can't pay too much attention to that; I'm distracted by Ben stripping my shirt over my head and dropping it on the floor along with my bra. By the way Mal's eyes move over my body, a ghost caress to follow the very real feeling of Ben's touch.

"Claire likes being watched." Jack looks up to meet my eyes as he says it, like we're sharing a secret.

Mal shudders again. I'm not sure if it's from Jack's words or the sound I make when Ben's hands come back to my breasts, skin on skin this time.

Jack lowers his voice more, until he's growling out the words. "Makes her crazy to know we're watching her, seeing how much she loves it. If you really don't want to watch, that's fine, man. But I don't think you really want to go. I think you want to see."

"See?"

"See what she looks like when she's making those noises you've heard at night. We want it too--all of us. We talked about it."

Mal swallows, hard. "Stop, Ben," he grinds out. His earlier hesitation is gone, his voice carrying a snap of command that has Ben's hands stilling immediately, that sends a shiver down my spine.

His eyes seem to burn in his face, dark and hot as they meet mine. "Do you want this, Claire?"

"If you do." I don't have to think about the answer. Once Jack and Ben forced me to acknowledge it, it's been all I could think about. "I don't--we don't want you to do anything you don't want to. But Jack's right. I like being watched. And we trust you. I--we want you."

His face softens and he nods thoughtfully, circling the table and taking a seat in a chair closer to us. One with a good view, I notice.

"Would I just be watching?" He leans back in the chair, arms and legs sprawled wide. "Or could I make-- suggestions?"

I can't hold back the shivers this time, imagining all the possibilities inherent in that word.

Ben's hands squeeze my breasts gently. "You like that idea, baby?"

I nod wordlessly.

Jack chuckles, drawing his own chair up on the other side of us, until we're three points of a triangle. With me in the center, which feels amazing and terrible. "Well, we all know how much you like being told what to do."

"Is that so, Claire?" Mal's eyes are even hotter, some-how. "You like that?"

"You guys are gonna kill me," I mutter. The low growl of his voice rasps pleasantly over my nerves. I have to close my eyes for a moment, unprepared for the edgy intensity that comes from adding Mal into the mix.

"What should we do first, Mal?" Ben's hands move ever so slightly. Just enough to make me squirm against him, desperate for more stimulation.

Mal waves a hand. "Go ahead and continue as you were. I'll speak up if I have any thoughts."

Without further ado, Ben leans down and captures one of my nipples with his mouth, making me gasp and arch back. I can see Mal and Jack out of the corners of my eyes, feel the warmth of Jack's eyes and the laser-focus of Mal's attention. But Ben keeps me grounded, using his hands and mouth to toy with my breasts until I'm moaning and grinding against him, desperate for enough stimulation to come.

I don't even realize I'm begging, an incoherent mix of curses and please spilling out of my mouth, until Jack growls, "That's it, sweetheart. Show Mal how pretty you beg."

"Please, Ben, fuck, shit, please." I'm babbling, trying to pull together enough focus to create a coherent sentence. But that must be good enough, because he catches one nipple between his teeth while squeezing the other just right, turning his name into a wordless cry as I come.

Hands slide around me--some part of me recognizes Jack's touch, the familiar callouses rasping lightly across the skin of my belly. He tugs me to my feet, getting my jeans and my panties off in one fell swoop.

In front of me, Ben strips off his shirts, shoving his jeans and boxers to the floor before settling back into the chair. He pulls me back into his lap before I have time to really think about anything, about the fact that I'm naked in front of all three of them.

Two of his fingers slide easily up into my pussy, the slick stretch making me throw my head back and moan. "Ready for me, baby?" he murmurs.

I can't quite put together an answer, but he doesn't wait for a verbal one. Lifting me slightly, he lets me sink down onto his cock in one smooth stroke, gravity pulling me down and spreading my legs wide around him. He groans and bucks up into me a little when I bottom out, making me grip his shoulders to keep my balance.

After that one involuntary movement he stays still, waiting for something. I roll my hips experimentally, barely able to brace my feet on the chair for leverage. He rewards me with a scorching kiss and the flex of hands on my waist, so I do it again.

"There you go, baby," he rasps. His hands slide down to grip my ass; not directing my movement, just holding me. "Let Mal see you ride me. So fucking beautiful like this."

The reminder of our audience has my eyes flicking over to Mal. He still sprawls indolently in the chair, but his eyes are intent on us. His pants are undone, his hand curled tightly around his cock. Slow strokes at first, but he picks up speed, matching my rhythm as his hand begins to move.

"Do you want me to tell you what to do, Claire?" His voice is deeper and rougher than normal and I can't look away, his eyes holding mine.

I swallow, my mouth suddenly dry, nodding wordlessly.

"Touch your breasts," he orders.

His eyes darken even more as I slide my hands up my stomach to cup my breasts, lifting them like an offering. Ben and Jack both make inarticulate noises, but I can't look away from Mal.

"Is that what you like?" he asks. "Is that enough for you?"

"No."

One corner of his mouth tips up. "I didn't think so. Play with your nipples. Show me what you like."

Sucking in a breath, I obey, squeezing my nipples lightly at first, tugging, scraping my nails lightly over the tightly crinkled skin. The sensation shoots straight to my pussy, building on the hot, thick pulse of Ben's cock, the grind of my clit against him every time I move. I shiver, but don't stop.

"How does it feel?" Mal manages to sound no more than mildly curious, like he's not jerking off right in front of me.

"G-good." I move faster.

"You should probably tell Ben," he muses, "since he's the one you're fucking."

Trying to make my brain form sentences almost has me sobbing. "Ben--shit, oh God, Ben. It feels so good. I can feel--"

He covers my hands with his, tightening my grip on my nipples. My head tips back, my eyes sliding closed, and I move faster.

"Fuck, yes, please, Ben, please don't stop, oh, just--yes, just like, yes, please, yes, fuck, yes--"

I come, shuddering, then again when Ben thrusts up into me, impossibly deep as he comes, too.

"You liked touching yourself for us, didn't you?" Jack's voice is low and intimate as he lifts me gently off Ben.

I nod as he bends me over the table, pushing me down to lie flat with one big hand in the small of my back. I'm still shivering with the aftershocks of my orgasm when he pushes inside me with one easy thrust. His hands circle my waist, which always makes me feel strangely delicate, even though I weigh almost as much as he does.

And then--nothing. He stands there behind me, his cock hard and throbbing inside my pussy, and does nothing.

I start squirming against him, but he just tsks at me, gripping my waist firmly and holding me still. "Something you want, sweetheart? Because if you asked for something, you'd probably get it."

"Want you to fuck me," I grit out.

"I don't know," he says. "I'm not sure you really want it. What do you think, Mal? Was that convincing?"

He'd pushed me down with my head turned toward Mal, so I can see him purse his lips, pretending to think. "I'm not entirely certain what you want, Claire. Perhaps you should provide details."

I have to fight to keep my eyes open and steady on Mal, although the blush is a lost cause. I'm fairly certain my entire body has gone pink. "Please, Jack, I want you to fuck me."

He pulls out slowly and pushes back in even more slowly, inch by agonizing inch. "That what you want?"

"Harder," I say.

He smacks my ass, just barely hard enough to sting, making me twitch. But he keeps moving at that same maddening pace, his cock dragging oh-so-slowly in and out of my pussy.

I'm shaking and whimpering. It feels so good, but it's not enough.

"Jack, please, harder," I finally beg. "Please, please fuck me harder."

He rewards me with faster, harder thrusts, his hands tightening on my waist to hold me steady so I don't bang into the side of the table. I can finally, finally feel my orgasm building, close enough to taste.

"You know what I want, sweetheart?" His voice is still remarkably calm, only the speed of his breathing to indicate he's fucking me over a table.

My mouth is so dry I have to swallow a couple of times before I can answer. "What?"

"Remember the first time?" I would've sworn there was no way he could make his voice hotter, more infinite, but there it is. "Remember the way you begged Benny to fuck you? I want you to do that for me. I want to hear the dirty words coming out of your pretty mouth."

I hesitate. Mal is right there, watching and listening. But Jack wants this, and even though I can feel myself flushing hotter, I want it, too. It embarrasses me, but I love it, the squirmy mass of embarrassment and arousal twisting together in my stomach. Nothing turns me on as much as when they force me to talk, to tell them exactly what I want in excruciatingly filthy detail. Knowing how it affects Ben and Jack just makes it better.

"Want you to fuck me, Jack." Holy shit, is that my voice, breathy and fucked-out already? "I love it when you fuck me, the way it feels when you bend me over and pound that big, thick cock into my pussy. Makes me so wet when you hold me down and fuck me."

He picks up the pace until he's pounding into me, just like I asked, hammering inside my pussy with each thrust. But for all the force of it, I can't look away from Mal, how much he likes this, how hard he's jerking off.

"Keep talking," Jack grinds out. "Keep talking or I'll stop."

"Fuck, yes," I moan.

His fingers tighten on my waist. I know he'll wince when he sees the bruises later, how he'll cover them in kisses until they heal. He can't seem to understand how much I like it, the proof that he wants me this much, enough to forget himself, enough to leave his mark on me. "God, Jack, love your cock, love the way you fuck me, always so fucking good."

Warm hands close over mine, pinning me more firmly to the table. I don't need to open my eyes to identify Ben's grip. I can just go limp, let myself sink into the relief of being helpless.

"Don't stop." Jack's breath is coming faster and faster.

"Benny's holding you down now. Can't go anywhere, can you?"

I shake my head, feeling almost drunk on it. On them. "Can't move. Love it when you hold me down, feels so good. Do anything you want to me, and I can't stop you. Makes me so--" I lose words as I come, riding it out. Jack fucks me harder, two, three more deep, powerful thrusts before he comes, too.

When I manage to pry my eyes open, Mal is sprawled bonelessly across the chair, his chest streaked with the evidence of his orgasm. Ben is lounging back in a similar pose in his own chair, a shit-eating grin on his face. And Jack's weight is pressing me into the table in a way that is rapidly becoming uncomfortable.

I shove myself up off the table. It takes two tries to dislodge Jack, who finally rolls to the side with a muffled grunt of protest. Ben pulls me into his lap and I go willingly, cuddling against him.

"Well," Mal finally breaks the silence.

Looking at him, I realize that, for the first time since I've met him, some of the tension has smoothed from his face, leaving him looking relaxed and maybe even a little happy.

"That was--educational." Before I can start to feel more than the tiniest stirrings of embarrassment, he leans over, placing a hand gently on my shoulder. "Thank you for sharing that with me. I am honored that you trust me so deeply."

"All right, feelings later," Jack announces. He finally stands up, stretching hugely. "Let's see if the lost city of Atlantis has showers."

ᛋᚱᚺ

As it turns out, showers in Atlantis are huge, luxurious affairs, bigger than some bedrooms I've had. We end up all four showering together--Mal makes some token protest, but I manage to convince him that I'm okay with it. More than okay, actually. That I trust him with it.

Given that he's seen me in much more charged situations, showering together isn't a big deal. Or that's what I tell myself. And it isn't--well, not in the sense that it's awkward or uncomfortable. But when Jack and Ben pull him into our little circle, when he joins them in washing me, gently and carefully--

Well, that feels like a big deal. Not in a bad way. But it's definitely something we're going to need to think about, and talk about, after this Trial business is sorted out.

Right now, though, we have just enough time to get dried off and dressed before the girl from before comes to bring us to dinner.

I'm not sure what I expected, honestly, but dinner is something unique. We follow our guide to a candle-lit table set on that same balcony overlooking the city where Rhea is waiting for us. There's more wine, served in glasses this time. There's a whole array of seafood, which isn't surprising, but also bread and vegetables, which are.

"We trade with the surface," Rhea says, passing a platter of gorgeously grilled shrimp to me. "Not that the people we buy from know who they're selling to. But when Atlantis first sank, we quickly realized that some things, grains especially, required far too much magic and work for us to grow ourselves. Much easier to buy from those with easy access to the sun."

"I noticed that it's getting dark," Ben says. He accepts the platter from me and serves himself before passing it over to Mal. "Is that artificial? We're deep enough that I wouldn't think sunlight could reach."

She smiles. "Very observant. The shield spell which keeps us hidden from the outside world also brings the sun's light to us. The problems that arose with artificial light made the time and magic expenditure worth it to us."

I can tell from Ben's face and body language that he has about a million more questions. For that matter, I have some myself. Finding Atlantis is like something out of a book I would have read as a kid. It doesn't seem quite real, even though the noise of the city is rising up from below us, lights shining through the twilight that's settling over the valley.

Before any of us can ask, though, Rhea fixes me with an intent gaze I can't look away from. "Have you made your decision? Will you face the Trials?"

The weight of her stare, of all of their eyes on me, feels

inescapable. I have to take a breath before I can answer. "Yes. I still think you're looking for someone else. But I'll do it. I'll try."

"Excellent." This time the smile reaches all the way to her eyes. "In that case, we will celebrate."

"But we have some questions about the Trials," Ben says. "What will she have to do?"

Rhea's face does something complicated. "In truth, we don't know."

"No one's ever tried this before?" Jack's face is the most skeptical I've ever seen it.

"Many have tried," Rhea says. "But those who fail have no memory of the events. It is as though it never happened."

I take another drink of wine. "Awesome." At least it's not one of those where you die if you fail, which I was halfway expecting.

"So, what?" Jack drains his glass as well. "How does she even start?"

"The Trials begin in the temple. The supplicant simply touches the Jewel. The spell does the rest."

Mal frowns. "Will she be transported elsewhere?"

"Her physical body will remain in the temple." Rhea swirls the wine in her glass. "But I cannot say where her spirit will go."

"So we can't help her." Ben slumps back in his chair.

Rhea smiles sympathetically at him. "Physically, no,

you cannot follow where she goes. But your bond may be more important to her than you know."

"Do you know anything helpful?" Jack's voice is just barely on the right side of politeness. I'm pretty sure Mal kicks him under the table, from the way he twitches..

"We believe the runes carved on the statue's base relate to the Trials in some way." Rhea doesn't change her tone, but the look she gives him has him sitting up straighter in his chair. "But as I said, no one has retained a memory of what occurred, so we have no way of confirming this."

Thinking about it, especially about losing another memory, has me fidgeting in my seat. "So I can just head down after dinner and touch the stone?"

"The spell is only active on the full moon." Rhea pats my arm. "You will return here in three days time and we can begin."

From the tightness around Jack's mouth, I can tell that he's not any happier about the delay than I am. Or maybe it's just that having another spell linked to moon phases is reminding him of what's coming.

Remembering what it was like in his head after he killed Khari just cements my resolve. I'm going to do this. For me. For us.

Three days.

26

Jack wanders into the kitchen just as I'm sliding a pan of something into the oven and snags a slice of bread from the loaf sitting on the island. "What's up?"

"Stress cooking." I close the oven maybe a little harder than strictly necessary. "We can't do anything until the full moon, and if I see another book or website talking about rune meanings, my eyes are going to cross permanently. So I'm making dinner. Lasagna will be ready in an hour."

"Well, hell," he says. "I was gonna make dinner. Now what?"

I shrug. "I still need to do the veggies and garlic bread. Dessert, too. You can help if you want, but I was here first. So you know what that means."

He raises both eyebrows. "What?"

Shooting him a smirk, I reach over and push play on my phone. "I get to pick the music."

"Fine," he says. Despite his best efforts, he's smiling as the bass beat starts thumping, low and rhythmic. "What're we doing first, boss?"

ᛋᚱᚺ

"Hey, something smells good." Ben walks into the kitchen about an hour later, Mal following at his heels. I guess they got tired of arguing over which of the seven-teen-thousand obscure rune meanings were most likely to apply to the Trials.

"Perfect timing." I hand Ben a stack of plates and nudge him toward the table. "Lasagna just came out of the oven."

He takes the plates and leans down for a quick kiss. "Have I told you lately that you're awesome?"

I grin up at him. "You might've mentioned it once or twice."

"And not just because you're an awesome cook, either." He leans back in for another kiss.

"Hey, I helped," Jack interjects.

Without looking away from Ben, I pat his cheek. "Yes, you were a big help, dear."

"You're damn right I was," he mutters.

Ben and I meet each other's eyes and somehow manage

to keep from laughing out loud as Jack picks up the lasagna and takes it to the table.

By unspoken mutual consent we keep the conversation light while we eat, trading funny stories and gentle teasing, just enjoying each others company. But once the dinner plates are in the dishwasher and the pie is reduced to crumbs, Jack clears his throat and asks, "Any luck?"

"It's pretty easy to find the meaning of the runes," Ben says. "They're standard Norse runes, part of an alphabet called the Elder Futhark."

"So what's the catch?" Jack looks from Ben to Mal and back again. "You don't sound excited enough for it to be helpful."

Ben smiles, but there's no humor in it. "The runes these days are mostly used for divination. Like tarot cards, but they're written on rocks or pieces of wood. Have you ever looked at the definitions for tarot cards? They can mean fucking anything."

"Give me a for instance?" Jack asks.

Mal pulls a piece of paper and a pen out of thin air. Or maybe a pocket, who knows. Setting it on the table, he draws a symbol that looks like two Vs on their side with one higher than the other, their ends tucked into the middle of the other one.

"This is Jera." He writes the name below it, but pronounces it more like "yare-awe." "It symbolizes a year, or a good harvest. If you're using the runes for divination, it

can represent a fruitful season, real-izing the results of earlier efforts, or a life cycle. And those are only a few possible interpretations."

Producing his own pen, Ben draws what looks a lot like an R, but spikier. "This is

Rye-though," he says, writing "Raidho" below it. "It represents travel, or seeing a larger perspective, or seeing the right move to make."

"And then we have Sowilo." Mal draws an angular s-shape. Or maybe it's a lightning bolt? "Which represents success, or health, or power."

"Fan-fuck-

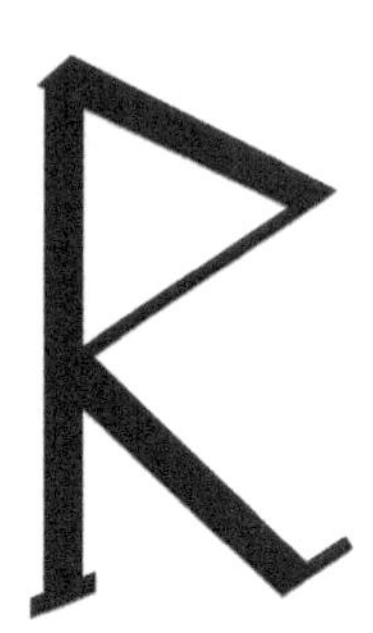

ing-tastic." Jack heaves a sigh. "So basically these trials could be anything. Or they might not even be related to these runes?"

Ben shrugs. "Pretty much."

"Look on the bright side." I poke at the remaining bits of pie crust on my plate. "At least I'll just lose my memory if it doesn't work. It could be the kind of trial where I die if I fuck it up."

"Don't even joke about that," Jack says sharply.

When I let him pull me into his arms, we both pretend

he isn't shaking.

There's not much more to say, really. We end up all piled together on the couch watching a movie, pretending we don't notice the way Jack twitches at every sudden noise, the tension in Ben's muscles, the way Mal watches all of us with worried eyes.

I couldn't tell you what the movie was about if you paid me.

ᛋᚱᚻ

THE MINUTE I walk into Jack's room that night he presses me against the wall, kissing me hungrily. I'm vaguely aware of the door closing next to us, of Ben's presence in the room. But most of my attention is taken up by Jack's tongue licking into my mouth, his teeth scraping lightly over my lip, his weight pinning me against the wall.

"Fuck," he growls. Tearing his mouth away from mine, he catches his earlobe between my teeth. I shudder against him as his stubble scrapes my neck, and he grins against my skin, using his teeth there, too. "Been wanting to do that all night. Thought about putting you up on that counter in the kitchen and licking that pretty pussy until you screamed for me. We could've let Benny and Mal have a taste, too."

"You should've." Ben crowds in behind him. "I bet Mal would love it."

"Some other time." Jack pulls back just enough to tug my t-shirt over my head and immediately starts unhooking my bra. "Got a surprise for you tonight, Benny."

Ben quirks an eyebrow, making quick work of my jeans and panties even though Jack is mostly in the way. "Oh, yeah?"

Jack smirks, shifting backwards enough to let me move away from the wall. "Show him, sweetheart."

Turning around, I bend forward slightly at the waist and brace my hands against the wall. I shiver as Ben's fingers skate lightly down my back and over the curve of my ass, spreading me wide to touch the base of the plug that sat there.

"How long?" His voice is rough as he traces the circle with his fingers.

"Since about half an hour before you guys came in for dinner." I'm grateful that Jack answers; I'm already having trouble forming words.

"Fuck." Ben curls a hand around my hip, pulling me back to lean against him. The flannel of his shirt is soft against my skin, warm from his body. "You ready for this, baby? Ready for both of us?"

All I can do is nod, anticipation curling hot and shivery in my belly."

"Gonna make it so good for you," he breathes. Hot air whispers over my ear as his big hands come up to cradle my breasts. I can't hold back a moan as he plays with my nipples. "We're gonna fill you up, make you scream for us."

My eyes slide closed, my hips moving helplessly, searching for friction as his hands on my breast build me higher and higher. I almost sob with relief when I feel Jack's lips on mine.

"Shhh, I got you," he murmurs. His fingers curl up into my pussy. I shudder as his thumb rubs over my clit once, twice, three times. I come just like that, pressed close between them, surrounded by them.

"Not nice to tease our girl like that, Benny," Jack chides. Tugging me over to the bed, he pulls me up to straddle him. He's naked already, sucking in a rough breath as I slide down onto his cock in one smooth motion. "C'mon, sweetheart, wanna see you ride me.

He grips my hips as I start to move. My eyes close and my head falls back as I savor the hot, thick slide of him inside my pussy, filling me up just right. After a few endless moments, he slides his hands up to my breasts, letting callused fingertips skim lightly across my nipples.

"Now who's teasing?" I gasp.

Ben chuckles, climbing onto the bed behind me, leaning down to kiss my shoulder. "Yeah, Jack. It's not nice to tease our girl like that."

I open my eyes just in time to see Jack smirk at both of us. Squeezing my nipples firmly, he rolls his hips up at the perfect time to let me grind my clit against him.

My hand shoot up of their own volition to grab his wrists, my nails digging into his forearms. I moan, feeling the electric sensation echoing from my nipples to my clit to where he's buried deep inside me.

"You like that, sweetheart?" He practically purrs the words, his arms flexing under my hands as he keeps toying with my breasts. "Want me to keep playing with your tits?"

Whatever reply I might have made strangles in my throat when Ben grips the base of the plug and pulls it out just a bit before sliding it back in. I shudder, clenching tightly around Jack, and he groans, too.

"Don't mind me." Ben's voice is rough already, his cock pressing hard against my hip.

Jack redoubles his efforts, matching me thrust for thrust. He uses everything he's learned about what I like to reduce me to incoherent babbling, unable to string words together in any kind of order. "Please" and "more" and "don't stop" and "Ben" and "yes" and "Jack" drop from my mouth almost at random. I come so hard I'm sobbing with it, shaking and shivering between them.

They coax me down together until I'm draped over Jack, chest to chest, skin to skin, heart to heart. He kisses me, long, luxuriant, sumptuous kisses. Like we have all the time in the world, like there's nothing else he'd rather be doing than kissing me, even though his cock is still hard, pulsing inside me.

Something clicks behind me, followed by slick, wet sounds. Then Ben's hand presses firmly on the small of my back, holding me in place as he slowly, torturously pulls the plug out.

Before I can react, his cock is nudging at my ass, warm, blunt pressure so unlike the cool, smooth silicon of the plug. "Relax for me, baby," he murmurs.

Jack kisses me again as Ben presses gently, inexorably inside. His hands rub up and down my arms and I let myself melt into his kiss, although nothing can completely distract me from the stretch as Ben thrusts slowly into my ass, the incredible fullness of having both of them inside me.

"So gorgeous like this." Jack's voice is tight, his hips making tiny thrusts up into me. "Doing so good for us--"

We both gasp as Ben finally stops moving, his hips pressed tightly against me.

"You okay?" he asks. His chest is heaving where it presses against my back, heart pounding like he just finished running, his hands wrapped around my waist in the way that always makes me feel tiny and delicate. Even more so like this, held between them.

"I think so." My voice is faint; I'm still trying to make sense of the sensations, trying to sort them out. I shift my hips slightly, testing, and both of them groan.

Ben's hands tighten around my waist. "I'm gonna move now."

He's as good as his word, fucking into me with slow, short digs of his cock. Each movement rocks me on Jack's cock until he starts to move, too, pressing up into my pussy. I'm so full, with just that edge of discomfort that sharpens the pleasure almost too intensely. Their hands hold me steady as I start shaking between them.

Jack's hand slips down between us, finding my clit. "Not gonna last long, sweetheart," he breathes.

"Me either," Ben admits. His fingers flex on my waist as he thrusts faster, deeper. "Think you can come for us like this, baby?"

"I...maybe?"

"So good," Jack's voice is ragged. "Always so good for us. Feels so good. Wish we could do this forever."

I shudder hard, my orgasm building back up again. Ben's hands slide up, finding my nipples, making me arch back against him.

"That's it, baby," he grits out. "Want you to come for us. Want to feel you clamp down on our cocks. Want you to scream for us."

My breath sobs out in choked gasps as they move together. Ben's hands on my breasts, Jack's fingers on my clit, Jack's cock pushing in as Ben's pulls out. I keen in the back of my throat as I come, vaguely aware that they're not far behind.

We stay like that for several moments, just breathing together, warm and sated. But finally Jack grunts, "next time, Sasquatch, you can be on bottom. But right now I can't breathe."

I whimper a little as Ben eases out of my ass. Brushing a kiss across my shoulder, he leaves the room. Before my sex-addled brain can do more than wonder where he's going, he's back, rolling me gently off of Jack and cleaning me off with a warm washcloth.

Once the cleanup is complete, he turns off the light and joins us under the covers. I don't know if it's the incredibly intense, athletic sex, or the comfort of them next to me, but sleep is a lot easier to find than I'd expected, even with the countdown in my head.

Tomorrow, we go back to Atlantis.

27

"Ready?" Ben asks.

I dry my hands on my jeans. It's too much to hope they won't notice, when all three of them are looking at me. I take a minute to look around me, to really take it in. The library, all the books on the shelves I haven't gotten to read or catalog yet. Jack, pretending the Mark isn't burning him up from the inside out. Ben, trying to hide his worry for both of us. And Mal, standing like he'd wait forever if that's how long it takes me to be ready.

But we don't have forever. And anyway, I'm being maudlin. Rhea said that the worst that could happen would be memory loss. I'm not going to die. It's fine.

"Ready," I say.

Jack and Ben each squeeze the hand they're holding at the same moment. Between one blink and the next, we're standing in the temple again, in front of the statue, with Rhea waiting for us.

Rhea smiles. "Welcome back. Are you ready?"

I bite back the snide question that wants to pop out. It's not her fault that I'm freaking out, wound tight and ready to snap. "As ready as I'll ever be."

"Very well." She gestures toward the statue and the Jewel. Maybe it's my imagination, but I think the colors are moving more than before. Faster. It's hard to look away.

"Wait." Jack's grip tightens on my hand, pulling me close. He tips my chin up and kisses me, a soft, almost chaste press of mouth to mouth.

I find myself clinging, and he doesn't seem to be in any hurry to break the kiss either. But eventually our lips part, both of us pretending we don't notice the suspicious shine in each other's eyes. Or maybe that's just me.

"I love you," he breathes. It's too quiet for anyone to hear, more movement than sound, but I know.

When I try to say it back, the words choke in my throat, but when I nod, I know he understands.

I step back and find myself in Ben's arms. I've never felt as completely surrounded by him as in this moment, like he's trying to make himself into a shield, to protect me from any dangers I might find. His kiss is just as soft, as gentle, as warm as Jack's. Neither of us speaks when we move apart, but I can see it in his eyes.

Ben turns me to face Mal, who looks uncertain. It only takes him a few seconds to come to a decision, offering me a hand. "May I?"

I take his hand, going willingly when he pulls me close, when his free hand gently cups my face and turns it up toward his. Kissing him is different, new. Even though I've only known Jack and Ben for a few months, so much has happened that it feels like it's been longer. With Mal, we don't have that easy familiarity yet. But there's something there. Maybe it's the fact that he knows Jack and Ben so well, or how intimate we've already been, but it doesn't feel strange to be kissing him. We just--fit.

"Good luck," he says.

Squeezing his hand, I let go, following Rhea up the steps to the platform where the statue stands.

Up here, the Jewel is at eye level, and the hypnotic effect is unmistakable. I can't take my eyes away to look at the runes chiseled into the plinth, but it's not like we haven't studied them over and over during the last three days. I could probably recite all the possible interpretations by heart at this point.

Not that it will probably do me any good.

Out of the corner of my eye, I see Rhea's smile. It's not a big one, but it is gentle and understanding.

"Don't worry," she says softly. "It doesn't hurt. And with time, not remembering becomes easier."

If there was room in my mind for anything but the Jewel, I would demand answers. I want to, to turn and ask, did she once think she was the Chosen? When did this happen? How many others have there been?

But my hand is already moving, my fingers inches from the surface of the Jewel. If it even has a surface. This close, it looks more like a bubble of liquid than a solid object.

When I touch it, I have a moment to be surprised by the cool solidity under my fingers before the Temple disappears around me.

ᛋᚱᚼ

ACTUALLY, it's more like the universe blinks for a moment. Or maybe I blink. Whatever the case, I'm still standing on the platform, but there's no statue, no Rhea, no Ben or Jack or Mal. Only a man who must have been the original inspiration for the statue, with a wooden staff on his back and a hood up over his head. All I can see of his face is one piercing brown eye and weathered skin, mostly covered by a bristly, steel-gray beard.

"Hello, Claire." His voice is low and resonant, almost seeming to vibrate my bones gently. "I've been expecting you."

"Well, that makes one of us." I clap my hand over my mouth, appalled at my inability to hold back the retort.

The man just laughs. Not mockingly, but like he gets

my snark and enjoys it. "Yes, I imagine this has all been a bit of a shock, hasn't it?"

I just nod, not trusting my mouth.

"I know you must have questions." He sinks down to sit cross-legged on the platform. "Ask, if you like."

"Are you Merlin?" I hesitate for a second, then sit, too. Looming over him feels weird, and I have a lot of questions. Might as well be more comfortable while I ask them.

He smiles. "That is one of the names I am known by."

"So you set this up?" I gesture vaguely around us. "The spell and the Jewels and the Trials and all that?"

"I did." He looks at me consideringly for a moment. "You want to know why."

It's not a question, so I don't bother answering. I just wait.

"There are many answers to that question," he says. "But some of them will not make sense to you at this moment. I put the Trials in place to ensure that anyone who took possession of the Jewels would have the ability necessary to wield their power. To be Earth's protector against the Fae Queens. To hold the balance, to create the magics, to do what must be done."

"Cool." I push myself to my feet. "Nice to meet you, thanks for everything, I'm ready for the memory wipe now."

He tilts his head to the side, observing me. The motion is unnervingly more like a bird than a human. "You don't know, then."

"Know what?" I probably shouldn't get snippy with fucking Merlin when he's in my head, but goddamnit I'm tired of being the person left out of the loop.

"What Talaith did to you--" he shakes his head. "The compulsion she laid on you, it cannot power itself. Without a source, it would fade away over time."

My stomach sinks like the Titanic. "Oh, shit. I'm not tied to Underhill, am I?"

"No, no. The Queens don't like to share power, and a tie between you and Underhill would not serve her purposes. If she had tied you to Underhill, she would not have let you out of her control." He reaches out, slowly, and touches the spot between my eyebrows, exactly where Mal's fingers had sat when he was trying to figure out my headaches. "No, she did something much simpler, and much cruder. She opened your mind to the magic here on Earth."

I blink at him for a second, but the words don't make any more sense if I think about them longer. "What?"

"Earth has ambient magic, too," he says. "If not quite so much as Underhill. All humans have the potential to tap into it, to use it, although relatively few learn to do so. Talaith found the pathways in your brain that were meant to touch that power and she opened them."

"Okay." Every time I think this whole "mind-fucked by a Fae Queen" thing can't get better, it does. I'm going to need so much therapy after this is over. "But what does that have to do with right now? The Jewels, the whole 'Chosen' bullshit."

He just looks at me for a moment, radiating infinite patience. "You can touch Earth's magic. And those same channels can be used for the power of the Jewels, since they are tied to Earth's magic, born of it. You can learn to wield it. If you choose."

"Oh, now I get a choice?"

His smile is tinged with sadness, and he pushes his hood back. With his face fully exposed to me, I can see that he's missing one eye, a jagged scar bisecting the lid, flat over the empty socket. "There is always a choice, Claire. Not always a good one, but always a choice. You can walk away."

"I really can't," I mutter.

"If you wish it," he says, "I can take your memories and with them, your compulsion. You can return to your life. Leave the Jewels to someone else."

I press my lips together to keep from blurting out my answer. Nothing is this easy, even if I want it so badly my whole body aches with it. Then something occurs to me. "Wait. You're the one who set up this spell, aren't you the one who came up with this bullshit about the Chosen? Don't you know what I'm going to pick?"

"I know many things. But your choices are yours, Claire. We change the future, every second, every hour, by our choices. No one, human or Fae Queen or god, no one can take that from you. This is the time. There is no fated prophecy to force you on this path. There is only you. Choose."

Closing my eyes, I pull a breath in through my nose. I need to focus. I need to think.

Without the compulsion, what reason do I have to go through the Trials, really? Sure, I might find a cure for Jack, a way for him to be free of Underhill, but I might not. And just because these Trials won't kill me doesn't mean I'll make it through finding all four Jewels safely. The smart thing, the safe thing, would be to quit while I'm ahead. Take the out, go back and live my life. If the guys were here, they'd tell me that.

Except.

The more I think about it, the madder I get. The Fae have used Earth as their playground for centuries, maybe millennia. They've toyed with people's lives, broken them and cast them aside like so many toys. The Fae are the reason Jack is afraid to sleep, the reason Ben sometimes has to touch Jack like he's not sure he's actually there. The reason behind the sadness in Mal's eyes sometimes. The reason I lost Jake.

"How much longer until the spell runs out?" I ask. "The one the Jewels are powering, that keeps the Queens away?"

Merlin shrugs. "These things are hard to measure. But it will almost certainly endure for the rest of your lifetime at least. You can live out your years without worrying that Earth will be overrun."

I bite my lip. The smart thing would be to back out. But I do have a tendency to make stupid, impulsive decisions. Just ask my parents.

"I'll do it."

He smiles. "Excellent. Are you ready to begin?"

28

ven though Merlin is still sitting cross-legged, not moving, there's a sense of power about him that wasn't there before, like standing in the path of a wildfire. Suddenly I understand, deep down to my bones, that this is Merlin, Arthur's legendary magician. I swallow the snarky remark that wants to come out and nod instead.

"Sit with me, then." He winks. "And it's all right. I like people with spirit, who are clever enough to talk back."

Returning his smile, I sit back down. "Okay. Now what?"

Lifting his hand, he sketches a familiar shape in the air. The rune hangs there, glowing with white light, two interlocking sideways Vs. "You have been studying the runes?"

"Yeah,." I swallow the rest of it, the thousand and one possible meanings. He already knows.

"So. Jera. Everything in its place, in its right time." He looks at me. "You have come here on the full moon, in your right time. To learn to use your magic, you need to understand its cycle. Magic flows through the earth, much like water."

I do my best to focus on what he's saying. "So it rains magic?"

He frowns, but not at me. More like he's trying to find the right words to explain it. "Not entirely. All living things radiate magic into the world. Some more, some less, but always there. It gathers, in streams and pools that you can learn to use. Here. I will show you."

I hesitate for a moment before taking his hand. If this is all in my head, I don't know what to expect. But his hand feels real, solid and calloused and scarred.

And then I'm not paying attention to his hand at all, because we're seemingly hovering in space, watching Earth spin slowly below us. It looks like every photo I've ever seen of it from space, glowing blue oceans, green and brown continents, and the white swirls of clouds over all of it.

"Look," Merlin says.

I am looking, but I resist the urge to say so. I'm not sure what he's telling me to look at, though. It all looks like I would have expected it to, if he'd told me we were taking this little trip.

After a few seconds, he sighs. "Think about the state you were in when you found Atlantis, yes? The trance?"

"Mal did that," I say. "I don't know if I can do it on my own."

"Oh, child." He shakes his head. As much as I don't enjoy being called a child, looking at his face, I know that's how it seems to him. "I'm sorry. I forget all that you don't know, all you haven't been taught. Close your eyes?"

It's a question, not a command, so I do it. Before I can get too bogged down thinking about whether I'm actually closing my physical eyes or if it's just me imagining that I am, he's speaking again.

"Think of this Mal. Think about how you feel when you are with him, of all the things that make him who he is. Hold those thoughts in your head, as strongly as you can."

After a few tries, I think I'm managing pretty well. My mind is a swirl of images and memories, like a montage in a movie. Mal's fingers touching my forehead, the cool wash of his power through my body. Mal's dragon body, his deep voice echoing in my brain as he patiently answers my questions. Mal's hand on me, anchoring me as I searched for answers.

"Excellent."

Merlin's voice almost makes me jump--or just makes me think I'm going to jump--but I manage to hold onto the feeling of Mal. I think.

"Now remember how he taught you to find the trance state. Imagine he is here now, telling you what to do."

Ignoring the question of whether or not I'm currently inhabiting my physical body, I start to move through the steps of relaxation, trying to remember then little mental twist it takes to enter the trance state. If I'd known there was going to be a test, I would have studied.

"Open your eyes."

When I do as he says, the first thing I see is the now-familiar beam of light leading me to the Jewel. It arcs down out of me, into the ocean. No, wait. There are actually four, each leading to a different part of the globe. "Are those--"

"The locations of the other four Jewels," he confirms. "With each you will face new Trials, new tests of your ability to use your power, to prove your worthiness to wield them. But this is not why I brought you here."

"Then why--"

The words catch in my throat as I finally really look at the blue globe before us. Where before it had looked pretty normal, now it's lit up like one of those photos of the world at night, lights glowing here and there. Places I know to be cities are the brightest, but there are other clumps of light, some dimmer, some moving around.

"All living things give off power, as I said." Merlin smiles at me. "Let's take a closer look."

With no more warning than that, we're hovering at about airplane altitude above the east coast; it takes me a few minutes to identify Boston. This close, the light is one solid blob, moving like ocean waves under us. When I start tracking the movement, we move to follow it. I may let out a very undignified noise at the sudden movement, but honestly, I think I'm coping with whatever the hell this is a lot better than could be expected.

"It takes a bit of getting used to," Merlin says. "But yes, you see? The power gathers, and even in a city this large, there aren't enough people who could use it without burning themselves to cinders. So it flows."

We follow the flow, watching as it grows faster and narrower, until it's a single, glowing thread of light, much like the ones attached to my chest.

"People have many names for these. The most common term is ley lines, something even non-magical folk have heard of."

"Where is it going?"

His eye twinkles as he grins at me. "Let's go see."

The line we're following occasionally intersects others, some larger, some barely-visible threads. Eventually, we come to a river, wide enough that even I can recognize it. "Is that the Mississippi?"

"It is." Merlin takes us lower. Or maybe I do. It's confusing, and right now, it's not important. "Here is the secret. Although the physical and the magical rarely inter- sect, rarely does not mean always. In the case of water, evaporation turns it into clouds which rain it back to earth, yes?"

"If I remember my third-grade science right."

He laughs. "Running water is known, in myth and legend, to ground magic. Most of the people who say this mean it as a fanciful term, but if you look closely--"

Doing just that, I watch, in awe, as the magic flows into the water, quite literally soaking into the ground. "So that--"

"Think of it as the magic cycle. Living things put off magic, it flows into the water, into the ground. Plants absorb it, and that energy is absorbed by the creatures that eat them, and those that eat them, and so on."

"Huh." I have the most irreverent urge to burst into "Circle of Life" but I manage to squelch it. Barely. "So this is the Trial? Learning how magic works?"

He shakes his head. "You know it's not that easy."

I sigh. "Yeah. It never is."

"Come."

Between one blink and the next we're hovering over Atlantis, the citizens going about their business below us. As much as I want to jet off to the temple, to see if Jack and Ben and Mal are all right, I have a job to do here. So I turn to Merlin, and I wait.

"What do you see?"

When I turn my attention back to the city below us, I can see the energy glowing around the people. It's brighter than I would have expected, though. "Why is there so much magic here?"

Merlin beams at me like my eighth grade math teacher

when I figured out how to factor polynomials. "Why do you think?"

Of course he can't just give me a straight answer. I look more closely.

Instead of flowing, like the magic we saw on the surface, this light is choppy, like waves on a lake. It tries to flow out, but bounces back from something invisible around the edges of the caldera, the currents mixing and melding with each other. It's almost painful to look at.

When I focus on the edges, I realize that I can see what it's hitting. A thin veil of magic hangs around the edges of the caldera, blocking the power that tries to leave.

"Is that the reason I couldn't see the city until I was right on top of it?"

"Correct." Merlin looks even prouder. "The shield is part of what has kept Atlantis safe for so long, Unfortunately, it has also trapped the magic put off by everyone who lives here."

I frown. "Wouldn't that just mean that there's more magic for people to use?"

"Even if every citizen of Atlantis could use the power, or wished to do so, they would burn themselves out before using up a fraction of it. The human body can only channel so much power at a time. And such a concentration of ungrounded magic is dangerous. Much more and the creatures, human and otherwise, who live here will start showing the effects. This is your task."

Great. A real-world pass/fail test. I think about it. "So,

the goal is for the magic to be able to ground itself naturally? It won't cause problems if most of it is gone?"

"The creatures living here will generate more than enough magic for anyone who might need it," he confirms.

"Okay." It occurs to me that maybe the solution is simpler than I think. "Wait, how do the Atlanteans get fresh water?"

He smiles. "There are stations set up along the borders of the caldera to filter the salt from the water. It travels through the city via aqueducts."

Well, so much for that brilliant idea. "The magic can't ground in that water?"

"The stone of the aqueducts acts as an insulator," he says. "Besides, it does not reach the earth inside the city. Waste water also leaves through filtering stations, but the magic of the barrier would prevent it from carrying the power out into the sea. For that you need fresh water, running in the earth."

"Okay."

This feels like the first day of grad school again, swimming in a sea of information, clinging desperately to the few scraps of knowledge I have and hoping I won't be swamped by all the things I don't know.

"So power can't make it past the shield." I'm thinking out loud, hoping a solution will come to me. "It needs fresh flowing water touching the ground to disperse it."

Merlin nods, but doesn't speak.

"But we're under the fucking ocean--sorry--"

He waves it away. "I rode with an army, more than once. Believe me, I have heard much worse."

I blow out a breath. "So we need fresh water under the ocean."

Something pokes at the back of my mind, some fact I picked up from somewhere. I keep talking, hoping it will work its way out. "And the aqueducts won't work, because the stone insulates them. Does it keep the magic out? Or keep it from grounding itself."

"An excellent question. Both, as a matter of fact."

"So if--" the thing I had half-forgotten pushes its way to the front of my mind. "Wait. Are there underground springs near here?"

Merlin smiles. "Clever girl."

"But if they haven't broken through to the surface, something's going to have to make a path for them, right?"

"Dŵr has enough power to do that," Merlin says. "But you recall what I said about the human body's limitations when it comes to channeling magic. If you try and aren't capable of handling that much--"

I flinch. "Will it kill me?"

"Perhaps." He meets my eyes squarely. "Or it might destroy your mind. If you are very lucky, it will only destroy your magical abilities."

I take a moment to think. Well. More than one, if we're being honest. Merlin waits patiently, not trying to talk me in one direction or another.

Obviously I'm not thrilled by the idea of dying, or becoming a vegetable. But all the reasons that I made this decision still apply. For me. For Jack and Ben and Mal. For the fucking world, all of humanity, everyone who's been fucked over by the Fae down the years.

In a way, I've been on borrowed time ever since I followed Jake down to Underhill. Forces beyond my control have been jerking me around ever since, pulling me one way and another. At least now I have a choice.

"Okay." I meet his eyes, doing my best to pretend I'm not scared shitless. "Let's do it.

ᛋᚱᚻ

I STILL HAVEN'T GOTTEN USED to the sensation of the world shifting around me, so different from the instant movement when Mal transports us somewhere. Suddenly I'm standing in the temple again. The real temple, with the statue. Jack and Ben and Mal are all talking at once, Rhea is smiling at me like a cat that just sneaked an extra treat. And I can't pay any attention to it, because the statue's hand is empty and the Jewel is in my hands.

"Have you completed the Trials?" Rhea asks, raising her voice to be heard above the noise.

As much as I wish I had, I know it's not the case. "I haven't even completed the first one. Dŵr here is just on loan until I do. But I need your help."

Rhea's face grows more and more worried as I explain

what Merlin showed me. "He's right. That level of power--it explains some things that I have noticed recently. But you have a plan to deal with it?"

"I have like, half of a plan." Holding the Jewel, I can feel water moving under my feet, can practically see it. "There's an underground spring near the surface here. With Dŵr, I can bring it the rest of the way. But the water needs somewhere to go, and I'd rather not be the person who flooded everyone in Atlantis out of their homes."

She nods. "Much appreciated, I'm sure. Let me show you something."

We follow her out of the temple, down to the base of the steps I saw in my vision, the guys staying thankfully quiet now. It's only been a few days, but it seems so long ago that I was seeing the city for the first time.

In person, Atlantis is even more beautiful than I remember. There's greenery everywhere, trees and bushes and low ground cover growing in what look like drainage ditches, flanking each side of the steps.

"Back when we first came here," Rhea says, "we brought the city as we would on the surface, including ditches for drainage. It took months and years to realize that it would not rain here, and to be sure the shield would hold the sea at bay. We try not to think about what would happen if it did not, but ditches would not save us. These still run throughout the city, and drain through the ground under the shield."

"And these plants aren't important for anything?" I

squat down to look more closely, brushing my fingers over a velvety green leaf.

She shakes her head. "Not as important as dealing with the excess of magic. I'd prefer not to be facing a crop of two-headed chickens, or worse. Besides, another source of fresh water would be welcome."

"Great." I get back to my feet, nervous flutters dancing in my stomach. "Do we need to maybe ask somebody? Get a permit?"

"My dear, you hold the Jewel of Water," Rhea says. I get the impression she's trying not to laugh at me. "Merlin himself set you this Trial; even the Council would not stand in your way. Besides, with the Jewel, no one in Atlantis could stand against you if we tried. Still, I suppose it would be polite to let everyone know so we don't cause a panic."

Touching her fingers to her throat, she stands for a moment, then starts to speak. Her words echo back to us from all over the caldera, and people stop to listen.

"Atlanteans, the Chosen has begun her first Trial. Do not be alarmed when the ditches fill with water; the Temple has the matter under control."

She turns to me expectantly.

"That's it?"

Her smile widens. "Every citizen of Atlantis knows our purpose. We have known since Merlin brought the Jewel, and we have been waiting. For you."

"Wait a minute." I push aside the weight of that expectation in favor of being my truest history nerd self. "Atlantis sank during the time of Plato. But Merlin and Arthur were, what, a thousand years later?"

"For someone with Merlin's power, wielding all four Jewels, time is--more fluid. Did you have more questions?"

I have so many, but I'm pretty sure she can't explain to me when my life became an episode of Doctor Who. Plus, holding something as powerful as Dŵr is making me feel a little uneasy. Even though I'm not used to magic shit, I can feel the power, pushing gently toward me. "They can wait, I guess. I don't suppose you have an instruction manual for this thing?"

She shakes her head. "I'm afraid not. But I will do everything within my power to keep you and the city safe."

Not as reassuring as I'd like it to be, but then again, I don't really have much room to complain. I want to turn to the guys, to ask them to hold my hands, to have Mal put me in that trance state again. But I don't know how that might affect them, what kind of danger it might put them in. Jack is already dealing with the Mark and everything that comes with it; I don't want to make things worse for him.

Taking a deep breath, I try to find that mental space again, focusing my attention on the stone in my hands. It takes a couple of attempts, but I know I've got it when the tracery of blue lines under the ground pops into my vision. Some are faint, barely visible, but the one under the temple glows so brightly I have to squint. Or maybe that's Dŵr--

it's glowing, too, swirling tendrils of blue-green-gray-white energy. One of the tendrils coils around my finger, and suddenly I can feel the water, too, the pressure that wears away at the stone keeping it from the surface.

Can we help? I ask Dŵr, feeling a little stupid and slow. *I don't know how.*

The answer I get isn't in words, but more of a feeling of confirmation. The tendril leaves my hand and reaches for the ditch, and somehow I can feel it like a part of my body. The Jewel's magic slips down through the layers of soil that hold the ground cover in place. The stone under the earth keeps it from going further. It pools there, shifting slightly, waiting.

When I try, it moves, kind of like moving my fingers, but without affecting any part of my body. I start with back and forth, but that doesn't seem to be having much effect on the rock. I can feel the power eroding the stone surface, but slowly.

Circular motion works better. After a bit of trial and error, I spin the power into a small, pointed cyclone, shrinking the tip smaller and smaller to drill down through the sedimentary layers. We drive deeper and deeper, closer to the water pressing up almost eagerly to meet us--

Like many big things, it starts small, a trickle of water dampening the dirt, too small to even be seen under the leafy plants, even though it's plain as day to me. But the pressure of the spring below soon breaks through, filling the ditch with water, flowing down into the city.

Rhea is saying something, but it can't penetrate the headspace I've found. I don't even have to move to repeat the process on the other side, whirling the power into a drill, letting the spring free. The magic almost seems to anticipate me this time, or maybe I've figured out better how to direct it. Either way, it only takes a fraction of the time before those ditches fill with water, too.

Dŵr's power curls around me approvingly, like a cat weaving through it's owner's legs. I want to bask in this feeling forever, but I know it isn't mine. I only have it on loan until I complete the Trials. And even through the high of using the power, I can feel it burning at my brain, searing through my mind. I turn, climbing back up the steps into the temple, placing my feet as carefully as I can. The statue's hand is open, waiting, and as I set the Jewel carefully in it, I swear I see the fingers tighten around it.

But I can't be sure, because that's when everything goes black.

29

I wake up back in the giant bed in the temple. For a second, I think I'm still having the craziest dream ever, but then it all comes rushing back. The Trials. Merlin. Opening up not one, but two freshwater streams in fucking Atlantis. And then, presumably passing the fuck out like a swooning Victorian lady.

Before I can dwell too hard on it, though, Ben sits down on the bed next to me, followed closely by Jack. "Hey. Welcome back," Ben says.

"What happened?"

His smile looks a little wobbly around the edges. "Well, I don't know what happened with you. From my point of view, you stood in front of the statue for about five minutes, then the Jewel was in your hands. And we walked out and you stood there for maybe a minute and then water came bubbling up in the ditches."

"And then you turned around and put the Jewel back in the damn statue's hand and fainted," Jack continues. "If Mal wasn't so fast, you'd have a hell of a goose-egg from hitting your head on that floor."

"Well that's something." I sit up, surprised to find myself shaking a little. "What's wrong with me? I feel like I just gave blood or worked out for three hours straight without eating."

Ben frowns. "Rhea said something about magic, that doing it uses energy. She said if you eat it should take care of the worst of it, but to come see her if not."

My stomach chooses that moment to attempt to devour itself. "Yeah, food sounds amazing."

"Here." Jack hands me one of the protein bars I keep around for after workouts. "Mal went and got some in case you needed them. Start on this while I see if they can bring you something."

He leans in to kiss me softly before vanishing out the door. I try to open one of the bars, but my hands are shaking too badly. After a couple of attempts, Ben takes it out of my hand and peels it out of the wrapper before handing the bar back.

As usual, the bar is a little dry, a little powdery, but the chocolate coating on the outside eases it down my throat. And honestly, I'm hungry enough that I don't really care. Ben hands me a glass of some kind of juice when I'm done, and with the sugar from that, I can feel my hunger easing a little. Even if the flavor combination is weird as hell.

"You scared the shit out of us, you know." Ben says.

"Sorry." I take another drink of juice. "Although now you know how I felt when the two of you headed out to deal with Khari. Or anything else, for that matter."

To his credit, he just smiles, sliding into the bed and holding me close instead of trying to tell me that as the men, it's their job to go out and hunt. I love his protective side, but if he tries to wrap me in bubble wrap again, I'm not above smacking him upside the head until he comes to his senses.

By the time I've finished a second protein bar, Jack is back with a tray full of bread and meat and cheese and fruit. At least, I think that's what it is. I'm eating it almost too fast to taste it, anyway. While I'm still inhaling the first slice of bread, Jack disappears again, presumably to bring back more sustenance. This is the kind of hunter-gathering I can definitely get behind.

They wait patiently while I eat what feels like my own body weight in food, but one or both of them is always touching me. Not oppressively, just a hand on my ankle, an arm wrapped around me, or a leg pressed against mine. But I can understand it. After what happened, I'm not too interested in letting them out of my sight, either.

Finally I slump back against the headboard, feeling less like my stomach is going to gnaw a hole through my body.

Apparently that's a signal, because Ben's voice is gentle when he says, "Can you tell us what happened? Do you remember?"

I can't blame them for being curious as hell; most of what Ben described sounded pretty boring. Besides, I need someone to share all of this with. Every detail is burned into my memory, shining with a clarity I've never experienced before. "No, I remember. I touched the stone, and I was still standing in the temple. But the statue was gone..."

ᛋᚱᚼ

"Wow," Ben says when I've finished telling the story.

"Yeah."

Jack's thumb rubs over my ankle. "And you feel okay?"

I stretch slowly, testing each group of muscles in turn. "Yeah, now that I've eaten."

"I mean--"

Before he can finish the sentence, someone knocks on the door. After a brief exchange of glances that's probably their version of rock-paper-scissors, Ben gets up to open it and let Rhea inside.

"Claire!" Her voice isn't loud, but her eyes crinkle at the corners from her smile. "You're looking well. How are you feeling?"

"Better now that I've eaten like three meals." I sit up a little straighter. "Did it work? Is everything okay?"

She crosses to the bed, laying her hand gently on my forehead. It's an automatic gesture, I don't think she even realizes she's doing it, but suddenly my throat goes tight with missing my mom, even with all her faults. "The water from the springs is flowing through the ditches. The engineering holds up, even if it is a few centuries old; nothing has flooded that shouldn't have water in it. I'm told the children are having a fine time playing in the water now that school has let out."

"I guess kids are kids everywhere." I can picture it, kids splashing happily through knee-deep water, flinging it at each other, floating boats and sticks and whatever else they can get their hands on. "I hope their parents aren't too mad."

"It will be fine." Rhea clearly has no such worries. "And even if they were bothered, a few wet clothes is a small price to pay for children who can grow up without being warped by excess magic."

I have no idea what that would entail, but I'm willing to live in ignorance for once. Every possibility my brain suggests is terrible enough that I don't want to risk finding out if it might happen. "So it worked?"

"My primary magics are in healing," Rhea says. "I cannot see the ambient magic as you can, or we would have known of this problem sooner. You tell me."

Giving Jack and Ben a warning look so they keep their mouths shut, I swing my legs over the edge of the bed. Moving cautiously even though the shakiness seems to have subsided, I make my way toward the doors and step onto the balcony.

I think I'm faster at finding the trance state this time; maybe practice really does make perfect. What I see is fainter than when I was with Merlin, but I can still see it. The glow of ambient magic is still there, but it's not the choppy, contained lake any longer Now it flows toward the streams of water criss-crossing the city, melting into the blue magic that carries it out into the sea. "It worked."

"Excellent." Rhea says. "Not that I had any doubts, but it's good to have confirmation. Now, if you'll return to the bed, I'd like to be sure you've suffered no ill effects from your task."

Ben and Jack both look relieved that she said it, but they're smart enough not to say so, or to hover too obviously as I make my way back inside.

I'm expecting something like a doctor's exam, but Rhea just holds her hands out flat a few inches away from me, moving them slowly over my body. Her serene expression never changes, which is both encouraging and frustrating, because I don't know what the hell she's thinking.

"You've recovered nicely from channeling the Jewel's power," she finally says. "I imagine by the end of the day you won't be feeling any further effects. If you do, though, please send someone for me. Will you stay here tonight, in case you need further help?"

Looking at Jack and Ben, I see my own struggle mirrored in their faces. I'd really prefer to go home for the night, to sleep in a familiar bed and wake up in our own space. But everything about my surprise magical abilities is a huge question mark. If something does come up, I think we'll all feel more comfortable having Rhea close at hand. "That's probably best," I say.

"Excellent." She stands up. "In that case, I will send someone with clothes for you to wear to dinner. The Council would like to thank you for your efforts, on behalf of Atlantis."

My feelings about that must be showing on my face, because she gives me a sympathetic smile. "Don't worry. It won't be as bad as you're imagining."

Before I can make an appropriately snarky response to that, Jack speaks up. "Um, I have a question?"

Rhea turns her attention to him. "Yes?"

"It's the full moon. And usually, I have--a problem on the full moon."

I suddenly feel like the worst girlfriend-slash-partner in existence. How did I get so caught up in all this prophecy stuff that I didn't realize the other significance of the full moon? But more importantly, why isn't he freaking the fuck out right now?"

"Your Knighthood," she replies. "I had wondered if you would feel an effect. Atlantis at large, and the temple specifically, are warded against the Fae. The spell that was placed on you is rooted deeply enough that we cannot cut off that connection, but we can, ah, stretch it somewhat. If you find it needful, you may return here during the full moons, even after the Trials are complete."

"Thank you." Jack's voice is husky, his face more raw and open than I've seen it since before he left to kill Khari. "I--thank you."

She reaches out, resting her hand gently on his head. "Earth's protectors are always welcome here."

And then she's gone before I can ask any more questions.

"Well. Dinner with politicians. Sounds like a blast." Jack stretches out on the bed next to me. "I think I need a nap."

"Nap sounds good." Ben joins us, snuggling close to my other side.

I can't argue with that, even if I am still feeling guilty for forgetting about Jack's curse. Now that I have a moment, thoughI realize what--or rather, who--is missing. "Hey, where's Mal?"

"He had to go deal with some family stuff," Jack says. His jaw cracks on a yawn before he can continue.

Ben picks up the thread. "From what he's said, his family is pretty traditional. Apparently he's young enough that they'll forgive him for sowing some wild oats, being friends with humans, but I think he's getting on toward the age where they want him to settle down and start having more baby dragon shifters. He goes back every so often, just to keep them off his back. But he said he wouldn't be gone long. Maybe he'll be back in time for dinner."

"Maybe--" It's my turn to yawn. My stomach is full, the bed is soft and comfortable, and I've got Jack and Ben around me to keep me warm. "Maybe so."

I think Ben says something else, but I'm already slipping into sleep.

ᛋᚱᚺ

"Well, that could've been worse." Ben closes the door to our room behind us.

Jack snorts. "Speak for yourself. The only way I was able to get through that dinner and all the formal shit was remembering that Claire promised to peel us out of these suits."

I take a minute to look them over again. I hadn't been sure what kind of clothing Rhea would provide, but I shouldn't have worried. For me, it was a floaty Grecian-style tunic dress. The skirt was made up of layers and layers of sheer fabric, enough to be opaque in combination, all split in different places to flash different views of my legs as I walked. But my favorite part of the outfit was the sandals, high-heeled but somehow still comfortable, with laces that criss-crossed up my calves.

The boys had much less elaborate get-ups. Their suits wouldn't have looked out of place anywhere on the surface, but they fit like they were made for them, accentuating their broad shoulders and tapering down to their waists.

"I did say that, didn't I." I walk slowly toward him, backing him up until he hits the wall. "But I think I've changed my mind."

"Oh yeah?" Jack swallows hard as I run my hands up and down the lapels of his jacket, and then again when I sink to my knees.

I smile up at him as I undo his belt. "Yeah, I think I'd like you to keep the suit on for a little while longer."

Ben settles into a chair, clothes rustling and furniture scraping over the floor, but I'm too focused on my task to look his way. Undoing the button on his slacks, I carefully pull down the zipper, easing the fabric away from where it's tented over his erection.

I tug the front of his boxers down gently, freeing his cock. Wrapping my hand around the base of his cock, I close my mouth over the head, sliding my lips slowly, slowly down the shaft until I can't take any more.

"Jesus fuck," he swears. One hand comes up to thread through my hair, the other slaps flat against the wall.

I hum slightly around him, just to get a reaction. My reward is the harsh sound of him sucking in a breath, the rasp in his voice when he says "I think she likes the suit, Benny."

Ben chuckles softly from the side. When I turn my eyes that way, I can just see him sprawled in his chair, jacket off, tie loosened, sleeves rolled up. "I think you might be right."

Swirling my tongue around Jack's cock, I swallow. His hips hitch slightly forward, then he sags back against the wall, like he's trying not to fuck my mouth.

"You keep that up, I'm not gonna last long," he warns.

Looking up, I meet his eyes and redouble my efforts, licking and sucking and swallowing.

"Fine, sweetheart, if that's the way you want it." True to his word, a few short minutes later his hand tightened in my hair as he comes, thrusting just slightly into my mouth.

I keep my mouth moving until he shudders and jerks away, tugging me up to my feet and into a long, deep kiss. Finally, he pulls back, his lips clinging reluctantly to mine. "I think Benny might be feeling a little neglected," he murmurs in my ear. "You gonna take care of him, too?"

I nod, turning toward Ben.

Before I can kneel in front of him, he shakes his head. "I've got other plans for you, baby. Not that I don't love it when you wrap that pretty mouth around my cock, but right now I want you to bend over and put your hands on the bed."

Doing as he says, I turn my head to watch him. Which means I see him pull his tie off in one smooth, almost menacing motion. I can't stop the shudder that runs through my body at the sight. The intensity of his eyes transfixes me, along with imagining what he plans to do with that tie.

"Hands together," he orders.

I drop obediently to my elbows, pressing my palms together. Leaning over my back, he knots one end of the tie around my wrists and secures the other end to the footboard.

"Now then," he murmurs. Running a proprietary hand up my back, he unties the sash wrapped around my waist, letting it drop to the floor before moving on to the ties on each shoulder. He makes an appreciative noise when the many-layered tunic slithers to the floor, leaving me in my bra, panties, and the high-heeled sandals--along with a garter belt and stockings.

"Damn." Jack is still leaning against the wall, his voice low and reverent. "If I'd known you were wearing that, we would've left dinner a lot sooner."

Ben runs his fingers over the waistband of my panties. "You were planning on us finding out eventually, weren't you, baby?"

I nod. "Only good part of wearing this stupid shit is that you guys like the way I look in it."

"Oh, we do." Ben all but purrs as he pulls my panties down, careful not to catch them on the high heels. "Ever since you put those sandals on I've been imagining bending you over and fucking you."

On the last word, he pushes two thick fingers easily

inside my pussy. "You're all ready for me, aren't you, baby? Did it make you wet, sucking Jack's cock?"

I nod wordlessly, groaning when he withdraws his fingers and replaces them with his cock. He slips inside me in one long, ruthless thrust, bracing his hands on either side of me and fucking me in long, deep strokes.

"I'm not gonna last long either." He doesn't pause as he speaks. "It was hot as hell, seeing you down on your knees, sucking Jack off. You did such a good job, took such good care of him. Now I'm gonna take care of you."

True to his word, he slips a hand around my hip to find my clit. Between his fingers on my clit, his strong, steady thrusts, and the endless, filthy litany of praise and endearments, it's not much longer before I'm shaking underneath him. I'm still shuddering when he pushes deep inside me and comes as well.

We lie draped over the bed for several long, breathless minutes, before Ben stirs reluctantly and pushes himself up. He reaches over to untie my hands, but Jack is already there, loosening the knots and rubbing my wrists to be sure they're not hurt.

"If I was five years younger, I'd be ready for another round," Jack says. "As it is, I'm thinking nap."

I open my mouth to make a smartass reply, but before I can speak, there's a faint rustling sound and Mal is standing there, looking very put out.

30

N ow is probably not the time for me to be noticing how hot Mal looks in a suit that matches Jack and Ben's. But I'm still turned on, my body vibrating with the force of my last orgasm, and he looks really good as he stalks toward us.

"You may find it interesting," he says, "to know that apparently we now have a telepathic connection."

"We do?" Ben's forehead furrows. "Wouldn't we know?"

Mal shrugs out of his suit jacket, hanging it over the back of a chair. "The bond is still very weak; I suspect that as it grows stronger, you will become more aware of it. I simply have more experience with this sort of connection, so for me, it is--remarkably visual."

I flush, suddenly very aware of what we were just

doing, of the fact that I'm sitting on the bed in nothing but my bra, garter belt and stockings, and high-heeled sandals. When I dart a glance at Jack and Ben, they wear identical smug smirks.

"Enjoy the show, Mal?" Ben asks.

Mal stalks toward the bed, every movement predatory. "It was very educational." His eyes are dark and intense as he stops in front of me. I don't think we've ever been this close, just the two of us, so close the smooth fabric of his slacks brushes against my stockings, catching slightly on the clasps of the garter belt.

He drops his gaze, raking it down my body until I feel it like a physical touch, then back up to meet my eyes. "May I?"

I swallow, my mouth suddenly dust-dry. When I look over at Jack, he shrugs, settling back against the headboard of the bed. "Up to you, sweetheart. Not gonna tell you what to do here."

Ben nods when I glance at him, joining Jack at the head of the bed. "Your choice."

Mal's fingers come to rest lightly on my arm, bringing my attention back to him. "I don't wish to pressure you," he says. "If this is not something you want, I understand."

He starts to back away, but I catch his hand before he can go far. "I want to." It takes effort, but I force myself to meet his eyes, to be sure he understands. "I want you. But I don't want to make decisions that affect this relationship without checking in first."

His eyes soften and he nods his understanding. When he relaxes, I suddenly realize how tense he had been, the way he'd been bracing himself for rejection since his arrival. He steps closer again, lifting his free hand to my face. "May I?" he asks again.

He waits for my nod before closing the distance and kissing me.

I know Mal has years, centuries, of lived experience, but after how careful he's been with me, I kind of expected him to be hesitant, a little uncertain. But he kisses me like he's done it a thousand times. The hand on my face slides back to thread through my hair and hold me in place, exploring my mouth with lips and teeth and tongue until I'm shivering against him.

He catches my lower lip gently between his teeth as he pulls away, making me shiver. His fingers catch as he slides his hand free of my hair, his eyes sharpening when I whimper a little.

"Later," he murmurs. His fingers skim over the edge of my bra where fabric meets skin, smiling when I shudder at the touch.

"I can--" I start to reach behind me, but he shakes his head.

"No, leave it on. I like seeing you like this." His voice is matter-of-fact, like he's commenting on the weather, but paired with the heat in his eyes, it still leaves a jittery warmth curling in my belly. "You look like a picture from a dirty magazine, but better."

I swallow. "Better?"

"Yes. Because I can touch you--" his fingertips dipped into my bra to tease a nipple "--and smell you--" he leans in until his lips are almost touching my neck and inhales "--and taste you--" he sucks gently on the side of my neck, making me moan "--and hear you."

"Damn, Mal." Jack shifts slightly, the covers rustling under him. "Thought we might have to give you some pointers about what she likes. But I guess you know what you're doing, huh?"

Mal smiles at him while ghosting his hands up my inner thighs, coaxing them apart. "You've given me opportunities to observe, Jack. Did you think I hadn't learned anything?"

He turns back toward me without waiting for a response. His hand goes from teasing, barely-there touches to a firm stroke up my center, opening me to his touch. When he slips two fingers inside my pussy, smooth and slick and messy from Ben's orgasm, I gasp, letting my head fall back.

"Ah." He adds a third finger, smirking a little as I make an inarticulate noise. "Talk to me, Claire. How does that feel?"

I do my best to engage the part of my brain that manages things like words. "Good."

He tsks a little, curling his fingers until they brush over the spot that makes me writhe. "You can do better than that, Claire."

With his fingertips stroking insistently inside me, it's hard to work up a good glare, but I try my best. "You're--ah--entirely too good at this."

"Told you." Ben's face is insufferably smug as he lounges back against the headboard.

"A few hundred years of practice, you pick up a few tricks." Mal pulls my attention to him, despite the deceptive mildness of his tone. "You still haven't answered my question, though. How does it feel?"

"It feels amazing." I don't have the brainpower to answer with anything but honesty. "I'm--oh, God--I'm going to come soon if you keep that up."

"Thank you." The politeness of his voice is kind of a mind-fuck, given that he has most of one hand buried deep inside my pussy. "What If I do this, too?"

His thumb strokes over my clit, unerringly finding the spot that makes my legs tremble, all while his fingers keep moving inside me.

"That--" I swallow down a moan. Barely. "That'll make me come even sooner."

"Good."

Cupping the back of my head with his free hand, he pulls me up for another kiss, not stopping until I'm gasping and moaning into his mouth. His fingers tighten in my hair, tugging gently, sending sparks of sensation dancing over my scalp and shivering down my spine.

I moan even louder, too far gone to care about the volume. The feeling of his hands on me, inside me, is almost too intense. I'm writhing against him, my body unable to decide if it wants to get closer or to pull away.

"Come for me, Claire," he rasps. "I want to see you."

Shuddering, I come at his command, unable to deny the absolute authority in his voice. He keeps his fingers moving inside me, his thumb rubbing my clit, fucking me through it. Until I'm so sensitive it hurts, until I manage to gasp, "Mal, stop, please, stop."

He freezes immediately, his forehead furrowed.

"It's okay, man," Jack says. I shoot him a grateful look, still trying to draw a full breath to explain. "Claire just gets really sensitive after she comes, don't you, sweetheart?"

I nod. My heart rate is finally starting to come down to something approaching normal, but it spikes up again when Mal leans in and murmurs, "I would really like to fuck you, Claire. May I?"

Another nod is all I can manage, but his eyes still light up. Pulling his fingers gently out, he brings them to his mouth and sucks them clean. "You taste so good."

I muster up enough energy to grab his tie and tug him down for another kiss. I can taste myself and Ben in his mouth, the flavors mingling with his and the lingering hint of Jack on the back of my tongue. All of us, together.

His hands slide down my back to curve over my ass, pulling me in until I'm grinding against him. I can feel the hard, thick line of his cock pressing against me through the fabric of his slacks. I'm getting them messy, but he doesn't seem to mind, groaning into my mouth and meeting me movement for movement.

Finally, reluctantly, he pulls away enough to undo his pants, pulling his cock free. "Are you ready?"

I can't help but laugh a little. His eyes sparkle back at me, like he understand. Like he feels it, too. "Yeah, Mal, I'm ready. Come fuck me."

Sucking in a deep breath, he obeys, pressing slowly and steadily inside me. His eyes never leave mine, and he never stops until he's completely buried in my pussy.

He leans down to kiss me, his hips making tiny, shuddering little thrusts. "I don't think I'm going to last very long," he breathes. "It--you feel amazing, Claire."

I reach up, smoothing my hands over his shoulders. "It's okay, Mal. It's not a contest."

"But I--" taking a breath, he starts to move. "I want you to enjoy yourself, too."

"I am. I will."

He seems to regain some of his earlier attitude, despite thrusting deeper inside me. "Still. Perhaps I should make sure. Do you remember me telling you about my water form?"

"Uh, yes?" Possibly it's just because my brain is sex-addled, but I can't figure out where he's going with this.

And then I can, because Jack and Ben both make surprised noises and there are--"Are those tentacles?"

The dark blue appendages hover on either side of me.

Mal looks truly uncertain for the first time since I asked him to stop. "If you don't want--"

I reach up to touch the tentacle on my right. Instead of the tanned-leather scales of his flying form, the surface is covered with smooth, slick skin. "It's all you, Mal. I'm good."

He searches my face, but what he finds there must be convincing. "Give me your hands, Claire."

A little stunned at the return of that authoritative snap in his tone, I obey. The right tentacle wraps around my wrists, pulling me gently but firmly down until I'm flat on my back, my bound hands pressed into the bed.

"Is that what you like?" He resumes his slow, steady fucking. "You like being held down?"

I nod wordlessly, my mouth gone dry.

One corner of his mouth tips up in that damn smirk. I suddenly realize I have no idea if he learned it from Jack or the other way around. "Talk to me, Claire."

"I like--I really like it when you hold me down and fuck me." I'm trying to goad him into moving faster, but all that gets me is the other tentacle gently stroking the most sensitive spots on my neck, over my collarbone. "Please don't stop, Mal."

He speeds up as I talk, one hand sliding down over my hip, urging my leg up to wrap around him. I moan at the change in angle as he pushes even deeper inside me.

The free tentacle manages to nudge my bra down, exposing my nipple to its teasing caresses. Another joins it, repeating the process with my other breast, but I can barely notice. Mal is driving into me, my wrists are still restrained above my head, and everything is melding together, nothing but sensation driving me higher.

When he slides a hand between us to stroke my clit, it only takes a few touches before I'm coming again. I'm still shaking under him when he makes a few last thrusts, burying himself inside me and groaning out my name as he comes.

It takes awhile for my breathing to slow down to something like normal, but it's nice, having Mal's weight on top of me, feeling his heart pounding against mine. But eventually my arm muscles start to complain about the position.

"Mal? A little help?"

"Huh?" He lifts his head from where it had been resting between my breasts. "Oh, sorry."

The tentacle around my wrists comes loose, and if his skin wasn't so dark, I'm pretty sure he would be blushing.

"Using your dragon shifter powers for kinky sex." Jack pretends to wipe away a tear. "I'm so proud. You're definitely part of this family.

The tentacle moves so quickly I can barely see it, wrapping around Jack's ankle and dragging him off the bed, dumping him unceremoniously on his ass. He sits there, looking injured, but all it takes is meeting Ben's eyes before I burst out laughing.

After a moment, Mal joins in, the surprise on his face

fading to merriment. Even Jack starts laughing eventually, all of us in various stages of undress in a temple bedroom in the lost city of Atlantis. For a second, I can forget about the Trials, about the Jewels, about everything but them.

In that moment, it just feels like home.

31

"A re you ready?" Rhea asks.

Realistically, I should be feeling more confident right now. I made it through the first Trial, learned how to use my magic and to work with Dŵr. I didn't die, I'm not a vegetable, I can still do magic stuff. The second Trial should be easier, right?

Because that's totally how anything works, ever.

But I've started this. I'm not going to wuss out before it's even halfway done. I square my shoulders before answering. "Ready."

She touches my hand lightly and steps back, leaving me standing in front of the statue with all three men. My men, as I've come to think of them, even though I'm still not sure Mal would agree with that. A conversation that needs to happen, for sure, but one for another time.

Jack kisses me gently on the lips. "Be careful."

"Pot, meet kettle," I joke.

He smiles just a little, squeezing my shoulders before stepping back to make room.

Ben's kiss is a little longer, a little more lingering. "Try not to pass out this time, okay? Jack worries."

I smile up at him. "Do my best, but no promises."

And then it's just Mal standing in front of me, still looking uncertain, even after last night. But when I step forward, reaching for him, he meets me halfway with a kiss that probably only stays light because of Rhea's presence.

"You can do this." His voice is firm, his eyes serious as he looks into mine.

Even with the many, many doubts flitting around my head, when I meet his gaze I believe it. Maybe it's some super-secret dragon hypnosis, maybe just the placebo effect. Either way, when I reach for Dŵr, I feel a renewed sense of confidence.

Hopefully I'm not fooling myself.

ᛋᚱᚼ

ONE OF THESE days I'll probably get used to the world rearranging itself around me. Today is not that day. At least I manage not to jump as the temple disappears around me, replaced by the empty room, empty platform. And Merlin.

"Welcome back, Claire." His smile is warm and

approving. "Shall we look at the results of your work before we begin?"

"Yeah, that sounds good. I tried looking on my own, but--"

He nods. "Your Sight will come easier with practice. In the meantime, I'm happy to help."

I assume that means he's going to take control like last time, taking us where we need to be to see, but instead I feel something tugging at my attention. Like a flickering at the corner of my eye, but it's nothing I see with my eyes.

"Your brain is trying to use muscles it has never possessed before," Merlin says. "It requires practice. Close your eyes."

When I do as he says, it's easier to focus on the thing I noticed. The feeling, the sensation, whatever. It takes a couple of tries, but eventually I--I don't know how to describe it. It feels like opening my eyes, only they're still closed.

But I can see.

I can see the warding spells laid into the walls of the temple, layer on layer, built and maintained by the priests for hundreds, thousands of years. I can see the blue threads of the underground spring I freed a few days ago, flowing toward its outlet and the ditches. Outside the temple, mostly obscured by the wards, I can see the glow, the power put off by the people of Atlantis. And most of all, I can see Merlin, power burning inside him like fire, tamed and bent to his will.

"Excellent," Merlin says. "Now take us up."

I open my mouth to ask how I'm supposed to do that, but apparently even thinking about "up" is enough in this state. I--we start to rise. I open my eyes for a second, then close them a little. I may know that I'm not in my physical body, but that doesn't mean I won't panic when I'm floating rapidly toward a solid stone ceiling.

We pass through the warding spells without a problem, and now I can see the city laid out below us. It looks even better than when I first woke up after the Trial. The power flows seem smoother, less like floodwaters rushing rapidly along and more like the normal movement of a stream. Always moving, always flowing, but calm and steady.

"Very good." Merlin pats my shoulder approvingly.

"How bad would it have been?" I ask. "If something hadn't been done?"

He frowns. "Excess magic reacts in unpredictable ways, but it can have effects similar to toxic chemicals. Deformities, babies born with powers that their bodies can't sustain, strange illnesses. Plants and animals tend to react first, but if you hadn't come along to take up the Trials, I would have had to find someone else to solve this problem. The citizens of Atlantis shouldn't suffer because of something so easily fixed."

"Wow." it takes a little bit to digest that. My first real magic thingy and I dealt with what sounds like the equivalent of something like Fukushima. "Okay. Well, what's on the menu for today?"

Between one blink and the next, we're back in the temple. Or maybe we never left? Magic gives me a headache if I think too hard about it.

Just like last time, Merlin sketches a rune in the air, the one that clearly evolved into the letter R. "Raidho." Just like Mal, he pronounces it *rye-though*. "Travel, the journey, the story."

"Why do these runes mean so many things?" I wince as soon as the grumble leaves my mouth, but Merlin just smiles.

"All the meanings are connected," he says. "Nothing means only one thing, no word in any language. There are shades and variations of meaning, from context, from language changing and evolving. Can you give me one word in English that only has a single meaning?"

Given the fact that I have a whole degree in English, I probably should try harder to come up with one, but I'm not about to argue with an immortal wizard. "No."

He smiles at me. "As you said, many meanings for Raidho. For those who use runes in magic, it can help them to find the correct path, to follow their inner compass. A sense of right and wrong is vital in those who wield magic. I believe a story-teller from your time created the phrase 'with great power comes great responsibility.'"

I goggle at him. "You did not just quote Spider-Man at me."

"Just wait until I start quoting Tupac." His eye twinkles at me. "But Stan Lee didn't invent the concept. Power in the hands of those without a moral compass is dangerous. This is why Raidho represents the right of kings. Nobility wasn't intended as a hereditary office. It was a recognition of worthiness to hold power. Arthur knew that."

"I think I get it."

He peers at me, his gaze sharp and piercing. "I believe that you do. But just as Arthur had to face more tests than pulling Excalibur from the stone, anyone who seeks to wield the Jewels must be tested."

That's all the warning I get before everything changes.

ᛋᚱᚢ

I'M NOT in the temple any longer, either the real one or the in-between space that Dŵr takes me to. When I recognize my surroundings, my heart starts racing.

It doesn't matter that I'm not a kid again. It doesn't matter that my self, whatever form it's taking right now, is standing behind my fourteen-year-old self. It doesn't even matter that no one seems to see or hear me.

I'm still here, somehow. Back in the one place I swore I'd never go again.

"Claire!" My father's voice is sharp, impatient. "Are you listening?"

"Yes, sir," younger me says.

The prompt reply doesn't appease him. Nothing does, when he's like this. But he doesn't raise his voice. Sometimes I think it would be easier if he did. "All you have to do is eat your dinner, and you can go."

My younger self dips a spoon in the soup in front of her, lifts it to her mouth. I don't remember this specific moment, but I don't have to. I know the flavor and texture of that soup, the nausea that rises in my throat as I try to swallow it down. Vomiting isn't an escape. We both know this. I find myself matching the shallow breaths young Claire is taking through her nose, doing her best not to taste.

"I cooked that," my father says. His eyes are sharp on me, on the me I used to be, watching for any signs of--I don't even know what he's watching for. Only that there's no way out. "It's good, healthy food. There are kids starving every day who would love to eat that. And you're so ungrateful that you want to leave it just because you don't like it."

There's no safe answer. Young Claire keeps her eyes down, takes another sip of the soup. The meatballs are long gone, nothing left to cut the acidity that's turning her stomach.

"I worked twelve hours today and came home to cook that for all of you," he continues. "If you--"

Somehow I manage to tune out his words, the sharp edges that still manage to cut me in passing. With the first shock past, I can see things that I never noticed as a child, as a teenager.

I can see the fear in his eyes. The anger is there, of

course. I always knew about the anger, feared it when he yelled, more when he was quiet. But I never looked long enough to see the fear.

"Yes." Merlin appears next to me, making me jump. "Good. Look more closely. What is he afraid of?"

"I don't know!" I regret my outburst as soon as it leaves my mouth. Too loud, too harsh. But being here like this has me on edge, tight with the tension of years. It weighs on my shoulders like it never left, like I never learned to live without it.

Merlin doesn't lash back at me, loudly or quietly. He doesn't even look disappointed, no matter how much I search his face, no matter how much I try to avoid seeing what's happening in front of me. He just raises his eyebrows and says. "Don't you? Look more closely."

Bracing myself, I look again. No matter how much I tell myself that it's not real, that this is more than a decade in the past, I still have trouble focusing. It takes a serious effort of will for me to look back at his face. To try to find the thing Merlin wants me to see. But try as I might, no matter how hard I look, I can't find an answer by the time teenage Claire finishes the last drop of soup and makes her escape.

"Very close." Merlin pats me on the shoulder. "We'll try another."

This time I'm braced for the world to reform around me. When it does, I relax a little when it becomes obvious that this isn't as fraught a situation as the last one. Just my siblings, gathered around in their pajamas for the nightly bedtime story my father would read us. But where--ah. There comes my younger self, down the stairs from her room, wearing the loose, baggy clothes I used to sleep in.

My father looks up and his eyes sharpen. This time it's easier to catch that flash of fear. "Claire," he says. "Go put a robe on. You know better than to run around the house in just your pajamas. Cover yourself up."

Teenage Claire retreats to her room, returning moments later with an old-fashioned house-coat zipped up nearly to her chin. But even though my father gives her an approving nod, the fear is still in his eyes.

"Is he--he's not afraid of me?" That's impossible. No matter how I turn it over, I can't make sense of it. There is no possible universe where my father was afraid of me.

"Getting closer." Merlin remains stubbornly quiet except for those two words as the scene changes yet again. I'm starting to feel like I'm stuck in a movie, watching highlight reels of the shittier parts of my childhood.

This time it's my everyday clothes. The skirt I've got on, even though it comes down past my knees, is too short. Too revealing, when I'm running. I need to wear something else. *Change.* I need to sit up, have good posture. It's not ladylike to drape myself over the chair, my head on one armrest, my legs on the other. *Change.* An awkward "date" with my father, where he tries to make conversation but ends up lecturing me on sin and sinful thoughts. *Change.* A stack of library books being confiscated for being inappropriate.

Maybe my brain finally makes the connection on its own, tired of waiting for me to do it. But suddenly the pieces click together. "He's afraid of losing control." I can taste it as the words leave my mouth, the truth of them resonating through me.

"Very good."

When Merlin's temple reappears around us, I take what feels like my first full breath in hours. Maybe days. "Holy shit. Was that really necessary?"

He looks apologetic. "The Jewels need to know what kind of person will be wielding them. The fate of the world, of humanity, is too important to risk that power falling into the wrong hands."

"And what does my fucked-up childhood tell you about the kind of person I am?" Yelling at him isn't one of my smarter choices, but this little trip down memory lane has me more shaken than I care to admit. "That I'm going to turn out like my dad, lashing out when I lose control?"

"Let's see, shall we?"

This time I'm braced for it, or maybe I've just reached some kind of weirdness quotient. We're back where we started, at the kitchen table. But this time, it's the whole family. My father, my mother, and five children I sort of recognize as older versions of my younger siblings. A girl who must be Mandy, her body starting to stretch and grow into puberty, is the first to notice us, but my father isn't too far behind.

"Who are you? How did you get here?"

Part of me wants to flinch, to cower in the face of his anger. I can see that reaction in the stillness of my siblings, the way Mandy is trying to disappear into her chair, the way Chris won't look up from his plate.

But he doesn't have any power over me. He hasn't for a long time. Even if I were physically here, I'm taller than he is now. Stronger, probably. I don't have to be afraid of him.

He should be afraid of me. And I know how to make him afraid.

"John." The fear in his eyes sharpens when I say his name, and part of me loves it, drinks it in like water. "I would say 'be not afraid' but you have a lot to be afraid of, don't you?"

He gapes at me, his eyes wide and terrified.

"You are not a Godly man, John McCalester. You abuse the trust your wife and children place in you and you call it God's will, but God has nothing to do with it. You are selfish, breaking them to satisfy your own need for control."

Jaws are dropping around the table, but I'm on too much of a roll to stop now.

"You've already driven your oldest daughter away, made her change her name, and your other children will follow if you don't mend your ways--"

"Who are you to tell me what to do?" he interrupts. The fear is still there, but he's covering it with a layer of bluster, trying to save face. "Who are you to tell me what God would want? You're nothing but a demon, sent here to test me! Whom the Lord loveth, he chastiseth--"

I wasn't planning to reach for Dŵr's power. It's just there, suddenly, filling me up to the brim, vibrating through me, begging to be used. It's the easiest thing in the world to reach out, to stop the words in my father's throat, to freeze him where he stands as I walk toward him.

Out of the corner of my eye, I notice that my hands are glowing, but I'm much more focused on the fear redoubling in his eyes.

"Love? Is it love to cut your children out of your life when they disagree with you? Is it love to control their every action like some sort of dictator? Is it love to make them ashamed, to feel like they're dirty and wrong? Is that love? Even Paul would disagree with you."

I feel like a giant, standing here almost nose to nose with him. With Dŵr's power swirling through my body, I can see his heart beating in his chest, his lungs working to carry air through his body.

It would be so easy. The power wants to be used. I could reach out with it, fill his lungs with water, or just stop his heart in his chest. He couldn't stop me.

Merlin could stop me, but he still stands where we were at first. Watching me. Waiting. I can see it on his face; he won't stop me.

When I turn back, my eyes move over my siblings--the ones that are left, anyway. They're all scared, too--well, that's fair. I would've been scared too, if a strange glowing woman magically appeared at the dinner table. But in every set of eyes, especially Mandy's, I see something else.

Hope.

"You have a choice," I say. My voice is surprisingly calm. "You can leave this house now, and stay away until you've learned how to actually love your children. Or you can die."

I give that a moment to sink in before I relax my grip on his vocal cords.

"Who--what--" he sputters. "I don't--"

"I need your answer."

His face hardens. "I rebuke you, Satan. In the name of Jesus Christ--"

For a moment, I don't know if I can go through with it. I hesitate. And in that moment, I see Mandy's shoulders slump, see the resignation in her body, the fear and pain and the knowledge that there's no escape.

When I stop his heart, quick and painless, I expect to feel regret, or sadness.

I don't. The only thing I feel is a weary satisfaction as he slumps to the floor.

"Will this cause problems for them?" I ask Merlin. "Should we take the body?"

"He suffered a heart attack," Merlin said. "There will

be no signs of foul play. And I will ensure that they do not suffer from the lack of his income."

I nod, turning to my mom. She looks dazed, like she's already blocking out almost everything that just happened. "Call 911. Tell them he just collapsed."

She doesn't move, but Mandy pushes out of her seat, going for the land line on the counter.

The last thing I see before we disappear is her looking at me, her mouth forming the words "thank you."

"Well." I sink down to sit on the platform. "Is it time for the memory wipe?"

"Why would you think that?"

I blink up at Merlin. "Um, because I used Dŵr's power to murder someone? Pretty sure that counts as failing the test."

He smiles, but there's an edge to it that reminds me of the scar on his face, of the fact that he stood at Arthur's side during battle. "You used the power to stop a man from further abusing his children. You offered him a choice, a chance to change. He refused to take it. What did I say to you before we began?"

"With great power comes great responsibility." The quote still feels incongruous, so much so that I barely manage not to roll my eyes.

"Your father was given power over his children. He did not take responsibility for the damage his actions caused. And when that damage was pointed out to him, he refused to stop."

It makes a certain amount of sense, but I still feel guilty, deep down. "Yeah, but--" I stop, not sure how to put that into words.

"You used your power to protect those who could not protect themselves. I did not create these trials lightly." Merlin says. "But I needed to know that, in protecting humanity from the Fae, I wouldn't be handing them over to someone far worse. Someone who would try to destroy others, rather than protecting them."

Despite everything, I think this is the moment that I first really grasp the magnitude of the Jewels, the power they contain. Like, really get it, deep in my gut and my bones.

"I don't know if I can do this." My voice is small, so quiet it almost gets lost in the weight of the silence that had fallen between us.

"I promised you a choice," Merlin says. His voice is equally quiet, his face utterly serious as he meets my eyes. "So I will tell you now; that promise will stand until you use the four Jewels together. Until then, you can return them to their safe places, leave them to wait for the the next Chosen. But once you take them up and use their magic together, they will be sealed to you for the rest of your life."

My mouth opens, then closes again without me speaking. Everything inside me is screaming to stop, to get out. Well. Almost everything. It's not that I don't grasp the situation. I really, really do. And I know any reasonable person would tell me to pass, to step aside and let someone else do the world saving.

But I've never responded well to being told what to do.

"Think about it," Merlin says finally. "You have time."

I open my eyes and find myself standing in the real temple, with Dŵr casting its shifting light on my face, Merlin's words echoing in my head.

Somehow I don't think I'll be able to do much else.

32

I pick up the last Jewel, holding it in shaking hands. I did it. I passed through the Trials, earned the chance to use all four Jewels. All that's left is to seal the Fae Queens back into Underhill, make all of us safe forever.

Hands close on my arms, harsh and implacable. Confused, I look from Ben to Jack and back again, but they aren't looking at me.

They're looking at her.

Even while I struggle, I don't know that I can blame them. Talaith is coldly, terribly beautiful, pale and cold as ice, unnaturally red hair cascading over her shoulders in perfect curls. Even knowing that she has enough power to squash me like a bug doesn't change the compulsion to look at her.

"Good work, my pet." She sweeps toward me, takes the

375

Jewel from my hands like I only exist to give her things. "Do you know, I never thought you could actually do it?"

"Why?" I choke on the word, but I force it out.

She shrugs one slim, gorgeous shoulder. "Why not? If you failed, I lost nothing important. Besides, it was amusing. Taking your memories, letting you think you were free. Letting you think they really loved you."

I do my best not to react, but her gorgeous lavender eyes sparkle with amusement.

"Oh, my dear." She purses her lips in mock-sympathy, patting my cheek. "Jack there was a Fae Knight. He knows the delight of serving a Queen. No human woman could compare. The changeling was always Fae-touched; you never stood a chance. And what sort of treasure could you offer a dragon that he would value?"

"You're lying." My voice shakes, one more humiliation, one more stone to add to the crushing weight of my failure.

She smiles. "I have no need to lie, little human. I've won. But you deserve a reward for serving me so well."

With a snap of her fingers, Ben and Jack start moving, pulling me along with them. I start to fight when I see where we're going, but I don't even slow them down.

The cage is made of gold and studded with gemstones, faceted into sharp points that scratch me as they shove me inside. I don't know what's worse, the way the gems turn red as they drink the blood they've drawn, or the blank adoration on Jack and Ben's faces as they turn back to Talaith, waiting for instructions.

She ignores them, reaching through the bars to drag a razor-sharp fingernail down my cheek, slicing my skin open. I refuse to give her the satisfaction of a noise, but my knees wobble as she runs her fingertip over the wound, bringing it to her mouth and sucking it clean.

"Just wait, my pet," she says. "I'm going to give you a front-row seat for humanity's enslavement. You, alone, will have your mind intact, the better to fully appreciate what is happening."

She pauses, her smile widening when I make no response. Without warning, she wheels toward Jack, a knife at his throat before I can blink. "What do you say, pet?"

I swallow, hard. Jack just stands there, his eyes empty., his throat bared and vulnerable as a thin line of blood trickles down from the blade.

"Thank you."

ᛋᚱᚺ

I WAKE up with a scream choked in my throat, shaking as I sit up in the dark.

"Claire! Oh, thank fuck." Jack drags me into his arms, holds me a little too hard. "I had the worst fucking dream."

"Not as bad as mine." Ben wraps around me from the other side, his grip just as fierce.

I hold them back as best I can, still shaking. "Must be the night for it. I--"

The bedroom door bangs open. I nearly scream before I identify the silhouette in the doorway as Mal, already stalking over to the bed. "We all did," he says. "The bond is growing stronger."

"Wait." Ben blinks, his lashes brushing against my face. "We all had the same dream?"

"I believe it originated with Claire," Mal says. He sits down on Jack's side of the bed with none of his usual grace, just collapses heavily. "But I was drawn in, and I sensed the two of you there as well. Although I could not reach any of you to break you out of it."

I sigh, as much as I can when I'm being nearly crushed between Jack and Ben. "Great. Now I'm sucking you into my nightmares. This is just a laugh a minute, huh?"

"It's not your fault." Jack pulls back just enough to look me in the face. "And honestly, after everything? Especially what you told us about that last Trial? I'd be surprised if you weren't having the occasional nightmare."

"Jack is correct." Mal's voice cracks on a yawn. His cheek is creased from the pillow, his eyes heavy with sleep. Seeing him like this is almost more intimate than fucking him, in a way. "I can teach you shielding techniques, if you wish, or ways to pull yourself out of such dreams quickly. But this is most certainly not your fault."

Ben yawns, too, pulling me back down to lie with him. "Tomorrow, though. Right now, I think we could all use some sleep."

"Of course." Mal goes to stand, but stops when Jack reaches for him, wraps a hand around his wrist.

"Stay," Jack says. I can't see his face, but from his tone of voice, I can picture what he looks like, the hesitant question in his eyes. "I mean, if you want to. No one--you shouldn't be alone after that. You should be here. With us."

Mal looks over at Ben and I, his face nearly inscrutable. But I've learned to read his eyes, or maybe it's the telepathic bond he keeps talking about. Either way, I can practically feel how much he wants to do as Jack asked. "If--are you--"

Ben moves closer to his edge of the bed, taking me with him. "Plenty of room, man. And Jack's right. You don't have to be alone, if you don't want to be."

"Claire?"

I tug Jack back against me, leaving him facing Mal, one arm stretched out invitingly across the space we've made. "Come to bed, Mal."

He only hesitates for a moment more before sliding under the covers, still holding himself a little stiffly. Finally, when Jack makes an impatient noise, hauling him closer and closing his eyes, he relaxes.

Which Is when I realize the reason I can see all of this is the light coming in through the open door. "Shit. Who's gonna close the door?"

"Not it." Jack and Ben both say the words at the same moment.

Mal just sighs, slipping a hand free of the blankets and waving. The door swings gently shut, filling the room with darkness again. "Good night."

I'm not expecting to sleep again anytime soon. The memory of Talaith's face, the malevolent pleasure as she licked my blood off her fingertip, as she held a knife to Jack's throat, is too clear, too vivid in my memory. I would rather face a thousand sleepless nights than see that again, ever.

Claire, Mal's voice rumbles in my head. *I will wake you if I feel you slipping into a nightmare again. I was taken by surprise earlier, but it will not happen again. Sleep. You need your rest.*

He's right. I know he's right. Tomorrow we go back to Atlantis for the third trial. Who knows what I might do, what mistakes I might make, if I'm sleep-deprived, my brain foggy with exhaustion. But every time I close my eyes, I see Talaith, smiling at me.

I see. Mal's mental "voice" is warm and sympathetic. *I can help you sleep, if you consent.*

I concentrate on forming the thought, on sending it in his direction. I don't want to wake Jack or Ben, not with this. *Please.*

Relax. I have you.

At first I'm not sure what's happening, but then it becomes unmistakable. Relaxation sweeps up my body, starting at my toes and rising like a warm bath. My muscles feel pleasantly heavy, sinking into the mattress.

The last thing I remember before slipping back into sleep is Mal's mental whisper, so quiet I'm not sure if I've imagined it or not.

Rest, love. I'll keep you safe.

ᛋᚱᚼ

I SHOULD PROBABLY BE WORRIED that having a dragon teleport me to the lost city of Atlantis so I can talk to Merlin about getting a magic gem is becoming so normal.

Hell, there are a lot of things I should be worried about.

But for right now, my attention is focused on the task at hand. I kiss my boys, give Rhea a nod, and reach for Dŵr. For once, I'm ready as the world changes around me, as I find myself in Merlin's temple one more time.

"The last trial," Merlin greets me. "Are you ready?"

"I have no idea." I'm pretty sure there's no point in lying to actual Merlin, so I don't even bother. "After the first two, I couldn't tell you what I expect. Was that the idea?"

He smiles. "I didn't do it on purpose, but I probably should have. Being ready for the unexpected is one of the best lessons a magic-user can learn. Especially one who plans to go up against a Fae Queen."

I sink down to sit cross-legged across from him. "Before we get started--will I see you again? If I make it through this, and I have Dŵr?"

"There are three more Jewels," he says. "And three Trials for each. But regardless of what happens here today, Claire, I promise. You have not seen the last of me."

"Cool." That sounds lame, but I can't think of anything less embarrassing to follow up with it, so I forge ahead. "What's today's rune?"

He sketches a lightning-bolt shape in the air between us. For the first time, I catch how he does it, the tiny flow of power he pushes out and leaves glowing in the wake of his finger. "Sowilo. The sun."

But that's not the only meaning, right?"

"Sowilo represents your energy centers, power. Victory." He looks me over critically. "You have no training, but your body is channeling magic instinctively. This will only take you so far, particularly with the power of one or more Jewels at your disposal, as you discovered after the first Trial. You must learn to use it consciously, unless you want to end up burning yourself out."

"From the way you said that, I'm guessing it doesn't just mean eating Cheetos on the couch in my pajamas?"

He snorts. "Indeed, not. As I warned you during the first Trial, the best scenario would be you losing your ability to channel magic. At worst, your mind, your spirit, might die. Or your body might simply burn up from the force of it."

I blow out a breath. "Cool. But you're gonna teach me, right?"

"I will endeavor to do so. But I can only teach you the

basic principles. It will be up to you to practice, to hone your power until it serves you like a familiar sword."

"Man, sometimes I forget you literally knew Arthur and then you say something like that." I grin at him.

He smiles back, but I can see the solemnity hiding behind it. And he's right. As nifty as this little time-turning pocket we're using is, I can't stay here forever. I'm going to have to work at this.

Good thing I've never been afraid of work.

"I know," he says. "That is but one of the reasons you are Chosen. But come. We have work to do."

He takes me to what must be a fjord, even though I've only ever seen pictures. Which didn't do it justice, by the way. The air is crisp and chilly, carrying the salt of the ocean up to as as we stand on top of a cliff.

"This is a powerful place," Merlin says. "Three elements meeting here, earth, air, and water. Can you use your Sight on your own?"

I feel like a kid coloring clumsily with crayons in front of a master artist, fumbling through failed attempt after failed attempt to open my inner eyes. But Merlin just smiles and nods when I finally manage, inside the glow of what must be his shields.

"Very good," he says. "Now I want you to look down at yourself. You've heard of chakras, yes?"

"Yeah." When I obey him and look down, I get a little lost in what I see for a minute. My body, yes, but overlaid with that is a small galaxy of energy, flowing out from the center and back again. Looking more closely, I see that my galaxy comparison is more apt that I thought. Hovering just above my breastbone is a spinning wheel of gold energy, a small sun radiating power out through my body. There are more, too. One over my stomach, one just below my navel and--"is that one on my butt?"

"Technically your tailbone." Despite the correction, Merlin doesn't look upset about my question. "There is also one on your throat, between your eyebrows, and at the crown of your head. You can't see them with your physical eyes, but I want you to look for them with your Sight."

I'm pretty sure complaining isn't going to get me anywhere, just like with any other impossible thing he's asked of me so far. It takes a bit of work, like everything else. But the Sight doesn't require me to use my eyes. Once I remember that, I do better, locating all seven of the chakras while mentally apologizing to every basic yoga bitch I've mentally mocked for using the word. Although I'm pretty sure they didn't have Merlin teaching them.

"Just as with your body's muscles, the more you practice, the more power you can channel," Merlin says when he's satisfied with my adventures in Sight. "You didn't begin with lifting hundreds of pounds. So we will begin with a small amount of power and continue until you can control it consistently."

"Okay." I roll my neck from side to side. "So, uh, how do I do this? Here? Atlantis has all the water it needs."

"Here," he agrees. "See the rocks down there, blocking the entrance?"

Now that he points it out, I can see the line of rocks jutting up out of the water. "Yeah, what happened? Earthquake?"

"Yes. Eventually the rocks will be moved, but in the meantime, the people who live near here will go hungry once there are no more fish coming in. So we will do something about it. And if your control slips, the only things around to be hurt are the fish."

Not exactly the most inspiring pep talk ever. I take a breath. "Okay."

"Close your eyes and see the power around you," he instructs. "Reach for it."

It's a little easier than when I was using Dŵr the previous two times, like flexing a muscle I've already found. I manage to reach out and make contact with the power swirling lazily around us, pulling it in until I feel like I'm about to burst from it, light exploding out of me.

"Excellent," he says. "Now take all of that energy, pick one rock, and aim it."

I'm expecting this to be hard, too, but it's much like shooting cans off a log back home. Gotta love that Southern upbringing. Make sure your aim is good, take a breath, and let go.

The rock I chose explodes with a sound a lot like a gunshot, dust rising in a cloud around it.

"Exactly!" This is the most enthusiastic I've seen

Merlin; for all his approval before, this is the first time I've really felt like I made him proud. "Now. Do it again."

We repeat the process over and over again, rock after rock, until I've blasted a narrow opening into the rockfall, deep enough beneath the surface of the water that fish can come and go freely.

"How do you feel?" he asks.

I take a minute to take stock, now that I'm not lost in the rhythm of pulling power, aiming, letting it go. "Okay? A little tired, but I'm not drained."

"Very well. Now let's talk about shielding."

Unlike channeling power into the rocks, shielding takes a bit more work for me to learn. No matter how Merlin explains it, I struggle with the concept. If I manage to spread the power into a shield in front of me I leave myself open behind, or overhead. The little seeds Merlin flings at me don't really hurt, but I'm starting to get frustrated.

"This isn't working," I finally say. I'd like to believe I'm not pouting, but I'm pretty sure that was a whine in my voice.

"No, you're right." He stops for a moment, looking off into the distance. "Sometimes I forget that the way I learned was not always the best. Perhaps another approach is called for."

I only realize my mouth is hanging open when it starts to dry out. I close it quickly, hopefully before he notices.

"Close your eyes."

With a carefully-hidden sigh, I comply. Sometimes it seems like all of Merlin's instructions start with me closing my eyes. But the salt air is kind of drying, so it's not the worst thing ever. Even if I am getting hungry.

"Notice your skin. Feel where it ends, and the air, or your clothes begin. Focus on that boundary."

I'm pretty sure I wouldn't have been able to do this a month ago, or even a week ago, even though I've had to develop a pretty good awareness of my body to lift weights correctly. But right away I can feel the difference between this and those failed efforts. My skin doesn't just contain my physical body, it contains the energy within it as well, holding it until I need it.

"Good, good." Merlin's voice almost startles me, I'm so focused on finding all the edges of my body, being aware of all of them at once. "Now pull that power over you, like another skin."

When I finally figure out how to do what he said, it feels a lot like Mal helping me relax the other night. Like warmth, rising slowly up until it envelops my entire body, cocooning me in safety. I don't even have to ask Merlin if I did it right; I can feel it, from the crown of my head to the soles of my feet.

"Yes!" A small flurry of seeds comes flying at me from all directions, but I don't even feel them as they bounce off my shields. "Yes, exactly like that."

Before I can make any kind of smug answer, though, I start to notice the telltale signs that I've over-exerted myself. My legs feel like they might give out if I take a step, and all of my muscles are quivering and shaky. The warmth of my shield disappears a few seconds later.

Merlin doesn't look disappointed, though. Or even concerned. "You remember what I said when we began? As you practice, your ability to channel power to your shields will grow. And you should practice, whenever you think about it. But for now, I should return you to your mates so that you can recover."

Before I can complain or protest his wording, he's gone, and I'm back in the temple.

With the Jewel in my hands.

"You did it!" Ben picks me up and twirls me around, setting me back on my feet with elaborate care, like he just realized I'm holding the magical equivalent of a nuclear weapon.

"I guess?" After the first two Trials, that seems kind of anticlimactic. No risk of possibly killing myself with power, no magical execution. Just--lessons. "He didn't say--but I have it, so--maybe?"

"Congratulations!" Rhea waits until Jack and Mal have both hugged me, not-so-subtly checking me for injuries or other problems, before moving in. "If you are holding Dŵr, I believe we can assume that you have safely passed all three Trials. Can the four of you stay for dinner?"

I exchange glances with Jack, Ben, and Mal, but I see my own feelings reflected in their eyes. "Right now, I'd really like to go home. Maybe we can come back another time?"

"You are always welcome here." Rhea kisses both my cheeks before letting go. "The city owes you a debt. If you ever have need of us, you only have to call."

Not sure how to respond to that, I just nod. "Thank you. For everything."

She steps back, smiling gently. "No. Thank you."

I take Mal's hand, cradling Dŵr to my chest with the other arm, and then we're gone.

ᛋᚱᚻ

"Well." I kind of want to set the Jewel down somewhere; holding it is making me nervous. But the idea of setting it down also makes me nervous. Like, this thing is pretty much the definition of tremendous cosmic power all by itself, never mind the other three. I can feel the power coming off it like heat off a stove. "So."

The guys all seem to share my hesitation. We've been standing like this ever since Mal zapped us back home, in a loose semi-circle in the library, just staring at it.

"How are we supposed to keep this thing safe?" Jack finally breaks the silence. "Not that we don't have some pretty heavy-duty protections on this place, but I wouldn't bet on them holding up to a Fae Queen. And if they find out we have it, more than one of them are going to come looking."

"We could take it to the Seven?" As soon as the words are out of my mouth, I want to take them back. I don't want Dŵr so far out of my reach. Not that I don't trust Ethan--okay, Ethan might conveniently "forget" where he put it, but I'm pretty sure I could get Tori to make him cough it up. But--the Jewel isn't mine, exactly, but the Trials have clearly formed some kind of connection between it and me. Leaving it with someone else feels wrong.

Mal clears his throat. "If I may offer a possible alternative? My hoard is protected not only by my magics, but those of my clan. Even the Queens are not powerful enough to challenge the dragon shifter clans for territory. And I could create a portal from here to there, so you could retrieve it whenever you wish."

Jack and Ben both look as relieved as I feel. "Yeah. Let's do tha--"

Before I can finish my sentence, a really rough-looking guy in a red hat appears in front of us in a puff of smoke. His eyes light up at the sight of the Jewel. "Talaith sends her regards," he says as he lunges for it.

All three guys move to block him, but he slides through like they're not even there, evading their hands-- and in Jack's case, his knife--with ease. He's inches away from Dŵr, from taking it--

--I reach for Dŵr's power, concentrating as hard as I can on stopping him--

--a wall of blue-swirling light springs up between us--

--he runs into the wall, going too fast to stop--

--light flashes, bright enough that I close my eyes.

When I open them, the only sign that he was ever there is the hat, rocking gently on the floor. It looks more red than brown, now, with bits flaking off and falling to the floor.

We all stand there, staring at it for a moment.

Well done, Merlin's voice says in my head. *You are a worthy protector. I will see you soon, Claire.*

"Huh. Apparently that was the last trial," I say. All three guys turn to look at me, eyes wide.

"Well," Mal says. "I think it's time to go."

33

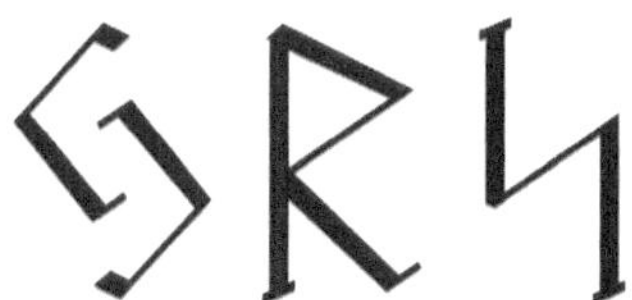

Standing in Mal's shielded spell room, I take a deep breath.

"Are you ready?" Mal asks.

"Ready to not have a Fae's hooks in my head?" I laugh a little. "Um, I've been ready."

It might be easier if you close your eyes, he says in my head.

Always with the eye closing, I grumble. I can feel his amusement when I do as he says, sort of warm and bubbly inside my mind.

Once my eyes are closed, my Sight active, he nudges at me. *Here. Let me show you.*

I let my point of view follow him into the sparking web of energy that it takes me a minute to identify as my brain. We spiral deeper and deeper until I see it.

Yes, Mal says. *The compulsion*

I suck in a breath. There's a tangle of dark, angry red wrapped around the paths of light, pulsing ominously. *Could you always see this?*

Not always. His mental voice is sad. *It was very cleverly hidden; until it was activated, there was nothing to see, although it is certainly what was causing the headaches. You are very strong, to have dealt with it for so long.*

I always was stubborn. I shrug. *Now what?*

Mal directs my attention to where the compulsion appears to be rooted, throbbing with the beat of my heart. *We will need to cut it free. You should warn Jack and Ben. The process may be uncomfortable.*

Speaking out loud takes a moment of adjustment. "Mal says this is gonna hurt like a son of a bitch. So don't freak out if I start making weird noises and stuff."

I can feel Mal's amusement even as I open my eyes. Neither Ben or Jack look excited about it, but they both nod their acceptance before I close my eyes again.

You will most likely want to draw on Dŵr *for this,* Mal says. *Water is best for cleansing, and you don't want to exhaust yourself.*

Okay. Reaching for my link with Dŵr, I let the cool flow of its power rush into me until I'm brimming with it. *Now what?*

Mal "reaches" for me somehow. *May I?*

Agreeing mentally, I let him guide me. Working

together, we form a blade out of Dwr's power, using it to slice through the root of the compulsion.

It burns, and I'm grateful Mal is there to steady me. My body starts to shake, little whimpers that I can't bite back.

I'm sorry. Despite the genuine regret I can feel, Mal doesn't hesitate, where I would've winced back. Wielding the power with surgical precision, he cuts the compulsion free, burning it to metaphorical ash. *If we leave even the slightest thread, the compulsion will remain. We--you would have to go through this again. It has to end. Now.*

So we end it, me feeding him the power, him searching out the insidious growth of the compulsion and destroying it.

I think maybe at one point I start to scream.

An eternity later, Mal says, *it is done.*

I open my eyes reluctantly. Even though it's probably psychosomatic, I feel a little hollow. Or maybe that's from channeling all the power. *Thank you.*

If there is anything you need from me, ever, you have only to ask, Mal says. *You are one of the strongest people I know. I am honored by your trust.*

Before I can come up with some kind of response to that, his mental presence retreats, fading back to the edges of my awareness.

"Is it done?" Jack asks.

"We have removed the compulsion," Mal confirms. "I

have stopped shielding Claire, and she shows no signs of needing to chase after another Jewel."

I open my eyes just in time to see realize I'm sagging into Mal's arms. It seems to take Mal by surprise too, but he manages to support me. Ben tries to help, but Jack goes to pull me into his arms at the same time. Somehow we all end up sitting tangled together in a pile on the floor of Mal's living room, relief so thick in the air that I almost choke on it.

"You did it," Jack says thickly. "I was so worried--and there was nothing I could do--but you did it. It's done."

"I mean, we do still have to find three Jewels," Ben points out. "And there are the trials. And--"

Jack smacks him lightly on the head. "Just--hush, okay? Just for a minute."

Ben grins at me, but he subsides, letting us savor the moment.

ᛋᚱᚻ

When we finally try to stand up, it quickly becomes apparent that Mal and I are weak-kneed, exhausted, and slightly dizzy from using enough power to burn Talaith's compulsion out of my mind. Ben and Jack support us, but they're kind of unsteady, too. We only run into walls a couple of times on our way out of the room.

Okay, five times.

Mal manages to shepherd us into his bedroom, graced

with a bed the size of two normal king mattresses. Not that it matters, since we all end up huddled together in the middle anyway, reluctant to not be touching.

Even though Ben and Jack hadn't officially been involved in the magic, they seem just as wiped out as Mal and I. Mal manages to get us all to take a few sips of water before Jack pulls him down onto the bed.

"Why am I so tired?" Jack asks.

Mal looks a little embarrassed. "With our connection, Claire and I may have drawn on you for the energy we needed to completely eliminate the compulsion. I apologize for doing so without asking you."

Jack shakes his head. "You never have to ask, man. Neither of you."

"Same. Now go to sleep," Ben says, his jaw cracking on a yawn.

"Way ahead of you," Jack murmurs. He buries his face in the pillow, one arm slung over my waist. "Do dragon shifters even sleep?"

"This one does," Mal mumbles. "Or I would, if you would stop talking."

I smile at Jack's disgruntled noise, giggling silently as it morphs into a snore. Ben opens his eyes long enough to smile down at me before he falls asleep, too, snuggled against my side.

Cocooned in their warmth, I succumb to the inevitable and close my eyes.

ᛋᚱᚼ

I DRIFT SLOWLY AWAKE, sprawled over Ben, his mouth gentle on mine. I sigh into the kiss, letting myself bask in the feeling of warmth and safety.

"There you are," he says. "How are you feeling?"

"I should be asking you that." I pull back enough to see his face. "I'm not the one who got accidentally magic-sucked without anyone asking."

He shrugs. "Been better, been worse. Any day we don't die, or come close, is a good day."

I let myself sit back a little, pressing back against his erection. "So you don't want to do anything about this?"

"I didn't say that." He grins wickedly. "Wanna play a game?"

"What kind of game?"

That grin widens. "The kind where we see how many times I can make you come before you get so noisy you wake up Jack and Mal."

I glance over to where Jack's face is pressed into the pillow. Mal is curled up behind him, one hand resting lightly on Jack's shoulder, even in sleep.

"What kind of incentive do I have to be quiet? If they wake up, they'll probably just join in. How do you know I won't wake them up on purpose?"

"Because," he says. "If you can come five times without waking them up, we'll all fuck you. If you wake them up, I'll just fuck you while they watch."

I try to hide the shiver that runs through me at his words. From the way his eyes darken, I don't think I managed it, but I have to try. "Either way, I get fucked."

He's full-on smirking now. "Bet you can't."

"Fine," I growl. Dammit, he knows I can't resist the challenge. "Do your worst."

"Oh, I plan to." He tugs my t-shirt up over my head. "Game on."

ᛋᚱᚺ

I BURY my face in the pillow, my breath sobbing out as I feel my fifth orgasm building. Somehow I'd managed to stay quiet when Ben pinned me down and toyed with my breasts, licking and sucking and biting, rolling the nipples between his fingers until I came.

For my second and third orgasms, he'd licked his way down my body and buried his face in my pussy, his shoulders pressing my thighs apart, no matter how reflexively I tried to close them as he took me apart with his mouth.

He fucked me with his fingers for number four, moving up so he could use his mouth and his free hand on my breasts, driving me crazy. Then he had me turn over and slowly, teasingly worked the biggest butt plug into my ass, taking his time. I'm seriously about ten seconds from begging.

Now he zeroes in on my clit, stroking with one hand. His other hand is firm on my lower back, holding me in place when I try to pull away from the sensations that are almost too intense, driving me up and up and up until I come again, barely choking back a scream.

"Good girl," he murmurs in my ear. Curling himself over me, his big hands stroke and pet me as I shake through the aftermath of my orgasm. "You did so well. You were so quiet."

"Very quiet," Jack agrees. "This asshole, on the other hand--"

When I can turn my head, I see him curled up on his side, his eyes hot on me.

"That was five, right?" He stretches like a cat, his body one long, lean line. "So do we get to play now, Benny?"

"I don't know," Ben says. "How long have you been awake?"

Jack grins. "Dunno about Mal, but I've been awake the whole time."

Mal sits up behind him, looking more rumpled than usual, "Likewise."

Ben opens his mouth to say something, but Jack raises his hand.

"But, Claire didn't wake us up. You did. So she still won."

"Fair enough." Ben shrugs.

Grinning, Jack pulls me in for a kiss. I whimper when my nipples rub against the soft cotton of his t-shirt, so keyed up that even that tiny burst of sensation was almost too much.

"Relax, sweetheart." Jack lays me back on the bed and pulls away to strip off his shirt. "We'll take care of you."

Mal nods agreement behind him, nimble fingers unbuttoning his henley and pulling it over his head.

I lean back against the pillows, watching impatiently as they strip. Jack shucks off his clothes in record time, stretching out alongside me, drowning me in long, deep, drugging kisses. A moment later, Ben is on my other side, nibbling at my ear and leaving a trail of long, sucking kisses down my neck.

When I pull back from Jack a little and open my eyes, Mal is standing naked at the end of the bed, looking more torn than he has since that first night in Atlantis, when Jack talked him into watching.

Jack notices him, too. "C'mere, Mal." He holds out a hand, still speaking in that low, rough voice. "Come give Claire a kiss."

Apparently dragon shifters aren't any more immune to that voice than regular mortals. Mal crawls up the bed toward me, muscles rippling under his skin. He hesitates just a bit when he comes to a stop, braced over me.

I slide my arms around his neck and pull him down for a kiss. He kisses me hot and wet, almost desperate, like he's afraid he'll be snatched away at any moment. Running soothing hands up and down his back, I let him take what he needs.

Finally he seems to calm, lifting his head to look into my eyes. "I believe Ben has a suggestion."

"Dude," Jack protests. "What do I keep saying about that shit?"

Mal rolls his eyes. "I did not invade the privacy of Ben's mind. He's practically shouting it; I'm surprised you didn't notice."

Ben grins. "We all know Jack's a little slow, Mal."

"Sometimes," Mal agrees.

He leans over slightly to murmur in Jack's ear. Jack's grin goes wider and wider the longer Mal talks. If I hadn't been watching so closely, I might have missed the goosebumps rising on Jack's skin, or the way he shivers just a little when Mal's lips brush his cheek.

I raise an eyebrow at Ben and he gives me a tiny nod in return. It's not just my imagination, then.

"Hey." Jack pulls my attention back to him. "You're thinking too much. Close your eyes."

I do as he asks, enjoying the feeling of warm, calloused hands sliding across my skin. Two tongues circle my nipples at the same moment a third licks across my clit. I gasp, my eyes flying open, arching up against three sets of hands that pin me firmly to the mattress.

Ben lifts his head from my breast, looking down to where Mal has just curled his tongue inside my pussy. "Lick her clit, Mal," he says. "Make her come one more time before we fuck her."

I start to shake and shiver when Mal goes back to my clit, licking a teasing circle around it.

"Yeah, right there," Ben says. "She's close, aren't you, baby?"

I open my mouth to answer, but Jack grazes his teeth across my nipple, Ben squeezes the other one, and Mal slips two fingers inside my pussy. Losing my words, I jolt up, screaming as I come.

Jack pulls me over until I'm straddling him, licking into my mouth for a deep, filthy kiss. "Gonna fuck you now, sweetheart," he murmurs. Pulling away, he positions his cock for me to sink down on. He smooths his hands up my back, holding me close against him. Kissing me again and again, he moves lazily inside me.

We both suck in a breath, breaking the kiss, as Ben eases the butt plug out. I let my forehead drop onto Jack's shoulder, taking deep breaths as Ben pushes slowly inside me.

He kisses my shoulder, rocking into me just a little deeper, making me whimper, overwhelmed by the sensation. "You ready for Mal, baby?" he murmurs.

Lifting my head, I nod, opening my eyes, shuddering when Jack and Ben begin to move inside me.

"Mal, get over here and fuck her mouth," Jack groans.

The bed shifts under us. I turn my head to see Mal move toward us. He kneels by my head, taking his cock in hand and lifting it toward my mouth.

"Open," he orders. I hurry to comply, swirling my tongue around the head. I can't move much, pinned between Ben and Jack like this. So I let my mouth go loose, let him fuck into it, slip his fingers into my hair, holding me in place for his thrusts.

It doesn't take Mal long to pick up on the rhythm that Jack and Ben are setting. Soon I'm lost in the push and pull of their cocks inside me. the wet, slick slide of Jack fucking my pussy, the dark, shivery feeling of Ben thrusting into my ass, the heavy weight of Mal's cock on my tongue.

Ben's hands find my breasts and I whimper, shaking between them. It's so good, so much, but my nerves feel scraped raw, strung tight and oversensitized.

"Can you come for us one more time, baby?" Ben scrapes his teeth over the side of my throat.

I nod as best I can, moaning when the movement makes Mal's fingers catch in my hair. He swears, tugging again on purpose, just hard enough to make me moan again.

"C'mon, sweetheart," Jack growls. He works his hand between us to find my clit. "Come for us."

Just like that, I do, groaning around Mal's cock.

My orgasm sets off a chain reaction, like all of them had been barely hanging on, waiting for me to come. Mal groans, thrusting just a tiny bit deeper, his fingers tightening in my hair as he comes, shuddering, the salty taste of him coating my tongue.

Jack throws his head back, his other hand tightening

on my hip, pushing up inside me as he comes. Ben's teeth close over my shoulder, his hands squeezing my breasts. He gives me a couple more hard, deep thrusts, before he comes too.

Limp and sated, I allow myself to be shifted around until the men are satisfied with the cuddling arrangements. I end up half sprawled across Jack, still flat on his back, with Ben curled up against my back. Mal settles on Jack's other side, his chest heaving, arm reaching across Jack to rest on my waist.

"Mal?" Jack says eventually. His eyes are still closed.

"Yes?"

"Are you hugging me?"

I look over just in time to see Mal roll his eyes. "We do share a profound bond, remember?"

"Dude." Jack sounds like he's complaining, but I notice he's not trying to get out from under Mal's arm. "You've got better people skills than this."

Mal just shrugs. "Given that I just had a sexual encounter with Claire, you, and your brother, it seems silly to quibble over a little skin contact."

Jack starts sputtering. "You...we..."

"Furthermore," Mal continues, "it seems that, if we were to continue this relationship in the future, we might eventually want to explore other positions."

Ben's chest shakes with laughter behind me. "What'd you have in mind, Mal?"

Jack's mouth gapes open wide.

"Oh, I'm not terribly experienced, as far as dragons go." Mal's eyes sparkle with amusement when they meet mine. "But I'm sure there are a number of ways four bodies could fit together."

Ben kisses the back of my neck. "I bet you're right."

ᛋᚱᚻ

34

A few months later

"**B**en! Not now!" Pushing him off, I turn back toward the counter. "I have to cook!"

"C'mon." Pulling me back against him, he kisses the side of my neck. "You've been cooking for the past three days. It's gonna be fine. Everything's gonna be great."

I roll my eyes. "There's a schedule. Your moms are going to be here in two hours, plus Jack's badass bounty hunter best friend that I only found out about last week. I have to peel the potatoes so they can cook in time, and the green bean casseroles have to go in the oven soon, and so do the pies, and--"

"Whoa, whoa," he says. "Baby, you are officially way

too worked up about this. Everything is gonna be great. You and Jack have already cooked enough food for three times as many people as we invited. Everybody is gonna eat their body weight in food and then pass out. It'll be fine."

Despite myself, I can't help smiling. "I know. I just--I know you guys didn't really get to do the holiday thing growing up, and I haven't bothered since Jake died. I want it to be nice. Especially since all these people are coming. I'm going to meet your family and it's making me jittery."

He takes me by the shoulders, turning me around to face him. "Hey. You're our family. Yeah, Grace and Michelle and Mattie are, too, but they're not gonna give you any shit. If they do anything that makes you feel bad, we'll stop it. Or if we don't, Mal will."

"Worst thing that'll happen is Mattie hitting on you," Jack predicts. I didn't even notice him wandering into the kitchen, reaching for the unbaked apple pie on the counter. "Good thing you're not into girls."

I slap his hand away. "That's not cooked yet. And what makes you think I'm not into girls?"

His eyes widen and take on a faraway expression. Ben just shakes his head, but his voice is suddenly a little lower, rougher, when he says, "Great. You broke him."

"I'm not going to start making out with random girls for you to get your rocks off, Jack. Definitely not if you don't leave those pies alone until they're done."

"So you're saying there's a chance!"

ᛋᚱᚻ

In the end, Ben's right, not that I'm going to tell him that. Grace and Michelle are super nice and make appreciative noises over the meal while telling amusing stories about various hunting-related mishaps.

After all the stories Jack told me about Mattie and her exploits--once he mentioned her existence--I'm expecting a cross between Black Widow and Buffy. But while Mattie looks like someone who could kick my ass without breaking a sweat or a nail, she's clearly trying to be friendly. By the time dinner is over, she's already had us all laughing until we cry with her story about a hot yoga class where someone had incredibly smelly farts, but no one could figure out who.

It's hard to be intimidated by someone who's red in the face from laughing about farts.

Too full to take another bite, I look up from my conversation with Mattie on the pros and cons of different spells for protecting cloud storage when Grace and Michelle start clearing the table. "You don't have to do that!" I start to get up from my chair. "I can--"

Jack's hand on my shoulder pushes me gently back down into my chair. "You can sit down and let other people clean up. You've been cooking all week. The rest of us can take care of it."

"Absolutely," Grace says firmly. "It's the least we can do after that delicious meal."

"Agreed." Mal reaches past me to pick up the pitiful remnants of the mashed potatoes.

Kissing me lightly, Jack whisks our plates off the table and carries them into the kitchen.

"I have to say," Mattie says, "I haven't had a lot of Thanksgiving dinners, but this one might be the best. How many people get to eat dinner in a library?"

"It is pretty awesome," I agree. "We eat in here a lot. Better than that stupid cafeteria-style table in the kitchen. I don't know where I found that thing, but I'm gonna burn it one day."

Mattie shudders in agreement. "I know what you mean." She glances around, then leans in and lowers her voice. "So, you and Ben and Jack?"

I try to stop the goofy smile that crosses my face, but I'm pretty sure I'm not having much luck. Besides, Mattie would probably see through me anyway. "Yeah."

"Good," she says firmly. "I'd about given up on those two finding someone who could understand that they're a package deal. And someone who's cool with Jack and Mal's whole--thing. You're serious about this, right? Not just looking for some random hunter loving?"

The phrasing is so incongruous coming out of Mattie's coolly perfect face that I snort out a laugh before I can stop it. "Definitely serious. I wouldn't have made nearly as many pies if this was just a hookup."

"Excellent." She steeples her fingers together. "So how

long should we string Jack along before we tell him we're not going to make out?"

"Oh, I like the way you think." I smile wickedly. "We should be able to manage at least another two, maybe three hours if we play our cards right."

Mattie returns the smile with interest. "This is gonna be fun."

Jack comes back into the library but stops dead, eyes wide, as soon as he notices us smiling at each other. "Don't mind me," he says. "Just go back to whatever you were doing. Pretend I'm not here."

His hopeful look fades into a confused one when we both burst out laughing.

ᛋᚱᚻ

"EVERYTHING WAS SO DELICIOUS, CLAIRE," Michelle says. She settles back in at the table, smiling up at Grace as her wife comes in with a cup of coffee for each of them. "Thank you so much for having us."

"We were so glad you could come," I say. The guys clatter the dishes in the kitchen, laughing at something Mattie said, since she abandoned me with a smirk. A small, scared part of me wants to find an excuse to go join them, but I force myself to stay in my chair. "I know it meant a lot to Jack and Ben."

Grace tucks a strand of blonde hair behind her ear and

takes a sip of her coffee. She and Michelle are a study in contrasts; Grace's blonde curls, sweet face, and curvy body in sharp contrast to Michelle's close-cropped hair, brown skin, and slim frame. But they move around each other with an ease born of spending years together, ease and familiarity that has a lump rising in my throat. I want that for the four of us, that comfort with each other, that confidence in the other people.

"It means a lot to us that they've found you," Michelle says. "They've always had each other, but you balance them. It's easy to see, even just being here for a little while."

Grace nods her agreement. "I don't think I've ever seen them this happy. We did our best for them, but we've always wanted more for them than just hunting. You're good for them, honey."

Something, maybe the unconditional acceptance on their faces, has me blurting out something I haven't even been willing to face in my own head. "What if I'm not? This stuff with the Jewels--it's dangerous. What if they get hurt because of me?"

"Oh, Claire." Michelle sighs. "These boys have been putting themselves in the line of fire for years before they met you. Do you know the story of how we adopted them?"

I shake my head; that's not something they've ever gone into any detail about. "They just said you saved them."

"Their foster parents were Fae posing as human, the

kind of Fae that sucked the life force out of children," Grace says. The bald, flat words sound strange coming out of her pleasant, motherly face, but her eyes are hard, remembering. "Neither of those boys had ever heard about the Fae before, but by the time we figured out who we needed to take out, Jack and Ben had already gotten the rest of the kids out of the house and gotten in a few lucky hits."

"It's who they are," Michelle says. "They're always going to fight. And this--this is literally the fate of the world. You couldn't keep them out of it if you tried."

Grace grins wickedly, an expression I've seen on Jack and Ben's faces too many times to count. They may not be related by blood, but I can see the way their mothers shaped them, a thousand little movements and expressions they share. "You might have fun trying, though."

"Baby, now you embarrassed her." Michelle shakes her head. "I can't take you anywhere."

My face is hot, but I join in the laughter, picking up my cup. "You're right."

"Good," Grace says firmly. "Just keep repeating that. It's an excellent quality in a daughter-in-law."

Mattie laughs louder in the doorway behind me as I choke on my drink.

ᛋᚱᚺ

"See, I told you it'd be great." Ben wraps his arm around

my shoulder as we say goodbye to the last of our guests. Grace and Michelle are headed to France, on the trail of a lead that might help us deal with Jack's curse, and Mattie has a contract to pick up an incubus that's been draining women in the Twin Cities.

"Yeah, yeah, you told me so." I roll my eyes. "Now I'm gonna go sleep for a week."

Jack smirks. "Want some company?"

I sigh. "I said sleep, Jack. Something I doubt I'll get much of if you join me."

"We'll make it worth your while," he murmurs.

"Promise." Ben falls into step on my other side.

Mal grins at me from behind Jack. "I have some ideas."

"Sure, why not?" I speed up, pulling them toward the nearest bedroom. "I can always sleep after."

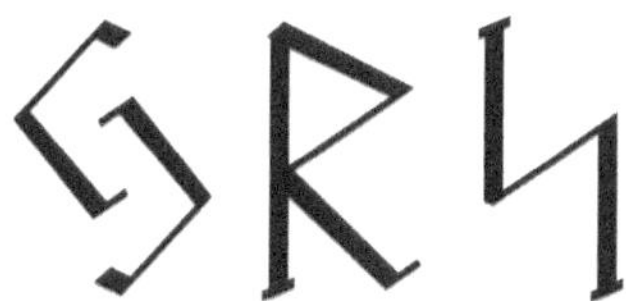

The half-feral Fae form a loose ring of nightmare monsters around the teenage girl, closing in one step at a time. A stupid person might think that the gaps between them offer a chance of escape. She knows better; her eyes dart toward the openings, but she makes no attempt to run. Just turns slowly, a futile attempt to keep them from getting behind her.

They stop moving. Hope flares in her eyes for a moment, only to die when the two Fae in front of her step aside, allowing someone else to pass through.

Unlike the horns and claws, teeth and tails, fur and feathers and scales of the Fae that have been hounding her, the woman looks almost human, if not for the cold, unnatural perfection of her features, the point of her ears., the aura of power that proclaims her a Fae Queen. Long, white-blonde *hair flows down her back in a silken cascade that reaches almost to her feet. The only point of color in her face is her eyes, an icy blue. She smiles as she walks forward, pale pink lips curving over perfect white teeth.*

The girl does not look reassured.

But she stands her ground as the Queen walks toward her, her chin lifted defiantly.

"Hello, my child," the Queen says. "You're going to help me find someone."

The girl shakes her head wordlessly.

The Queen's smile widens, becomes as cruel and predatory as any of the minions behind her. "Oh, I think you will, love."

At a gesture, two of the creatures take the girl's arms, holding her immobile. She tries to fight, but is helpless to move as the Queen lifts a hand, delicate fingers curled around a shard of ice.

Stabbing it into her chest in one swift motion, the Queen smiles as the girl screams.

BEN'S SCREAMS wake me up. He's sitting bolt upright in the enormous bed Mal had brought over from his hoard, eyes closed, screaming like he's being flayed alive.

Jack and Mal each have a hand on one of his shoulders. Jack talks to him, an endless stream of words that don't make any sense to me but probably would to Ben. If he was listening, and not screaming. Mal's forehead is furrowed in the way that tells me he's trying something magic to wake Ben up.

And failing.

He's also shivering, maybe because the blankets are in a tangled mess at the foot of the bed, so I wrap myself around him. His muscles are like iron under me, every one of them tensed.

And he still screams.

When he stops, abruptly, my ears ring with the suddenness of it. I pull back enough to look at him. His eyes are open now, confused when they take in my face. I probably look scared out of my mind.

"What?" he snaps. His body starts to shake.

"Dude, you were screaming," Jack says flatly. "Full-on blood-curdling horror movie screaming."

I tighten my grip, buring my face in his chest. "We couldn't wake you up. Even Mal couldn't--"

"I wouldn't," Mal corrects me. "You were not asleep, but in a trance. I felt it would be unwise to bring you out of it before it ended normally."

Ben scrubs his hands roughly over his face. "It's back," he says. "I had a vision."

Keep reading for information about how to keep up with new releases from Sierra Lane, plus sneak peeks at other books by her and other awesome authors!

ACKNOWLEDGMENTS

This is one of those things where I'm pretty sure I'm going to forget somebody, or a lot of somebodies. But I'll do my best, and if I forget you, know that it's not malicious, it's just that my brain is a leaky bucket right now after writing all these words.

First, to Taylor; if you hadn't introduced me to Supernatural, none of this would ever have happened. It's all because of you!!!

To everyone who commented on the fic that grew and metamorphosed into this novel, thank you for loving it and believing in it.

To the Epic Library Writing Group (of DOOM!) for being the first readers for my early chapters and helping me figure some stuff out. And for not judging me on my fithy, filthy smut.

To Ivy, for being SO EXCITED about this book that it helped propel me forward.

To the SPCOA, for listening to me gripe about this book over, and over, and over, and over, and over. For cheerleading me all the way to the finish line. I love you all!

To Kjerstin, Hannah, and Galen, for looking at the early draft and helping me figure out the problem areas. To Jenny especially, for calling me out on my first draft and helping me make it a better book!

To Tay and Tammy and Shelly for also listening to me whine and vent all of my feelings on so many occasions.

To every member of my online support system, you mean more to me than you know!

Always and forever, to Alex and Brittany For supporting me, believing that I could do this, reminding me that I have done it, for watching the kids when I needed to write or edit and picking up the slack. For talking me through my panics and holding me when I cry. For being there. I love you.

ABOUT THE AUTHOR

Sierra Lane has been making up stories ever since she was old enough to know what they were. As a child, she entertained her younger siblings and cousins by retelling books she'd read and inventing some of her own. Despite life throwing bumps in the way, she's always come back to writing, especially when that writing allows her to explore magical and fantastical worlds.

Sierra always assumed that she'd lead a conventional life with a husband and children. So imagine her surprise when she found herself happily partnered with not one, but two people. She and her partners live in the Ozarks with their ridiculously perfect number of children and a couple of bunnies for good measure.

If you want to keep up with Sierra's upcoming releases and sales, you can sign up for her newsletter or follow her on Booksprout or BookBub. And if you'd like to receive free early draft chapters and advance copies of her books before anyone else, you can support her on Patreon. To join her ARC team, see early cover reveals, and more, you can join Sierra's Sassy Sweethearts on Facebook.

SNEAK PEEK! HUNTED

BY SIERRA LANE

I can't help sighing a little as I scroll through Anne's Instagram photos. The beautiful beaches where she went with Donal and Susan for their honeymoon are a far cry from the small coffee shop where I sit, waiting on my latte. Not that I don't like Common Grounds; the coffee is good and the music selection is usually decent. But it's not Tahiti.

I feel another sigh bubbling up just as a blonde woman sits down in the chair across from me. I blink at her for a few seconds before I realize who just showed up. "Mattie? Weren't you a redhead last time I saw you?"

"We don't have time for banter," Mattie says. She's smiling at me like we were planning all along to meet for coffee, but her voice is quiet and her eyes never stop moving. "You need to come with me right now."

"Is this—"Nothing about her suggests that this is a joke, so I cut that question off and mentally kiss my latte goodbye. "Okay."

Grabbing my bag, I follow her down the back hallway, past the restrooms and through a door I've never tried, which she unlocks quickly—or I think she does, since I don't actually see a key. Behind it there's a small, windowless storeroom, walls lined with shelves full of boxes and bags. Mattie flicks the light switch on and closes the door behind us, muttering a quick locking spell under her breath.

"Okay, I think I've been pretty patient with the Terminator routine, but seriously, Mattie, what the actual—"

I stop in mid-sentence, my mouth falling open when three men literally walk through the back wall like it's nothing but air. Three very attractive men, I notice vaguely, clearly muscular even under their clothes. I'd probably be paying more attention to their looks, quite frankly, if they weren't carrying what looks suspiciously like a dead body between them, all wrapped up and oblong.

"What the actual fuck is going on?"

Oh, look at that, I found my voice after all. Great. But seriously. With Anne on her honeymoon, the only reason I was planning to leave my apartment this week was for coffee and groceries. Getting pulled into cramped back rooms and meeting hot guys carrying dead bodies was decidedly not on the menu.

"There's a contract on you," Mattie says, gesturing to the guys, who lay the body-thing down on the floor. "Capture and delivery preferred, but kill if necessary. You're lucky I took it before someone else could."

"So, what, you're gonna kidnap me? Or kill me?"

One of the guys winces a little, which is when I realize my volume and the pitch of my voice have both risen sharply to something that could be considered a screech. But I think I'm allowed, honestly. Someone wants me captured? Or dead? What the *fuck?*

"No, of course not," Mattie says matter-of-factly, kneeling down to unwrap whatever the fuck the thing is on the floor. "We're going to use this simulacrum once it's spelled to look like you and I'm going to deliver it to the client. Hopefully they'll buy that it's your body, but if not, at least I'll figure out who's behind this."

"You don't know who hired you?" One of the guys speaks for the first time, the one with the warm brown skin and smile lines around his eyes, eyebrows raised skeptically.

His good looks are especially surreal in contrast with the vague, unformed shape of the simulacrum on the floor. Only the face and part of the chest is visible, but that's enough to see the waxy, vaguely moist-looking surface, the featureless, hairless oval of its head. I've never seen a simulacrum up close before, and I kind of wish I hadn't now. I'm pretty sure I'm going to have nightmares about this.

Mattie shrugs. "Contracts are usually handled through

an intermediary. This one came from someone high up in the Fae courts; that's all I've got right now. Here, Wynn, give me some of your hair."

It takes me a second to drag my sickly fascinated attention away from the simulacrum and realize why she's asking, but I finally yank out a few strands of hair, hard enough to make my eyes water, and hand them over. Mattie presses them to the simulacrum's forehead, murmuring under her breath. Symbols appear, glowing over its surface with a queasy-looking shine. I blink and then it just looks like me, lying there on the floor, my messy hair spilling out of the wrappings, my favorite lipstick red against the pale skin. Still and silent and dead.

It's fucking creepy.

"This won't throw them off the trail for long," Mattie warns, straightening up. "Especially not if you're where they expect to find you, in your apartment or your usual neighborhood. You need a place to hide, so you can lay low until I can figure out why they're after you."

"Oh, okay, I'll just go to my other house." I'm acting like a petulant brat, but this is a strange enough situation that I feel a little justified. "What are you gonna do, put me in witness protection? I don't really have anywhere to go."

Mattie smiles, gesturing toward our audience. "That's where they come in."

Oh yeah. The three super-hot guys who are still

standing there, watching me have a complete breakdown. Great. Perfect. Way to make a good first impression, Wynn. "Are *they* going to put me in witness protection?"

"Not exactly. But we can keep you safe," the tallest one says, smiling, and fuck me, he's even hotter when he's smiling, gray eyes lighting up with it, dark brown hair pulled back in a messy bun.

"They owe me a favor," Mattie says dismissively, wrapping the simulacrum back up.

As many questions as I have, it's a relief not to see what looks like my dead body sprawled on the floor. Even more of a relief when she murmurs a spell and it vanishes from the room.

Of course, that means there's no longer anything else to distract me from the three guys that I'm apparently going to be staying with. They're all incredibly hot in their own ways. The guy who promised to keep me safe looks like any hipster I'd see around the neighborhood at first glance, with his man-bun and shirt-sleeves rolled up, but even through the button-down I can tell he carries a lot more muscle than your average hipster. There's just the slightest edge of ink peeking out from under his sleeves, and I have to drag my eyes away before my stare becomes super creepy.

"I'm Jamie," he says, offering his hand.

"Wynn," I answer inanely as I take it, like we're being introduced somewhere other than a coffee shop storage room where I just found out about a contract on my life. His hand is big and warm as it wraps around mine. He doesn't try to crush mine in his grip like a lot of guys do, but he also doesn't treat it like a dead fish he can't wait to get rid of. Look, I've had a lot of creepy handshakes in my day, way more than I've had good ones. Even without the fact that Jamie looks me in the eye instead of checking out my rack, this is definitely one of the better ones.

He smiles at me as he lets go, stepping back just enough to be out of my personal space bubble so he's not looming over me "Nice to meet you, Wynn. This is Gabe and Max."

Gabe, aka laugh-lines, grins, holding out his hand. "Always a pleasure to meet one of Mattie's friends."

"Did I say we were friends?" she asks mildly, leaning against the wall and looking vaguely bored with our human social rituals. Mattie's not Fae, or at least she says she isn't, but she does Fae better than anyone I've ever met.

"Nah, but you wouldn't use up this favor for just anybody," Gabe responds. Clearly he knows her well enough to get that, and not to be bothered by her attitude. "Right, Max?"

Max shrugs, still kind of hovering in the background. He looks like an Abercrombie & Fitch model, all clean-cut features, blond hair, and warm brown eyes. In contrast to Mattie's air of being above it all, he looks exactly like me when I get dragged to a party where I don't know anybody. I kind of want to pat him on the arm and tell him it's okay if he wants to leave. Except I guess I'm the one who's going to be leaving.

"Time to go," Mattie says, right on cue. "You can finish up introductions later. I'll check in as soon as I can, but until I do, promise me you'll stay put until I let you know it's safe."

For a second there, I'd somehow managed to forget that apparently this is a matter of life and death. Looking into Mattie's eyes strips that illusion away. Maybe I met her at the most hilariously awful yoga class of my life, maybe she comes over to my place for good takeout and bad movies, but this is what Mattie does. She's a bounty hunter. I don't have a problem with that normally, since the people she goes after have done very bad things.

I just never thought she'd be coming after me.

"Am I going to be okay?" I ask her, my voice wavering.

"I'll make sure of it," she promises, moving in for a quick, blink-and-you'll-miss-it hug. That, more than anything else that happened in the last ten minutes, is terrifying. Mattie doesn't really *do* physical affection. "Now go."

Jamie offers me his hand again. I bite back all the questions bubbling up—*who are you? where are we going? how can you be sure I'll be safe there?*—and take it. He's got a nice hand, really, and just like the handshake, he holds mine carefully, just the right amount of pressure to be comforting but not painful or scary.

"We'll keep her safe," he promises Mattie, turning

toward the same wall the three of them walked through in the first place. "I swear it."

"You'd better," she says, her tone mild to anyone who doesn't know her.

Max holds out his hand, one pinkie extended. Out of this entire surreal day, watching my badass bounty hunter friend solemnly link her pinkie finger with this random dude is one of the most surreal parts. "Promise," he says softly.

"I know," she replies, her face softening a little. "I wouldn't be sending her with you otherwise."

He nods back, like he understands what a big deal her trusting him is.

Mattie lets go of his hand and murmurs under her breath again—she's used more magic in the past ten minutes than I've seen her use in the entire two years and change I've known her—nodding to herself before opening the storeroom door just wide enough to slip out. It closes behind her with a solid, final-sounding thunk. The snick of the lock turning, without anyone in the room touching it, is just the icing on the cake. Now it's just me, alone with three random strangers. This is great.

"Ready?" Gabe asks me. His eyes are warm and compassionate, like he can see exactly how close I am to a screaming meltdown. When I dragged myself out for coffee, I was not expecting this level of mindfuck.

"I guess?" I shrug helplessly, only then realizing that Jamie is still holding my hand. "I don't know what the fuck I'm supposed to be ready for, or how I'm supposed to be ready for it with just the stuff in my bag. I guess a quick stop at my apartment is out of the question?"

I had to ask, but I know the answer even before Jamie shakes his head. "That's one of the first places whoever it is will be looking for you. Mattie would skin me alive if I let you go back there. After a few days, if the heat dies down, one of us can pick up some of your things. But honestly, we can get you whatever you need once we're there."

It's on the tip of my tongue to ask where "there" is, and they must read it on my face. Gabe smiles, opening his mouth to speak, but closes it again when Jamie uses his gentle grip on my hand to steer me toward the back wall.

"It's easier just to show you," he says, glancing down at me. His mouth quirks up at the corner into a crooked smile. "You good?"

I shrug again. "Let's do it, I guess."

His smile widens, warms. Out of the corner of my eye I can see Gabe and Max moving in on either side of us. Like guards, or something.

I have no idea where I'm going, or what I'm going to do when I get there. I have no idea why anyone would want me kidnapped or killed. I'm about to leave my favorite coffee shop with three hot guys I've never met before—I mean, I guess if I have to go into witness protection or whatever, at least the view's nice, but I never even got my fucking latte.

It's definitely Monday.

Jamie squeezes my hand, pulling me out of my downward spiral. I step forward when he does, forcing myself not to flinch, and walk through the wall.

Read more on Amazon!

SNEAK PEEK! GLAMOURED

BY JOELLE GREENE

With a final coy smile, I headed offstage. The click of my towering heels was lost to the DJ's voice pouring through the overhead speaker. I was always a little… maybe sad wasn't the right word, but when I was done dancing and reality flooded back in, I kind of wished it wouldn't.

Kendra stood at the side of the stage, waiting to go on. She caught my arm as she peered past me, out into the club. "How is it tonight?" She had to shout over the sound of the DJ announcing her booming through the room.

I glanced back as well. "Not bad for a Thursday." I lifted my hand, full of bills, to demonstrate. "I've had worse starts." There were a good number of shifters out there, their coiled energy calling to me from the edge of the stage. They were just as drawn to me as I was to them, so that probably had something to do with it.

She adjusted the hem of her booty shorts. "Fucking hope so." A brief smile lit up her face before she slipped past me, out into the hazy light.

I hustled back to the dressing room. I didn't need to rush before my next set, but I wanted to call Eddie. Being a witch meant I was immune to most of the viruses that went around the club, but it didn't mean I couldn't be a carrier. Kelli had called out for the third night in a row. Our floor manager said the club was all about fantasy. No one's fantasy included a runny nose and chest-shaking cough, so he didn't mind that she missed work.

But her absence didn't come before passing on her cold for me to take home to my son. When Cam had started sneezing that morning, I'd been tempted to call out myself. Opal usually babysat for me. Before she'd hooked up with some of the Pride, we'd been careful to arrange our days off for different days so we could exchange babysitting. I'd watch her toddler, and she'd watch Cam. That meant I only had to pay a sitter three nights a week instead of five.

Kelli calling out meant Opal had come to work. She didn't have to worry about the childcare thing anymore. Eddie, one of her partners, he'd started watching her daughter while she worked. I'd freaked out when Opal had called to tell me she couldn't watch Cam, but they'd both assured me over and over again that he'd be fine with watching Cam, even if Cam had a little sniffle. I just wanted to check on them.

Opal waited by the door to the dressing room with her phone in her hand and a concerned look on her face. My heart sank, my mind already churning with anxious thoughts about my son. "Eddie called," she confirmed. "Said Cam is really having a hard time breathing."

"Shit." I pushed my hand through my hair, shoving it back from my face. I looked around the room, taking in the concerned eyes of the other girls. "What do I-" I needed this job. I *needed* this job, and I knew Sean wouldn't exactly be tickled if I just dropped my scheduled sets. But I couldn't just abandon my son like that.

"Go. We'll cover for you," Jazz, one of the other dancers, offered.

Opal gave my arm a squeeze. "It's fine, Cammy. Go get your baby."

"Thank you." Tears of gratitude flooded my eyes, and I impatiently dashed them away. Stage makeup was built to last, so at least I didn't have to worry about smearing it. I tucked my money away and quickly shed the heels, pushing them into my bag. I didn't bother taking off the makeup, instead just pulling off the skimpy bottoms that made up my costume.

I got dressed as quickly as I could, and gathered my hair behind me so I could pull the hood of my plain black hoodie up over my head. We weren't to break the fantasy while we were at work, and technically I'd be leaving during work hours. I didn't want someone to recognize me in the parking lot and bitch about it to Sean.

I made sure I had my phone in my purse before yanking the strap up my shoulder. I could sort out my locker tomorrow.

"Call me when you know what's going on," Opal told me firmly as I passed her on my way out.

I nodded and gave her a quick hug before heading into the narrow hall.

Andre was the bouncer who watched the staff entrance most nights I was there. The Pride owned the club. He wasn't a member, but he was affiliated – someone's brother or cousin or something. He made sure no one came in to harass us or get up in the Pride's business.

Concern pinched his face when I approached. Andre was good people. He wasn't *big*, but he was tall and lean, and he had that same predatory grace that all the cat shifters I'd met seemed to. "You taking off?"

"Yeah." I jerked my thumb back toward the changing room. "They said they'd fill in for me."

He glanced around before his warm brown eyes came back to me. "I can't walk you out to your car, but I'll watch from here."

"Thanks, Andre." I managed a quick smile for him.

"Sure, sweetie." The term of endearment wasn't personal; Andre called all the dancers that. "You take care."

I nodded, slipping outside while he held the heavy door for me. It was drizzling, a fine sheen covering my hands almost immediately. I kept my head down as I dashed across the employee parking lot to my car.

It was cold inside. I hurled my bag and purse to the passenger seat before shoving the key into the ignition with slightly shaking hands. I turned it, but it just revved without catching. "Come on!" I'd gotten my little blue car super cheap and used as hell, and I knew it was definitely on its last legs. And it always seemed like it was when I was in a hurry that it acted up.

I tried it again, then again, promising it that oil change I'd been putting off if it just let me go and get my son. Nothing. I pulled my shoulders down from around my ears and took a breath. I had enough cash on me to call for a ride if I needed one, and the baby carrier in the backseat would come out easily enough. That was just one more complication I didn't need.

The glimpse of something over by the large, green dumpster eye caught my attention. A tall frame, hooded eyes, an impressive set of shoulders… Someone I hadn't seen in a little over a year. Someone I desperately needed *not* to see. "Come on!" I ducked my head and almost frantically tried the key again, and at last the car started.

A glance at Andre showed he was still standing there, waiting until I pulled out. I couldn't look, I couldn't risk letting *him* see me, but I had to know if my past had finally caught up to me. I lifted my head and looked at the dumpster, but no one was there. I did see an old office chair with two bits of stuffing sticking out that might have looked like eyes.

The tension in my muscles eased as I pulled out of the lot and into the road. I told myself that had to be it, just a chair and the shadow from the overhead light. Andre hadn't looked like he'd scented or heard anything. A whisper of doubt in the back of my mind gnawed at me, urging me to get out, to run, just like I had so many months ago.

I gave myself a firm mental shake. Cam needed me to be present, to take care of him, not to be startling at imagined ghosts. With one hand on the wheel and my eyes on the road, I reached into my purse and pulled out my phone. As soon as I stopped at the first red light, I looked down to unlock it. "Call Eddie," I told it as I put it in my lap and set it to speaker.

"Calling Eddie," it replied in what always sounded like a faintly snarky voice. Phone lady was judgy as hell.

He picked up on the second ring. "Hey," he greeted, his voice a mixture of concern and relief.

"Hey. I'm on my way. How is he?"

"Not good, Cammy." He paused. "You might want to take him to the hospital tonight."

"Shit." My hands tightened on the steering wheel until my knuckles stood out pale against my skin. Helpless tears stung my eyes, and I stared hard at the rain-dark road in front of me. "Okay. Can you get him ready to go?"

"Sure thing. See you soon."

"Thanks, Eddie." I glanced down to make sure he'd hung up, and let out a long breath. The hospital down on Sixth was friendly to shifters and witches, so I could take him there. Normally I passed Cam off as human, or half-human with no presenting witchiness, but anyone who gave him medical care needed to know he was half-shifter.

That was enough to make me hesitate too – especially after the fright I'd given myself in the parking lot. What if someone there knew Cam's father and word got back to him? I knew a witch I could take him to, someone who wouldn't ask questions or make records. She was a nurse in her day job, and after-hours she'd help the rest of us out.

But I couldn't. As anxious as it made me, I needed to do this officially. That way if Cam's father ever did find us, I could prove I was providing adequate care. Not that I expected him to go through the courts to sort things out, but *just in case*.

I was probably speeding all the way to Opal's apartment building, but I was barely aware of the drive. I hardly took the time to turn the car off and pull the key out of the ignition after finding a space in her parking lot. My footsteps rang out through the night as I took the stairs up to her second floor apartment two at a time.

Eddie pulled open the door just as I got there. He must've heard me coming. He had the same predatory grace as Andre, but he was a little shorter, a little more burly. And he was part of the Pride. He wasn't wearing his cut over his plain t-shirt, but I knew it would be somewhere around the apartment.

"Hey. He's sleeping." He shut the door after I stepped inside and followed me down the short hall to where the portable playpen was set up in the living room. "I tried to feed him, but he just threw most of it back up."

Worry gripped my heart in a vise. Even in his sleep, Cam's chest labored with short, shallow breaths, and there was a lot of crackling going on. "Fuck. I hope he doesn't get Lana sick."

"Don't sweat it, mama. Lana's not half-human." He gave my shoulder a comforting squeeze.

It was on the tip of my tongue to tell him that Cam wasn't either, but I couldn't tell him that. I couldn't tell anyone that. If *anyone* guessed who his dad was and word got out... "Is it okay if I sit here with him for a minute before we go?" I couldn't hold him in the car, but skin to skin contact would help him feel a bit better.

"Sure, whatever you need. I've got all his shit all packed up." He gestured to the diaper bag sitting on the floor beside the playpen.

"Thanks, Eddie." I took my hoodie off and had one arm out of the sleeve of my t-shirt when I paused. I looked up at him, a bit embarrassed. "Sorry. It needs to be skin to skin."

He laughed, scrubbing his hand over the top of his bald head. "I've seen your tits, Cammy."

That was a little different. I was working, then. I was

Cami the dancer, not Camilla the worried mom wanting to snuggle her baby. But if he didn't care, I wasn't going to either. Besides, I had a sports bra on under my shirt.

I finished pulling off my shirt and leaned down to pick Cam up. "He's a little warm." I gently pressed him to my chest. He stirred and made a little noise, but he didn't wake up.

Eddie appeared behind me. He pressed the back of his hand to Cam's forehead and nodded. "Yeah. Better than he was. I gave him some Tylenol at about six, if they ask."

I balanced my baby against me and unsnapped his onesie. I got Cam stripped down his to diaper with Eddie's help, then sat on Opal's battered gray couch with him pressed against my chest. "Sh," I soothed when he fussed a little, kissing the top of his head.

I wasn't a very good witch. I was good at glamour, which was pretty much a necessity when I stripped down to practically nothing five months postpartum. But all witches knew a little about healing; it was one of the first things we did. Siblings, or parents, or friends, or pets… Skin to skin contact, and I traced the sigil for healing on his bare back and pushed a touch of power through it.

Eddie stood and watched us, arms folded. "When's your next day off?"

"Sunday." I always had Sunday and Monday off.

"I'll call Sean, tell him you'll probably need some more time off." Sean was our manager.

I shook my head. "You don't have to do that." Some of

the tightness in my shoulders eased when Cam stopped struggling quite so much to breathe. But I couldn't sit with him all the time. He still needed to go to the hospital.

"I'll take care of it. I know you're still pretty new, and he won't give me any shit."

"I don't..." I took a deep breath. Opal was always telling me to let other people help me, but I couldn't help but be suspicious. "Why are you..." I gestured to him. "I mean, it's one thing to watch Opal's kid, but you don't know me."

"I'm starting to know you pretty good. And since we're both such big parts of Opal's life, we're gonna know each other more." They'd been together for about three months, Opal, Eddie, and Dax, her other partner. They'd started doing their thing shortly after I started dancing. When I gave him a skeptical look, he grinned. "Opal would have my balls if I didn't."

I smiled a little at that. That was probably true. Opal didn't take shit from anyone, badass motorcycle club or not.

"It's like this, Cammy." Eddie skirted the couch to sit on the other end. "Opal said you're her family. That makes us family." He gestured between us, his eyes wide and earnest.

The words made sense, but I wasn't sure I understood the logic. I'd known them for the same amount of time, and I didn't consider us family. Opal said I had trust issues.

She wasn't *wrong*, but I couldn't help but wonder how they were so willing to just draw me into the fold.

I swallowed any further protest. Arguing wasn't going to do me any good, and I had enough going on. "Okay. I should get going." Cam had probably gotten about as much better as he was going to just from that.

Eddie reached for Cam, and I handed him over after just a second's hesitation. I needed to get both of us dressed, and that would be easier if I had my hands free.

Cam immediately started fussing. He normally liked Eddie, but he just had to be feeling so miserable. My heart broke for him. I rushed through getting both of our clothes back on, and picked him up to snuggle against me.

"You want me to ask one of the guys to take you down there?" Eddie sat on the arm of the couch, his hands loosely clasped in front of him. He still looked concerned.

Family or not, help or not, that was where I drew the line. Not to mention I was pretty sure none of them would want to sit around a hospital waiting room for *us*. "No thanks." I had to juggle everything – my purse, Cam, the diaper bag – but I'd had practice with that. Eddie held the door for me, and watched from the walkway as I went back down to my car.

Read more on Amazon!